T0285961

The Constant Listener

published with a grant

Figure Foundation

The
Constant Listener

Henry James and Theodora Bosanquet

an imagined memoir

Susan Herron Sibbet

with Lady Borton

Swallow Press * Ohio University Press * Athens

Swallow Press
An imprint of Ohio University Press, Athens, Ohio 45701
ohioswallow.com

Jacket art: Photograph of Lamb House and Henry James courtesy Wikimedia Commons
Photograph of Theodora Bosanquet © National Trust / Charles Thomas

Jacket design by Beth Pratt

Printed in the United States of America
Swallow Press / Ohio University Press books are printed on acid-free paper ∞ ™

27 26 25 24 23 22 21 20 19 18 17   5 4 3 2 1

Library of Congress Cataloging-in-Publication Data
Names: Sibbet, Susan Herron author. | Borton, Lady author.
Title: The constant listener : Henry James and Theodora Bosanquet—an imagined
  memoir / Susan Herron Sibbet with Lady Borton.
Description: Athens, Ohio : Swallow Press, 2017. | Includes bibliographical
  references.
Identifiers: LCCN 2017023530| ISBN 9780804011839 (hc : alk. paper) | ISBN
  9780804040785 (pdf)
Subjects: LCSH: James, Henry, 1843-1916--Fiction. | James, Henry,
  1843-1916--Friends and associates--Fiction. | Novelists,
  American--Fiction. | Bosanquet, Theodora--Fiction. | Book editors--United
  States--Fiction. | GSAFD: Biographical fiction | Historical fiction
Classification: LCC PS3569.I24 C57 2017 | DDC 813/.54--dc23
LC record available at https://lccn.loc.gov/2017023530

To all the listeners and
creative support people in the world,
for their invaluable roles in helping
make great art possible

We who knew him well know how great he would have been if he had never written a line.

—Edith Wharton, letter to amanuensis
Theodora Bosanquet, March 1, 1916
(two days after Henry James's death)

A Note about Style

Attentive readers of Susan Herron Sibbet's imagined memoir will notice British spelling, the unusual contractions and punctuation of quotations from fiction by Henry James as published more than a century ago, and the inconsistency of that published style with the style of James's concurrent handwritten letters, with James's plays published three decades after the Master's death, and with the narrative style used by Theodora Bosanquet writing in the late 1950s. Attentive readers will also notice that the afterword, acknowledgments, and notes bring the reader up to modern times through the use of current US style.

Lady Borton

Contents

1

"The Tragic Muse"

October 1907

If it be ever of interest and profit to put one's finger on the productive germ of a work of art, and if in fact a lucid account of any such work involves that prime identification, I can but look on the present fiction as a poor fatherless and motherless [sic], a sort of unregistered and unacknowledged birth.

> —Henry James
> Preface to "The Tragic Muse"
> The New York Edition, volume 7

It seemed to take hours, but at last the train to Rye slowed and pulled around the final curve, and the tiny station came into view. I leaned over to look at it, almost a doll house of a station, lemon yellow with white trim, bright colours that would never survive in London. There, on that bright October morning, those colours looked just right.

I stood up eagerly, but I still had to wait with the other Rye passengers for the train to stop. I carried my bags and bundles down the steps after the guard had opened my compartment. I looked around and saw at once the large figure of Mr. Henry James coming towards me, his arms stretched high in the air, and I waved back, a small wave with my one free hand. As we met, he took my hand and shook it warmly.

"I'm so glad to see you made the train, so very glad, really, Miss Bosanquet, most glad." His warm words made me feel conspicuously welcome as I stood awkwardly among the strangers at the station.

"Now, your things! Oh, yes, I hope you will not mind walking up the hill. It's but a few steps. I always make my guests walk, to take in the feel of our wonderful Rye. Really, it's so old, you know, quite ancient, nothing like it for venerable," Mr. James went on as we passed out through the doors of the station. Once we reached the curb, I was startled to see an old man in soiled clothes coming directly towards us, noisily shoving his muddy wheelbarrow into our path, but Mr. James greeted him.

"Oh, good, George, here's our Miss Bosanquet, and I expect her trunk is up waiting on the platform. Is that right, do you have a trunk?" He turned to me, and I was alarmed that my expression of confusion and repulsion was there for him to see. He went on quickly. "Oh, I am sorry, Miss Bosanquet, I forget that down here in the country we might look a bit rough to you city folk. I assure you that George is the gentlest of men, and he nearly always re-members to clean out the inside of our garden wheelbarrow before he brings it down to fetch my visitors' things. Would you like to have your bundles carted up along with the trunk?" Mr. James took my bundles and lunch basket and gave them to the gardener, with instructions to take them to my room.

"I hope you don't mind, Miss Bosanquet, but I've arranged for you to have your own tea waiting for you with your landlady, and so we'll go straight to Marigold Cottage. I'm afraid that my domestic arrangements at Lamb House are not all that could be desired this afternoon. I have a very simple household with a housekeeper, who cooks for me, but she's quite unreliable, and today appears to be a bad day. Then, there's George to take care of the garden, and then of course there is little Burgess, my manservant—he came to me when he was a boy, and he's not much bigger now—but you'll meet them all soon enough. Now, then . . ." He led me across the wide street that ran beside the town's high wall with its round, embedded stones.

"Is this not just the thing?" Mr. James patted the stones as we walked past. "They say that villagers began building the town wall on this side of Rye in 1194. Hard to think of those poor fellows over seven hundred years ago laying stone on stone right on this spot. And I think my work goes slowly, step by step! Not a patch on these fellows, I'm sure."

At last, I was to hear something of the work to be done. I remember leaning eagerly towards Mr. James, listening to his smooth and endless flow of words as we climbed up the steep, cobbled street between the houses leaning side by side in the dusky October light.

The next day, that first morning, I found my way up to Lamb House. I realised, in spite of all my preparations, that I knew nothing of what was waiting for me beyond the heavy, copper-green door. I was afraid to knock. I had been too nervous to sleep well or eat a proper breakfast, worrying over that first day. Though I was confident of my skill with the typewriting machine, I was concerned how my bad ear, left over from a childhood illness, might affect my ability to typewrite correctly in an unfamiliar situation. I had always been the one at Miss Petherbridge's secretarial bureau to set up the arrangements of table, chair, and machine in relation to the person giving dictation. I had hoped to arrive at Mr. James' house early, but at least I was there at the appointed hour, ten-fifteen, in spite of the weather. My walk up the hill had been very short but very wet, with the steady rain obscuring all the house fronts and making the cobbled street quite treacherous. Now, I lifted the heavy brass knocker and thumped it twice.

I'd had to wait two months after the interview and Mr. James' kind offer in his first letter before he could make the arrangements for me to come to him. I had answered yes and then waited until, at last, his second letter arrived. I felt ruffled at my flat in London that morning when the early post brought Mr. James' reply, the heavy cream envelope with its Rye postmark and the smell of the leather writing desk and the sea. I opened it along the edge and slipped out a single, folded page.

His remarkable script seemed strong but shaky, the elegant black ink flowing smoothly over paper stippled cream in the light. The reassuring kindness was set out so that each word was distinguished, but the ending blurred and slid off into the ache of his fingers:

October 9th, 1907

Dear Miss Bosanquet,

I rejoice to hear of your arrival tomorrow & shall give myself the pleasure of meeting you at 1.28 at the Station. You shall have every facility ~~of~~ [sic] for trying my machine. I have just got a new & apparently admirable one.

Yours very truly,
Henry James

After what seemed like a long, silent wait, Mr. James' copper-green door swung inward, and I was startled to see Mr. James himself. He was dressed less formally than for our first meeting, this time in a blue-belted jacket and bright, striped shirt with a cheerfully red spotted tie, his clean-shaved face shining pink out at me as I stood hesitating on the doorstep, while the rain poured down. He stepped back, inviting me in, and I stammered something in return to his warm welcome. Then, as I came in with my dripping coat and umbrella, I was so alarmed I could scarcely speak. Was I really meant to hand over my dripping umbrella to Mr. James? Was he really going to help me out of my very wet macintosh? As I hesitated, I was aware that I was dripping all over the black-and-white tiles of shining marble in the entrance hall.

It all seemed so unlike Miss Petherbridge's secretarial bureau. Never before had a client greeted me. Instead, there had always been time to settle myself, to put away my street things and take on the appearance of calm assurance and competence that Miss Petherbridge had taught us girls. But as Mr. James hung my coat and umbrella on the hall stand, I wondered: Whatever was I to do about my wet galoshes? Pull them off right there, in that beautiful entrance hall? Mr. James noticed my discomfort and led me to the kitchen and to the chair where apparently he himself removed his muddy foot-wear; there was a paper spread, and so I was able to pull off my galoshes and collect myself, for the moment, while he spoke to his housekeeper. He introduced me to Mrs. Paddington and then went on to give her instructions for his lunch—to be ready at one-thirty, a moment that seemed endlessly in the future.

Mr. James then led the way back to the hall and up the front stairs to the large corner room where we would be working. I wondered again how it would be to work with Mr. James in such close quarters. Lamb House did not seem to be very large, and it looked as though Mr. James' own bedroom was right across the hall from the room where we were to work. Quite convenient for him, I thought, when he had an idea for something in the middle of the night, but it did seem somewhat improper.

"We call this the Green Room," Mr. James announced as he preceded me into the room, "from the colour of the paint on the wainscotting." He went to one of the windows and pulled back the heavy curtains, making the room much brighter, much more welcoming. Hesitantly, anxiously, I waited, hardly able to take it all in as he waved towards a large cloth-covered, lumpish mound on a dark metal stand set up conveniently at the end of a large desk.

He went on, "I am not quite ready for you, so please make yourself comfortable. Arrange things for your convenience, have a look around at my books, whatever you like," and then he turned away and began sorting through a large pile of papers.

I avoided approaching the dread machine and instead turned and looked around at the graceful room with tall, curtained windows on two sides and the sounds of the rain streaming down outside. I liked the small fire already glowing in the tile-rimmed fireplace. There was an easy chair placed nearby and two large writing desks, one set before the window, one against the wall. Every other bit of wall was filled with waist-high bookcases. I went closer to where the light fell on the titles. There were books by Edith Wharton, George Bernard Shaw, Joseph Conrad, Turgenev, other Russians, the French—everyone.

I could not resist—I took down one delicious novel, then another, only to be amazed to discover that each one had been signed by its famous author, dedicated, and autographed with effusive notes for Mr. James; his collection was immense and personal at the same time. I was delighted to come upon a book by Paul Bourget, someone I had always wanted to read. As I turned the curious pages, with their texture like felt and the ruffled edges where they had been torn with a paper knife, their thick weight and pale ink pressed deep, and the soft words, it all seemed so different from our crisp, English-made books. I tried my French on the first paragraph and was glad to see I could read it—Oh, thank you, Mlle. Brun.

I was startled by the sound of a metal clang against the grate; Mr. James was leaning over the fire and giving it a poke, which only made the sullen flames disappear. He looked up as if appealing for help and found me guiltily trying to stuff Bourget's book with its bright yellow wrapper back onto the shelf, afraid it might not seem proper for me to be looking at such writings. Mr. James, in an expansive gesture with the poker, waved me on as if he wanted me to keep the book.

"Oh, good. Good old Paul Bourget, I see. Perhaps you can use my books here to help you through the pauses in dictation. Sometimes I can't go straight through a piece of writing but, instead, must think for a bit. The man who first took my dictation would read the newspaper during the intervals. My dear Miss Weld would knit while she waited for me. You don't knit, do you, Miss Bosanquet?"

"No, I never could—I didn't have the patience."

"Well, then, please help yourself to any of my books at any time, and you can read through the intervals. Now, tell me, what do you think of my machine?" He left the poker and walked to the mysterious, cloth-covered mound. As he swept off the cover with a flourish, I was startled to see how shining and new, how large and complicated this Remington looked. It was not at all like the old model I had practised on back at Miss Petherbridge's. I went over to it and said in my best business voice, "It's fine, sir, such a new one." I tried touching a key, and it flew up alarmingly.

Mr. James brought a plain wooden chair over for me. "Well, we might as well begin and see how it goes." He pointed to a large stack of fresh, white paper on the writing desk. "Here is the paper. I don't pretend to have the slightest idea how this glorious machinery works. Please take your time getting ready for me to begin. I've written out for myself what we will be doing today, so let me know when you're ready."

I moved the chair to what seemed the best angle for hearing him, sat down, and began by tucking two pieces of his beautiful, heavy paper between the rollers. Everything was different, but I knew that with my good understanding of machines, I could do this. I looked for the tab key and the space bar—at least they were in the right place. The rollers moved silently, and the return lever was not the same as on the machine I knew. But, yes, I could do this.

"Yes, I'm ready."

"At the top, please put Capital V, *Volume,* Capital *I.* New Line—the widest space between the lines, if you please, Double Double Space."

There was a pause while I struggled to find the lever that adjusted the lines. Finally, I had to stand up and walk around the machine to look and feel blindly, desperately, until I located the lever on the far side. Mr. James was still waiting patiently for me, a sheaf of paper in hand. He cleared his throat and in his warm, clear voice slowly began to dictate:

"All Capitals, *PREFACE,* Double Space, Capital I *I profess a certain vagueness of remembrance in respect to the origin and growth of* Quotation, Capital T *"The* Capital T *Tragic* Capital M *Muse* Comma, End Quotation*," which appeared in the* Quotation, Capital A *"Atlantic* Capital M *Monthly* End Quotation*" again* Comma, *beginning* Capital J *January 1-8-8-9 and . . ."*

Here, there was a pause in the tapping of my keys while I hunted for the numbers *8* and *9.* I had not practised numbers, and they did not come easily to my hand. There!—But he had gone on.

"I'm sorry, sir." I interrupted the flow. "Could you please go back?—I lost some of the words . . ."

"Go back? Where? What?"

"I stopped at the date, at 1889."

"Oh, yes, I see. Well, I will slow down, I must not rush you along so—this is your first day. I hope it will come easier when you are more accustomed to the machine." And he went back again: *"January 1-8-8-9 and running on* Comma, *in-or-din-ate-ly* Comma, *several months beyond its proper twelve—"*

Mr. James stopped his pacing to look at me. I glanced up, waiting for a full stop or more words. Was that to be the end of his long first sentence?

He went on. "Full Stop. Capital I *If it be ever of interest and profit* . . ."

Oh! This was a new sentence—Or was he talking to me?

". . . *to put one's finger*" (I began typing furiously to catch up) "*on the productive germ of a work of art* Comma, . . ."

The work went on in fits and starts to the bottom of the page—my page, for his page seemed to be bottomless.

As he passed behind my chair, he continued, ". . . *and I remember well the particular chill* Comma, *at last* Comma, *of the sense of my having launched it in a great grey void from which no echo or message whatever would come back* Full Stop."

He paused, as he seemed to notice that it was time for a new sheet of paper.

"Let's halt here," he said, "and see how it's going. By the way, at least for some months, you and I will be working on prefaces for a New York edition of my collected works in more than twenty volumes. Since the publisher is in the United States, we'll use American double inverted commas—what the Americans call 'quotation marks'—as a small concession, but wouldn't you agree that we should honour accepted British spelling and use a space before semicolons and colons?"

I was very glad to have that breather with his directions and his nod to our British style, for I was feeling terribly out of sorts, perspiring, even shaking from the strain of working his new machine and from the hugeness of Mr. James' presence. I hurriedly rolled out the sheet, glad to be done with that page at least. But in looking over the typed sheet, I was horrified to find so many misspelt words, over-struck letters, uneven and faint letters, and smudges.

Mr. James took the sheet from my hand and made an unconscious grimace at the messy page. I looked away and bent to the machine, struggling to put a fresh sheet in place.

"It feels good," he said, "to be dictating again this way after so long. I lost my last amanuensis, Miss Weld—perhaps you know her—when she decided to marry. And then I went travelling for many months without being settled enough to dictate. It is a great relief to me now to hear the *tap-tap* of the typewriting machine, Miss Bosanquet. I have become accustomed to this method. In the old days when I would be writing a serial like 'The Tragic Muse,' I would write out my text in longhand with my favourite dip-pen and inkwell and send out a section of it as it was written, off on the first boat to the New York publishers, and they would have it typeset and send the galleys back by return boat.

"And so, it might be a month or more before I would see my work again. Of course, I could correct only the most glaring errors that way, and of course by then I was hard at work on the next instalment. Think of it, weeks between—really, it is most remarkable that these old pieces fit together at all. Now, it is all so pleasant—I write out my notes, dictate from them in the morning, and then I have the typewritten pages even with a copy so that I can correct and amplify the pages that night, almost before the ink has dried. Well, of course, the typewritten word doesn't have quite that glorious damp and fresh-ink smell of my old pages, but really it is a most remarkable system."

He had been pacing back and forth across the room while he was talking and apparently keeping a close eye on my progress with reloading the machine, for as soon as I was done, he said, "Ready then, Miss Bosanquet? Onward:

"Capital I *It seemed clear that I needed big cases* Dash—*small ones would practically give my central idea away* Semicolon *; and I make out now my still labouring under the il-lu-sion that the case of the sacrifice for art* Underline *can . . .*"

I was stumped again. How was I to underline? Oh, yes, the upper-case dash—but now, where—Oh! Had he stopped when the machine stopped? I hoped so.

". . . *can ever be* Comma, *with truth* Comma, *with taste* Comma, *with discretion involved* Comma, *apparently and show-i-ly* Quotation *"big* Full Stop, End Quotation.""

It all went smoothly for several more pages, even past Mr. James' spelling out in a low aside, "'The Newcomes'—one word," as if I had never heard of Thackeray or the other characters and titles Mr. James used so often as examples. It made me wonder what impossible sorts of secretaries he had been accustomed to. And yet I was glad that I had done my homework, had spent the month waiting for that job by reading over his novels, especially "The Tragic Muse," so that the names of his characters, of the reluctant artist, Nick Dormer, and the aspiring actress, Miriam Rooth, and their strange friend, Gabriel Nash, would land safely from my fingers, even if Mr. James had not carefully spelt out their names.

I was surprised, after the first panic had subsided, that I was able to do this, to take his dictated words and, yes, too slowly, and, yes, with too many errors, place them on the typewritten page. I was surprised, too, that I could understand him, could follow his argument as he dictated, and see what he was trying to communicate. Oh, not at first, when I could not even find the right keys, but soon enough I could listen and think and typewrite simultaneously. I was thrilled to be there, to hear his words and thoughts before anyone else, to be their engraver, their recorder, even sometimes their midwife.

It is true that at times Mr. James would stop dictating suddenly and, instead, pace the room, struggling to improve a word or phrase. That first day, I was extremely uncomfortable with his long, weighty pauses, since I had no way to tell if this was one of the times when he would prefer me to be engaged otherwise, rather than panting like an eager retriever at the hunt, waiting for Mr. James to throw his words out again. I had brought the Bourget to the table, so I leafed through the pages and tried not to look up at the tense figure across the room. Happily, these pauses were brief because he had prepared most of his text for that first day.

Later that week, when I was retyping those first smudged and much corrected pages, I remembered how at times his words or phrases surprised me. Sometimes, my disquiet was caused by his phrases, such as calling "The Tragic Muse," the unpopular book before us, his "*maimed or slighted, the disfigured or defeated, the unlucky or unlikely child.*" Suddenly my mind flew away to home and my poor little brother, Louis.

Or when he proclaimed that the book's best points to him were things I had barely noticed in my reading—its "*preserved tone.*" Mr. James was most happy not with the novel's pacing, its balanced treatment of the interesting artists and the Paris theatre scene but, rather, that he had succeeded in hiding what he saw as a flaw in the book's composition. He thought he had gone on too long in the first parts, where he set the stage, the scene, and supporting characters so that the last act—the real story—could be enacted. He went on at great length to explain that what he had really cared about was his theme. After all, nothing should be more important to Miriam or Nick or any aspiring artist than to be free to create art.

I was surprised at the vehemence of his language when describing his characters' sacrifice for art: "Capital T *There need never* Comma, *at the worst* Comma, *be any difficulty about the things advantageously chuckable for art* Semicolon *;*"

He went on, and then he startled me: "*Nothing can well figure as less* Quotation *"big* Comma, End Quotation,*" in an honest thesis* Comma, *than a marked instance of somebody's willingness to pass mainly for an ass* Full Stop."

I believe that moment was the first time I had ever typed any language remotely like "*ass.*" I must have looked up, and he did seem a little embarrassed, but he did not stop. Clearly, this book and its theme of what a man must sacrifice for his art had meant something important and, to him, perhaps even disturbing.

I wondered at his assurance. It was easy for him to talk about artists suffering for their art while he was there in his lovely house filled with antiques and oriental rugs, snug in quiet Rye, easily visited by all his famous, wealthy friends. For me, it was different: I wanted my writing, my art, to be out there, to make a noise, so that I could become famous myself. What, then, was I doing with my own life, there with Mr. James?

But in the midst of his words I had no moment to pursue that thought.

As our appointed three hours drew to a close, Mr. James seemed to be enjoying himself more and more, perhaps not wanting to stop. He went out for a few minutes to ask Mrs. Paddington how long before his lunch would be ready, and I looked over what we had done so far.

I wondered for the first time how hard had it been for him to become a writer. Was his family like mine, not wanting him to be miserable, poor, and struggling? Even now, Father still hoped I might yet give up my career and marry, for my own good. I think my telling Father that I was training with Miss Petherbridge and was going to live with my friends in a London flat or even my telling him I was going to Rye to take the job with Mr. James had been easier for him to accept than my telling him that I hoped to be a writer.

Mr. James came heavily back up the stairs and, with some chagrin, announced that we would have to stop. The housekeeper was adamant: her lunch would not wait.

I stacked our finished pages and pulled the cover over the machine. As I stood, Mr. James urged me to take the Bourget book, and I did.

Soon, bundled and cautioned against the continuing bad weather, I was back outside in the gloomy day. The rain had lessened, but it was still wet and cold. Where was I to find my lunch? What was I to do with myself now? The arrangements with my landlady were for one hot meal in the evening, but I was on my own until then, and so I made my way down to the shops and found a dark loaf of that morning's bread, a small yellow cheese, and a good bottle of ale. I took the purchases back to my room, tore off chunks of the cheese and slabs of the bread, arranged them on a piece of clean paper, and drank from my tooth cup (for of course my room came with no amenities of dishes or cutlery). I threw away the paper, rinsed out the cup, and looked around at my small, nearly windowless room, at the low brow of the eaves that blocked the light, the narrow bed, the dusty old spread, and the rusty corner sink. I washed out my shirtwaist, soot-stained from the train journey the day before, and spread it out to dry on the chair back.

I thought again about Mr. James and how his conversation had gone from a nervous, stilted defensiveness to, perhaps, real enjoyment. Even the way we ended had a hopefulness. Oh, he had not liked how poorly I typed, but he could see my work was improving with each new page, and I liked it when he added references to "us," a collective we of readers and writers. I had noticed that usage when he dictated, "... *and we look in vain for the artist* Comma, *the divine explanatory genius* Comma, *who will come to our aid and tell us* Full

Stop." Mr. James had smiled, seeming almost hopeful, and I had smiled in agreement. Only time would reveal to me more about what I could do for him, with him.

The second day seemed easier than the first, since now I began to understand what he was doing. The New York Edition of his collected works was his artist's canvas enlarged. He was a consummate and totally conscious, even self-conscious artist. The work we were doing on the prefaces was meant to frame and display, to varnish and polish his conscious art. I was in awe of these explanations of his process, and I wanted to learn everything I could from them.

From the moment I had heard his words being dictated to a typist down the hall all those months before, I had dreamed of sitting there beside Mr. James, helping him to achieve his dream and learning from the experience how to become a successful writer. Perhaps I might someday show him some of my work, but for now I was happy watching him exclaim proudly about every difficulty he had overcome, about how he had met all the challenges he had set for himself, handling such a large canvas combining art and politics in the same novel, steering his complex story through to its conclusion.

He had paused and then gone on. "Capital I *I fairly cherish the record as some adventurer in another line may hug the sense of his inveterate habit of just saving in time the neck he ever [sic] undiscourageably risks* . . ." There Mr. James was, the adventurer, pacing our small room or even sitting or standing at his desk—I could imagine him in the role, and my ambition increased with each new revelation, each new discovery.

It was inspiring to hear him talk of his two main characters—Nick Dormer, painter and politician, and the beautiful actress, Miriam—who, against all odds, fell in love. Mr. James seemed almost to be channelling his actress's quandary, with his—or was it her?—impassioned speeches:

"Capital S *She is in the uplifted state to which sacrifices and submissions loom large* Comma, *but loom so just because they must write sympathy* Comma, *write passion* Comma, *large* Full Stop."

I felt that, without being aware of it, Mr. James this time was speaking directly to me and my aspirations: art, passion, sympathy—What wasn't I capable of?! Those words made me wonder what sacrifices I might have to make for the life of writing.

He paused, his hand in mid-air, as if he were an orchestra conductor stopping in mid-beat. "Miss Bosanquet, it seems you're so attentive that you hear my voice drop for each parenthetical phrase, and you catch the silent beats in a compound sentence. I think I don't need to dictate each and every comma but only the other punctuation and unusual commas. And a full stop surely alerts you to a capital for the next word." With that, he went on:

"*Her measure of what she would be capable of for him* Dash—*capable, that is, of* Underline *not asking of him* Dash—*will depend on what he shall ask of* Underline *her, but she has no fear of not being able to satisfy him* Comma, . . ."

He paused, and I thought to myself: Ah! If only life could be like that.

But there was no time to think, for he continued:

"*. . . even to the point of* Quotation *"chucking* End Quotation*" for him, if need be, that artistic identity of her own which she has begun to build up* Full Stop."

I felt a little shiver of apprehension and typed to the end of the page.

2

"In the Cage"

August 1907

The action of the drama is simply the girl's "subjective"
adventure—that of her quite definitely winged intelligence ;
just as the catastrophe, just as the solution, depends on her
winged wit.

> —Henry James
> Preface to "In the Cage"
> The New York Edition, volume 11

It was no accident that Henry James and I met in the summer of 1907, though I had known nothing of him beyond the revelation of his novels and tales. That heavy morning in August 1907, as I sat in a top-floor office near Whitehall, compiling a very full index to the "Report of the Royal Commission on Coast Erosion," my ears were struck by the astonishing sound of passages from "The Ambassadors" being dictated to a young typist. Neglecting my Blue-book, I turned around to watch the typewriting-machine operator ticking off those splendid sentences, which seemed to be at least as much of a surprise to her as they were to me.

When my bewilderment had broken into a question, I learnt that the novelist, Henry James, was on the point of returning from

Italy, that he had asked to be provided with an amanuensis to type-write his dictations, and that the lady at the typewriter was making acquaintance with his style. Without any hopeful design of supplant-ing her, I lodged an immediate petition that I might be allowed the next opportunity of filling the post, supposing she should ever abandon it. I was told, to my amazement, that I need not wait. The established candidate was not enthusiastic about the prospect before her and was even genuinely relieved to look in another direction. If I set about practising on a Remington typewriting machine at once, I could be interviewed by Henry James himself as soon as he arrived in London. Within an hour, I had begun work on the machine.

Of course, that morning, when I first heard of the possibility of working for Mr. James and went after the job with all my heart, I'd had little experience of working for anyone. I had graduated from university the year before, with my degree in geology but without any clue as to how I was to make my living. I was only very sure that I did not want to become a teacher as my friends Nora and Clara from Cheltenham Ladies College had reluctantly trained to be. No, I had already tried the local dame school while waiting to pass my university entrance exams, and I knew I could never do that again. Like Nora and Clara (and unlike most of my other classmates at Cheltenham), I knew that I would not be marrying any time soon, if at all. Instead, when we finished our training, Nora, Clara, and I went to London and shared a flat. While Nora became the administrator of a small girls' school, Clara and I looked for other possibilities.

It was Clara who found Miss Petherbridge and her establish-ment to train educated females for practical jobs in the White-hall government offices that were now at last opening up to young women seeking employment. Miss P. was a middle-aged spinster, ambitious and kind, who happily kept us practising away in rooms she had found near Whitehall. No matter what level of education we had upon arrival, Miss P. started us all at work on the very lowliest of government tasks, and so I was there training to be an indexer—not a stenographic typist or any sort of typist.

Saying that I knew nothing of Mr. James beyond the revelation of his novels and tales actually means that I knew quite a bit about him. Mr. James had been part of my life ever since I was able to read his work by myself. His characters were my friends, his heroines aspired to the same high goals I did and had the same wishes and dreams that I did. I eagerly devoured each new book as it came out, delivered to us by Mudie's Lending Library.

I remember the lost afternoons when I first found "The Portrait of a Lady" and devoured it, lying in my bedroom, weeping silently, feeling the great promise of that brave girl and how the cruel and more experienced, unscrupulous friends surrounded her with their selfish schemes and blinded her to what might bring her happiness. I loved all Mr. James' poor, blighted young girls—Daisy and Nanda and Maisie and Fleda Vetch, even poor little wild Flora in "The Turn of the Screw." I believed Mr. James gave me, with his stories of the pain and power of cruelty and of love, of open deceit and agreeable divorce, of new and old wealth, a more realistic idea of what went on in the drawing-rooms of Belgravia and maybe in the girls' bedrooms at Cheltenham than had any sermons in my father's church.

And so, after I went to Miss Petherbridge to ask for the chance to work with her esteemed client, Mr. James, she agreed that if I would practise and be patient, soon enough she would arrange for the promised interview with the famous author.

Our offices near Whitehall were too noisy and public for meeting prospective clients. Because Miss P. and Mr. James were old acquaintances, she arranged for our appointment to be at her flat late one afternoon on a long, hot August day. I walked the few blocks in the hopes that stretching my legs would calm me. The hot sun glared off the hard, white house fronts; as I climbed the steps, I could feel my shirtwaist sticking to my back, where the heat had made it quite damp. I banged the knocker and was shown into a sort of anteroom to wait. Miss Petherbridge and Mr. James were talking; I could hear their low voices from beyond the closed door, and then the door opened.

Miss Petherbridge came out, all cool and comfortable in a crisp, beige linen dress, which I had never seen her wear at the office. She apparently had dressed up for this meeting. She had done her hair differently, too, not all pulled back into a bun but with side curls, softer, more attractive. Since she was tall, taller even than I am (and

I am nearly six feet tall myself), it seemed strange for her to look so delicate. I put my hand up to my hair and its combs and pins, afraid to think how I must look after my hot walk.

Miss Petherbridge seemed more excited than usual. Her voice was high, and the words came fast.

"No, no, my dear, you look fine, come in, don't keep Mr. James waiting for you." She held the door for me to go into the front parlour. Her introductions were quick. Then she was gone, and I was alone with Mr. James.

I stood speechless in panic, but to my relief, I found I would have time to retrieve my composure, time even to study this great man, for he immediately began to speak at length, and apparently he expected no response, since he left no pauses.

He was standing beside the fireless grate and gestured for me to join him and sit down. As we settled ourselves into the two chairs set facing each other, I noticed that he was dressed in a rather peculiar combination of the properly dark morning coat and trousers worn with a most un-British sort of soft and flowing silk tie in a brilliant red and blue spot, and with a broad, expansive waistcoat of a comforting yellow check. It made me wonder who chose his clothes. I knew he had never married, but it did make me feel a bit more relaxed to see his not-infallible taste displayed. Perhaps even Mr. James was a victim of his own enthusiasms; perhaps after all his years in England, he had still not quite got the hang of our English taste. Perhaps there *was* something I could do to help him.

As he continued to express his apparently deep and long thoughts about his pleasure in making my acquaintance, I looked into his open face and was quite struck by his handsome, bright look. His eyes were clear, grey, penetrating and now were slightly twinkling at my own apparently staring, curious gaze. He was tan, quite burnt actually, and his light hair was only a fringe about his beautifully shaped, shining head.

I wondered where he could have been travelling, to be so tan, and as if reading my mind, he went on, saying, "I'm just back from a month's motor-flight with my dear friend, Mrs. Wharton, in her amazing automobile, speeding along that glorious hilly spine of

Italy. With her usual good fortune, even on the voyage home we enjoyed the best weather."

I thought then that he had the look of an experienced sea captain, with his brown skin and those direct, sharp eyes, but I wondered at the mouth, such a sensitive, expressive feature. No, no sea captain would have survived with so much of his soul revealed as Mr. James. He was still talking in his beautifully resonant voice, with neither a British nor an American accent, I noticed.

"Miss Bosanquet, I want to be sure you understand the special circumstances, the arrangements I require for someone to come to work for me. My home is in the most provincial and adorable of towns, the ancient village of Rye, on the Sussex coast, a perfect antique town, but very quiet, nothing there for a young woman to entertain herself. Well, there is golfing, I suppose, but then you perhaps don't aspire to that most daunting of sports."

I was so amazed at his gentle, kind manner, his apologetic tone that I could barely pay attention to what he was saying. Was this the great novelist, the author of the terrifying "The Turn of the Screw," the shockingly risqué "The Sacred Fount," the deeply disturbing "The Golden Bowl"? Here was that looming presence, the mind that had put forth such monumental works, novels of such depths and heights—cathedrals, even. Now, was he asking if I desired to play golf? I could hardly believe my ears.

Mr. James went on. "The work itself will not be too taxing, I trust. We will work every day, including Sundays, for three or four hours, from ten to one. There may be other typewriting projects for you after our mornings together, making clean copies, corrections, but those morning hours of ours will be sacrosanct. Perhaps Miss Petherbridge has told you of my current project, that I have embarked on a massive effort, the revised edition of all my most important works. I will include only the pieces I deem worthy, and there will be corrections and revisions to be made, but most of our time will be used to dictate the prefaces for each volume as I come to them. At present I have the first seven prefaces completed, but now I need to pick up the pace.

"As you will find out, I like to write while standing up, moving about, dictating to a steady typewriting machine; I like the ease of speaking these essays of memory, these excursions into my thoughts about writing itself. I got into the habit of dictating about ten years ago, when I had something wrong with my right hand and arm. It happened part way through a short novella—'The Awkward Age,' I believe—and the new procedure seemed an aid to my imagination. I liked it, though there are those who don't agree. My brother says he can tell exactly where my dictating began."

I could only nod my understanding, my appreciation of his problems then, his huge project now, but some small voice was niggling away in me, asking: What was I letting myself in for? How many years would I spend doing someone else's work when all I really wanted was to work on my own writing? Ever since my dearest friend, Ethel, had encouraged me to use my brain, to follow my aspirations, I had dreamed of writing. I did not know what, exactly, but I knew that I would have to earn my own way, and it would be a struggle. But now, should all my time and energy be given to someone else's writing, even to someone as famous as Mr. James? Yet I wanted to be there, I wanted to learn, to be inspired in his presence. I wanted to be generous, and so I pushed those thoughts away, and with my whole being, I kept nodding, agreeing, ignoring that little, selfish voice.

Mr. James described the arrangements he had undertaken for the comfort of his amanuensis: There was a boarding house called Marigold Cottage quite nearby, with an accommodating landlady, Mrs. Holland, whom he understood to be a good cook and who would provide me with a room and meals. We would work at Lamb House. He had arranged for delivery of a fine, new typewriting machine, a Remington, the best, he had been told, all in order to make my work even easier. He went on in his quite charming way, in spite of my shy, frozen silence in response.

Soon enough I was back outside on the dusty, bright London street, having agreed to everything, even the very low rate of pay he was offering. I knew nothing of payment—I had never yet been paid for any of the work I had done on the indexing, since I was still in training. In fact, I had no idea of whether Mr. James' arrangements were good or even proper. Should a single young woman go to a man's rooms, even such an older man, to take dictation to his typewriter (as we stenographers were called in those days)? It was all a new business to me, for I had only worked for a few months with Miss Petherbridge and her "girls," as she called us.

In 1907, Miss Petherbridge found us girls, or sometimes we found her. We were that new phenomenon: university-educated young women, women who wanted more from life than to wait at home and pull taffy until we married. We were what the newspapers called the "New Woman." No one quite knew what to make of us.

The infernal typewriting machine was changing everything. At first, the machines were a mere substitute for the local printer down the street or the copyist who worked late nights to ensure that a court brief or financial agreement had the correct number of copies. But as more typewriting machines appeared, the arrangements of work-rooms and offices had to shift, because the stenographers became women willing to work for lower rates than male secretaries and copyists.

Previously, most novelists, including Mr. James, had written quickly in longhand, with the first version the final version. They were accustomed to sending their pages straight to the publisher to have the lines typeset; perhaps even Mr. James was never truly sure what he had written until the galleys came back as proofs to be corrected. Now, with the typewriting machine, all that had changed. Thoughts of personality, handwriting, and female circumstances meant nothing when a man could dictate to the typewriter. We would take down all the man's words and arrange them into one clean copy ready for his immediate corrections and our retyping.

This was the new method Mr. James was in love with, the machinery he wanted me to be his agent for, yet when he interviewed me, I still had not learnt more than the rudiments of that process or how to use a typewriting machine.

I went to Miss Petherbridge the next morning to report on my interview and to hear from her what the financial arrangements to which I had agreed really meant.

"Oh, dear, Miss Bosanquet, you have let him take advantage of you, if I do say so myself. Even if he is my old friend, I am surprised at him. What did you ask?"

"I didn't ask anything. In fact, I think I hardly spoke a word; he seemed to do enough talking for the both of us."

"Well, perhaps I should have prepared you. When Mr. James came to me, asking for a special sort of young woman to be his amanuensis, he even admitted that it was because a woman would be less expensive than a man. This enormous project of his—it's weeks, months, perhaps years of work! Poor Mr. James was concerned how much it would finally cost, and a woman does require far less, after all, than a man who might have a family to provide for. But my dear, I am glad for you! You must have made a good impression to have him make up his mind so quickly. Well done! Congratulations!"

"But Miss P., there is one difficulty—I've only the barest idea of how to use the machine. Can you suggest someone to give me lessons or perhaps a book I could use? Can I learn to typewrite quickly enough? He wants me to come to him in a few weeks."

"I know what you need," Miss Petherbridge said in her usual brisk way, and soon enough I was seated in a private office at the end of the hall before the large, shiny, black-and-gold apparatus, and a book, "The Curtis Method to Speed Typewriting," open to "Lesson One: Familiarise Yourself with the Machine."

I prided myself on being good with machines. At my home near Lyme Regis, it was my responsibility to keep the bicycles in good working order. I kept my own tools, wrenches, grease can, and oil can in the tool shed, and many times I would go out there when I wanted some quiet, away from my father and his little voice practising his sermons or reading out articles of interest from the weekly paper. In the tool shed, I could take my bicycle apart, spread the pieces all over the floor, and work for hours, happily forgetting all about his demands. Because I was famous for my knowledge of bicycles and other machines, even my most proper friend, Ethel Allen, and her sister often asked me to come down to St. Andrew's to look at their bicycles. Usually it was some mechanical problem, nothing very complicated, often a loose chain or brake pads to be tightened. I always dropped my own tasks and sped down the hill from Uplyme for any chance to be with Ethel.

I suppose in those days, still in the reign of Queen Victoria, it was unusual for a girl to be interested in machines, but I always had been. They made sense to me, somehow—logically constructed, beautifully put together. Unlike with people, if something went wrong with a machine, using attention and patience, I could figure out the problem and make everything right.

This machine I was facing was formidable but not daunting. I soon learnt that I would have more time to practise, for Mr. James could not arrange for my room and board with Mrs. Holland until October.

"The Curtis Method" seemed very clear and logical. Soon enough, as instructed, without looking at the keys, I was practising away, typewriting, but only the silly nonsense words for those first lessons. I opened the book:

```
bab    cab    dab    fab    gab
bob    cob    dob    fob    gob
```

I thought how strange English letters and words could be. Whatever makes us speak as we do? My mind would wander off, my hands would slip to the wrong keys, and I would have to start again:

```
cat    cot    cut    dot    dat    dut
```

This project was becoming less and less appealing. I did want to work for Mr. James, even for his low rate of pay, but why did the typewriting have to be so boring?

However, I did improve as the days of practise went on. Soon, I was ready to try sentences, paragraphs, even whole pages, but I found that going for speed had its disadvantages. Not looking at the keys but, instead, using the home keys was actually quite difficult. One slip and my typewriting turned into

```
qw294lit rqw5, e3lig34q53ly,
2ihou5 e3lidqdy, 5 h3 435u4n.
```

What I had typed did not make any sense! My fingers had been on the wrong keys. I moved them and tried again. All was well, until I lifted my hand to throw the carriage return and once again came back to the wrong keys. Perhaps I needed to abandon Mr. Curtis. I did not have time for this. I tried looking down at my fingers for several words—my words!—and it was better. I could still use the home-key method, but if I could look to find the less familiar keys—the O, the P—it was much better. I hoped if Mr.

James were simply dictating, I would have a chance to look down, and I might be able to typewrite for him without so many mistakes.

One afternoon, in frustration, I pulled a newspaper from a pile and began using the typewriting machine to copy the first article I saw:

The New Woman

Special to the "Gazette" by M. Perry Mills, on assignment in America, August 1, 1907

It is only at the end of the last century that women have entered the professions or gone into business. Among our grandmothers it was an unheard-of thing for a woman of good family to earn her own living. If her husband died, or if she were a spinster with no money of her own, she was taken care of by the next of kin in the masculine line, or scraped together a scanty living doing embroidery or some other "ladylike" task. It never even occurred to her that she could fit herself out for work, enter public life or the professions. . . . Such a suggestion would have been met with exclamations of horror as something truly impossible and unfeminine.

My thoughts went to my aunt Emily and the box of books our "maiden aunt" always brought along with her when she was required to come and stay with us. How I suspected she might have longed for an education.

Reading on, I skipped down to

How different conditions are today! Girls go to college with their brothers, take their degrees and sally forth into the world to struggle for themselves, if not on quite equal footing with men, yet every day more and more attaining that end. It is the age of "working women."

And yet such a state of affairs did not come about suddenly, nor is it wholly the result of women's discontent with domestic life. It is rather more the outgrowth of the times—the natural evolution of womankind in the history of the race. The increased cost of living, the higher standard required of young men entering the professional and business life, and the consequent necessity of prolonging the period devoted to preparation for that life, are heavy factors in the movement.

That nine women out of ten would prefer marriage and the making of a home for themselves to achieving success in any profession is just as much of a truth today as it was a hundred years ago.

I stopped typing and made a rude noise, then looked around to see if anyone were still in the office, but it was so late that the office was empty. I laughed and said out loud to myself, "This is one to show to Nora and Clara back at the flat!" Then I bent my head back to my exercise book. Meaningless letters were easier to deal with than some idiot's rantings about the New Woman.

After another hour of practise, when the evening light was nearly gone, it was time to stop and go back to the flat or do something fun. I rubbed my hands, stretched my fingers wide apart, curled my fists, and, with a groan, stretched my tired arms over my head. I heard an answer to my groan.

"That bad, is it?"

I turned to find that Clara, my closest friend in London, had come in behind me. She came over to give my shoulders a quick, comforting squeeze. I must have seemed tired. She looked as fresh and bright as when she had set out that morning from our flat for her job as secretarial assistant to Lord Milne. Her perfect frock was without a wrinkle, her heavy gold hair was still perfectly smoothed up into its high combs, her clear white skin was as flawless as ever. I put my hand up to my chin, where I knew there was another inky blotch. Clara laughed her light laugh and held out my jacket from the rack by the door.

"About ready to go? We can stop for a quick bite at the pub and still reach the theatre in time."

I collected my things into my string bag. "I'm so tired. I'm not at all sure about this . . ." and I showed her the exercise book. "It's been weeks, and my neck hurts, my fingers are sore, and my back aches. I actually like it when the machine breaks down. I know how to fix the blessed machine—but I don't know how to use it."

"Now, now, Dora, you always underestimate yourself. You're getting really good. Look at this!" Clara pulled a sheet from the waste-paper basket and read in her melodious voice, "Pap nap tap sap, pip nip tip sip, pop mop top sop. Not one mistake! Oh, look at this one!" Clara picked up several half-filled pages lying on the table beside the machine and read out loud,

The Tattler Tells All

The Huntsman's Ball was honoured with our most brilliant young debutentes, Miss Georgina Sedly and Miss Maria Whitworth, but the person most talked about this lively season is the handsome raven-haired, blue-eyed Miss Margaret Haig Thomas. . . . It is rumoured that Miss Thomas, one of the wealthiest daughters of the land, may soon be leaving our glittering dinners and gorgeous balls for the less than brilliant weather of Oxford and the dingier halls of Somerville.

"Dora, what made you type that one?"

"I don't know. It caught my eye, someone very rich who leaves the social scene to go to university—It seemed different."

"This is good typewriting. You're getting better. The only mistakes here are in the spelling of 'debutante' and in the spacing."

I put the cover over the machine with one motion, then gave the cover an extra tug. "I hate the space bar. I hate the machine. I wish I could secure this job some other way."

I took Clara's arm as we walked side by side down the long hall, past the empty rooms. "You know, Clara, there really are not enough jobs. Even if all of us go to university and complete our degrees, there will not be enough work for women unless men open up the rolls and hire women to teach in men's classes, hire women to write and edit the newspapers and books, fill the publishing houses, hire women to be the lawyers and clerks and agents."

Clara stopped and turned to look at me. "Dora, you surprise—You, the shyest woman I know, you're starting to sound like one of those militant Suffragettes."

"But, Clara, I'm stuck. I have no money of my own, only a little more than the hundred pounds a year my mother left me. And my old home is no longer my own, now that Father and his new bride are all caught up with planting the garden with exotic shrubs. The only future Father and Annie can imagine for me is to teach horrid little girls or find a husband or move about again and again to all the cousins. I guess Annie still believes I will find someone to marry someday. After all, I might have the same good luck she did, catching someone older and settled, like my father."

"Can you try to talk to them, tell them that what you want is different, that you want to be on your own?"

"Oh, no, no. I feel muffled up and invisible when I'm there. I don't dare even speak. But what I really want is to write. The real excitement of this typewriting business is that now I can typewrite my own stories and make them look quite professional, as if I had hired a secretary. It's curious what the typewriting does. I can feel my writing all so much more clearly when I am typing my own words. It flows out of my fingers; it's so different from writing with a pen. I even practise on the typewriter on pieces from my diaries. Maybe I'll send them to you and Nora when I am with Mr. James. Oh, I don't know how to express it, but taking this job seems to be changing everything."

Clara was a little breathless, trying to keep up with my longer legs as we walked quickly along the street towards the entrance to the Tube. "I've always liked what you write, Dora—your letters are wonderful, and your essays and stories. Someday you'll be published, I know. Only, I wonder, if you do get the job, what will Mr. James think of another writer in his room?"

"I would never tell him. I could never tell him. I imagine he will think I really don't know very much, that I'm only a girl who happens to be there to be the extension for his hands. I don't think I would want him to know much about me, about what I do know. That will be my secret."

"How can you keep yourself secret? You're so obviously intelligent and capable."

"But you see, I wonder if he would want anyone for his amanuensis who was too smart, too able. My father used to say that I should hide what I think, that men never like it when a woman seems to know too much. Besides, it will be easy for me to be quiet with Mr. James. I probably will not be able even to speak around him for days."

3

"What Maisie Knew"

November 1907

*No themes are so human as those that reflect for us, out of
the confusion of life, the close connexion of bliss and bale, of
the things that help with the things that hurt . . .*

—Henry James
Preface to "What Maisie Knew"
The New York Edition, volume 11

When I began with Mr. James, I was not much of a typist, and I wonder whether that fact altered his method somewhat. With the others, the experienced Miss Weld, the very fast Mr. McAlpine, Mr. James apparently still worked out everything—every plot twist, even his layers and layers of language—in his notes based on jottings of initial inspirations in his note-books before he began dictation. With Miss Weld, Mr. James was working on the later novels; surely he must have prepared voluminous notes in addition to the note-books I had caught sight of when he used them to help him remember certain details of past compositions. The note-books were always stacked about the room when we were working on the prefaces.

I always imagined the note-books to be filled with treasures, helpful techniques, and startling inspirations waiting for some ambitious young writer to find later. Perhaps I hoped it would be myself, for I was such an ambitious young writer. I had been writing for years, had even seen my essays in print in the weekly paper, but only in our little Uplyme, not down in Lyme Regis. I had tried stories and poems, even some plays, which we put on for the local children. I liked the feeling of seeing my words printed out and having my friends tell me how much they enjoyed my writing. Now, I was going to have the chance to learn more, right from Mr. James himself. But of course I certainly would not let Mr. James know anything about my own literary aspirations.

Mr. James always spoke of his past amanuenses with affection and a little condescension. He was humourous and kind, but it was clear to him that they had never had the slightest idea what he was about, nor did he want them to. It was better, he explained, to have this blank wall echoing back his words exactly as he spoke them. He often told the story of the young woman typist who, sitting in for the ailing Miss Weld, apparently was uncomfortable with Mr. James' long, thoughtful pauses (which could become excruciatingly long when he was struggling to find the right word). She became so concerned for the poor man's agony that she made the shocking mistake of trying to help by suggesting a word to solve his dilemma.

No, it was a blank object, not a person, whom Mr. James had expected when I first came to be his amanuensis, and so I made the effort to become a null, a nothing.

How does one become a null? I think Miss Weld could do it because she had her whole other life away from Lamb House, away from writing altogether. Years later, after I was comfortably settled in Rye, I often met her friends, who told me of Miss Weld's charming tea parties, her generosity to St. Michael's Ladies' Guild, her wonderful knitted garments distributed to the deserving poor, and the triumph of her happy marriage to the local young worthy who had been fortunate enough to win her over—a solicitor or a medical man, I've forgotten. It's surprising that she and I never met over the years, but perhaps it's that we were part of two very different circles of friends, even in tiny little Rye's society.

When I left my old friends behind in Chelsea to go to Rye and Mr. James, I still had my whole life's work before me to figure out. Perhaps in my inexperience I was something of a null, but I had ambition, I felt pain, I had dreams. I knew I wanted to write, and I believed that working with Mr. James might help me become a writer. I came to listen, pay attention, be involved with his work and, by that labour, take to myself something of his methods and inspiration, which might be helpful to me in my own struggle.

I wonder what he saw in me those first days. When did he first suspect that I was not another sweet, smart, pliable Miss Weld (only taller) but some other order of young woman altogether? Oh, he was so observant. I'm sure he knew from our first interview that I was different—How could he not see? It was not simply my height, for I was always the tallest of any group of girls. No, everything about me was the opposite of the "dear girls" I was expected to resemble, with their sweet faces, dimples, soft and agreeable smiles, tender and delicate voices, quiet manners, graceful movements—Oh, no, I was much more than tall.

I was strong, with good shoulders (from my days of championship matches in tennis and cricket) and good, strong legs (I could bicycle steadily the mile and a half up the hill from Lyme to Uplyme without breathing heavily). Of course, my usual complexion was brown and shiny from some outdoor escapade, my hair would never stay neatly up, and I wore no jewellery or ribbons or powder. I was a plain, solid, practical girl and proud of my strong, boyish ways. I think I would have been glad for him to see all that, but not my ambition. No, that I tried to hide for a long time.

At first, Mr. James went very slowly, word by word, from his elaborately written notes. He usually paced back and forth, never looking my way, especially for those first weeks. But one morning I noticed our relationship undergoing a change as we were working with the novella "What Maisie Knew," that heartbreaking story of a tender, young girl. I remember that I was uncomfortable with his discomfort. He kept looking at me—what was he thinking, imagining? Now, when I look back over my old copies of the prefaces, re-read the words, I can almost hear his voice.

That day had begun rather badly. When I first arrived, the house was in turmoil. The housekeeper met me at the door, saying, "Mr. James is not ready, he will not be ready for you for quite some time—" and then she was interrupted by a frantic Burgess, the valet, hurrying through the front hall, rushing past me, still in his shirt-sleeves, his thin arms and legs flying, shouting back over his shoulder to an invisible Mr. James, apparently not yet downstairs, "I'll get him back for you, sir, the little monster," and then Burgess was past me, out through the still-open front door.

Maximillian, Mr. James' precious little long-haired dachshund, terribly quick for all his short legs and round belly, had got loose again. Then Mr. James appeared, buttoning his waistcoat, his tie flapping loose. "Miss Bosanquet, I am so sorry, there's been a terrible tragedy, our little Maximillian has escaped again, and it takes at least two of us to corner him."

Mrs. Paddington handed him the leash, and he started past me.

"Shall I come too?" I found myself saying to my surprise. "I used to be good at catching my father's little dog when she got out."

Mr. James spoke over his shoulder, "Yes, come on, then. You take Church Street, Burgess usually goes up by the Wall, and I'll take the lower regions," and off he went breathlessly calling out for Maximillian.

I tried to imagine what a round-bellied, short-legged little dog like Max might be drawn to on a cool, wet morning. I remembered that it was delivery day at the butcher's down on Queen Street and headed off in that direction. Sure enough, there Max was with the other, bigger town dogs but apparently accepted as one of them in spite of his elevated status in Mr. James' household. Max was so preoccupied with his ruffian friends that I was able to scoop him up.

In triumph, I brought Max back to a still distraught Mr. James, who apparently had already given up the search as a lost cause yet was waiting hopefully at the open door. He was exceedingly grateful to me, and then he took Max in his arms and simultaneously declared that Max was the worst blackguard, while feeding him blackmailing bits of biscuits from the tin open on the stairs. After a few minutes of this, Mr. James handed the little rascal to Burgess, and we went upstairs to try to do some work.

Once we were settled, the morning had a different feeling to it. Mr. James was dictating from a handful of notes, and now for the first time he glanced down at me while he dictated. Oh, he still paced back and forth, and clearly there was an ending he kept looking towards, but now the meanderings were more noticeable and dominated our proceedings.

I was unsure at times on that morning as to whether Mr. James was "writing" his preface or talking to me about his memories of the ways he used to work and of his methods those many years before.

He was working on that volume with its two novellas, "What Maisie Knew" and "In the Cage," plus one long short story, "The Pupil." I was already familiar with "Maisie," which had puzzled me when it first came out, whereas "In the Cage" had been a favourite of mine since it first appeared. When I look back over that preface for "Maisie," I hear again his conspiratorial tone reciting those humourous and yet somehow revealing anecdotes. I still thrill to remember how he spoke directly to me, dictating to me as if he and I—we—were in this together with the struggle of the author, as he dictated,

"Capital T *That is we feel it when* Comma, *in such tangled connexions* Comma, *we happen to care* Full Stop. *I should n't really go on as if this were the case with many readers* Full Stop."

No, he went on that way because I was there. I felt it in his pause, his shuffling of pages before he moved on to the next story. Even now, thinking back, it seems as though he is still here with me, something my friends these days probably cannot even imagine.

In the Master's careful, meticulous prose, I can still hear his striving always to be fair and just and even modest in his self-examinations and yet celebratory about his triumphs over the slightest difficulties of scale or point of view (often self-inflicted). Always, there was the struggle to keep to his "small" subject, to produce the necessary "short" story, a struggle that so often had ended in failure. His stories inevitably became novellas, and the novellas grew to novels, never the other way around.

That day, he was proud of his process, using young Maisie to tell her own story, keeping it all within her own limited, muddling consciousness. He dictated:

"*I have already elsewhere noted, I think, that the memory of my own work preserves for me no theme that . . . has n't signally refused to remain humble* Comma," and then he referred to the very large theme of little Maisie's story with a charming image drawn from our morning adventure. I remember how impishly he looked at me and then dictated,

"*Once* Quotation "*out* Comma, End Quotation," *like a house-dog of a temper above confinement* Comma, *it defies the mere whistle, it roams, it hunts, it seeks out and* Quotation "*sees* End Quotation" *life* Semicolon *; it can be brought back but by hand and then only to take its futile thrashing* Full Stop."

We shared a good laugh over that clever bit, both of us in on the joke.

What was remarkable about those days and stories recorded in my diary and letters, why I can remember them even now, fifty years later, is the shift in Mr. James' manner towards me. We were to become better, closer allies as time went on, but it was that early exchange, working there on those stories about modern young women struggling to make their way in this treacherous world that we became—Oh, "collaborators" is not quite the word. It's more as if it felt like we were co-conspirators.

We both understood something about Mr. James' story, his theme, his characters, and their inner worlds, which others did not. And so, I became his constant listener, his faithful companion as he struggled ever deeper into the mire of explanations of his processes, his themes, his ambitions for those ignored works.

I was aware of his understanding, and he was aware of mine from a look or a phrase. We knew that we were somehow united on the same side, even as different as we were, separated by age, by temperament, by nationality. We knew that each of us had watched, felt, suffered, understood. During his dictations, we went about the business of getting others to see what he saw, and to understand.

For, you see, what I sometimes forget now in the world's acclamation of Henry James—the Master, as his friends referred to him—is that when I came to him in 1907, he was hardly read. Not the previous books, not the new collections. Not by the great public, not even by book reviewers. No, he had become that terrible spectre of the famous Great Man left behind in his immense age and stature with no audience. It was to be several painful months before I would wholly understand his desolation and the bitter taste of ash—all that was left of his great fame and power. In my first enthusiasms, I believed his friends read his books, as I read them, and that seemed enough.

Well, almost enough. At first, I did have some doubts about myself. Did I truly understand his work? But also I began to have my doubts about Mr. James. Did he understand what I needed as an amanuensis? It was true my speed increased with each day, and I slowly brought my nerves under control. My hand no longer shook while Mr. James read over each finished page, and soon enough, he simply paused while I pulled out the typed page and rolled in the fresh paper.

With each new page, I was exhilarated. There were so many wonders. Mr. James poured out ideas that burst on me like fireworks, stories that broke my heart—lost loves, secrets revealed. I happily typed away, silent as Patience sitting on a monument, usually content and waiting for the next surprise.

But not always. No matter what I have said about my thrill at being there, there was still a part of me that was young, proud, well educated, knowing everything, thinking I knew even more than Mr. James. I had studied my rhetoric, I had read the ancients, I knew what good writing sounded like, and I felt sometimes that this old man was off on some extravagant escapade of language or memory. Of course, I would take it all down because, after all, he was paying me to, but there was that proud part of me who knew better, who wanted to correct his excesses.

Sometime during our first weeks, his love of alliteration got to me. Mr. James apparently adored the sound of words, especially how his own words sounded in his own voice with repeating letters, and even with certain letters—*L*'s were a favourite, and those pesky *P*'s. I remember one of the first prefaces. It was for "The Awkward Age," and he was speaking of his first idea, the "germ" of his story. I was quietly tapping away, imagining along with him,

"The seed sprouted in that vast nursery of sharp appeals and concrete images which calls itself, for blest convenience, London Semicolon *;"*

Some layer of my mind was agreeing with his description, Yes, that's it, London is filled with possibilities.

". . . *it fell even into the order of the minor* Quotation *"social phenomena* End Quotation*" with which, as fruit for the observer, that mightiest of the trees of suggestion bristles* Full Stop."

But now, I was lost. "*Nursery*" . . . and then "*fruit*"? And now, a tree with "*bristles*"? Yet, nevertheless, my fingers tapped correctly in automatic response to his endless voice.

"*It was presumably present* Comma, *a fine purple peach.*"

His voice went on, but my mind was growling: Peaches are not purple, Mr. James. There's too much of the letter *P*, Mr. James. But of course I kept on going, never saying a word. At least, I was cautious enough for that.

The very next day, Mr. James came back with his corrections inked over the words from the day before. It was as if he had over-heard the distaste in my mind for his alliteration, for he had changed that purple phrase, though it took a double negative to get him out of trouble, and he had kept most of the *P*'s, had even added to them: "*It was not, no doubt, a fine purple peach, but it might pass for a round ripe plum . . .*"

I felt a surge of pride, my judgement exonerated.

4

"The Awkward Age"

December 1907

. . . the quite incalculable tendency of a mere grain of
subject-matter to expand and develop and cover the ground
when conditions happen to favour it.

—Henry James
Preface to "The Awkward Age"
The New York Edition, volume 9

A telegram from my aunt Emily arrived, announcing she
was to arrive in Rye the next day. She said she happened
to be visiting with a friend and hoped to come over to spend the
afternoon. Mr. James had asked for an entire morning's work. That
meant that the afternoon would be mine, and I could take her to all
the sights in Rye. But, oh dear, she wanted to meet Mr. James and
see where I was working. I could not have that happen. He would
seem such a strange sort of person for Aunt Emily's niece to be
spending time with.

Aunt Emily had always held high aspirations for me. Oh, not
marriage and social position as the other aunts on my father's side
did. No, Emily was my dearest aunt, my mother's sister-in-law. And
I think I was always her favourite, too.

I am not sure why I was special to her, because I was the wildest of all the cousins. Perhaps she liked me because I had most needed her help, or perhaps it was because I was quite different from what was expected. But whatever the reason, my aunt Emily always took notice of me, though I do not believe she understood me any better than any of the other aunts did, and there were plenty of other aunts, all of them aunts by marriage. My mother had only suitably business-minded brothers, six of them. They all were married, and Aunt Emily was married to the youngest, my uncle Ras, and lived in a big house in Kensington. As much as she liked me, not even Aunt Emily seemed to understand what I thought or cared about, even while I was young and still living with my father. No one understood why I enjoyed repairing bicycles. And I am sure that no one at home ever read one of Mr. James' novels, for they hardly read any books at all.

"Home": What a strange-sounding word now, after all these years settled in London with Lady Rhondda—*my* Margaret—and with the Second Great War more than a decade behind us. Where was my home then, in those days when I first went to Rye? I was startled then if Mr. James suggested I go home on the days when his struggle to find the right words overcame him, when it appeared to me that he had spent too much time away from his dictation and had lost the thread.

Even then, I thought it strange to call my boarding house and its cramped, cold room "home." When forced to return home to that room, I was miserable; it was noisy and through the thin walls I heard voices, but those were voices of no one I knew or wanted to know. I felt quite lonely there. On cold winter days, that room was dark and even damp, and the old wall-paper was yellowed, greasy, while the one low-browed window opened only onto an unkempt patch of grass and the alley with its cans for cinders and rubbish.

When I was young, I used to have a lovely room in our old, brown house across the road from my grandfather's big house filled with Bosanquet uncles and aunts and cousins in Swansea, the older, more fashionable part of the Isle of Wight. My father was the youngest boy of eight. His eldest sisters, my aunts Bessie and Bert, were much older. I am sure they never approved of me, especially when I wanted to go to university, for they had very definite ideas about what a young lady—a well-behaved young niece—should be, and whatever that was, I was not that. I wish I had met my father's younger sister, Georgie. She was most unusual. I had always heard that she'd never married, wore her hair cut off very short, rode horses, raised dogs, and was not at all like the other sisters. But she never came to visit.

At first we lived near my Bosanquet grandfather, and I grew up believing the Bosanquets to be the busiest, most energetic of families, with our golf games at dawn, cricket before luncheon, croquet tournaments in the afternoon heat, and tennis round robins at tea-time.

My father was happy and busy in those days, when he was assistant vicar in a big, popular church. I don't remember his being at home often, fortunately not enough to notice much about me. I was an ungainly girl afraid to make many friends. My older cousins across the road, Queenie and the boys, fascinated me, but often they were busy, and so I would read or play alone with my cats; we always had two or three feline generations, mother and daughter and granddaughter, and they were my best friends.

My mother and father liked it best when I was quiet. When my father was home, he was usually doing something in his study, and my mother was often in her room with the door closed. She always rested after lunch, every day of her life, a real rest, not a few minutes of sitting down with her eyes closed. No, she went up to her room (and of course she and Papa never slept in the same room in those less-demanding times) and had several private hours without interruption. By unspoken agreement, the household protected her. Everyone told me to keep quiet and be good; even then, my mother's health was not strong.

Her room was cool and dark in the early afternoon, even in summer. She had the shades drawn and the curtains closed, doubly dark there in her cave of shadow and bed and dresser. She always slept under a cover of some sort, a soft knitted pink blanket in winter and, in summer, the most beautiful coverlet—crisp and white, made of embroidered linen and lace, an impossible dream of a bed cover. When I was young, my mother seemed to me a very silly woman, but I understand, now that I am older than my mother was when she died, that she wanted only to have beautiful things always around her, that she wanted her life to be beautiful, too, and so she made a little ritual, I realise now, of going up to her darkened room at the same hour every day.

"For a little bit," she would announce at the luncheon table. "I'll go up now for my little rest, for a few minutes. I always feel so much better after I've had my rest. Please forgive me. Perhaps you both should take a rest as well. I think it's best for us to save our store of energy, while we can," and so, with a coy wave, up she would go.

I always felt a little lost when my mother was sleeping in the middle of the day. I had too much energy to lie down at midday when I was young. The maid could not persuade me to stop playing and rest for a few minutes even if she promised to look at a picture book with me, but once I was old enough to read for myself, I would take my book and disappear outside, and no one could pull me back, even for meals. And then when I got my first bicycle, oh heavens, I was free at last to go wherever I could imagine, flying down those sandy lanes, my long legs out on each side, my short hair loose, blown back by the breeze I had created.

Though I understood even then that my mother was not well and needed rest to save her energy, nevertheless, her door was closed all too often when I wanted her. There were some good days when she would be in her sitting-room by the window, writing letters or painting with a tiny brush some water-colour scene on stiff paper the size of my hand. She and Papa wrote and illustrated a story book for me, a rhyming version of "The Three Bears," but it was such a strange little book that I was afraid of it, I think. I did not like how it portrayed what happened to bad little girls. Goldilocks looked terrified by the huge bears, and even the youngest bear frightened me when his little wooden chair burst under him, with the sharp splinters flying everywhere, the way my parents drew the story. I guess they thought I would laugh at his predicament. I don't think Mama ever understood my fear of meeting strangers, or of the dark, and so I had to pretend to be strong and brave for her. No matter how hard I tried, I could never be the good little girl my parents had wanted.

Sometimes, though, my books would not be enough, and I would escape that quiet house to go across the road and find my cousins. I thought I must be a bit of a Bosanquet after all because I did like to run outside and play games, especially with my boy cousins, especially cricket, which was their favourite, too. Because I was tall and strong and fast, they always let me into their games. We felt that playing cricket was our birthright, for, as Bosanquets, we were extremely proud of being related to our famous cricketer cousin, T. A. Bosanquet, whom we admired much more than our philosopher cousin, Bernard Bosanquet.

As we grew older, the boy cousins became more uncomfortable when I came out to play, but I always believed that it was because I had grown taller and was faster than they were. I was proud of being chosen to be on my school teams, but my strength and fame at cricket only seemed to embarrass my mother. I remember her scolding me for rips in my play skirts and grass stains on my knickers. She would worry that I was playing too rough and too wild for a proper sort of girl. I tried to reassure her by bragging that they loved what I did at my school. Even Cheltenham Ladies College, the bastion of propriety and wealth that the family had packed me off to, could be happy with such an excellent cricket player.

But then at the end of my first year, when I came home from Cheltenham, I found things to be very much changed. My family had left our beautiful big brown house, left our cats and cousins, and moved to Dorset and a new house, the Hermitage it was called, and a new parish, Uplyme. My mother seemed even more tired, and there was a new baby brother.

They never explained to me what had happened, why the birth had been so difficult. Now, I wonder if perhaps my mother was too old. My parents always seemed old to me, and they had waited for a long time, even for me, and I was already ten when Louis was born. Perhaps something had gone wrong, for my mother was never well again, and poor little Louis—We all felt that there was something not quite right about him. Our house had to be kept absolutely quiet, for once the baby began to cry, there was no way to comfort him. We went through a succession of nurse-maids and other servants, who did not want to stay on. Louis was always the most beautiful and the most difficult child. Perhaps I did not help much either, since I moped about the new place, complaining, wishing to be back at my grandfather's, back with my friends at school, anywhere but there.

In that regimented quiet, once again I found my only freedom in books. I read all the time, so that my parents could not say I was making too much noise. Instead, days would go by when no one heard a word from me.

I think it was like that, too, when I went to Rye, far from my family and friends once again. No matter how lonely I felt, I could still lose myself in books and, this time, in Mr. James' library. As he looked over my shoulder, he saw me finishing book after book, and he would even suggest what I should read next, so that I might go ahead to his new stories, or look at a play he was going to revive, or even go back and see what his newly dictated prefaces were like. I was happy to think I had more, new, unpublished writings by Henry James to read.

After all this time, I can still remember the shock of pleasure I felt as a young girl when I read my first James story. That was one night when a more experienced girl at Cheltenham smuggled to me that strangely affecting ghost story, "The Turn of the Screw." I remember turning the pages, slowly at first, mystified, then hungrily devouring the book, and eagerly seeking out all the rest—novels, novellas, stories, everything. When I had to leave school because my mother was very ill and needed me at home, I was glad I had books for comfort.

My mother was taken from us when I was twenty. It was Aunt Emily, her brother's wife, who came to help. I think she must have felt sorry for me, a young girl left alone with a small brother and a bereft father. Of course, I thought that I was grown up then; after all, I had been in charge of myself and of our household for the long months of my mother's illness. But I remember that during the time the different aunts stayed on with us after the funeral, it was Aunt Emily who could make me cry—her voice sounded so much like my dear mother's—and she tried to comfort me, something my father never tried to do.

It was also Aunt Emily who was there and who knew what to do when I fell ill. A bad head cold suddenly turned terrifyingly worse—high fever, headaches, and then my ear was in excruciating pain until suddenly, with a feeling of intense pressure, then release, my eardrum burst. I was ill that time for several weeks and needed Aunt Emily to take care of the household and keep me from complete despair, but as things do, I got better, and she could return to her own family.

The next year, when I went to prepare for the exams for university, only Aunt Emily listened to me talk about what I was about to do. I wondered if she wished that she herself had gone to university, but of course when she was young, there had been no real opportunity. After I received my degree, I think she was proud, though of course she never said so. She only glanced at the piece of parchment I had tacked up on my bedroom wall; she touched the Latin words, then went on talking of her garden and the weather.

It was against my father's wishes and the other aunts' dire warnings that I shared a flat in London with my school friends and went to work with Miss Petherbridge in Whitehall. Even that outrage did not seem to faze Aunt Emily. She would invite me to dine with her and my cousins at Honiton Street, and though she never asked about my work and I never really spoke of it, I am sure that she knew. Her present for my birthday that year was a very smart leather belt, with a note indicating that I was to use it to look handsome when I was on the job. I was very pleased that she might approve of me, because all the other aunts were in a dither over my working at all. They were at my father like a flock of sparrows, but of course he did nothing, said nothing; soon enough, he had his new bride and their new house. My father was the last person to be concerned about me, about what work I was doing or even where I was living. Even before I was twenty-one, when I left to go to university in London, he informed me that I was to be on my own since I was so smart. From then on, I would have to make do with my mother's inheritance; once he re-married, he and Annie would not send me any more funds.

Now, all these many years later, I see why writing this is so difficult. I can't seem to stick in one place. I keep wanting to write as if I am talking to someone, but that feels too personal. I am afraid there are things I should not be saying, afraid there are people I will hurt, even though my father has been dead now for thirty years, and my poor dear aunts have been dry and dead even longer. My cousins, even the youngest ones, Queenie's children and the others, have long given me up. I believe they think I am stranger than even my aunts thought; they whisper about me across the cocktail table whenever I attend family gatherings. So what do I care if I tell things that might hurt people's feelings? And what do I care if I tell the truth? But I do care that it makes sense. I do care that I tell it well, and not this haphazard sort of unstructured writing—I suppose I can always return later and clean it up, but that was not the method I learnt at Mr. James' knee, or should I say, at his elbow.

I did not mean to be writing about my father or even my aunt. I meant to be writing of those first days with Mr. James and how what I was doing there was unusual for a young woman, but now, all these years later, who could understand that? These days, young girls go into unrelated older men's houses and do all sorts of things every day and night, and no one thinks anything of it. But in 1907, so soon after the Old Queen died, so soon after King Edward, that wild royal, had become the leader of the Empire, well, who knew what to think?

Certainly Aunt Emily did not. And that was why she came to Rye so soon after I began to work for Mr. James. She had decided I needed a family visit. When she arrived, I was still up in the Green Room, trying to finish. I heard the knocker thump, and she was brought upstairs.

"Dora, my dear," she exclaimed as she took off her tiny brown suede gloves and lifted her fashionably dotted veil to look around, "what a charming place your Mr. James lives in. And how hard you must be working!"

"Aunt Emily! You've surprised me!"

The room was strewn about with open books, piles of papers, ink pots, red and black, and I was still rudely sitting at the type-writing machine.

"Let me finish this line," I said. "You're so early!"

I went to help her with her things and to lean down to give her my customary kiss on her soft, papery cheek. She was dressed in her favourite colour, that rich cocoa that set off her dark eyes so well.

Even after she removed her delicate little hat, her silvery hair was still its usual perfection in its braids and elaborate coils. She smiled, and I thought that her face showed a little tiredness from the journey, for her pleasant smile lines had deepened and her skin was not its usual perfectly transparent rosiness. She was telling me she had caught the earliest train.

"I was that eager to see you, my dear. And we're all so curious about what it is you're about here." She looked around the room with its mess and books everywhere, so different from her tidy, plush-velvet Kensington home. "I'm afraid we're all worried about your Mr. James, and what it's like for you here all alone, without friends or family. My dear, whatever were you thinking?"

And so for the hundredth time I had to try to explain to someone, and even worse, a woman from my mother's generation, what I was doing there with Mr. James. I was not homesick and was certain I would be fine once I was accustomed to the typewriting machine and to Mr. James and his unusual working style. By now, he almost seemed to be more like me than anyone in my family. But I could not tell Aunt Emily that! Looking around his masculine, leathery book-lined study, I could barely speak. My reticence had once again returned.

"Aunt Emily, I'm not sure—I need to work, I need to be on my own. As you know, my father—"

"Oh, don't speak to me of your father, I'm not thinking about your father. He'll do fine with that nice new bride to take care of him. No, Dora, it's you I worry over. What are you doing here? Won't you come back to the aunts and let us try once more to find you a husband? You know, you barely gave us a chance last summer before you hurried back to London and took a job in that secretarial bureau. Aunt Ellen and I were mortified. Really, my dear, none of our other nieces has ever done any such thing. Even Cousin Freddie when she went down to Swansea to teach in a boys' school did not surprise me as much. Have we really failed you so badly?"

I knew I had to answer something, for my dear aunt had my best interests at heart, but what could I say? I could not explain how I had come to be there, instead of making the rounds to all the aunts and uncles, repeating the circuit until someone found the right man for me to marry. Well, I knew that would NEVER happen. When I was younger, my deep love for Ethel had made that clear to me, even if no one but my friends believed in me. But how could I tell this dear aunt the things that I had held silent in my mind and heart for so long, for years—a lifetime, it seemed—the things that would disturb her so?

While I was hesitating, Aunt Emily moved around the room, nervously fingering an object here, a piece of paper there, lifting up a book to look at the title by the light of the window, then putting it down with a shake of her silvery head. She turned again to me. "I suppose I'd better come right out with it. What we really want to know—Is it proper, do you think, for a gentleman's daughter to be here, doing this sort of work? You know we're not at all familiar with what it is you are doing here."

I tried once again, explaining my work as literary secretary to Mr. James, helping with his correspondence, of course nothing personal, and then his real work, writing the prefaces, the stories, and the plays.

"Aunt Emily, I imagine as he dictates to my typewriting machine that he is talking only to me, as if I were his friend and we were sitting together over tea. He tells me about how he got his ideas or where he ran into trouble—it's as if we are partners or old friends. He seems to tell me everything."

"But Dora, is it proper? Is it right for a young, unmarried woman to be here in a man's house, alone with him, upstairs, up in his room? I've never heard of such a thing!"

I had to think for a minute why it seemed right to me. Of course, I had been uncomfortable at first. It was a small, intimate house and very much arranged for the comfort of the elderly bachelor who lived there, but then I thought back to why I had wanted to work with Mr. James from the first instant I heard about the job.

"Oh, he's fine, Aunt Emily! Ever since I was a girl, I've loved his books. Maybe some things I could not understand, some subject matter was too old for me, and some things I still don't understand. He is very deep, Aunt Emily. But always I've felt that Mr. James had a special gift, a way of making complicated things clear, as if he were writing for me or girls like me. Maybe it would help if I could show you."

I went to the shelves to look, and Aunt Emily went to sit carefully on a small, old chair beside the writing desk. But first she had to move a book, which had been left there; she turned it over, with its yellow wrapping, its foreign-looking cover and French title, and she put it down carefully without checking inside. Then, looking around, frowning at where my typewriting machine made an ugly shadow on the floor, she folded her hands to wait.

I found the page. "Here, one of his young heroines is talking about how hard it is to grow up in this day and age. You've watched my girl cousins and me struggle. Listen . . . Here in this morning's preface, Mr. James has young women in mind:

"'One could count them on one's fingers (an abundant allowance), the liberal firesides beyond the wide glow of which, in a comparative dimness, female adolescence hovered and waited.'

"Mr. James goes on to describe the 'inevitable irruption of the ingenuous mind' ; and then says,

"'The ingenuous mind might, it was true, be suppressed altogether, the general disconcertment averted. . . . A girl might be married off the day after her irruption, or better still the day before it, to remove her from the sphere of the play of the mind ;'

"Can you see, Aunt Emily? It's as if he spoke our hopes aloud, finding words for us young women:

"'That is it would be, by this scheme, so infinitely awkward, so awkward beyond any patching-up, for the hovering female young to be conceived as present at "good" talk, that their presence is, theoretically at least, not permitted till their youth has been promptly corrected by marriage—in which case they have ceased to be merely young. The better the talk prevailing in any circle, accordingly, the more organised, the more complete, the element of precaution and exclusion.'

"Aunt Emily, if we younger women can only find our own way, a way out of this ridiculous set of impossible expectations. Can't you see?—Whenever I read this, it makes me feel that he sees us. He wants to help us, here in our preposterous position, caught between what we want and what is expected. He describes one of us, a young woman of 1907, kept modest and ignorant, and yet she's still expected to know so much. We're supposed somehow to stay innocent and yet understand every innuendo, to be good and also wise, to act helpless and yet to be strong, to appear beautiful and at the same time completely artless."

Aunt Emily had moved uncomfortably in her chair. She did not like my use of "innocent" and its implied, unspoken opposite. She raised her head and protested, "But Dora, the old ways were there to protect the young girl—"

"My point exactly. Now, we are without protection. Everyone claims to admire the New Woman, but then no one knows what to make of us. What do we want? And what does it mean when we're brought up among such contradictions, when we are encouraged to try for good jobs and independent incomes, then required to give it all up if we ever marry? Or we're supposed to remain innocent and pure yet can attend university with our brothers and argue about biology and economics, educating ourselves, but for what? For glorious disappointment. And now we have those impossibly idealistic Suffragettes, trying to persuade the public that all women, except the Irish, should have the Vote. They make beautiful speeches with their classical allusions, their goddesses and martyrs and glorious hand-embroidered banners—and all the time they're divided among themselves as to when or whether they should blow up Parliament. Oh, it's all so confusing—But I know that when I read Mr. James, I feel safe, I feel understood. Working beside him, I feel useful, I even feel a little like I might somehow learn to understand myself."

After my outburst, Aunt Emily shook her head, and I changed the subject to ask after the new baby cousins I was sorry to have missed at the holidays. My aunt stayed on to share the tea Mr. James had arranged. I gave her sandwiches and a cup of tea, but probably it was not her usual flavour. I am afraid that the sort of biscuits Mr. James usually provided seemed rather small, and his sharp-flavoured cheese crumbled. I can see her familiar, exquisite gesture as she brushed the crumbs off her delicate fingers with her handkerchief, then folded her hands in her lap and looked around, still silent. In the face of all my words, she was too perplexed to speak.

But later that day, when Aunt Emily had gone and Mr. James had returned from his afternoon away, I realised that something had changed. Somehow, my aunt's unspoken questions had been answered. It was not by anything I had said, I was sure. Perhaps it was Mr. James' lovely home, Lamb House itself, with its solid evidence of rank and presence and position, that reassured her. Before she left, we took a turn up and down the gravel paths of his walled, formal garden and looked at the neatly labelled beds of perennials, the prize-winning rose-beds, and his awards (earned by his gardener, George!) proudly hung on the wall of the glass house, each medallion engraved to "Mr. H. James, Esquire." There, in the cool winter afternoon's light, surrounded by the grey stone and ancient pale-rose brick walls, everything was orderly and snug in Mr. James' well-tended and protected winter garden.

And so, my aunt left me with a long hug, pressing a specially wrapped package into my hands, insisting that I open it after she had left. It contained several of her large, and justly famous, plump currant scones along with her hastily written note explaining that I was to share the scones with my employer.

5

"The Spoils of Poynton"

1908

*The horizon was in fact a band of sea ; a small red-roofed
town, of great antiquity, perched on its sea-rock, clustered
within the picture off to the right ; while above one's head
rustled a dense summer shade, that of a trained and
arching ash, rising from the middle of the terrace, brushing
the parapet with a heavy fringe and covering the place like
a vast umbrella. Beneath this umbrella and really under
exquisite protection "The Spoils of Poynton" managed more
or less symmetrically to grow.*

—Henry James
Preface to "The Spoils of Poynton"
The New York Edition, volume 10

As it turned out, after the excitement and strain of Aunt
Emily's visit, I was needed to help Mr. James keep on
the narrow track, back to the prefaces. As the dark winter days short-
ened, our work seemed to slow. We were poring over several volumes
containing all his short stories, struggling mightily to fit them into a
new arrangement. The publisher thought the volumes would be too
long with the way Mr. James had so carefully divided them.

Some mornings, I could see that Mr. James was tired, even when we started. From the quantity of new work he had readied for us by hand, apparently the night before, I wondered if he had slept at all. It was on one such morning that he seemed to be having more of a struggle to locate the exact word, and his usual slow pacing before the windows became halting, even agonisingly blocked. Finally, he stood at the mantel, his bent back to me, apparently thoroughly stumped for the word, audibly searching among the many possibilities, ones that sounded the same, ones that had the same rhythm of syllables, ones that meant somewhat the same:

"... *the air as of a mere disjoined and* lass—lassitudinous ... asinine ... [long silent pause] ... acerbated ... exacerbated ... exasperated ... aspiration ... aspirated ... [longer silent pause] ... ulcerated ..."

Through that struggle, my mind began to wander, since my chosen book that morning had not been good enough for such a long pause. I looked down at my shirtwaist, with its crisp white pleats, and tried to brush away a smudge from the carbon paper.

Mr. James spoke. "Now I've got it: *disjoined and lacerate-d lump of life* ..." Then he went back to his notes, and we marched endlessly on.

Shortly after one in the afternoon, Mr. James put away his notes. His tone was kindly. "I believe that's a goodly amount for today, Miss Bosanquet. I wouldn't want to appropriate your afternoon as well. We'll begin again tomorrow at this spot."

I pulled the cover over the typewriting machine and stacked the good copies and carbons.

And then I was free to return to my rooms and try to wash out the smudge, for this was my last clean shirtwaist, and I had no time or money for the laundry.

I had been well trained by Miss Petherbridge to watch every detail of my appearance. I was most particular whenever I went to Mr. James. I had only a small dresser mirror in my dark little room at the back of the house. I could slant the mirror up to fix my hair or slant it down to try to see if my hem was straight or my stockings had gone baggy and wrinkled. I never have wanted for much of a mirror, but I remember that room and that mirror as a particular trial. Getting ready in the morning, I would actually change my shirtwaist several times and turn back and forth before the mirror in that cramped room, trying for the best effect, that desired combination of crisp, tailored efficiency and tender, helpful femininity. In those days, I still had hopes for some possible combining of the two very distinct and combative parts of my nature.

"My nature"—What a strange phrase that is, implying so much of what I was born with, like a wild animal, and yet also with a meaning of what I myself added, what I brought on myself.

"My nature"—I am flooded with all that phrase contains—my family and how they struggled with my wild nature, how my mother tried to make me appear sweeter, smaller than I was, bedecking me in frilly dresses, pulling me close in those old photographs. And my wild behaviour: No one could rein me in, not even when my mother was ill, not even after she had died. I roamed the cliffs and hills of Lyme Regis, met my friends secretly and helped them to write and perform plays.

I was a puzzle to my parents. Only my cousin Queenie really understood. Once when we were all together at our grandfather's, she told my fortune, using the latest fad, phrenology, to read my character from the bumps on my head. Meanwhile, she helped me do my hair, putting it up for the first time. It was that sad, lost Christmas when my mother was quite ill, and so I had gone to Queenie for help. She was the girl cousin closest to me in age, one year older but much more experienced. She lived in London, and she went to parties all the time.

I can remember the feeling of her brushing and brushing my unruly hair, and then she surprised me by her comments, saying I had an interesting head, and that she could read my character from its shape and its various bumps.

I held very still, and she moved her soft, delicate hands through my hair, gently massaging and talking in her beautiful, low voice.

"Dora, I can feel that you are jealous and a flirt."

"I don't believe you." She was right, but still I had to act sceptical. "How can you tell that?"

"No, wait, I can do more. You are generous, sulky . . . you have no religion but some affection."

I knew she was even more correct, at least about being sulky, as my poor father could attest, and about having no religion; I thought of all the missed Sundays, the giggling through chapel. I relaxed even more into the wonderful feeling of her hands.

And certainly I was a flirt—ask my friends from Cheltenham Ladies College, that very particular finishing school my parents had, with great hopes, sent me to. Sometimes we would have a dance with ourselves, no men, after a formal dinner in the Great Room at Holyon House, and we would all dress up in our long white gowns, practising with each other the different steps. I loved to dance, and I went from girl to girl, wanting to dance with everyone. During our secret cocoa parties, after the lights were supposed to be out, going to each other's rooms, I would go to so many different rooms that my friends would tease me about being an outrageous flirt. But I liked being friends with all the girls. I did not mean to flirt; it's that I have always been curious about other people. I want to understand what they are really like.

I suppose Queenie was right. I did want to be generous and affectionate, but then that jealous part would come in and make everything complicated. I remember wailing to Queenie, "Why do my friends not like each other, too, as I like them? Why do they always want to have me all to themselves?"

Her only answer was to continue her report: "And you are very independent in some things."

I liked to hear that; I knew I was named after my father's father, Theodore Whatman Bosanquet, but I used to pretend I was like Empress Theodora of Constantinople, that brilliant strategist famous for her bloodthirsty appetite.

I asked Queenie, "Do you think I've had too much freedom? I sometimes behave as if I were a boy, but I've been alone so much, I don't know. I wonder if deep down I'm not all mixed up. Maybe I really don't care about what people think about me and how I act. I've always liked being odd, liked being the one to fix machinery, and to be really good at cricket when girls are not even allowed to run. I like to write my own bloody adventures."

Queenie went on touching the surface of my head and along the ridges behind my ears, then moving up to the tender area along the temples. "I can feel that you are artistic and not at all practical."

How could she have thought that? Whenever I tried to draw, it came out looking strangely flat and dead—like my old fossil-rock drawings from the Lyme Cliffs or the sketches of dissections I used to do with my father. I have always wanted to be around people who are artistic, but until recently I was a little afraid of them, too. Where do they find their ideas? They seem so self-sufficient, so centred on themselves.

I wanted Queenie to go on, and I asked her if those two characteristics, being practical and being artistic, had to be opposites. I certainly felt practical, if being practical meant keeping track of the details of daily life, such as knowing how much money was left in our household account when my father left me in charge. To my mind, being practical meant listing the pantry order perfectly before the household ran out of things and before my father shouted at me again for forgetting. But being practical also meant teaching myself to refrain from turning silly and sentimental about my feelings, such as missing my mother, or my pashes at school, or worrying over whether anyone really cared for me.

But by then, Queenie had finished pulling my hair up into an elegant French twist. She shook her head at my questions, and with a hug, she gave me one of her own black velvet bows to cover all the stray wisps that still escaped from the combs no matter how hard we tried. And so, beautifully together, we went down to join the family.

Now, standing before that impossible mirror on Mermaid Street in Rye, how I wished Queenie were nearby or at least that I had one of her clever velvet bows with me. What a struggle it was to put my hair up into a simple twist that day, when I was to dress for my first rather large-scale social occasion in Rye, a literary tea-party given by some woman I had not yet met, a friend of a friend. I certainly did not feel very independent or flirtatious. Instead, I felt nervous.

I wondered if I might see Mr. James there, and as I pulled and smoothed my hair tightly back, I had to laugh at the sudden thought of his broad forehead, his smooth skull—What would Queenie have made of his character? I never could induce her to say whether someone could be artistic and practical at the same time. I certainly was learning about Mr. James and his practical, methodical approach to his writing with each new day, but I was not seeing much of what I would have called his artistic side.

I wondered about his other characteristics. I knew Mr. James did not go to church, because he expected me to work on Sundays. I had seen him being quite affectionate with his little dog, Max, worrying over every whimper and squeak. I suppose the world saw Mr. James as a famous man. His books had made him wealthy and independent, but of course he'd had no contrary expectations to fight off, as I had with my family. He seemed quite settled and happy in his successful literary career. And sulky? When things did not go right for Mr. James, like that morning when Mrs. Paddington kept interrupting with one household problem after another, I had seen him annoyed, but with good reason. I could imagine him as a good, devoted friend but not as a flirt, not as a jealous lover. I was quite sure that, at age sixty-four, he must have been too old to feel any of that.

That afternoon tea was my first such invitation, sent by a Mrs. Dew Smith, a friend of my old friend Nora Wilson's family—and therefore she was probably very rich and very well-placed. I wanted to make a good first impression, and part of me was also nervous about the possibility of meeting my august employer there; it might be the first time Mr. James and I would meet socially, outside of our working arrangements.

I carefully chose my deep blue cashmere because it was almost clean and the colour would set off my eyes. I laughed to think of Mr. James noticing the colour of my eyes—Had he ever yet really looked at me? I hoped to impress him that I, too, could be a part of Rye's social scene and prove to him that I was more than the body behind the typewriting machine.

As I walked down the hill and across town, following Mrs. Dew Smith's instructions, I felt again the conflict between my two sides—hard, ambitious, and practical or tender, creative, and passionate. Which was I?

What was I doing in sedate little Rye, pretending to Mr. James that I was a competent, self-possessed working woman, quietly and calmly sitting before him at his typewriting machine? What did he know of me? Only what Miss P. had told him, and what did she know? I had hidden my wild nature from her as well, combed my unruly hair up into rolls and pins. I had worn a tidy skirt and shirt-waist to work in her establishment and had kept to myself, never talking with her about my real life with my friends, Nora and Clara, reading each other's writing, sending off our hopeful stories and poems signed with made-up names.

As I had learnt from Mr. James' prefaces, he prided himself on his sensitive consciousness and might have missed nothing in his apprehension of other people, but I liked to think that I had fooled him, at least before that afternoon.

When I arrived at Mrs. Dew Smith's, I could see that her house was big and appallingly new, on the Romney side of Rye with a view of the yachts and the golf course. Apparently she had plenty of money and did not mind showing it off. I arrived a little early— Well, I was exactly on time, but that was early for what we used to call a tea-fight. I introduced myself to my hostess. She was full of gossip about our mutual acquaintances, Nora's parents, and I was glad I did not have to make much explanation of my employment, of what had really brought me to Rye.

Looking around the room as more women arrived, bedecked in their lace and feathers, velvet and ruches, I did not see any others who looked as if they had ever heard of the New Woman or of working for a weekly salary. Mrs. Dew Smith chattered on and filled all the space, and when others came in, I could move away gracefully.

I was glad the constraint of meeting my hostess was over and I could hang back, for timidity had overcome me again like a huge wave and I was floundering beside the tea table, hoping my cup and saucer would not slip from my hands, wondering how to juggle the sandwiches, biscuits, iced cakes, napkins, little plates, tiny forks, sugar tongs, and all the other paraphernalia of the tea table spread before me.

I heard that familiar voice first, then saw that Mr. James had come in soon after the crush had reached its height. Our hostess was clearly thrilled with his presence. She rushed across the room, her shrill voice blaring her pleasure. With pride, she brought him through the crowd, introducing him wherever it was necessary, though I noticed it was not often necessary, for he knew so many people. The slow procession was making its way straight to the tea table—and me—and my hand began to tremble. Would he make a fuss, embarrass me, shame me? Or would he not acknowledge even knowing me and shame me even more?

I put my cup down with a rattle and snatched up a sandwich and bit into the cold cucumber, the smooth creamy mayonnaise, but then the dryness of the white bread was too much. I could not swallow, and then he was there before me. I secretly wiped the mayonnaise from my fingers on the table cloth, knocking several of the biscuits to the floor. I gave one a little kick to send it farther under the table in the nick of time.

But as Mrs. Dew Smith began to pronounce my name, Mr. James took my hand with a great friendly roar of laughter. He was clearly glad to see me, surprised, and yet not totally surprised, all the while keeping my hand in his and easing all discomfiture.

"Ah, yes, my dear Miss Bosanquet, how wonderful that Mrs. Dew Smith should have invited you as well, and we can meet this way. Now, I hope to hear some of your words for a change. You are so efficient and steadfast in our work, listening to mine," and he paused, waiting for my reply.

Of course, now that I was to answer, I was choking and could only sputter and mumble and nod in a friendly way, but he let go of my hand and went on, turning to our hostess, covering my embarrassment, my gulping of tea, swallowing.

"I feel so blessed to have Miss Bosanquet with me. I was struggling with this project, could not find the right sort of assistance, and a very old, very dear friend brought us together—" Mrs. Dew Smith nodded encouragingly as he went on, telling her all about his enormous, ambitious project of revisions.

I was glad he had been so friendly towards me, but I was a little startled, too, at the picture he painted of his long relationship with Miss Petherbridge, but then I realised they must have long been old friends in some way for him to accept me as unquestioningly as he had. While he continued talking, Mrs. Dew Smith piled up an ample plate for her famous guest and led him to a large comfortable chair near the other worthies of the town, between the short, red-faced man I knew to be the mayor and a handsome young sportsman, who apparently was visiting, from the look of his golf-course plaids and casual air.

I happily swallowed another gulp of my tea, feeling quite pleased that Mr. James had shown his friendship for me and that I had not been required to say anything.

"That was a close call," a young woman said from the corner nook behind me.

I turned and saw Miss Bradley, tall and blonde, with large dark eyes that took in everything. I had met her several times at her parents' intimate afternoon teas. I nodded, and she went on.

"You know, he's quite sweet when you're used to him, but I remember that my first conversation with our local famous man was terrifying. I was a little girl when he would come to our house and talk and talk. I was afraid he wanted me to respond, but now I know he only means to be kind and to make everything go well. Mr. James has long been an old friend of my father."

Miss Bradley standing there before me—a vision she was—gestured towards an old gentleman who had replaced the golfing youth sitting near Mr. James.

"My father and Mr. James can talk Shakespeare for hours." She turned back to me. "I've known Mr. James all my life. Miss Bosanquet, ah, Theodora, or should I call you Dora? Oh, why don't you just call me Nellie?"

And so, we began an easy conversation, so easy that I was comfortable even when Mr. James came back to talk with us and refill his plate and cup.

"Miss Bradley," he said, "you are back from your studies in Paris, I see."

"How good of you to remember. Yes, I am home again."

"And how is your painting? There is so much to see here in our lovely Rye—the old houses, the water, the light—Ah, our sky has been 'done' so many times. But I'm sure you bring us the latest techniques. I hope for your father's sake, that you're home to stay."

"I want to stay—If only I can find a proper studio, where I might give lessons."

"Ah, yes. I have such happy memories of my own youthful painting days back in America at the side of my artist friends so many years ago. Oh, you must find your own place, mustn't she, Miss Bosanquet?"

He turned to me for support, and happily I found my voice and spoke of the places I had seen in Chelsea, the studios and rooms my friends had set up, and the women whom I had seen painting, sculpting, even writing there.

Our conversation went on easily, openly, for somehow Mr. James made opportunities for me to speak, and my restraint disappeared. I was entranced by the lovely Miss Bradley, and it seemed Mr. James encouraged our friendship, even promising not to work me so hard so that I might have more time for visiting. Later, I wondered if perhaps Mr. James had known what I needed to make me happy—a new friend, the possibility of friendship.

Mrs. Blomfield came over and was introduced, and Mr. James seemed so casually to remark, "I hope you find a chance to show my young friend your lovely home at Point Hill. I shouldn't spoil the surprise, Miss Bosanquet, but when you do visit, I hope you'll pay special attention. Perhaps you may see something that will interest you after we begin the next preface, the one for 'The Spoils of Poynton.'" With that, he turned away to speak with our hostess, who had brought over one last offering to his altar.

In a low, conspiratorial tone, Nellie Bradley admitted that she had never heard of that most interesting novel. "Now, I can tell you. Actually, I've never heard of any of his stories or novels. I've never read a word. I don't like to read, but I do like to be read to while I'm painting." She paused meaningfully and then added, "Perhaps some afternoon you might come to me?"

And so, we made the arrangements.

6

"The Story in It"

1908

*I hasten to add, the mere stir of the air round the question
reflected in the brief but earnest interchange I have just
reported was to cause a "subject," to my sense, immediately
to bloom there. So it suddenly, on its small scale, seemed to
stand erect—or at least quite intelligently to lift its head ;
just a subject, clearly, though I could n't immediately tell
which or what. To find out I had to get a little closer to it.*

—Henry James
Preface to "The Story in It"
The New York Edition, volume 18

"*Everything counts, nothing is superfluous in such a survey ;
the explorer's note-book strikes me here as endlessly receptive.*"
I had read that sentence one evening in 1908, when I was looking back at the first page of the first preface, which had been typewritten by someone else. I was trying to catch up to where Mr.
James and I were by reading over the earlier, already completed
work. How that sentence stopped me!

"*Nothing is superfluous.*" I was afraid of the sound of those
words. I leafed through the preface pages, nineteen of them, which

he had needed to explain his first novel, "Roderick Hudson," one of his shortest.

Originally, Mr. James had planned to write sixteen prefaces, but by the time I came to him, he had finished only six. Part of me was glad for the work, while part of me was groaning at its endlessness. Yet there, on the first page, Mr. James expressed an understanding of the danger that he might go on and on in his *"art of representation,"* which *"causes the practice of it, with experience, to spread round us in a widening, not in a narrowing circle."* Even so, he was fearless, and I liked his bravado from the first, his claims that such a retrospective would be a good story, *"a wondrous adventure."*

Unlike my excited obliviousness on the first mornings, after several weeks, I now felt doubts, wondering how he saw my part in his adventure. It alarmed me to imagine that we had embarked together, already far out to sea, the two of us alone on this little boat, floating on the sound of his voice, swept along by the flow of his memories, which were moved also by some unknown current, some deep upwelling of inspiration. Who was the steersman? Where were we going? What made us move?

Even in those early prefaces, I had my questions when I saw Mr. James name his mysterious wellspring—*"that veiled face of his Muse which he is condemned for ever and all anxiously to study."*

Did I believe him or think he was like all the other old, grey-bearded authors who claimed their own private and mystical source of inspiration, somehow vaguely female, the silent, veiled figure that was their angel? They glorified her to be watching over their writing, while they often had a real, unrecognised figure facing them, like Mr. Browning's dying wife, like Mr. Coleridge's ignored and brilliant daughter, or even like Milton's amanuensis-ing daughters, who took down his words when he lost his eyesight.

When my famous author referred to his muse, he might have meant it literally. After all, we were set up to work, I and my sister typists, sitting there before him, our faces bent over our machines, waiting in silence for his every word.

But of course when I first began, I had no such idea. I was much too nervous. To me, when he mentioned his *"Muse,"* she became another character in his story, his adventure. And my job was not to inspire him. No, I was there to keep him on the narrow, nautical course and bring him back safe.

As we continued with the prefaces during November and December, I found more to worry about. Our adventure seemed threatened by his constant fear of becoming lost, but then an old note-book would help him find his way, like an ancient navigator's rudder or an explorer's sketch map. From the first, I longed for the chance to look inside one of his note-books whenever Mr. James pulled one out from the pile of battered old composition books as he prepared for our next new work. I soon learnt how important to his process those old note-books were. In their pages he had written out moments, scenes, and ideas to remember for future projects: anecdotes someone had told around the tea table, whispered bits of ancient gossip, some scene observed while walking along a gravelled path in St. James Park, names that might work in some future story. It had all gone into his note-books, awaiting the right moment. From those bits he could look back to reconstruct the moment of creation and describe it for the prefaces. As I was to learn later, from those bits he might also launch a new story, dictating first a long composition of notes to outline it while pacing and holding the note-book.

It occurred to me then that I might make use of my diaries in that same way, as a repository of any delicious bits I came across. Perhaps my diary would inspire me if I thought of it as my muse while I was writing every night.

My diary—How much it already meant to me! I had begun to keep it on the day my mother died, when I was twenty. That year, when I met my friend, Ethel Allen, it was my writing she loved. She expected so much of me, even suggesting I use the diary to record my progress through the list of books she had made out for me to read. When she was forbidden to see me—her family objected to our special friendship—she told me to use my diaries as my place to write down everything I thought about, everything I saw around me.

I wondered: Is it only men who have their own muses? Is a muse always female? I remembered noticing those graceful female sculptures that shimmered on the dark staircase and in the dusty corners of the Slade Wing of the University of London, where I went to study after my mother died. Early in this century, all the female students, even those in the sciences and medicine, had to go up to the Slade School of Art to share the one small Commons Room. I used to watch the lively young artists in their soft clothes and bright colours, so different from the garments worn by my drab, overworked female colleagues studying medicine or geology. But those plaster casts of famous Greek and Roman sculptures—why were sculptures so often of flowingly graceful women?—the mythic Muses on the stairwell, each one apparently enlightening her own academic or artistic sphere, whether history, dance, music, painting, or poetry.

And why were they veiled? Would a face have made them too individual, too self-possessing, so that whatever they gave was somehow still their own, not belonging to the man who received it? I wondered if Mr. James had been afraid to look too hard at his muse, to speak so easily of her, lest she withhold her gifts or disappear. Perhaps I could learn from him how to look for my muse, how to listen for her voice.

However, it was only his voice I heard inside my head in those first long weeks of working together. After finishing two or three prefaces, in December we changed our schedule to make use of more than the morning, as I had first agreed. Mr. James was pleased with my work, and I was typewriting much faster, with almost no mistakes. And so, he had me return in the afternoons to work on another, quite different project, to make corrections on and copies of a play for the London theatre. We took his recently published tale, "Covering End," and prepared it for the stage, reworking it into a three-act play called "The High Bid," all because Mr. Johnston Forbes Robertson, the West End actor and producer, had asked Mr. James for it.

First, Mr. James dictated the changes. Then, after I had typed those, he had me mark the pages with a ruler and red ink, underlining the stage directions in red and leaving the dialogue plain. In my more judgemental moments while listening to this new work, I did not think Mr. James' play-writing was up to his novels and stories. Yet he seemed enchanted by this new project, and I was charmed by his enthusiasm.

He was much more animated with that dictation, pacing the whole room, speaking in different voices for the different characters, using gestures and pauses saturated with emotion. Sometimes I had to add the stage directions as he performed them, because he would forget to spell them out for the written page. We were that comfortable in our work.

At the time, I knew a little about stage productions but not because I had seen very many. No, it was because, while I was with my father up in Uplyme, my friend Ethel and I would dress up and put on little plays for her sister, when Ethel and I were still allowed to be together.

I remember the day when I thought to bring some old clothes of my father's and grandfather's to use for costumes. I carried them out of my house, hidden in a big basket, then rode with them on my bicycle down the hill. How Ethel and her sister and I howled when each of us dressed up in trousers, vests, hats, moustaches, and beards. I was the best at it, not only because of my height but also because I could move like a man, and my low voice was a distinct advantage. Usually, I could barely speak aloud, especially with strangers, but it was so different when I was acting. How I loved to play the swashbuckling pirate king or the evil, caped stranger. I always drew the villain's part.

Sometimes, we would write out our version of "Cinderella" or something we had made up; once it was "The Creatures of Impulse." (Of course that was my idea for the title!) We would put on several shows for the local children and invite the neighbourhood.

How I loved remembering this as I typed, and then I could bring all that experience to Mr. James and his play. I liked it when Mr. James seemed to be counting on me, but I did not really know how the play would seem to a sophisticated London audience. I thought some of his language seemed stilted, melodramatic even, but perhaps it was that I was only able to hear it. I missed having the charming actress, the handsome actor to embody the story.

It was especially apparent when he was dictating the plays that Mr. James had a beautiful, unusual voice, with its rich baritone colouring the clear and warm phrasing. I enjoyed our play-writing sessions very much. Listening, almost forgetting to work the typewriter, I wondered if the producer would ever find an actor who could play his hero with such a sweet and thrilling sound.

I wondered, too, about Mr. James' apparent nervousness when he began to dictate each new act. He was slow, hesitant, almost stammering. For the first time, I thought that Mr. James might be shy, even as I was, and so his struggle was intensely interesting to me.

It was an enormous effort to wrench that play into shape for the producer, Mr. Forbes Robertson. Each change, each cut had been a wound for Mr. James and took hours of pacing, dictating, hearing me read it back, then trying again.

Once or twice in that pressured time, I believe, I proved of some help in those revisions, even more than in adding red-ink underlining to indicate the stage directions. I especially loved the American heroine and her spunky ways. I had noticed that at one crucial moment, Mr. James had not given her a reason for one of her speeches. Something had been lost in the to-ings and fro-ings of the various copies and versions of the script.

But how to comment on his mistake, that a character was suddenly acting and speaking in a way that was too brash? I waited for a moment when all was going well and Mr. James seemed in a bright mood. I gathered my courage and ventured, "I wonder if the heroine might be a little too outspoken here. Are we to think of her as a little too charmingly forward? Perhaps—"

He bristled a bit. "Ah, Miss Bosanquet, these rich American women set loose with their father's or dead husband's piles of money. Is there anything they don't think they can say or do?"

I hesitated, then plunged on. "Still, I do think she needs—we need—more of a reason for her brashness here. What was she feeling about that beautiful house, about its handsome and puzzling new owner? Do we know?"

"Ah, I see. I've left out a step. This is not old Shakespeare, I mustn't have her confide her secret passion to the audience in front of the curtain. No, you're right, I have lost something here. Let me think—"

I waited expectantly, my fingers arched over the keys. And then:

"No, I mustn't. In fact, I believe I'll need more time, and I don't want to waste your time, our time." Gathering his notes, he went on, "So then, we are done for today. We will take up here tomorrow. Or perhaps it might be next week. I will send for you."

That's how it often was. I was glad to help, but there I was with my next day's pay lost and no way to make it up.

But soon Mr. James was able again to dictate easily, no more stammering, and, perhaps, it seemed to me, in the early scenes his women came even more easily, especially his heroine, Mrs. Gracedew. I believe he had based his imagination of his character's speaking voice on the American actress we all admired, Gertrude Elliott, since he hoped (as Mr. James explained in a low aside) that he and Mr. Forbes Robertson (who happened to be her husband!) could tempt her into the part.

Once, during a short break for changing the paper, I got up my courage to tell Mr. James how thrilled I was to think I might to be the first to hear the words Miss Elliott was soon to speak on the stage. He laughed with me, for I was blushing.

"You, too, adore her, I think," he said to me as he went on dictating her lines. The Master's voice—that beautiful instrument—changed again, becoming warmer, sweeter, more like Miss Elliott's famous low and musical tone with all it promised of inner strength and beauty and passion. I imagined that he became her, and I imagined the scene with her in it.

That afternoon, there before my machine, I felt the easy flow that now and then happened between us, as his story unfolded and my fingers tapped smoothly, confidently. I wanted nothing to interrupt the flow of that voice, the gradual unveiling, the revelation of that heart and mind to me, as his characters came alive there on the stage in my mind's eye, while I typed on and on.

7

"The Real Thing"

January 1908

*The question, I recall, struck me as exquisite, and out of
a momentary fond consideration of it "The Real Thing"
sprang at a bound.*

—Henry James
Preface to "The Real Thing"
The New York Edition, volume 18

In many little ways, Mr. James encouraged my growing
friendship with Nellie Bradley, asking after her, speaking kindly to me of her family, and recalling his first visit to Rye
many years before, when he had rented the house on Point Hill
to finish one small book, "The Spoils of Poynton," and then to
begin another.

I remember now how busy Mr. James and I had become that
cold, wet winter. While we were still working on the prefaces and
revisions of the novels and tales, we were putting the finishing
touches on "The High Bid," even while the play was already in production with Forbes Robertson and nearly ready to go for its first
run in Scotland. Perhaps thinking of the scenic or dramatic method

he needed to write a new play was making Mr. James remember that time years before, when he had tried writing for the theatre—and, I understand, had tragically failed.

"The Spoils of Poynton" was the first piece of writing he had successfully completed after his most public, demoralising theatrical disaster. I understood little about that painful incident when he dictated to me the preface to the piece written soon after that blow. Of course, he avoided mentioning his dramatic failure. In fact, in collecting all his most admirable works and in writing his prefaces, he left out his attempts at writing plays and focused, instead, on everything else. Only later would I come to understand the reason.

Yet with this work, with "The Spoils of Poynton" and its preface, he really let himself go, describing for me in his wildest metaphorical style the process from its idea and spark all the way to the last words of the novella.

We had been steadily working our way through the stacks of his novels and tales, and we often began with where he found his plots. And so, it was on that dark winter morning when he first talked of the germ of the story for "The Spoils of Poynton." This time, the germ was an anecdote taken from gossip at a dinner party. I was struck by his unusual choices of violent language, by how, in general, his sources of inspiration were becoming appallingly clear: He stole his inspiration from real people's stories, stole from his friends, stole their tiny terrible moments, their lost dreams, hidden lives, broken promises, cruelties, and lies. He took for his own any chance revelation. Mr. James apparently believed it was the right thing to do. He had not taken much, he dictated to me; he had used the tiniest part of someone's story—". . . *the prick of inoculation ; the whole of the virus, . . .*"

As I typed steadily to the sound of his voice, I wondered: Was what he did right? Was that the technique I wanted to learn from him? Why was I reluctant to take on the challenge of Mr. James' methods? Could I steal, take my friends' stories, and use them that way? Why not? Was it my lack of courage, my lack of having the necessary, cold-hearted hunger for gobbling up my friends' stories and spitting them out again?

As Mr. James paused to poke the fire, I wondered: In my diary, had I not been using something from Mr. James' method? Even on our longest days, I had usually been able to keep up my daily-page habit, recording what had transpired that day.

Mr. James was pacing again, dictating his justifications to my fingers:

"*Life being all inclusion and confusion, . . .*" and a long pause, then, "*. . . and art being all discrimination and selection, . . .*"

I wanted to remember those phrases, for it was curious to think how, in general, diary entries can become the truth, somehow promising a basic honesty, a tell-all quality. I had been thinking, I'll write this down before I have a chance to censor myself, my actions, his words—the old fly-on-the-wall, the *témoignage* quality that professors and gossips rely on to bring to life their dry recitations of facts and dates.

But I had no time to muse, for I had to type on and record his reasoning:

"*. . . life has no direct sense whatever for the subject and is capable, luckily for us, of nothing but splendid waste.*"

I admired the balance of his phrases. Yes, this was how a great writer told of his method of drawing from life, I thought, as I bent again to my machine, thinking how in the evening I was slaving over my diary pages, their steady pace, the even slant of letters, the nearly identical length of every entry—how it was all calculated, all controlled, no sudden scribble on some evening after too much brandy. No, even then, I knew I was writing those pages—my "private diary"—for public consumption.

As that first winter passed and as I heard and concentrated my mind and fingers on more and more of the prefaces, I was also listening carefully for my own benefit to Mr. James' well-thought-out theories of composition. It was in my diary notes that I first endeavoured to make use of his rules and suggestions as I understood them while taking them down.

As he described the germ for "The Spoils of Poynton," I was caught in his spell when he told me of the story's inspiration on that Christmas Eve, that brown London night. It seemed as if I were also there at that dinner table, eavesdropping. I was caught. It had all begun with his friend, another guest at the table, telling him of someone she knew, a good lady of the north, freshly widowed, who was engaged in a fierce family battle with her son over her dead husband's will. Naturally, under entailed British law, the son was to receive everything the mother and father had owned together, even his mother's precious house and her priceless collections. Everything was left, entailed away, exclusively to the son. Mr. James had thought that this one hint from his dinner companion was enough and dropped out of her conversation to let his mind begin to work out the rest of the story for himself.

As he dictated, describing his curiously (to me) ghoulish practise of picking over the bones of a tragedy, building his art on the ruins of other people's broken lives, I found myself becoming more and more alarmed.

Again, here was foolish Life, who was notably female—

"*I saw clumsy Life again at her stupid work.*"

He continued, recalling that he had been forced that Christmas Eve to listen to more of the woman's story. At some point, I must have made some sort of unconscious, protesting creak with my chair. I could not type it out as he dictated. Mr. James then came closer and, in the most deliberate, even diabolical, of tones, went ahead dictating, forcing me to face the bloody work necessary to reach a story.

He had been caught by the guest's anecdote, but her first few words—"*but ten words*"—were all he needed to know, as he thought to himself:

"*One had been so perfectly qualified to say in advance : It 's the perfect little workable thing, but she 'll strangle it in the cradle, even while she pretends, all so cheeringly, to rock it ;* "

His own murderous cheerfulness flowed on as he described to me how he stopped his friend from finishing her tale so that he might extract only the tiniest germ, the one viable cell, and throw out the rest. I was dumbfounded to think he'd had no desire even to attempt to tell the whole story, even to try to deal with the "*fatal futility of Fact,*" as he alliteratively called it. Instead, he went on blithely to describe how he played with his characters, choosing which ones to throw together, which to send their separate ways, with his main concern apparently over the scenic construction of the story, as if it were a play on a stage.

Yet I could see that, for myself, once I had begun copying from my diary entries and rewriting them for my friends in London, the subject of my diary became Mr. James and his work and how I was doing in his work. Though I would carve out my words and slave over them, I was not writing fiction. I would not let Life take over my pages. And so, though I had described for my friends the first time I met Nellie, as I went on to spend more and more time with Nellie (and thought about her more and more), she appeared less and less in my tell-all diaries.

I noticed that, in contrast, Mr. James cared not a bit about what happened to whom but, rather, cared about through whose eyes, by whose artistic consciousness the author would enable the reader to see. I felt a shiver at the cold-bloodedness of his method.

He was bubbling over with his enthusiasm for this story about Poynton. Clearly "Spoils" represented some sort of dividing line for him, after which everything was different. He wanted his readers, his listeners, and me to understand its importance. In his description, he compared himself to a doctor, to a scientist with his data, to an architect, a master builder, to an artist, who then at last *"renews in the modern alchemist something like the old dream of the secret of life."*

That day, we halted our work on the preface to "The Spoils," for, by some curious coincidence (or was it by one of Mr. James' conveniently encouraging arrangements?), I went to visit the Blomfields' house on Point Hill for the first time.

Mrs. Blomfield greeted me at the door and ushered me into the house. I could see that her home was filled with beautiful things. Then she took me, strangely enough, back outside to the terrace, saying that Mr. James had wanted her to be sure to show me Point Hill's terrace and its view of the harbour. "Though," she said, "why you would want to see it now, in January, I can't imagine."

It was cold and gusty on the small, paved terrace hanging there between the house and the edge of the cliff, but I obediently walked about, holding my jacket close against the wind. It was a lovely view—the small red-roofed town opposite, with its tiny houses climbing the hill up to our familiar church steeple, and when I turned, there was the seaward view, all that long, low horizon. The wind was cold, but as I turned for one last look, suddenly I knew why Mr. James had wanted me particularly to be shown this spot. It was there that he had written "The Spoils of Poynton"—right there on that terrace with that view before him, as he had told me in his preface. Suddenly his words became real to me: I could picture him gathering his papers, dip-pens, and inkwell, settling to his work, happy to be writing a story again after his struggles at the theatre, happy to be back again in his own art form.

But why had I nearly missed seeing it? Why had I not understood right away? Something about his description did not fit this reality of house, terrace, and view. I thought back to the way he had described the tree, a great ash overspreading his writing table, shading and protecting him through those lovely, long summer days of good writing in this very spot so many years before.

But of course in January it was different, for the huge old tree was a bare clacking noise of bent sticks whipping in the wind, so pale and lifeless that I had missed it when I first walked outside. My reality of this spot was very different from his memory and from the happy scene he had created for the reader in his preface, and I was struck by its difference.

Amazing to think now that his famed "*scenic system*" had germinated with "Maisie" and then bloomed there on that terrace, where I had stood. Even then I think I had a glimmer of understanding, when I saw how that spot itself was theatre-like. As I looked out over far-off Rye and the busy boats dotting the horizon, we became the audience for the world's show. Observing from high above in our safe balcony seats, we could see it all acted out below us, without any need for editorial comment or omniscient narrator.

Or perhaps that terrace was not for the audience but for the actors. Perhaps it was the stage itself, like in those old-fashioned theatres, where the proscenium stage with its trap-doors and props protrudes out into fleshless air. Perhaps the terrace was where the whole drama was rehearsed, perfected, and enacted.

Writing there, Mr. James had imagined his characters in a series of scenes, like the Ibsen plays we were beginning to enjoy on the London stage. How thrilled he must have been to find all his secret love of the theatre, his long apprenticeship, even his past failures at last in his hands again in a way he could put to use. We can read those last great novels of his, and in our minds' eyes and ears it is as if they are being performed before us. We are moved by their intricate stories enacted in all their complexity, their tangled webs of blind stumbling and sudden sight.

I could see now how "Spoils" and the rest of his work made a different sort of Reality for us to muddle with. Perhaps that is what Mr. James meant with his repeated mistrust of the old ways and his insistence on using only simple observations of the *"secret of life"* as our subject. Only sometimes I think he missed the old ways, wanted it still to be possible simply to describe some experience, some place, and hand it over to his reader. I believe he wished he could do the Real Thing, tell the Truth just once.

That afternoon brought what at least for me was a surprise visit by Mr. James to Mrs. Blomfield's tea-party, though as I think back, I realise that his arrival was probably one of his life-plot diversions, in this case to tease me. Of course, I immediately retreated into my shy self, which no one else would have noticed amidst Mr. James' flurry of bantering words.

But the next morning, when I arrived at work, Mr. James greeted me gleefully: "Did you see it? Were you surprised? Did I not describe it perfectly, the terrace, the expanse of the sea, the old red-roofed town, the rustling ancient ash tree with its exquisite protection?"

I did not have the heart to tell him how I had nearly missed seeing his sacred writing space in that wintry terrace scene the day before. Instead, I enthused, "Oh, yes, Mr. James, it was all there, exactly as you had described! You got it down in every detail, so amazingly, exactly as it was."

8

"The Ambassadors"

Spring 1908

*Never can a composition of this sort have sprung straighter
from a dropped grain of suggestion, and never can that
grain, developed, overgrown and smothered, have yet lurked
more in the mass as an independent particle.*

—Henry James
Preface to "The Ambassadors"
The New York Edition, volume 21

Sometimes I surprise myself when I remember how I
behaved that spring, when I was so young and eager,
every morning going to work for Mr. James, then going about day
and night with Nellie Bradley. At times I must have truly shocked
the good citizens of Rye. But they only knew the outside. Inside,
I think I would have been even more shocking to them, with my
hugely ambitious dreams, my wild thoughts, my improper curiosity in trying to find out everything about my mysterious and secretive employer, Mr. James. In fact, my imagination had to work
overtime because Mr. James was so private, so secretive about his
own life.

At first, I believed he was letting me into his deepest memories and thoughts. His effusively emotional words sounded as though what he was dictating came from some deep feeling, but as we went on with each preface, with each book's genesis and every memory sounding equally palpitatingly heartfelt, I began to suspect—and then to be sure—that his real affections, his real passions, his caring for real people, if he ever did, would never be revealed.

And I was frightened because I was completely dependent on this man whose character I could not read. Perhaps that uneasiness, that deep fear explains my near *faux pas* over his mail. I certainly had puzzled over those letters, over what was correct behaviour.

It all began that first time Mr. James left me to work while he visited friends in the countryside. This was before I had become accustomed to his ways and still had not received complete instructions for every circumstance. He was to be gone for several days and so left me with plenty of work to copy, more corrections to add. Yet after only a few days the mail was piling up on his desk, and each day he was away brought even more. I wondered if he always received this many letters and telegrams. Somehow, I doubted that he did—How could he ever find time for his own writing, if he must be answering all these insistent, persistent friends? Why, some of them had written him twice a day, and on one day more times if you counted the telegrams.

I was certainly impressed with the famous names on his letters: Ford Madox Hueffer, H. G. Wells, and Mrs. Clifford. But Mrs. Wharton was the worst. That week she had written from Paris over and over. And it appeared that she was not afraid to use the telegraph, for she also had sent fat wires, two or three in an hour, it seemed. To send even a short wire was so costly, I could only imagine her wealth. Or was it her style to wire to Mr. James from America, from the deck of her ocean steamer, from Paris—from wherever she was?

I tried to organise the piles to be ready upon his return, dividing the unopened envelopes into stacks according to each writer, guessing from the outside whether it was personal or business. I was fascinated by the personal letters: I knew how carefully he guarded his private life, and I knew that once I had separated the private letters from the business correspondence, I would never again catch sight of those fascinating bundles of real letters, with their fat envelopes of pale cream paper, their elegant grey or blue or even violet ink. I thrilled even to imagine breaking open the wax seals and looking inside the special folds and other secret-keeping devices. But of course I always had to leave all those letters as they were.

As the piles grew, I soon found my simple system failing, especially for one of his most devoted correspondents, a Mr. W. Morton Fullerton. It was unclear where Mr. W. Morton Fullerton fit. I could not tell which letters were business and which were personal. The envelopes were typed or addressed in a firm, masculine hand in black ink. All of them were long, white envelopes printed with the return address of the Paris bureau of the "Times," with Mr. W. Morton Fullerton's name penned in above in the best business-like manner. However, if I held one of his letters in my hand, I could feel its weight, feel that it contained many sheets, much more than a business letter. I wondered if Mr. Fullerton was sending more of his writing, perhaps one of his own articles for Mr. James to read. I had helped Mr. James with quick typewritten responses to some of his friends but never to Mr. Fullerton. I had noticed that when Mr. James looked through his mail, he would put the envelopes from Mr. Fullerton aside. Apparently those letters represented something more than a professional friendship. I was curious, for that young man had not yet appeared in Rye. And so, after seeing Mr. Fullerton's name so often, I began to look out for his articles in the "Times." When I did find his work, and this was infrequent, it seemed humourous and clever but not at all in Mr. James' league.

Looking at the Paris postmarks, I wondered if it was Mr. Fullerton's friendship with Mrs. Wharton that was the attraction— How well did those two know each other? For the hundredth time, I wondered about Mrs. Wharton; I still had caught only the barest glimpse of her. I looked again at the two piles of letters on the work-table: Mrs. Wharton's was high, but Mr. Fullerton's was even higher, and only from that one week. All this flurry of mail made me wild with curiosity: What could be happening over there in Paris? What was it that Mrs. Wharton, Mr. Fullerton, and Mr. James were all involved in?

Even in my few months with my employer, I had gathered from Mr. James' chance remarks that his friend, Mrs. Wharton, was a handful. One day, after one of her visits, I remember his talking about her:

"Mrs. Wharton? Do you know her work? Excellent, excellent. I've known her a short time, but she is Edith Jones Wharton. Her father was one of the Joneses, one of the richest families in America. Do you know the American expression, 'Keep up with the Joneses'? That saying started years ago in New York as a reference to *her* family."

I, too, felt the charm of Mrs. Wharton's money, but in observing Mr. James' enthusiasm, I realised that her appeal had to be based on more than her money. It had to lie in the other things about her: her talent, her success, her freedom to go wherever she desired, her courage to travel without her husband, her choice to live in Paris and to live well.

Paris—I had always dreamed of living there someday myself. In school I had learnt everything I could about its streets and shops and cafés, its writers, its enchanting women. My favourite fantasies came from reading Mr. James' books about Paris: "The American," written before I was even born, so impossibly romantic and tragic, and his late novel, "The Ambassadors"—my favourite, another romantic story, but with all the complications that made me feel I was there, walking the streets with its hero, my hero, Lambert Strether. What a coincidence that it was his corrections to "The Ambassadors" that Mr. James had left with me.

And that pile of letters and telegrams from Paris—How I wished I could open one of them and, for a minute, have a peek into that world. For an instant I held one up to the light—surely Mr. James would not mind, perhaps he would not notice—but then I came back to my senses. Of course, he noticed every little thing. And so, I did nothing. Dutifully, reluctantly, I left the letters and returned to my copying work on changes to "The Ambassadors."

I saw that I was nearly done. I could slow down, take time, and actually read what I had been typing; I was glad to recognise a passage, one of my favourites. Mr. James had been describing his middle-aged American hero, Lambert Strether, on his first and last visit to Paris.

Speaking to a young man who was starting out, Strether was trying valiantly to express his own feeling that life was passing him by. I could see from Mr. James' cross-outs where he had struggled with the words, could tell that changing this part had been important and that the old version written in 1900 had been difficult to fix. I could see that he had tried a whole new version handwritten in the margin, but then he wrote me a note to go back to the original, published version. The words were stark and intense. His description of Strether and Strether's sudden realisation was heart-breaking in all its bare simplicity, as Strether speaks to his young friend, Little Bilham:

"There were some things that had to come in time if they were to come at all. If they didn't come in time they were lost for ever. It was the general sense of them that had overwhelmed him with its long slow rush."

Seeing Mr. James' struggle to find new words for the pages of "The Ambassadors," I felt so strongly his sorrow. I wondered why he was so sad—Why did he need to deny himself and his hero any chance of happiness? Of course, I was young, and so I did think of him as very old, too old to be in love. I could not imagine my august employer to be like any other mortal able to suffer a broken heart; I could see only the elderly Olympian figure who had chosen Art over Passion, living alone, perfecting his stories into the night. I think I even imagined that he had succeeded in removing emotional interruptions from his life. I think I believed in his sad stories of artists and writers, for whom it was impossible to feel love or to feel at home in this world.

I was beginning my struggle to find my own way, perhaps even trying to follow his example. What if I had opened one of those letters? How little did I know of such worlds? No, it was better that I only watched and cared for my Great Man from a distance, believing that Mr. James was old and sad and alone in his work.

If I had understood more, perhaps I could have been of more help in the months to come, when Mr. James was troubled over his lack of success and when his writing ceased to keep his spirits up, and then he fell ill, and then his family arrived and pushed aside all his old friends. But first came that summer and fall of 1908 and the visit of his brother, William, which brought such upheavals. Yet I missed all the early signs. And so, later, I was completely unprepared for Mr. James' depression, his illnesses, his demoralisation, and the eventual cessation of his work that was to come.

Much later, only after I came to know Mrs. Wharton for myself, did I learn why Mr. James had remained in England far from his family and country, why he stayed on in dark, provincial Rye long past the time it was a comfort, a home for him, even after his isolation and depression in Rye were making him ill. But I am getting ahead of myself. I did not open the letters. I did not understand, and I can only be a little sad now over how long it took me to see that in Lambert Strether's speech, Mr. James might have been speaking for his own lost self.

There, with his—and Strether's—warning reiterated before me, I wonder if I saw Mr. James' hand helping me to go forward, urging me to follow my heart. Seeing his sadness, did I see the danger of losing my chance for happiness? With his words, I was warned off of trying too hard to behave well by the world's standards, to be good, and miss out. I think it was then that I first understood: Mr. James was helping Nellie and me in his own secretive way, inventing errands, arranging meetings, making sure we took the chances he had never had, even supporting Nellie's effort to find a studio where she and I might be alone.

But now, years later, whenever I re-read "The Ambassadors" and watch Strether's moral choice to gain nothing by his adventure but, instead, to return to America empty-handed, it seems to me the saddest part about that brave call to "*Live all you can ; it's a mistake not to'*" is that Strether himself did not yet see what was really happening there in Paris with his young friends, nor did he believe that he might still have a chance, Oh, not to be happy like those wild, young fellows, no, but he did still have the chance to be himself and to be happy with Maria Gostrey, his friend.

But that was not the book that Mr. James had written.

Soon, I hoped, he would come back from the visit to the countryside, and we would move on to Maria Gostrey and her scenes, and so I kept sorting Mr. James' letters, working on the corrections and still saving enough time for the messy task of cleaning and oiling the Remington, which I had postponed long enough.

I have always loved good tools, loved being able to fix things. It made me feel of use, and there were plenty of such opportunities with Mr. James, for he had not the slightest idea of anything mechanical, from the workings of the handles of the fireplace flues to the simplest refilling of a fountain pen, when he finally agreed to try that latest invention. Worst of all, of course, was our Remington typewriting machine. As the months passed, it became completely my responsibility to keep the Remington oiled and working smoothly. From time to time, opening it up to do the job thoroughly became necessary. At such times, it was good if Mr. James was out, for then I could completely spread out and have a go at it. I would appreciate the silence as I worked, surrounded by the orderly array of metal bits and parts set out on an old canvas square. Working there quietly with no voice rumbling in my ear, it was pleasant and peaceful, and I found that I could think for myself for a change and let my mind wander as it would.

All in all, that late winter morning, I felt our months of work had gone well; I knew Mr. James liked me, and I liked the work very much. Mr. James really needed me, of that I was sure. I took out my supplies from my special box in the hall closet, lifted the cover of the Remington, and began to brush and oil the hinge joint of each key, being careful to slather oil over every moving part.

Then I left the hinges to absorb their glistening oil, and I turned to replacing the old ribbon. I unwound it and lifted it off of its spindles; as always, I was surprised at how thin, grey, even twisted it had become after all those key strokes, all those hours and hours, all those words running under my fingers and against the fabric, turning into ink on the page.

I unwrapped a bright new package and began carefully to loosen the inky black ribbon to fit it into its proper place.

The metallic spool clanged as I put it on the left spindle; I lifted the spool and clanged it again, simply to enjoy the sound. I thought of how Mr. James had left me with more changes to this version of his preface to "The Ambassadors," and I wondered again about Lambert Strether and his friend Maria Gostrey.

Would it really have been so wrong for Strether to have received something from their sudden, sweet friendship? Mr. James' discussion of his *"drama of discrimination,"* as he had described it in his preface, had taken an hour of intense dictation. The passage consisted of less than one hundred words, but every phrase was meticulously balanced, extended, withdrawn.

Even though I was alone in what Mr. James called his "working room," I imagined his voice still dictating the preface as I unwound the ribbon from the new left spool, passing it through the two stiff prongs and onto the right spool, being careful to tuck the end under:

"As always—since the charm never fails—the retracing of the process from point to point brings back the old illusion. The old intentions bloom again and flower—in spite of all the blossoms they were to have dropped by the way. This is the charm, as I say, of adventure transposed—*the thrilling ups and downs, the intricate ins and outs of the compositional problem, made after such a fashion admirably objective, becoming the question at issue and keeping the author's heart in his mouth."*

I clicked the cover shut over the well-oiled machinery and then looked down at my hands, now black with carbon, ink, and oil. I called to Burgess to ask for some hot water.

And what about Maria Gostrey, whom Mr. James had called *"the reader's friend,"* who acts with such exemplary devotion? Her character had achieved *"something of the dignity of a prime idea"*—but what about Maria herself?

Burgess knocked. He brought in steaming water in a white china pitcher and a basin for me, as he did so often for Mr. James.

I followed him into the bedroom—such a nice room, panelled and quite simple, with two charming silver candlesticks by the bed and a very good old mirror against the wall. One or two late, ragged blooms of the white pillar roses were still visible through the small window looking out over the garden.

It was a lovely afternoon, and once everything was tidy again in Mr. James' study, I went down to his protected little garden for a short walk.

Mr. James did think highly of me—I remembered a note I had typed for him one morning, when his hand had been especially stiff with too much revision for him to write for himself. It was to his brother, William. At that time, I was still struggling to learn the

Master's ways. I think he meant to be praising me and, in his own round-about way, meant for me to hear his defence of my work, our work. But still, I was startled by this:

"*I shall have to tick-out my love on this so public-looking system— which I am returning to, for general labour, after eight month's [sic] severance from it, with deep and particular appreciation.*"

I wondered if this "*tick-out*" would do for my life's work. Were these thrilling ups and downs of transposed adventure, or were they no more than finger exercises?

I had come to understand that my mouth was best kept shut. If the day's dictation went on too long, Mr. James would select a chocolate bar from his box, strip off the silver foil, and lay it beside my machine, meanwhile hardly missing a semicolon.

What, I wondered, would Maria Gostrey have given Strether in return?

Down in the Master's garden, walking between the high, green hedges, I heard the rhythmic *snip-snip* of garden shears and noticed Old George up on a ladder, trimming the thorny long canes of an old climbing rose. The pale blush petals and clipped branches fell past the shaggy, cracked bark.

"Look out, Miss," he called out.

"But they haven't finished blooming," I protested.

Old George put aside the shears, sniffed, and wiped his nose on his sleeve. "These here, they're regular climbing sports. You've got to cut them back in the bloom, right in the bloom. The new growth will come right if you cut right." He looked around the wintry garden and at the last few blooms on the old climbing roses.

"Mr. James, he understands the roses, cuts them right back, cuts the crossing branches but leaves the one centre." His voice lowered. "He cut them himself, a while past, to carry down to you when you were sick, his favourites, the Bourbon roses."

The gift of the old Paris blooms, the old Paris of Gloriani, Strether, Little Bilham, gathered into a handful of deep pink. Out there in Mr. James' tended garden, I felt even more the sense of names in the air, of ghosts at the windows, of signs and tokens, a whole range of expression all around me, too thick for prompt discriminations. I felt as lost as poor Strether.

I want a Maria Gostrey for myself, I thought. And I would never leave her behind, with everything still unsaid, leave her to wait for word to come, for her friend's beautiful letters, to read them laid out on the dark mahogany table under the shining brass lamp in her perfect Dutch-tiled dining-room.

I stopped beside another of the old roses. Where else could I see such blooms, the boss of yellow stamens, the deep rose corolla fading to a pale cream centre, the leaves crinkled and coppery, the thorns so handsome, so difficult, so meticulously placed?

9

"The Saloon"

April 1908

. . . yet with the constitutive process for each idea quite
sufficiently noted by my having had, always, only to say to
myself sharply enough : "Dramatise it, dramatise it!"

—Henry James
Preface to "The Author of Beltraffio"
The New York Edition, volume 16

"This is never going to work," I thought as I turned
over the pages of the short story Mr. James had
given me to read. And as it turned out, I was, in a way, correct.

"Forbes Robertson wants another of my plays," Mr. James had
announced happily before he left on another of his jaunts. "He
wants a one-act to open for 'The High Bid' when they bring it to
London. I've been re-thinking a ghost story, which might work.
Why don't you read this story over, and we can begin on the play
when I return?"

I had never heard of "Owen Wingrave." Mr. James had brought
the story out only in American magazines, and that was before I
began to work for him. As I turned the pages, I wondered why he

would choose to remake that story into a play. I liked the hero, a handsome young man, who did not believe in the sacred power of war, even though he came from generations of soldiers. I liked Owen's courage for not giving in. He would not become a soldier even though family pressure was on him to do so: His dying grandfather threatened to disinherit him. Even his beautiful fiancée accused him of cowardice and threatened to break off their engagement because of his pacifist beliefs.

But somehow I could not see the drama in the story, could not see his struggle as something to portray on stage. Indeed, a few days later, when we began to work on the play, everything seemed oriented inward, and what is worse, the battles in Owen's noble mind occurred before the curtain rose. For the first twenty minutes of the play we did not even see our handsome hero or hear the dreadful argument during which Owen had been disinherited.

How was Mr. James to persuade our suburban audiences to care about this young man?

Soon, his longer play, "The High Bid," would no longer be travelling from town to town in Scotland and out in the provinces. Mr. James wanted to be sure the play would be staged in London. He seemed to feel he needed something more to make it irresistible to Mr. Forbes Robertson and his American actress-wife, Gertrude Elliott. I suppose it was the ghostly aspect of "Owen Wingrave" that encouraged Mr. James to try to make it into a one-act curtain-raiser, which he hoped would be popular with the crowds!

I knew Mr. James was still worried about "The High Bid" and its problems. Was it possible that Mr. James thought Owen and his ghost story could prepare his audience for the strange turn-about of the hero in the three-act play? The beautiful lead actress for "The High Bid" had said she'd felt the audience was restless and disturbed by its favourite actor playing a character who almost literally turned his back on the common man when he decided to return to the old traditions and to hold onto his ancient estates, his piles of money. And yet, in spite of it all, he still got the girl.

Why add this ghost story to the confusion? Did Mr. James think this show of Owen's courage, his vision of the blundering cruelty of the world, would set up the audience for the next play with its idealistic hero and heroine? It all seemed very complicated and even more problematic. Wouldn't there have to be only one stage set for both plays? Or could they stage a whole new set in the short interval between the two performances?

After some paper shuffling, Mr. James announced that we would start with dictating his amplifications to "Owen Wingrave" as a play to be called "The Saloon," beginning with a thorough description of the set. (In those days, "saloon" was a common spelling for "salon," not be confused with "pub" today!) He told me he did not like that the tradition in England was only to go and see a play and never to read it in print. "How I wish the English—and even the American public—would learn to appreciate the written form of my dramatic offspring. The French understand written play scripts so much better."

I did not dare to tell him that the first play I'd ever read was in a book by Racine. That play had seemed so French and romantic there in its grey-and-purple printed paper covers, but then I remembered no scene-setting and no stage directions whatsoever.

Yet as he went on, it seemed Mr. James was up to something else. Were his detailed descriptions designed to help the production designers create the right set? Why so much about the slightly worn rigidness of sofas and chairs, the family portraits of colonels, generals, all the military ancestors, a glass display case bristling with swords and shakos and epaulettes? Yet I could see as he was setting the scene so that everything he described would be easy to roll out for this play and then quickly roll away for the next, his beloved "The High Bid." I had not yet seen how the set designers for "The High Bid" had created Mr. James' beautiful marble hall, with its impressive, curving central stairs. But now, apparently, this other set for the one-act had no such thing, no stairs at all!

Mr. James began dictating "The Saloon": "*. . . a plain but ample country-house of an October night* ;"

But how would he make the stage seem right away like a haunted house? No, perhaps that was to be gradually revealed.

He went on, glancing at his notes: "*. . . what is important being rather a highish clear window, not directly accessible from the floor, and not curtained, . . .* "

Mr. James paused, looking up at me, then continued: "*The whole place betrays a little its having been a much older and formerly much lower, in fact quite low-browed 'hall,' more or less fundamentally renewed and modernised. The high window appears even a survival from some upper storey, perched aloft and alone, after the reduction of the two storeys to one.*"

I wondered how the set builders would make that strangely high-up window seem mysterious or haunted, like a hidden doorway to some long-forgotten part of the ancient house.

Well, of course the dialogue would explain the window and the room haunted by some past violent upheaval of passions, a room then destroyed to make this modern hall, or "*saloon*," as Mr. James described it. I remember wondering as I typed the Master's play: Did Mr. James know how to make the old house seem haunted enough, but not too much? And how would he make us believe in a character who was not visible, his Demon, his Terror, his intangible Ghost?

We kept on with other directions for the stage-setting until the end of our session. His struggles made me think how much easier it is to make us believe in ghosts we can read about in a short story than see—or not see—on stage. I closed up the typewriting machine. Later, as I walked down the street through the gloomy afternoon, I thought back to his earlier ghost story, "The Turn of the Screw," and how each appearance of its ghosts was revealed only to the governess through the actions of the children. When Nellie, my friends, and I found ourselves reading those pages faster and faster, we came to believe that there really were ghosts—but, at the same time, we came to wonder about the governess. Had all this only been in her strangely disturbed mind?

Of course, in a story everything is words, but in "Saloon" there had to be something real. Obviously, Mr. James would never stand for some sheet-flapping figure as his ghost gliding about before the audience. Perhaps, I thought, he might go for the complication of a Pepper's Ghost or simply use a sudden darkening of the stage.

When I arrived at Nellie's little Watchbell Street studio, as I was setting everything out for tea after Nellie finished painting, I found a new concern: What if there were people in Mr. James' audience who might truly believe in ghosts and haunted rooms, not as something from a psychologic upset but with a real, deeply buried fear of some frightening, powerfully imagined presence who might overcome them. Strange things have been known to happen, and sometimes people really do believe—Well, there was my own Nellie, who still could not walk past Gibbet Hill or the old grave-yard after dark because she had been told too many ghost stories.

Further, what did *I* believe about ghosts? It's true, I had gone with Nellie to visit her medium and sat with the two or three others that night, some of us more ready to believe than the rest. The medium began by asking us to close our eyes and think of the dead, of those who had gone before us. Of course, I found myself in my usual state of not wanting to do what I was told. Instead, I kept my eyes open and looked over at Nellie. She was in tears! Who was she thinking of? I tried to imagine. For me, I faced a great blank, since I refused to think of my mother.

The medium then asked us to open our eyes and sit quietly in the darkened room. Indeed, there were some strange sounds, moans, thuds, creaks, all the stuff I had heard of from ghost stories or other séances, when suddenly my Nellie cried out, "I'm sorry! I'm sorry, I tried my best!" She collapsed into loud weeping.

I ushered her from the stuffy room and out into the fresh air of the hallway, where I gave her my almost fresh handkerchief. She wanted to tell me all about it, how her very old grandmother had died. But now, she saw that death scene differently: "My mother sent me to stay with her, alone. Grandmother had been unconscious for days, it seemed, only this time her eyes flew open and she stared straight into my face. She spoke, as clear as could be, 'Don't do that ever again. Don't! Be a good girl!' That was the last thing she ever said."

Nellie was wailing. "It's us, Theo. I know she meant us."

"Nellie, how could she have known about us?"

"I don't know, I just know—I heard her voice again tonight."

That was our ghost story. The warning of Nellie's grandmother from the Beyond was enough to freeze my Nellie's affections towards me. It was weeks before I could coax her to do anything private and sweet with me again. But eventually she let her grandmother's caution recede, an event I certainly did not record in my diary.

I pride myself that I was much more scientific in my researches on ghosts and the psychical occult than Nellie. I liked reading about past lives and trying out trance writing or sendings, but since I did not want any of my ghosts telling me what to do, for a while, that was my last psychical experiment with Nellie.

Later, after Mr. James and I finished the changes for the one-act play and sent it off, he settled again into the next preface, the one for the volume of early short stories about writers and artists, "The Author of Beltraffio." I had not read those stories, and he had not yet provided me with their corrected pages. He spoke on and on about his process, this "*so bare an account of such performances*," how he had moved from the tiniest suggestion to realise the whole story. Again and again, it seemed he was talking to himself with an almost disembodied glee, boasting how he magically transformed the most innocent incident into exactly the shocking story he wanted.

"'*Dramatise it, dramatise it!*'" he dictated enthusiastically, as we moved on to the story of the author whose wife objected so intensely to her husband's disreputable stories that she hysterically abandoned their son to die from a raging fever rather than allow the boy to grow up and read his father's horrors. What a terrible story! I even wondered if Mr. James' story might actually be based on something real—how one author can ghoulishly reveal another's tragedies and ghosts.

The next preface, which was for the collection of stories, "The Altar of the Dead," was full of such horrors; I was glad when we returned to finish up a few changes in the script for "The Saloon." Apparently Mr. James had been struggling over the last scenes. I, too, still had my doubts. His hero was so noble, and the other characters hardly mattered, including Kate, the hero's girlfriend, when she violently accused Owen of being a coward. I wondered if Owen would even care what she said.

It all seemed a bit muddled there in the darkened room of the play's final scene. I listened as Mr. James struggled to get it right—to move the girl out of the room in such a way that she could make another dramatic entrance to end the play with the dead young man in her arms. To me, the chance of success seemed unlikely.

Mr. James was pacing that morning. I knew he'd been having trouble.

"Miss Bosanquet," he said, "I can't make up my mind—how real does this ghost have to be for the duffers in an audience to understand what I'm trying to say?"

He walked again to the window. It was growing darker, the right atmosphere for our work on this play.

"I know!" he said. "I'll have Owen speak to the Horrors themselves, to the paintings and portraits of his terrible, dead relatives." With that, Mr. James was once again full of enthusiasm. "Here, let's work on the stage business, two pages before the end."

He added more stage directions for the hero: "... *he turns to the portraits, dimly seen, on the wall* Semicolon *; addressing them as his Family and his Contemners [sic], and letting loose at them the full wave of his denunciation and defiance* Semicolon *;*"

"I think that will work. Our handsome friend, Mr. Forbes Robertson, is very good at defiance and denunciation, don't you think?" Mr. James paced. "It's as though Owen sees his ancestors come alive. They are his ghosts. Of course, his stupid Kate sees nothing." He continued the stage direction:

"... *which embraces thus the whole place, its inmates, its imputations, its immediate rather gruesome aspect, all its ugly actualities and possibilities, that bears him up and on to the end.*"

"Oh, dear, Miss Bosanquet, is it possible some mistaken director might read this direction and think I mean for the portraits to come to life, to come out of their frames and down into the murky room?"

"No, no," I assured him. "Anyone who has read the terrifying apparitions of your ghost stories knows it's far more frightening to watch our hero as he alone sees what no one else can. The actor must act out for us that these are his horrors."

"Yes, and so I must move that girl off, away from centre stage—I've got her stumbling and moaning to him, but I want his speech to be strong."

He was silent for a few moments and then said, "I like this—let's pick up the dialogue again at the speech where Owen is gesturing and addressing the ancients in their dusty portraits on the wall." He dictated Owen's words:

"*What do I care for what you 'see,' if it makes you all Stupid and Cruel? What do I care for your narrow minds and your pitiful measure of Life?*"

"No, wait," Mr. James said, "I suppose he is speaking both to the family portraits and to the girl, so I must keep her in the scene."

"Yes, yes—" I had to speak. "It works that he is not really speaking to her, but she hears it that way."

"Ah, yes, I'll have the two characters speaking away from each other—at cross purposes, only the audience can see it all—and then that climax. I'll have him even name it—" and Mr. James dictated,

"*What do I care for the* Capital D *Demon himself* Open Parenthesis *(at which* Comma, *as throwing herself back horror-stricken* Comma, *KATE gives a piercing shriek* Close Parenthesis*) except for the joy of* Underline *blasting* Dash, Exclamation Point—*!*"

"Somehow," Mr. James said, "right here, the lighting designer will have to figure out how to make the stage even darker."

He thought for a minute and then went on dictating more directions, for the stage was to be "*caught up and extinguished in a great quick* Capital B *Blackness of deeper* Capital D *Darkness . . .*"

I typed quickly, happily: The ghosts were there. The play might work. Kate called out, recognizing her own part in the tragedy that Mr. James dictated,

"Capital D *Dead of the* Capital D *Death* Exclamation Point*!*"

10

"The Lesson of the Master"

1908

"The artist—the artist! Is n't he a man all the same?"

—Henry James
"The Lesson of the Master"

Even when I was first listening to Mr. James dictate, I did not always understand. Little did I know then that I would end up spending my life as a writer and an editor. It seems so strange looking back at my struggles to think about becoming a writer, when I look around our Book Room now and enjoy my old comfortable chair, my desk piled high with my own old, yellowed manuscripts—poems, speeches, half-finished stories, odd scraps of scenes I tried and rejected. I can hardly remember what it was like to try to write back then, when I never had a room or even a table, nowhere to start an idea and then leave, hoping I could return to it easily and soon.

Here, in my very own working room, I have shelves filled with my favourite books, and today I have covered the floor around my desk with distinct piles of the Master's books, those beautiful leather bindings of the New York Edition, the later stories, and the last novels, each with its fluttering white slips of paper marking passages and phrases to remember, scenes that have become important in my life—so many markers. I find it hard to keep in mind that I did not always know what those passages meant, why it was that I love to re-read a line, why I go back to a story again and again.

But I did want to write even then, though I did not know what it was I wanted to write. I had so few living models of women writing: we all loved the writings of Olive Schreiner with her brave novel of life on an African farm, the first writing I had read about a successful, independent young woman. I did try writing some domestic essays for "Hearth and Home," like the ones I had written for the little hand-made newspaper my friends and I passed around when I was still living at home in Uplyme. I remember writing my piece on "Manners," which revealed how horribly bashful I was and how I made use of my bad, unmannerly behaviour to get my way.

At the Hermitage, alone with my father and the servants, as long as I prepared his meals, I had time to myself to read and write. Even when my father seemed to be paying little attention to me or the household, somehow, there was money enough so that I could order from the stores and pay the bills. Later, after I had left home and gone to London and the university, I had to find paying work— and probably something that would take up every day, take me into the rooms of a stranger, sitting hunched over his typewriting machine, listening for his every nuanced word.

When I was first in Rye, I had very little time for myself, even after I had finished my half day with Mr. James. It was very seldom only a morning's work. Some days, when we would need to go on longer, he would suggest that we stop for a few minutes for a cup of tea, but then we would push on.

Back in my dingy little room on Mermaid Street, I would have to sit on my narrow, lumpy bed to write, or fold my long legs into the window seat to catch the last light. But I did write. From there, I would write long letters and sometimes pieces for my friends or for the local women's pages, things that I hoped were clever vignettes about local worthies and provincial triumphs. After sweating over them, inky fingers and all, at last I would send them forth in a clean hand-written copy. I am so glad all my teachers at Cheltenham had insisted I work diligently on my handwriting so that my short articles were quite legible. But I worried that those pieces still looked like unprofessional, schoolgirl scribbles. I wanted something better.

And then, one day the answer appeared when I was sent on an errand for my employer down to Mr. Rix, the stationer. There, shining forth in his window in its black-and-gold splendour, was the solution to all my problems: the new, improved, and, best of all, portable Oliver typewriter, a smaller version of the massive Remington I was using. At once, I knew I must have it. I went inside and tried out its smooth motion. As I leaned over the machine, Mr. Rix suggested that I could have it, if I could make a series of small payments. I figured that if I could put aside something every week from my meagre salary (my usual three shillings a day, so much less than a man would have received), I might make the payments.

That Oliver would be the right size, perfect. I could keep it in my room or take it with me, unlike the heavy, awkward Remington, as big as a credenza and only to be moved by two men, and not often.

I placed my order with Mr. Rix, and I brought him a little bit of payment each week. Happily, on those visits, he allowed me to become acquainted with the Oliver, sometimes even a little touch on the keys to feel its smooth action, its lovely shining finish. I began to imagine it on its own little table in my room, imagine how I would take it up to London, take it with me when Mr. James was otherwise occupied, wherever I was to go, even take it with me for a stay at the Bradleys' house if I were so lucky as to be invited for the weekend. My own machine meant I could find other work besides waiting on Mr. James, and even more to be desired, I could work on my own essays, make my own writing more professional, more saleable.

The weeks piled up, and owning my own machine came closer. That winter of 1908, when the Cause—women's suffrage—came to Rye, I became even more inspired. With courage (and the Vote), a woman could make her way in the world alone; she did not have to be married and depend on a man. I wanted to have my own career, my writing, and to be living with my own Nellie. All this was dependent on that little Oliver!

At that time in provincial little Rye, it was impossible for two young women even to dream of such an unconventional life. Of course, Nellie and I had no privacy, no place to be alone, since she still lived under the watchful eyes of her parents, while I was in my grubby boarding house with the ever-vigilant Mrs. Holland listening for my comings and goings, waiting to entrap me on the landing, suspiciously demanding her rent money every week, for there were weeks I did not have money. Some weeks Mr. James was away, and some weeks he would forget.

One particularly bad patch had come when Mr. James kept stopping our work on his prefaces, first for the play in Scotland, and then with his other distractions and commitments with his friends. I had been so pleased that at last we seemed to have moved on to one of the longer novels, "The Ambassadors," but then suddenly we stopped the novel and returned to his play, "The High Bid," preparing for Edinburgh and the try-outs.

All those times he left me without work, as I gnashed my teeth in frustration, I knew it did not have to be that way. There would be the glory of owning my own typewriting machine. When I had saved enough, when I had it at last, then I would be free of Mr. James' whims. I could find other copying jobs to fill in when he was dithering over a passage or, worse, when he left to go on a motoring jaunt with his well-off friends.

It seemed that year we saw more and more motor cars on the roads near Rye, for the rich enjoyed travelling more often between their country estates and the city. I soon learnt that Mr. James loved to be driven about in someone's luxurious car. Whenever invited, he would make time for travel, whether for extended trips on the Continent or to motor about the English countryside, visiting friends for lunch.

I suppose it was Mr. James' rich American friend, the famous writer, Mrs. Wharton, who was the worst. Any trip with her in her gorgeous motor car, a very modern Panhard Levassor, was a great inducement. It must have seemed so easy to slip away, leaving all his word struggles behind, and fly across vast distances with Mrs. Wharton at his side.

It was the car that caused Mr. James to describe Mrs. Wharton as the Fire Bird herself, the Angel of Devastation: She cared nothing for interrupting whatever work he was deep into. She left ruin in her wake, yet in the heat of the moment, he seemed to think he was blessed by her slightest invitation.

With all this travelling, Mr. James took advantage of his longer absences to arrange with the workmen to have the more unpleasant sorts of work done to poor old Lamb House—the drains mucked out, or all fifteen chimneys swept, or even some more major project, often leaving me in charge to check in on the progress and send off daily reports.

Once, the project was to electrify Lamb House—the scheme had, of course, come originally from Mrs. Wharton, again the harbinger of change and uproar and primary author of the deemed revolutionary compendium, "Decoration of Houses." The experiment was costly, I am sure, and was making a great mess besides, during all those weeks of construction. For most of the summer, the workmen were everywhere inside the house: in the cellar, in the attic, up and down the stairs. Their black wires humped across thresholds, crossing and recrossing the hall again and again. Doors could not be closed to them; the wires lay thick and twisted in the way. There was continuous noise—the sounds of plaster falling, the ripping of old wood—and so Mr. James had been correct: The house was no place in which to do our work. It was decided that only when the mess was cleared would I send him word, and then Mr. James would return to throw the switch.

I wondered if the imperious Mrs. Wharton had first suggested the project as her way of persuading her older friend to escape with her for a longer-than-usual motoring trip away from his beloved Lamb House. Mr. James was sometimes able to resist her invitations because of the needs of his writing, especially our extensive revision project, for he hated spending long periods away from his typewriting machine and our work. But what with the plaster dust sure to lie thick over his papers and the constant sound of destruction drowning out his soft voice giving dictations, he soon agreed to join the Angel of Devastation and her pack sweeping along the dusty roads of the English countryside.

His notes back to me were full of sunshine, country air, and gentle entreaties for me to keep to the tasks he had left me. Some fat letters were filled with new pages of revisions to our work; I could see his enthusiasm, see that though he was enjoying all the sunny comforts of that rich American socialite's life of luxury, he still seemed to be eager to return, especially to something of his own, to a new work for which he had high hopes.

That summer, even in usually fog-bound Rye, we had long days of sunlight, bright and glaring on the pages as I worked alone under the tall, arching windows of the Garden Room, a separate, small building across the garden from Lamb House. The workmen had not disrupted the order there, since Mr. James had decided against bringing electricity out into that bright, large study. He had been very clear; he wanted the electric light in rooms of the house for the dark days of winter, for his upstairs guest rooms, for the entry hall and the stairs, and of course, for the kitchen help below-stairs. He liked to think of himself as living on the brink of the Modern Age and would make use of every new convenience, especially when his rich, young friends so insistently pointed out to him the brash, bright ways of the future.

One morning, I went to the street door to check on the final stages of the project. The workmen were feeding the last of the thick black wires through holes in the walls, then attaching round brass covers to cap off the disconnected gas outlets.

The ugly modern electrical fixtures protruded from the walls on each side of the first-floor rooms, and a single, clear bulb hung from the ceiling of each of the rooms upstairs, slightly swaying in the draught from the open doors. The circular metal covers over the unused gas jets were smooth and rounded, almost a female shape, with a lovely curve and a slightly raised bump in the centre. I wondered what Mr. James would make of them, gracing the walls of his very much old-bachelor-style rooms.

At last, the workmen were finished and had begun to clear away the mess. And so, at last, one evening, we were expectantly awaiting Mr. James' arrival, as it began to grow dark. I thought it would be a lark to greet Mr. James with all the household staff lined up, as if to welcome home the Master, or for a hero's triumphant return, as if his homecoming were a victory celebration or the Jubilee. Whether it was out of superstition or in consideration of his feelings, no one but the workmen had yet tried the electricity, and in case of failure, we still had ready the old iron candlesticks with their candles in place from the weeks of working with the gas off.

As we waited at the appointed hour, the sound of the motor car echoed off the walls of the other houses at the turn up the narrow, cobbled street. Mrs. Wharton was in her usual hurry. Her driver left the motor running, while he climbed down to help Mr. James out. Burgess hurried to collect the luggage from the high rack behind. Mr. James took Mrs. Wharton's hand, and they murmured their good-byes in the shadows before the house.

As we waited in the slight dark of the hall, I opened again the pamphlet "Basic Instructions for Your Electrical Safety and Convenience," from the Central Power Authority. The tiny print of the pages was legible in the dim candlelight.

Mr. James greeted each of us with a handshake. "Well, what's this?" he said. "Why all this darkness?"

I spoke for us all. "Welcome back, sir. We've waited to save the lighting of the new electric lamps for you. If you would care to throw the switch, the device is there on the wall." I pointed to the small ceramic box near the staircase.

"I've been looking forward to this for quite some time," Mr. James said as he moved towards the fixture.

I had a moment of panic. What if the workmen had not finished but had been interrupted? What if there were something they had forgotten to tell us? I reached out to stop Mr. James, holding out the pamphlet. "Perhaps you should look this over first. They seem to think electricity needs quite a bit of explanation and precautions before we begin."

Mr. James took the pamphlet and held its small print up to the light from the candles. "I can barely read this—let's try this Modern Age for ourselves and see what it's all about."

He quickly flipped the switch, and the room sprang up at us from the dusk. Each piece of furniture leapt out of its long-held place. The stairs curved and throbbed; the ceiling lowered. Beyond the window the night was black. With every surface lit, every unevenness became flat, hard, bright. The glass of the pictures and bookcases glared, the candles became tiny flickers of orange lost in the whiteness.

We all gasped and blinked. The light revealed our faces as pale and flat, colourless squares or circles. Our clothes were stiff, our hands and feet like cardboard. We watched as Mr. James reached again to the switch and firmly snapped the lever off. Suddenly the dark was back, the room connected, stretching away into the rest of the house. The stairs floated up to the mysteries of other dark rooms; the night was thick and comforting, and the candles hummed their light into the silence.

"I always hate it when I'm told too much," Mr. James said.

He moved on into the rest of the house.

We each took a candle from its place and walked in its circle of light to other rooms, to our work, and to the business of the night.

11

"The Bostonians"

July 1908

*She [actress Elizabeth Robins] has lately hurled herself
with ardent conviction into the Suffragette agitation,
but not in the obstreperous, police-prodding or umbrella-
thumping way of many others.*

> —Henry James
> Letter dictated to Theodora Bosanquet
> For William James

It was a lovely stretch of days, when Rye was flooded
with sunshine and late-summer visitors. Fresh from his
Continental tour with Mrs. Wharton, Mr. James seemed happy to
be back at work. Still, it seemed to take many hours for him to shift
back into our old routine, and I was worried that we might never
settle down again. I badly needed the money, and I was frightened
at how financially dependent on him I had become. Being paid by
the hour was not a practical arrangement for me when Mr. James
had trouble writing.

After several false starts and rambling pauses at the mantelpiece,
at last Mr. James reached a good rate, and we moved quite well into

the preface for the volume of short stories with "Daisy Miller." I was entranced again by that story of a lively American girl and her first foray into the more sophisticated world of Europe. I knew that it had been his first story to sell well and the first to give Mr. James hope that his work would become popular. He had been telling me this as we finished for the morning, while I spread the cover over his typewriting machine, collected the new pages, and straightened them into a stack for his usual stint of revising later that day.

"Shall I come back after lunch for the corrections?" I asked.

"Oh, no, but thank you. I must entertain my young niece just over from America. Another interruption, I'm afraid, and I don't know what I'll do with her. Peggy used to be such a dear child, but now—Now, she has come over to spend time in Oxford, while Professor James and her mother are there for his lectures. Peggy must be close to your age, Miss Bosanquet, about twenty, I believe. Perhaps you can suggest some entertainment for her. Can you help?"

I thought about my own plans for the evening and rashly offered, "She might be interested in going with Miss Bradley and me to Mrs. Dew Smith's house and tonight's talk on votes for women. I'm sure she would be welcome, and perhaps Miss James might find it amusing to observe our little English town's reaction to that universal, burning question. I understand the speaker tonight is supposed to be quite wonderful."

Mrs. Dew Smith, our local *grande dame,* regularly sent round invitations to her soirées to hear the latest fad speaker. The month before, her guest had been the mesmerist Professor Schlenk; now, she was presenting a bright young woman, who had come all the way from Australia to speak to us on the question of justice and women's suffrage.

Mrs. Dew Smith was not a defender of rights for women; she only knew what might be of interest to her friends. The Suffragettes had been in all the London papers for months, with the February Mud March that had brought out three thousand women marchers and then, in June, another march of ten thousand to honour Mrs. Fawcett. The previous month, on Women's Sunday, there were reported to have been thirty thousand marchers on behalf of women's rights.

Provincial little Rye had not yet been organised or even rallied, but apparently, now, this young woman and her hostess, Mrs. Dew Smith, were ready to give it a try. I, for one, was not going to miss this event.

Mr. James at first seemed delighted with my suggestion for his niece, but then he must have had second thoughts, saying, "Why, yes, I was invited. It does sound quite interesting, but do you really think, do you suppose—I mean, I really don't think her parents, that is, I'm sure my niece wouldn't be interested in that."

I could not contain myself. "Of course she would be interested! The topic tonight is of great importance to young women everywhere—America, Australia . . . How could she not be interested?"

"But I'm not sure that that sort of talk would be appropriate for such a young woman. It might become too frank. I've heard—"

I was remembering how he had once dictated to my typewriter "*the Suffragette agitation . . . with its obstreperous* Comma*, police* Hyphen *-prodding or umbrella* Hyphen *-thumping ways.*" How could I forget those phrases?!

I spoke calmly. "But I'm sure that Mrs. Dew Smith would never allow such an ambiance to develop at one of her soirées—never." I was gaining courage with every sentence. "Really, you must bring Miss James!"

"Well, of course you're right. I'm sure our trusted neighbour will not disappoint us—and we must not disappoint her." And so it was agreed. I would return to Lamb House to meet Miss Peggy James in time so that we could all walk together down the hill.

My first impression of Peggy James then was a quick introduction in the street in front of Lamb House that evening. She was a pleasant and intelligent-looking young woman in her stylishly round horn-rimmed glasses and piles of dark hair looped up in the complicated style so popular in America. She seemed eager to make my acquaintance, shaking my hand firmly—no caution there—and we walked side by side down the narrow street with Mr. James following us, exclaiming about the clear evening sky, the unusual warmth of the day, all the usual weather-y sorts of talk.

I was surprised to hear Miss James cut right into one of Mr. James' longer phrases. Perhaps he was winding up to present his opinions on our hostess or to expound a bit about Rye history. His niece began to speak over top of his words, with neither apologies nor perhaps even awareness of her apparent lack of respect: "Miss Bosanquet, I understand from my uncle that you're quite a reader. Are there any new books over here you would recommend? I love to read about the aristocracy, the lords and ladies. Who is your favourite author? Have you read Mrs. Lucy Clifford's latest?"

Of course I had—We all loved Mrs. Clifford and devoured her romances, but I did not want to admit as much in front of her uncle, and so I attempted to shift the conversation to other topics that might interest Miss James. Remembering my cricket-playing days, I thought of asking her about sports; she looked strong, as if she might play, but I was wrong, for in answer to my question, she exclaimed, "Oh, cricket? Is that not for boys? I have never cared a bit about sports. That was all for my brothers and my father. They like to tramp all over the place, up and down mountains, but I would rather stay at home and read, or perhaps go out to a lecture or to the Chautauqua and watch all the well-dressed rich and famous people. Are there not quite a few famous writers living around here? I think my uncle said Robert Louis Stevenson used to live here before he got so sick. Who else do you know?"

I was afraid I could be of little help to Miss James, for the only famous person I knew was her uncle—and another I hoped to add soon, her father. I looked around for Mr. James, but apparently he had met up with acquaintances and was stopped at their door-step. We paused for a moment to give him a chance to catch up. I asked Miss James about her father's work in psychical research, some of which I had read and which I had heard a little about from one of Mrs. Dew Smith's speakers.

"I don't know," Miss James said. "Which work do you mean? My father has so many different experiments going on—I can't follow them all. Does that sort of spiritualistic thing interest you?"

Now it was my turn. "Yes, I would like to try something like automatic handwriting one day," I admitted, hoping my employer was not paying attention, but no such luck. He had caught up again.

"Ah, yes, the Great Eternal Mind—Wouldn't it be grand if we all could tap into it, and then the Great Eternal Mind would write all our books for us—"

"Oh, Uncle Harry, you shouldn't make light of it. Father's quite taken up now with his psychical phenomena, and Mother, too—She's even more of a believer, I think." Apparently the literal-minded Miss James could not detect when her uncle was only having a bit of fun with us, perhaps because it was at the expense of her father.

As we turned onto Watchbell Street and headed uphill towards Mrs. Dew Smith's, a heavy silence fell over us. I thought frantically through possible subjects—Mrs. Dew Smith's recent travels, Mr. James' recent travels. No, I thought, I suspect Mr. James would not want me to mention his extravagant friend, Mrs. Wharton. We could talk about Rye and its old houses, but I knew that Mr. James had already given his niece the whole, exhausting tour and—well, there was the weather—

"It's been so lovely," I began, and at the same moment, Mr. James began, "What a heat wave—"

Peggy certainly was not reticent. She interrupted again. "But Uncle, it's hardly what I'd call a heat wave. You know in New York City, where Brother Harry works now, it's above ninety degrees every day for weeks at a time. Here, I've hardly seen the sun at all—or were you making a joke? Oh, I seem to have missed the point. Really, Uncle, you must give me a signal or something. I never understand what you mean when you use that dry English humour."

At last we were at Mrs. Dew Smith's door and soon enough were greeted, introduced around, and seated, the three of us in the front-row seats of honour.

Mrs. Dew Smith clapped her hands for quiet, beginning straight off to describe her newest discovery. As she spoke of her prize guest's beauty and courage, I could see for myself, but with the buzz and hubbub of the crowd and with my deaf ear, I missed her name—I learnt it later—Miss Muriel Matters. She was a small, fair woman, quite young to have accomplished all the adventures Mrs. Dew Smith was reading from the notes in her hand:

"Quite well-known for her eloquence in her native land, and perhaps you've read of her exploits here last week, up in a balloon to call attention to women's plight, so often left up in the air." There was a polite titter from the audience. Mrs. Dew Smith pushed on.

"Miss Matters is known best in her native Australia, where she and others, like her devoted friend, Miss Smith, have already achieved some measure of freedom for women."

As our hostess gestured towards her speaker, I noticed with increasing interest that Miss Matters had brought along a companion, another young woman, who appeared completely devoted to her. I wondered when Miss Smith, like us, had been caught and held by the very real field of magnetism surrounding Miss Matters.

At last, Miss Matters began in a low voice to speak of her work back at home and what she had learnt in England. I bent forward to catch her every word. Miss James leaned forward, too, but only to whisper to me, "She is lovely. That dress, I'm sure, is made of the most expensive silk. That turquoise would be the perfect colour for me."

I let my hand sway, indicating that she needed to be quiet, and we listened without interruption for nearly an hour to Miss Matters and her views, including a most shockingly frank discussion of the conditions for fallen women, the women of the streets. I felt Mr. James shift and stir uncomfortably as Miss Matters went into some detail. Mr. James must have been concerned, I imagined, about his niece and what she might be thinking at such a graphic presentation of the horrible conditions for quite young girls, some only nine or ten when forced out to make a living on the streets. But he need not have been concerned. From my seat on the other side of Miss James, I could see that she was secretively making a list on a scrap of paper she held under the flap of her handbag: "Clair— Belgian chocolates. Aunt Fanny— Cherry cordial." Mr. James need not have worried. Miss James was impervious.

But I certainly was affected by Miss Matters, more than by any previous suffrage speaker. Perhaps it was that she was young, or perhaps it was the foreign turn to her speech. She spoke so clearly about the plight of the single women who seek financial independence, who still had so many unjust barriers put before them by the men who wanted to keep everything the way everything had always been. Why was it that women still could not hold property, or vote, or run for office, or have their own bank accounts, or, if widowed or divorced, even keep their children, their homes, or control their children's finances?

Miss Matters was logical and persuasive. Her rallying cry—"Be just and fear not!"—was soon being repeated by others in the audience, as we were more and more with her. By the end, the supportive questions from the audience—"When can we hear you again?" "I'd like to bring my husband to hear you." "How long will you stay?"—made it clear that her eloquence had won at least us over to the Cause.

Miss Matters announced that she would be speaking the next evening down on the Town Salts, the open area below the cliff. As we rose to applaud her and then to talk among ourselves, I vowed to go down that evening to hear more. I wondered, too, knowing the town of Rye even a little, if she might not need help with that very different, probably rowdier sort of audience. As retiring as I was, I thought: I must go.

Mr. James and his niece, however, were not to be of our party. I noticed that as Mr. James stood up, he took his niece by her elbow, as if she might want to linger, but she seemed as eager as he to seek the hostess and the door and return to Lamb House and their dinner. Mr. James gave me an embarrassed little wave as they left, but I was glad to see them go, for I wanted only to hear more and see more of Miss Matters. I listened to Miss Muriel Matters and saw her at ease with her profession, saw her with her second self, Miss Smith.

The question of where Nellie and I could spend our time together had become quite a problem for us, now that we were inseparable friends, real "chums," as Mr. James called us. That day, watching Miss Matters and Miss Smith, I knew what I wanted, and I knew the Oliver typewriter was central: If I did become successful, then I might be able to afford a real place of my own. And then perhaps I could persuade Nellie to come live with me, as I had so often dreamed.

The next morning, my landlady rapped on my door when I was still in bed, feeling my monthly worst, and there was still no work up at Lamb House to make me get up and on with my usual day.

"Miss, miss, you must come down at once, there's a man here at the door asking for you!"

I was startled, alarmed: Was there something wrong? Could it be that something had happened to Mr. James? Or might it be the treasured Oliver I'd been awaiting for so long a time? I dressed hurriedly in the clothes I had thrown on the chair the night before and pulled my hair back into its combs as I hurried down after Mrs. Holland, who was complaining all the way.

"Miss Bosanquet, he will speak only to you." She was affronted, for her domain had been invaded. "I told him it was a mistake— there were no crates or boxes ordered here. It's not right, his insisting on delivering it only to you, whatever outlandish thing it could be."

I laughed a little, relieved at least now that I knew nothing had happened to Mr. James. I tried to soften her outrage at the effrontery: imagine, having something so huge and awkward, even possibly improper, delivered to her respectable boarding house.

Two men with a wooden crate stood at the door. The label said "Miss T. Bosanquet, Marigold Cottage, Rye," and I could see on the side that it had come from Mr. Rix and the Oliver Typewriting Machine Company.

At last—

After they had hauled the crate into the vestibule—with Mrs. Holland fussing about and complaining with her "Be careful!" "Watch out!" "Watch the paint!!"—they pried off the top and lifted out my shiny new machine. I gave them a little extra and asked them to carry it up the stairs and to my room, where I'd had a small table ready for weeks, it felt like.

It took only one of the men to lift the precious machine out of the crate, as if it weighed nothing. I hoped I would be able to carry it as easily, but it did look larger inside my small room, once it was enthroned on its table.

After Mrs. Holland and the men left, I sat there, waiting to catch my breath, thinking, Here is my salvation—if only I can do this on my own.

I took out my tool kit, with its wrenches, my oil can, and soft, dingy rags and began to ready the machine for use. The familiar clean smell of the oil filled my small room, and I felt my muscles relax, my worry diminishing. I know how to do this, I said to myself, I am a trained typewriter and secretary. I breathed again. I can do it. But, oh! Maybe it will be too difficult to find my own small jobs and somehow fit them in, considering Mr. James' current, sporadic working schedule. As I moved the small parts, added a little more oil to the shiny hinges, the compact levers, the even array of keys, though, I just knew it felt right.

I put in the paper I had ready and began to type. I would write to my friends back at the flat, to Clara and Nora, telling them my joy at being independent, ready to work anywhere, any time. I loved the look of the crisp black letters on the white paper, the words clacking and clicking their way across, the *ding* at the end of the line, and that wonderful smooth shove of the return lever and the roller flying back, ready for another line of my words.

But then, after the excitement of at last possessing my Oliver, there was more excitement to come.

Down on the Salts that evening, the gathered crowd was much larger, perhaps as many as a hundred, and included many of the town's young toughs and bullies ready to make a laughing-stock of any speaker who showed the least sign of weakness. But soon Miss Matters had this crowd, too, in the palm of her hand, and by the end we all formed an impromptu torch-light parade back up to the town with calls and shouts back and forth: "Votes for women!" "Be just and fear not!"

What I had heard that evening and the evening before inspired me to write, and when I came back to my room, I typed the title, "A Suffragette." I went on to write a long article about what I had learnt and felt, especially now that I could type it without having to ask permission to use my employer's machine.

I was pleased when I finished the article and rolled out the last page. The piece did look quite professional. I sent it right off and was proud to have it accepted by the "Westminster Gazette" and in print in a week's time, much to Clara and Nora's amazement.

Clara wired me, "DORA HURRAH FOR YOU STOP NOW IT BEGINS YOUR OWN WRITING CAREER."

Nora's note was as positive, humourous, and clever as ever.

For the next few weeks, Miss James stayed at Lamb House while she waited for her parents to arrive in England. Often, Mr. James would ask me to spend time with his niece; apparently entertaining such a young woman was a demanding encumbrance for him. Nellie happened to be away with her family on holiday, and so I was always free to be included in Mr. James' plans for his niece. He sent us off on walks about the shops, or she borrowed her uncle's bicycle to ride with me down to the shore or to take tea at one of the pretentious little tea-rooms over on the side of town near Nellie's house.

We seemed to strike up a friendship of some sort, but Peggy (we were "Peggy" and "Dora" that summer) never did find my remarks amusing. I remember I did try to introduce her to other girls, especially to one of my Rye acquaintances, Miss Amber Reeves, a very sweet young girl at Newnham College in Cambridge, since Peggy was to be at Oxford and might like to have a friend not far away. But it was not to be. Peggy James came back more concerned than before, saying, "Dora, how could you? That Miss Reeves was not a bit of a 'sport' as you said English girls are. She was frightfully academic and so conceited."

I tried to imagine what muddled trans-Atlantic exchange had led to that misunderstanding, and then I had to laugh at myself. How was I to explain to a young American girl (and one of Mr. James' own family) what it was that a young English girl had meant to say or meant to do, or even to describe how I was sure that she had not been trying to give offence? Perhaps it had been a sort of Daisy Miller story in reverse. I thought it might have been fun to share the joke with Mr. James—but not yet, no, not yet.

As to my own ambitions, I continued to be inspired long after Miss Muriel Matters left Rye. We did form a local Women's Suffrage Society, and I found myself elected the secretary, because of my typewriter. But neither Peggy nor my own Nellie ever wanted to have anything more to do with the inspiring Miss Matters or her ideas. Nellie had been particularly sceptical of Miss Matters' supposed balloon-flying, protesting that there had probably been no hot-air balloon at all, and she must have posed in a fake balloon to make her speeches, all for the benefit of the papers. Nellie would never listen seriously to someone like that, and so—not for the last time—I went on my adventure without her, and she resented my fun. Still, Nellie was pleased with my success publishing the article. What a thrill that small cheque brought!

That fall of 1908, it seemed that Mr. James still disappeared whenever he chose, leaving me idle. I was delighted with my beautiful little Oliver, for now I could apply to anyone for copy work, typing away wherever convenient. It was Nellie who brought me my first new client—her father!

From our first meeting I had known Nellie's father, Professor Bradley, to be a well-known local author of lengthy and well-respected tomes, except that, as Mr. James had intimated to me, it was probable that they did not pay. I think I might have taken the hint right then about my own employer's concern with work that would pay, but at that time I was more interested in Miss Nellie Bradley.

Nellie and I were hopeful that I might profit from her father's long-windedness, for if I made enough money, we might take rooms together. I packed up the Oliver and took it to the Bradleys' one slow morning when Mr. James was busy with his niece, visiting Hastings and the battlefields.

Nellie brought out a long chapter, which her father had said was ready to send off, only needing to be typed up into clean copies. I was ready to try, but I wondered if I could do that sort of copying—Would it be too technical? Was Mr. Bradley a foot-note-ing, tables-and-graphs sort of man? Nellie assured me that her father's work, although entirely boring, was of the straight-forward sort. All I had to worry about was his atrocious spelling, and I knew I could handle that from the years of copying out my father's sermons.

We set up the machine in Nellie's bedroom on a small rickety table we had found, and I began to look through the manuscript. At first, I had trouble with Mr. Bradley's handwriting. Strange as it may seem, I had gotten used to Mr. James' loose scrawl and elegant script, almost like a mannerist painting in its suggestive obliqueness, leaving out so much. But I had the advantage of knowing Mr. James' subject matter well. I am not sure I ever knew what it was Mr. Bradley was writing about, but his cramped, faint handwriting made it even more difficult. I had to keep calling Nellie back into the room for help with translation, until, at last, with an exasperated sigh (she was trying to paint the background of her portrait of Mrs. Dew Smith's little pug dog), Nellie suggested she come sit with me, even read the troublesome parts aloud.

"That's it, dictate to me!" I jumped up and took her arms and led her to the mantel. "You be Mr. James. Here—Stand here; hold the papers like this." I demonstrated an imperious pose, one hand holding the papers, the other gesturing magnificently, even with a Napoléonic grandeur.

"And then you must pace up and down," I went on, striding back and forth across the room, reading a few words.

"Now, here, you try it—" I thrust her father's pages into her hands.

"Oh, Dora dear, you know I can't do it that way." Nellie was almost wailing, but she did try, coming back to sit beside me and dictate over the quiet ticking of my little machine. It was a lovely morning of good work, and we made our way through quite a pile of paper. When we took it back to Mr. Bradley, he was very happy, promising to write a cheque soon, asking if I would like to do another set. Then, he disappeared into his study to bring me more.

When he came out, he was carrying a huge stack of papers, many more chapters to copy. Looking over the pages, my heart fell. I realised there had to be weeks and weeks of work here. I knew I could not be the one to contract with Mr. Bradley for so many pages. I felt strongly that my first loyalty had to be to Mr. James, no matter how often he left me without work. I still believed in him, still owed it to him to be there whenever he needed me, ready to drop everything else at his first gesture.

Sadly, I handed back the papers and packed up my machine to take it back to my room. But as I walked up the hill, I found myself earnestly wishing that Mr. James would return to a more regular schedule, wishing that his family would leave so that Mr. James and I could resume our old routine.

However, I did hope to meet Mr. James' famous philosopher brother, Peggy's father, Professor William James. I had long wanted to meet him, ever since I had come across that paper on trance writing, or maybe it was one of his earlier essays on dreaming and consciousness, or maybe when I first read his book, "Psychology." Perhaps I might encourage him to talk to me about séances and mesmerism, about the occult and all the other things I had wondered about.

12

"The Reverberator"

September 1908

The face of the work may be small in itself, and yet the surface, the whole thing, the associational margin and connexion, may spread, beneath the fond remembering eye, like nothing more noble than an insidious grease-spot.

—Henry James
Preface to "The Reverberator"
The New York Edition, volume 13

I had to keep one of my larger handkerchiefs in my lap to dab at my forehead. It was that hot, even out in the Garden Room, where we were still working, though summer had ended. There, the light slanted through the trees, and the windows were all open to catch any movement of wind, the sounds of birds busy in the berry bushes, the rose bushes.

Each summer, we would move our dictation out of Lamb House when the weather became too warm for working inside. On hot days, it was much cooler out there in the Garden Room, a handsome brick outbuilding with its large windowed room, its open airy space larger than any room in Lamb House. It saddens me whenever I think of the Garden Room, for it is no more, having been destroyed during the Nazi bombing.

Mr. James loved to entertain his visitors with stories about Lamb House and that separate building, telling them that in Rye the mayors often had to do business away from domestic entanglements, for the town's reputation had been principally as a smugglers' and pirates' haven. The main house had been built centuries before as the residence for Rye's mayor. Because of its narrow staircases and ground-floor kitchen, the cooking heat and kitchen smells in summer would come up most insistently right beneath our upstairs working room, the Green Room. In winter, that extra heat was welcome, but in the summer it was wonderful to be cool out there in the garden, within its high, shaded brick walls. I loved working in that cooler room, under its elegant arches of light, and I loved looking out past the kitchen garden to the deep green of the Lamb House lawn.

That particular morning, I thought how well Mr. James had begun. He had gotten back into the work after his brother and family had left for the rest of their journey.

Yet the words seemed to be coming more slowly, and I could hear the birds' quarrelling intensify. Suddenly there was a loud metallic clatter; with that, the birds flew off. Mr. James stopped his pacing and went to the open door, reaching into his pocket for his handkerchief to pat away his perspiration. Once the rattling moved farther off, Mr. James came back to his usual place and began again, going back to that time of writing "The Ambassadors," when he was most warmly affected with his invention of his *"reader's friend,"* Maria Gostrey:

". . . or that no less a pounce is made on Maria Gostrey Dash— *without even the pretext, either, of* Underline *her being, in essence, Strether's friend. She is the reader's friend . . ."*

Then he fell silent, in one of his longer pauses, and I was glad that I now knew enough to keep my silence as well.

The rattling became a muffled *clatter clatter clatter,* then pause, and I noticed in our silence the scent of cut grass.

Clatter clatter clatter, pause. I pictured Old George pushing the mower up, turning, pushing the mower back, back and forth across the soft green miniature lawn of the Lamb House garden.

It was not so large an area as I used to mow when I was a girl, when my friends and I took over a part of the large lawns and gardens down at Ethel Allen's house. She was my special friend that summer when I was twenty; we spent every moment we could together, away from her sister and away from my father's demands.

She and I had wanted to set up for lawn tennis, the latest fad, and had persuaded Ethel's gardener to let us mark off a rectangle on her family's noble lawn for us to cut very short and roll level and smooth. Then we would put up a net and invite all the neighbours for a round-robin tournament. I was younger and stronger, so I began the mowing. It was hard work, and I felt sweaty and most unattractive as I shoved the heavy lawn-mowing machine back and forth, slewing it hard around the turn, *clatter clatter clatter,* pause.

Once we had defined our rectangle of light green grass, we hauled out the lawn roller from the shed and pushed it, the two of us rolling it back and forth. I remember the fragrance of crushed grass, the feeling of Ethel so slender and vibrant there beside me. Of course, we could not speak, for we were too out of breath, and it was too noisy with the clang of the roller.

When at last the lawn was as smooth as velvet, we removed our wooden, gut-strung rackets from their presses and searched for the newer balls the dogs had not yet chewed. It was a glorious romp. And we were safe, for if we were playing game after game of tennis out in the fresh air and sunlight, then her mother and sister could not complain that we were too much together and behaving unhealthily, as they had accused us before. I was a good player, and so I could let Ethel's younger sister win often enough to grow bored and leave us alone. But Ethel, dear Ethel, with her weak heart even then, she would tire quickly and need to rest.

We could stop and sit and talk of the books we were reading and the list of books she had made for me to read. I was happy to follow her direction. We would talk of the future—how I was sure I was never going to marry, no matter how many times my aunts found young men for me to meet. Ethel reassured me that she was sure I was going to be somebody, if only I would keep on with my reading, keep on with my writing. She believed in me, in my writing. Some afternoons, I would bring her my journals, and she would read aloud to me what I had written. Even though she left out the parts I had written about her, I knew she was pleased. She would laugh or smile so sweetly when she handed the notebooks back, as we sat there in the warm sunlight beside the fresh, green grass.

Clatter clatter clatter, pause. Now, the sound of Old George at work came faintly through the open door. Mr. James broke his stillness with a slight sound, the intake of breath that I knew as the signal that he had found his words. I sat up, ready:

". . . *in consequence of dispositions that make him so eminently require one* Semicolon *; and she acts in that capacity* Comma, *and* Underline *really in that capacity alone* Comma, *with exemplary devotion* Comma, *from beginning to end of the book.*"

And so I bent to my machine, and we tap-tap-tapped on once more.

But I found myself wondering: Ever since his family had left, Mr. James seemed to be having difficulty working steadily. Or did I have it wrong? Had his family's visit distracted him, or had his work become a struggle, and so he welcomed the interruptions? It seemed to me that he was glad to have new stories to be engaged in, for we spent less time that fall on the prefaces and revisions. He had rushed to prepare everything in his precise way for the newest volume, and yet when it was complete and the publisher sent the proofs, it was a struggle to coax Mr. James into work on the final revisions. I could barely send the proof he had read and the edited copies back to his publisher in time.

At times, I wondered if I did not have some serious misconceptions about my employer. Perhaps he was trying to mislead me about his work habits, his seriousness of purpose, even his desire to complete and send anything off! As I walked home after a puzzling sort of a day, I would find myself mulling over all that I knew of him, all that I had observed and wondered, as I tried to lay the contradictions out in some scientific and orderly way.

Mr. James sometimes said one thing and did the opposite, but not from any sense of polite obligation that I could see. I never saw him tell little white lies even for social convenience. No, what I was seeing was a series of what were to me much more puzzling behaviours: He hated to be interrupted, and yet every time the door-bell rang, he would hurry to the window to see who it was. He despised gossips and worriers, yet he was the first to pass on the really bad news concerning the Madox Hueffers' marriage and disastrous public quarrels in the street. He believed that the very best way to travel, with the most chance for gathering impressions, was by First Class train, and yet the very minute Mrs. Wharton turned up with her elegant Panhard touring car, he was ready to chuck it all for the chance of a ride, leaving me in mid-sentence if necessary. He might complain of her lack of warning, her bad timing, her non-existent schedule, and he might growl, "When does the woman work?" He might be envious of her chauffeur and scold his own little Burgess, telling his manservant to stand up straighter and put on a cleaner jacket whenever Mrs. Wharton was expected. He might think her velvet cloaks and elegant furs were too much, she was immensely too much, and yet he always went whenever she beckoned. He came back late, exhausted, still complaining, insisting he would not go the next time, but he always did.

Personally, I could not understand her great attraction; in fact, during my first months with Mr. James, I had never even caught a whiff of her Paris perfume. Nevertheless, I could feel her wake, as if I were some row-boat left bobbing in the tumult after her oceanic departures or ignored in the chaos around her arrivals.

I remember one morning, when we were finishing one of the prefaces for "The Middle Years," that collection of stories about aging writers, and Mr. James was rushing through in order to drive off with Mrs. Wharton yet again. I was excited that this time, surely, I might meet her, if only she would arrive before we finished our work, but it was not to be. Mr. James concluded the section early and dismissed me without a moment's thought.

Another morning, I had hopes of catching a glimpse of her, or at least of seeing her famous car, but when she came, no luck: Mr. James had sent me to the post office to mail off the latest preface, and so I missed her again. When I came back to the empty house, Burgess was nearly speechless with joy over having been asked to help the chauffeur with the spark, whatever that was, while I was left again with no work for the next day or two, during which the peripatetic couple would presumably be away.

I wondered how old she was. What did she see in my employer? What attracted her? Perhaps it was that they were both born rich and American. I had heard at Mrs. Dew Smith's tea table that Mrs. Wharton was the only child of an immensely wealthy American family, new money, more money than was good for them, and I was intrigued by hints that she was very attractive for an older woman—she had to be at least forty—and always dressed richly in the best Parisian fashion. My informants went on and on about her elegant furs and her fine car with its beautiful leather seats, its polished shine. I was beside myself with wanting to see her.

I suppose I had heard of her novels before I came to Mr. James, but I began to look at her works with an eager interest. By then, Edith Wharton was a most famous authoress, a phenomenon producing several popular books—travel memoirs, short stories, novellas, and novels—a year in both England and America. Often, one of her stories would be serialised beside one of Mr. James' in the same magazine. I knew she had presented Mr. James with many volumes of her work. Before long, I, too, was caught by her spell, not in person but through her writing.

My curiosity led me one morning to choose one of her novels to read in our pauses during dictation. I found that I liked her writing: Her characters were most interesting in spite of the despicable situations she seemed determined to place them in. Her style was much more straight-forward than Mr. James'. Mrs. Wharton's detractors said she imitated Mr. James, but I could not see this. I sensed a cut-throat quality to her plots that his never had. And I found that once I began one of her books I could hardly bear to stop.

That fascination led me one afternoon to make what might have been a terrible *faux pas*—at the very moment Mr. James was finally dictating the outline for a new short story. We had put aside the last of the endless parade of prefaces in hopes of writing something that would "pay, and pay well," as Mr. James put it.

I knew that he had also become desperate for paying work: I was there when, finally, the first royalty cheque arrived after he had finished two thirds of the work on the New York Edition and after the early volumes had been out for months.

Mr. James showed it to me with laughter and ironic scorn. "Look, it's all of two hundred eleven dollars," he gaily announced, but I knew he was upset. He must have expected much more for all the work we were doing. He then hastily arranged with his publisher (actually, he and Mrs. Wharton shared publishers) for a new book of short stories, and we were happily working away, except when we had to stop while he searched for a word or a phrase that had escaped him.

I was ready for his pauses now, and so I opened my book—Mrs. Wharton's most recent novel. Soon enough, I was lost in her pages, quite impossibly lost. Only Mr. James' tapping on the window to chase a cat away from his roses brought me back; I could only hope he had not noticed, had not tried to dictate some of his story and failed to secure my attention. I felt like such a traitor, caught up with another writer's work, that I tried to slip the book with its scarlet cover under some loose papers, but I believe his bright eyes caught me at my deception all the same. I realised I would have to be more careful.

As the autumn turned cold and dark, Mr. James began again to have whole days when the work did not go well, and I noticed that the bad days often followed a visitation from Mrs. Wharton. I remember one such day when Mr. James sent Burgess to tell me not to come that morning but to wait until after lunch. I was disappointed, because I had planned to arrive early. I had hoped to have a chance to do some repair work on the Remington, which had been giving me trouble.

When I arrived and set my coat on the hall bench as usual, I noticed that something about his hat collection was amiss. While most of the other hats—the Tam o' Shanter, the opera hat, the fedora, the deer-stalker, even the turban—were hanging neatly on the hat-rack near the hall mirror, the pith helmet had been left out on the bench. I knew that Mrs. Wharton, the Angel of Devastation, was to have swept through our peaceful little Rye, scooping up Mr. James on her way, and I wondered if the white huntress, perhaps, was her favourite role. Why did she need more victims, with her immense popularity, all her simultaneous serialisations, her money, and her fame?

I hung up the pith helmet with its swaths of perfumed veiling on the hook between the derby and the beret. I knew where it belonged, for I had often studied Mr. James' extensive collection, that mixed family of headgear so temptingly arranged and draped and furled across the enormous rack, and I would note its increasing number as I passed by on my way up the stairs. Now, I wondered which had been his choice to wear that morning on his drive with Mrs. Wharton.

I climbed the staircase and went through the open doorway of the Green Room, where Mr. James sat with his hands on his knees, glowering before the grate with its fitful coal fire. In the dark room, there was no appearance of any writing about to be done, only a surprisingly empty space where our huge, familiar typewriting machine usually stood.

He glanced up at me and announced in the most gloomy of tones, "You'd said the blessed Remington was not operating properly. I've had Wilton Rix come out. They've taken the Remington away and lent us a replacement machine, a stuttering Smith—" He gestured despairingly towards a strange, shining machine waiting on the desk in front of the window.

"I am not able, I am sure I will not be able to dictate to the sound of its keys. I am not accustomed to it—it is an alien machine." Mr. James stood heavily, pushing himself up from his heavy, oak armchair with both hands. He went on.

"I am sorry, Miss Bosanquet, but it may take some time until the Remington is returned. Until then, I can't work. You might as well go back to your friends in London and wait until I can begin again—" With that, he walked to the window and began to look out, while holding the curtain back, smoothing the heavy fabric between his fingers. "If I ever can begin again."

I must have answered something, but I was completely devastated. Another break in our work! How was I to pay my bills? Still, I kept a careful tongue, turned, and went back downstairs. He came with me and graciously, apologetically, took my coat from the bench and helped me put it on.

I don't know what possessed me—Perhaps it was my utter frustration with his silliness over the different sound of this new type-writing machine, perhaps it was my worry over my pay, or it may have been that particular dark blue of my coat or my catching sight of that familiar dome-shaped hat. Suddenly, I was inspired to try something, anything to make him go back to work.

I spoke up in a bright, perky tone completely unlike my usual, quiet voice: "You know, I've never tried one of your famous hats. What's this one?" From the rack, I took the dark blue dome—the London bobby's hat—and pulled it on, arranging it as I looked in the oval mirror of the hat-rack. The hat fitted closely, covering all my hair, making me feel rakish, even daring, as if I were dressed up again as the brave hero or swaggering villain in one of our theatricals back home.

I tilted the bobby's hat to the official angle and put my thumbs in my pockets, turning to give Mr. James my sternest look. "And is it true you have not done your writing stint for today but have been carrying on, traversing about the countryside in a fancy automobile, alone with a married woman of renown?"

"Yes, but . . ."

"And is it true you have abandoned your poor bit o' work here at home, left it waiting because you can't abide the sound of a chattering Smith to replace the chattering Remington? No, sir, we simply can't have it."

Mr. James grinned and reached for the most disreputable example of the hatter's trade on the rack—the poor boy's checkered cap. He pulled it down, soft and loose, covering all his high forehead, right down to his now-smiling, grey eyes.

He bowed. "Well, guv'nor, I beg forgiveness, sir." He ducked his head and touched the brim in a salute. "And if the guv'nor so wishes, we can return to the study and give it another go."

And most amazingly to me, he turned, still wearing the cap, and began eagerly to climb the stairs. I settled my bobby's helmet even more firmly and followed him.

13

"The Private Life"

1908-1909

The sight of him at that moment was illuminating, and it kindled a great backward train, connecting itself with one's general impression of the personage.

—Henry James
"The Private Life"
The New York Edition, volume 17

My cousin Queenie was right. I am easily jealous of attentions shown to my loved one or attentions that my loved one pays to someone else. In the early months of my work with Mr. James, I did not realise how attracted I was to the Master—Oh, not that way exactly, no, but after a year with him, I, too, was in his sway. I was one of his court, and he was our sovereign, our ruling Famous Man. All of us there at Lamb House paid him homage in our various fashions, from the cook preparing special cuts the way he liked to Old George tending his choicest blossoms and even his man, Burgess, who did everything Mr. James wanted for any moment's desire.

Of course, Burgess worshipped Mr. James and jealously guarded his power, making sure no one else did anything for the Master, from bathing and shaving and dressing to packing and unpacking, even arranging the movements of writing tables, desk chairs, and the massive typewriting machine. Burgess was the one to collect the mail and bring it to Mr. James each morning and afternoon, and if Mr. James was away, he would give it to me to sort and tend.

Even after the Remington was repaired and Mr. James and I tried to return to our work, things did not go all that well. Apparently, this was still a difficult time for Mr. James. And it was also a particularly bad time for me: I was penniless!

One afternoon, when he was away, I let myself into Lamb House to see if he had sent any new pages for me to work on in his absence. Suddenly, I was struck by my predicament—I had so little money. I usually had so little money that this penniless state did not seem unusual, but in fact, this time, I had nothing to fall back on.

I had learnt that the small, quarterly cheque of inheritance from my mother had not arrived because the bank holiday had interfered with the usual arrangements, and I had counted on Mr. James to pay me before he ran off with Mrs. Wharton. Apparently, he had forgotten. He hardly ever sent work for me while he was away. This time, he had left me with only a few pages of revisions to finish and no money to pay for them.

I do not think Mr. James ever understood my circumstances. He apparently had always had money or could easily write stories that made money, and when he was starting out, his father—so unlike mine—had sent him remittances.

The first money I ever earned in my life, in fact, was for my first week with Mr. James, and he paid me only a shilling an hour, which was not very much even in those days. I knew that, but I had not cared, for as long as there was steady work, I believed I would make out all right. I was accustomed to spending very little money; I did not travel like Clara and Nora, my better-off friends from Cheltenham days; I did not buy things. I kept close accounts at the back of my calendar diary, down to shillings and pence. I knew I was not extravagant.

No, the only thing I did that might be called an extravagance was to like my cigarettes too much. Not many other girls smoked then, in 1908, but I had begun early, even before I was at university.

One week-end a fascinating lecturer, Dr. Charlotte Green, had come to Cheltenham to speak to the older girls about the future of women in medicine. Because I was to go to university in science, she singled me out for attention, invited me out to the garden to talk with her while she smoked. Of course, when she offered me a cigarette from her slim, silver case, I had to try one. It was not as pleasant as I had thought it would be, but since she made it look so elegant, I went on trying. I knew enough not to breathe the smoke in but only to hold it in my mouth a little and then let it out. I did not want Dr. Green to think I was an inexperienced little ninny. I wanted her to think I was old enough, smart enough to follow her example out into the real world.

I liked the feeling of the slim cylinder in my fingers, I liked the sophisticated way my hand looked holding it, the way the tip glowed, the way the smoke drifted around the two of us there in the corner of the courtyard between Founders Hall and the new Science Building. But that cigarette lasted only a few minutes, and then we went back inside to the others. Happily, my heroine was staying with us for several days. Soon enough, before the end of her stay, I had become quite a smoker. It was Dr. Green who walked me down to the tobacconist to buy cigarettes for myself, telling the man behind the counter that two packets would be required, remarking that cigarettes were good for a weak heart. My heart was not weak, but only very much smitten with Dr. Green.

By that morning in Rye, I had been smoking for years. I was a shameless smoker, and I was desperate. I needed cigarettes, needed money, and so I went to Lamb House, looking for the cheque Mr. James had forgotten, looking for help. There was no answer to my knock; the servants must have taken advantage of the Master's holiday. I was glad I had remembered my key; I let myself into the back of the empty house.

Once I entered, I realised that I was alone in Lamb House for the first time. It seemed strange to find it so quiet, so still. All the furniture was covered with dust sheets, and the shades were drawn, giving the familiar rooms a mysterious, waiting quality, as if in the setting for a play. I was not surprised to find there was no cheque and no new work. There was only a note mailed in a hotel envelope and sent to me, saying that I should keep checking back every so often for the expected new galleys for the prefaces.

That meant that I was still without money, without hope of money, and without hope of a smoke. Being there in the familiar rooms, I felt the desire even more strongly. I was surprised, for I had not realised how much I had come to rely on Mr. James and on his easy supply of cigarettes.

I suppose I had gotten used to smoking his cigarettes when I was there with him. Often, when he was working on a particularly troublesome passage, Mr. James would smoke while he walked up and down, silently and then audibly searching for the missing word. I would breathe in his smoke and soon begin to wish I could have a break so that I, too, might have my cigarette. But of course we did not smoke companionably together, at least not during those first weeks, for at that time it was not proper for a young lady to smoke with a gentleman—or, for that matter, to smoke anywhere outside her own rooms.

In fact, at first I tried to keep my smoking hidden from Mr. James, but of course he found out. He came upon me smoking desperately in the garden one cold winter afternoon when I was supposed to have run to the corner post. He only laughed, for as he explained, he had also come out to smoke in peace, away from the housekeeper and her complaints over his wayward ashes. I felt we were partners in crime as he lit one of his favourite, rich-smelling, French cigarettes and leaned over to offer me one. After that, he would sometimes offer me his own brand from the silver cigarette boxes he kept everywhere.

But now, where could I find a cigarette? Would he have left any in the boxes placed about the rooms of the lower floor for the con-venience of his friends? I rushed from the hall to the front parlour, the dining-room, and even the telephone-room, lifting the dust sheets and finding the boxes, but every box was a disappointment, left empty in Mr. James' absence.

Then I began to search the less obvious places, along the wide mantels where there were decorative boxes, carved ivory jars, small ebony chests, hoping to find some hiding place. Somehow, I did not think about what I was doing, shamelessly searching through his rooms. Perhaps I believed it was not that bad: I was not looking upstairs or actually opening anything that might really be private.

I wondered if Mr. James was ever as in need of a cigarette as I now felt myself to be. The fruitless search had made me even more determined to find one. Where, then, might he have stashed away an extra pack in case he ran out? I began to search more frantically, opening every glass-fronted cabinet, even feeling behind the books on the shelves, but I found nothing.

Then I thought there was a chance that he might have set aside a half-empty packet, forgotten somewhere by accident one day, though I had never seen him do such a thing. I ransacked all the closets but found nothing among the dark masses of fur-collared or velvet-trimmed overcoats and fusty umbrellas. I even felt in the pockets.

I was desperate.

At last I did something I would never have thought I would do: I began to go into the drawers. Oh, not his dresser drawers upstairs, no, only the drawers of all the desks and cabinets downstairs, where it seemed more public and so in some way still not prying. I opened one after another, even the locked ones. I knew how to wiggle and shift those old locks in the right way to make the drawers open, and still I found no sign of a cigarette. Finally, I sat down before his big mahogany desk. I remembered seeing Mr. James sitting there and smoking while writing his letters near the drawing-room fire in the evenings, when I would bring him the corrected chapters.

The desk was massive and lovely, its old dark wood like satin, and it was loaded with drawers and cubby-holes. I began to yank open the drawers, to pull out the papers that I could see, being very careful to keep the piles separated and organised so that I could be sure to put them back in the right order. I knew from having searched through my father's papers how to return Father's pages so he would never know they had been disturbed. It was the only way I could find out what Father intended to do after my mother died and I was left to handle the household accounts. My father would never tell me anything, not until it was too late to prevent his whims, so I would wade through his letters, looking for the important correspondences with the banks and house agents. Prying had been my only defence against unpleasant surprises, overdraughts, and enormous bills for something Father had bought without considering whether we had the money to pay for it.

Now, I carefully went through Mr. James' papers, pulling them out to see if there might be a scrunched-up old cigarette pack forgotten at the back of the drawer. Of course there was nothing— only voluminous letters from his nephews or his brother waiting to be answered and an old receipt or two.

But then in one of the loosely locked drawers, as I lifted out the pile of letters, a single yellow half sheet, an old telegram, fell out, folded in such a way that of course I could read the pasted letters: "Arriving tonight boat train STOP Apparently bribery successful STOP At last we are free STOP How I hunger for your sweet words of affection STOP" No date, no signature.

Who could it be?

I was mad with curiosity and had forgotten all about cigarettes.

I wondered if it might be his brother—but, no, Professor James was even older than my Mr. James! Far too old to be involved with sweet words of affection. Perhaps it was a fond niece or nephew whom I had heard him speak of with affection, who might be in trouble, who might have come to him for help and write him with such endearments, but I doubted that. My imagination went wild. That is the trouble with being a writer; your mind can run rampant over the smallest words: "bribery"— "hunger"—"sweet words."

How I envied him and his exciting life, which led to such friendships!

Then I realised that the logical explanation had to be his present companion, Mrs. Wharton. He had been travelling with her when I first came to Rye, he had known her for a time, she was rumoured to be in trouble, and now he was off again with her, throwing deadlines and commitments to the wind, leaving me to finish his galleys and to deal with his publishers. Of course, it must be Mrs. Wharton!

I had met Mrs. Wharton briefly and, of course, had seen her car coming and going, had caught glimpses of her tall, straight form, her elegant hat with its veil pushed aside, her tanned and wrinkled face. Most unattractive, I often thought. But I knew more about her from rumour, from the gossip columns in the papers. Mrs. Edith Wharton was famous for her scandalous novels—a rich American, and so rich, apparently, she did not care what scandal her novels might stir up, with their tales of illicit love, even of divorce. She herself was even seeking a divorce, they said. I wondered if it might be Mrs. Wharton herself who had been threatened with bribery, who had needed to be rescued.

I looked at the telegram once more, noting that it could have been written either by a man or a woman, with no clues as to which it might be. Mad with curiosity, I pulled out all the other papers, thinking they might give me a hint, but there was nothing to be learnt from the letters stuffed in with the telegram. They did not seem even to be from that same time.

And so I carefully put all the papers and the telegram back into the drawer. I could only swallow my consuming curiosity and wait. I knew Mr. James and his lady friend would be back at the end of the week. Perhaps then I might have a chance to observe them together. Then I could see if my guess was correct.

And the cigarettes? Maybe if I went back to my rooms I could persuade Nellie to lend me a little change until Mr. James remembered to pay me. That was unlikely—but, then, it had already been a most surprising day.

If I added that mysterious bribery telegram to all those bundles of letters, I had new puzzles. I continued to worry over it. Was it Mrs. Wharton who had sent it? Who was bribing whom and about what? What indiscretion had been committed? And what was Mr. James' part in it? Or could it be one of Mr. James' other friends, one of those handsome young men whom he helped out so often? I had watched and imagined friendships, more than friendships, but I could never be sure.

I continued to puzzle over that telegram. But several weeks later, a possible story came together—or so I thought—when another mystery telegram arrived after Mr. James had gone up to London with Mrs. Wharton. This time, he had left me work to do. I was there in the Green Room, working on galley proofs early one morning when Burgess entered.

"Mr. James has a telegram, Miss. Reply paid, extremely urgent. But the Master is not due to come back until tomorrow." Burgess handed me the yellow envelope.

I had a premonition, a very strong premonition, and I even thought that it was a good thing I felt closer to my employer than a few months earlier. By now, I knew Mr. James was depending on me to deal by myself with any emergencies. And so I tore open the telegram and read it with growing alarm. It had come from Mr. James' sister-in-law, saying that Professor William James had fallen ill, and they were returning sooner than expected. Mr. James was to meet them at their train at five o'clock the next afternoon, which was that very day!

"Tell the man the reply is 'Yes,'" I said to Burgess. "I will go right away. There will be someone there to meet them."

It was of such urgency that within minutes after I had opened the telegram, I was packed up and on the next train, on my way to find Mr. James at his London hotel. As I was being jerked and bumped along in the old train from Rye to London, I began to fit together some of the pieces. My concern for them—for Mr. James and Mrs. Wharton—grew stronger. Now, I knew what I could do for Mr. James.

It had all happened so fast; some part of me was thrilled. Now, I was perhaps to see for myself the relationship between Mr. James and the famous Mrs. Wharton. They were to stay at the Terminus Hotel, since no women were allowed to take rooms at Mr. James' club. Within three hours, there I was in London, waiting at the hotel's marble counter for the clerk to return with the room number for Mr. James, or at least with a way to send a message to him. It was taking a very long time. I did not want to touch the counter. It felt greasy and slick with use, from too many strangers having leaned across it to sign the hotel register with lies or to receive their mail, perhaps to receive a note to set the time and place to meet, a letter saying "Good-bye," saying "Never again," saying "It was all wrong."

I leaned away from the counter, trying to find some place to wait that was not so open and public. I felt so out of place that I had barely spoken to the shirt-sleeved young man at the desk, who was probably much younger than I. I could not imagine leaving a message for Mr. James with this stranger, but it was important that Mr. James receive this news right away. The wire had been insistent that he must meet his brother and sister-in-law's train that afternoon. No mistake about that: Mrs. James was worried that the Professor would be over-tired from the uncomfortable crossing; she would not stand for any other arrangement.

At first, I had thought how convenient that Mr. James should already be staying at a hotel near the station where the boat train would come in. He had left his itinerary with me, saying that he planned to see off his young friend, Mr. Morton Fullerton, who coincidentally was leaving London at the same time as that Mrs. Wharton. The Angel of Devastation was returning to her apartment in Paris for the winter season.

Then it occurred to me how Mr. James' family might view the idea of Mr. James with a woman, both staying at the same hotel. This made me even more determined to prevent Mr. James' ever-so-proper sister-in-law from seeing him with Mrs. Wharton.

I looked around the empty hotel lobby once again and was surprised to notice that it was not empty. In a shadowy corner I could see a man with his back turned. I recognised the familiar shape and knew it was Mr. James standing there alone, with his hand to his eyes as if he were trying to brush something away.

Now, the odious young clerk was leaning over the counter and saying, "I'm sorry, Mr. James has already checked out, as has Mrs. Wharton. I have no listing for a Mr. Fullerton."

Then, when I turned back to look for Mr. James, the lobby was empty.

A few minutes later, I was hurrying through the crowded streets into the cold, cavernous station, with its echoing bells warning of trains arriving, hoarse voices calling out departures, and under it all, the rumble of huge engines pulsing, hardly held back, the floors vibrating. Crowds blocked my vision, and I had to stretch to look over the heads of the mass gathered beneath the huge board announcing the departures and gates. There it was, Mrs. Wharton's train to Southampton leaving on Track 12. When I pushed over to the Arrivals board, at first I was glad to see that Professor and Mrs.

James were to arrive on Track 14 at nearly the same time. That would make it easier to catch Mr. James and alert him to his brother and sister-in-law's changed plans.

But then I realised with a shock of apprehension that their two trains were too close together! What if Mrs. James came upon her brother-in-law paying court to Mrs. Wharton, a woman no longer socially acceptable, living apart from her husband, perhaps even already divorced? I hurried and pushed past the crowds in the concourse to reach the gate. There Mrs. Wharton's train was, but now where would I find Mr. James? The steam was bursting from the engine at the head of the long line of cars, and there were clusters of strangers at the doors of the First Class carriages. I walked along the platform past one and another until at last I caught sight of Mr. James' familiar, solid form, his shining bald head, for he was holding his hat and bending his head close to the dark, shining furs and feathers of a woman. Of course, Mrs. Wharton would be strikingly dressed, no hiding for her, no veils and muffling capes—she had nothing left to hide.

But as I drew closer, I stopped when I realised it was not only Mr. James with Mrs. Wharton, their heads bent towards each other. As Mr. James stepped back, she moved to take the arm of another gentleman, whose distinguished-looking back was facing me. I was mad with curiosity. Surely this was not her possibly divorcing husband whom I had never seen. No, this tall, graceful man seemed familiar to me. As he laughed and turned his sunburned face, I recognised those beautiful eyes, the handsome beard of Mr. Morton Fullerton. Were they leaving together, he and Mrs. Wharton? And now Mr. Fullerton was embracing Mr. James, who seemed overcome. They were parting, and Mr. Fullerton helped the Demon Woman up the step and into their compartment. Now, Mr. James closed their door, and I felt relief as he turned away, for now he was safe from discovery by his sister-in-law.

I called to him and he stopped, turning heavily like an animal in pain, lost, confused, turning to the sound of my voice.

"Mr. James, I'm here." I went to him, putting my hand on his arm.

His face was tear-stained; his voice, rough and low. "Miss Bosanquet, what are you doing here?"

I felt in my pocket and pulled out the telegram from Mrs. James. "It's this wire—I'd hoped to catch you—Your brother and his wife, they are arriving today, right here, and she expects you here to help them—"

"Here? Today?" His face went completely white. "When?"

"Now. Their train is already in. On the next platform."

He seemed to be staggered. Was it by the near miss?

As we turned to walk, we caught sight of the familiar, tall, thin figure of his brother and the smaller, rounder one of Mrs. James. They were quite near us at the end of their platform. They apparently had been standing there for some time, waiting, looking about. What had they seen?

The Professor caught sight of us.

"Harry, Harry!" he shouted. He walked towards his brother, hands outstretched in his unembarrassed American way. And then the brothers heartily shook hands.

Mrs. James seemed to hang back even more drawn into herself, holding her skirts away from the dirty train platform, her face unreadable under her veil, her back stiff, her head high.

I watched as Professor James shook his brother's hand once more, and they both started talking at once. Then I noticed that the Professor's wife was staring not at the two brothers but, instead, across the track at the window of the First Class compartment, where I could see Mrs. Wharton's furs and her back pressed against the window and could also see Mr. Morton Fullerton gazing out at the James brothers.

Mrs. Wharton and Mr. Morton Fullerton's train was beginning to move. Its grinding noise was deafening, as the last calls went out and the doors slammed.

I was consumed with worry. Now, Mrs. Wharton would turn to sit down. She would look out the window and show her well-known face. Now, both of Mr. James' friendships would be betrayed to his disapproving family. But no, Mr. Fullerton was shifting, helping Mrs. Wharton with something—her coat, her furs—blocking the window. He was pulling down the shade, and I imagined that he was holding her in his arms, for she must have been overcome with sadness to be leaving Mr. James.

But it was still all so puzzling.

14

"The High Bid"

March 1909

*And if you waylay me here, as I infer you would be disposed
to, on the ground that we "don't want works of art," ah
then, my dear Bernard Shaw—*

—Henry James
Letter dictated to Theodora Bosanquet
For George Bernard Shaw

"You, there! You with that package! Put it down and
come over here; I need you NOW!"

The man's voice was imperious, booming, somehow familiar,
not to be resisted. In the dark gloom of the empty theatre, I could
not see who was demanding that I come over, or even quite where
I was to go. Was he in the orchestra pit, up on the empty stage, or
behind the half-dropped curtain? Yes, there he was, at the side door
where the light from the hall fell in a square. I put down the package of finished, revised Act Two for "The High Bid" and hurried
over. As soon as I reached his side, the man insisted that I lift the
long piece of wood he held by one end.

"Higher, higher," he said. "You're tall enough. There. That's the effect I want." He took a hammer and gave the wooden archway several hard smacks.

"Thanks, young man—" He stared at me. "Oh, I am so sorry, Miss, I didn't see you well in the dark, and I assumed—You are quite tall, and really, you are strong enough."

But I was also staring at him, at none other than the great Mr. Forbes Robertson himself.

"I'm here from Mr. James," I stammered. "I'm his secretary, Miss Bosanquet. I've brought you the final revisions for tomorrow's dress rehearsal. Mr. James wanted you to have good copies of the changes in the last scene."

Mr. Forbes Robertson gave the fake archway another shake as if to make sure it was solid. "I think I'm done here. We've been rushing to pull this set together. I've had quite a time finding men to finish the work."

We walked back up the aisle to the seat where I had dropped the package. "Let me give these to the others," he said, taking the copies, "and then I would like it if you would let me take you out for tea or something to eat after you've come all this way. Perhaps a drink? What would you like?"

"I would like that, thank you."

Before long, I found myself seated in the red-plush, gold-fringed parlour room of the nearest pub, while my favourite actor treated me, going up to order beer and cheese. He came back to the table where I was waiting and sat down with a sigh.

"I never thought when we agreed to produce Mr. James' 'High Bid' in London that it would come to this. We can give it only a short run and only afternoon matinées. Oh, I'm sure the ladies will love it, and my wife is delighted to have this juicy part—Mr. James does give his heroines the most wonderful lines. But damn, there's not enough time."

Mr. James had had high hopes for "The High Bid" during his talks with the great Sir Johnston Forbes Robertson and even hopes for staging "The Saloon" as a curtain-raiser. The modest success of "The High Bid" while on tour in Scotland had boded well, and so Mr. Forbes Robertson had agreed to add "The High Bid" to his company's winter repertoire. But the search for a large theatre had not gone well. Only His Majesty's would do because "The High Bid" needed a proscenium arch tall enough to accommodate a very large set, in this case, to boast an entire English manor house. Unfortunately, Mr. Forbes Robertson had already booked another play, "The Passing of the Third Floor Back," with himself as the lead actor for His Majesty's Theatre.

Mr. James had blustered that Jerome Jerome's "The Passing" was a slight thing, which would surely fail and fall off the boards in no time, leaving a clear field for his own work. But, as it turned out, "The Passing" was an appealing play about a mysterious visitor to a London boarding house, with the visitor being a reincarnation of Jesus. As the daughter of a pastor, I am embarrassed to admit this, but I was amused when Mr. James muttered to me, "Jesus Christ is the main character, and of course one has to realise that *He's* a formidable competitor."

The Jesus play was immensely popular and made Mr. Forbes Robertson a wealthy man. By the time "The High Bid" was to open, "The Passing" was in its sixth month of sold-out shows. That was the reason an afternoon matinée with a run of not even a week was all Forbes Robertson could provide for Mr. James' "The High Bid." As for Mr. James' one-act curtain-raiser, it seemed clear to me from the Master's sputtering comments under his breath that "The Saloon" had never been a play Sir Johnston Forbes Robertson actively imagined producing.

Nevertheless, "The High Bid" would have its brief run, starring Mr. Forbes Robertson and Mme. Gertrude Elliott. I was thrilled to be part of the flurry, carrying Mr. James' many corrections to the theatre, hoping I might glimpse the great Forbes Robertson or, even better, my heroine, Gertrude Elliott. I couldn't wait to see the play itself and hear the actors saying the words that had passed through my fingers.

Not yet able to believe I was sitting opposite the great Forbes Robertson in a pub, I murmured something sympathetic and then asked, "Will you tell me how it is going? Do you think the critics will like 'The High Bid?'"

I knew Mr. James was concerned, because he had announced to me that he would not attend the opening or even the dress rehearsal.

That decision was strange, since the previous year he had travelled all the way to Scotland to watch the first try-outs for "The High Bid." The two of us had come up to London for these last-minute changes. Mr. James had even had me working up in my old rooms in Kensington Gardens to ready the script in time. Then there came a postponement, and now he had fled to his room at London's Reform Club, leaving me to wonder.

"Is there some problem?" I asked Mr. Forbes Robertson. "I'm wondering why—"

"Why Mr. James isn't here? Even as an afternoon matinée, I do think it will have a good, solid run. He needn't fear on that account. But that's not what keeps him away. Really, Miss Bosanquet, have you not heard about the first time he brought his work to a London stage? What a disaster! Everyone involved should be damned in hell for that night! Surely you've heard the story."

I had heard something about a weak beginning, a play that was too wordy, something about the curtain call, things being thrown, the actors—

Mr. Forbes Robertson rushed on. "The theatre was a circus in those days, ten years ago—maybe it was fifteen. New plays were opening every week and closing nearly as fast. There were conflicts between the writers and the producers, between the actors and the audience, there were cliques and fights—Oh, it was a difficult and lively time! Old Queen Victoria was still alive; everything was different. You probably don't remember, but the theatre was a disreputable place, and everything depended on the whims of the public. A playwright could be famous overnight, but then as soon as the crowd's love affair with a writer's leading lady ended, his play would be finished, done with, and the writer would be out on the street. This was when that scoundrel, Oscar Wilde, had three plays in three different theatres, and every one of them sold out for two shows a day! What a time that was! Poor Mr. James, he never did figure out what happened."

"Was his play that bad?"

"Oh, no, my dear, his play was beautiful, elegant, delicate, a wonder. The actors, the critics, we all loved it!"

"Then what was it? What happened?"

"In those days, the theatre was not the sedate, well-mannered scene we have now. No, in those days before cinema, there were even pitched battles at theatre performances between warring factions. George Alexander played the hero's role for Mr. James. Mr. Alexander was usually well-liked. But his detractors had filled the balcony to rain down their disapproval. The rabble out-numbered and out-shouted Mr. Alexander's fans."

Mr. Forbes Robertson sighed as he topped off our pints.

"When the curtain came down—and with it the call, 'Author! Author!'—the performers led Mr. James out to take his first bow on a London stage. I could tell he was immensely pleased and justifiably proud in his modest way. But then the rabble-rousers booed and catcalled, and, oh, it was awful." Mr. Forbes Robertson took a sip of beer. "Miss Bosanquet, you may know that we actors are hardened. After all, no matter what happens on stage, we have disciplined ourselves to keep on being someone we are not. That evening was not the first time Mr. Alexander had been booed off the stage, and not the last, either. But Mr. James—"

Mr. Forbes Robertson pushed the cheese about on the plate.

"But Mr. James, he turned this way, that way. He didn't know what to do, whether to bow or to exit stage right or stage left. He looked terrified, immobilised. Mr. Alexander graciously ushered Mr. James off the stage. The hooligans in the balcony hurled insults. The words they slung pelted Mr. James. But our dear Mr. James—He had no words."

We two sat in silence amidst the pub chatter. I felt short of breath, as if I had been struck in the chest. I started to speak. "I, I didn't know—"

But Mr. Forbes Robertson went on. "I tried to talk with Mr. James, tried to explain that the booing and catcalling had nothing to do with him and everything to do with actors and their jealous fans. Nothing and everything. But he would never let me broach the subject. He's so voluble and facile. Any conversation is always Mr. James' conversation. Miss Bosanquet—" Mr. Forbes Robertson turned the cheese plate slowly. "Are you coming to the opening?"

"Why, yes. Of course!"

"Mr. James always speaks so highly of you—how he could not do his work without you, how attentive you are, always listening. In terms of Mr. James' work, I think you may know him better than anyone. He trusts you. Could you do me a favour? I've wanted you to know the accurate story. For context. You don't need to mention any of this to Mr. James."

Mr. Forbes Robertson's expression turned cheerful. "'The High Bid' will seal the past in the past." He raised his mug, holding it out towards me. I raised my mug as well.

"I'm pleased that you'll be at this opening. Afterwards, you'll have the chance to see Mr. James often. Will you help him realise that this opening is different? Please do this for the rest of us. You are Mr. James' listener, but you are also one of the few people to whom Mr. James listens."

Two days later, I felt anxious as I waited while Nellie fussed at the entry-way mirror in our shabby room in a ladies' hotel. Nellie was pushing and pulling the ribbons at her waist and around her hat, fluffing, patting. It seemed as if she would never finish getting ready, and I hated to be late.

"Wait a minute, Dora," she insisted. "I'm sure the play will not start without us. Surely Mr. James has let them know that he has asked us to go, that we will be coming. Oh, I'm so excited! Imagine! Mr. Forbes Robertson himself! You do think that after the play Mr. Forbes Robertson will come out to meet us, don't you?"

I did not think Mr. James had done anything but give us tickets for the play's London opening matinée. Nevertheless, I humoured Nellie all the way to the theatre. Even I felt a thrill as the usher showed us our seats. They were magnificent: centre stall, not too close. I looked around at the glittering audience, thinking that the attendance was rather sparse, but then, despite all Nellie's preparations, we were rather early. Maybe the Afternoon Theatre Matinée Series was not yet well-known, since it had only recently been established so audiences could while away the slow, dark afternoons before gathering for late tea and dressing for dinner parties.

Sitting in the darkened theatre, waiting for the curtain to rise for "The High Bid," I felt a twinge of guilt, of disloyalty, for Nellie and I had purchased tickets for the next day's performance of "The

Passing of the Third Floor Back," starring Mr. James' formidable competitor: a popular rendition of Jesus Christ. What if Mr. James heard that Nellie and I had gone to see that play‼ I squirmed in my seat, relieved that the theatre hall would be dark.

The orchestra interrupted my worries, changing tempo from the quiet overture. Then there was the rushing whir of the huge curtain rising slowly, majestically up into the shadows to reveal the set for "The High Bid."

And what a set it was! This was a period when we paid great attention to theatrical sets. The audience gasped and broke into applause. There, before our eyes, was the old oak paneling, the glowing stained glass and the silvery carved stone of a centuries-old English country house. The house even had more than one room: towering up into the back of the stage, reaching out into the wings were several storeys of the central hall represented by high, lead-paned windows, faded tapestries, and huge oak beams. The vast estate was hinted by the stage-left entrance opening out to the bright colours of a summer garden and what appeared to be acres of lawn. But central and looming over everything was a wide, curving, stone staircase, which seemed to lead to other, unseen wonders above.

We ceased our applause and watched the silent entrance of Chivers, the white-haired, much-darned-and-repaired, perfect servant of the house as he crossed the room, stopped, and listened.

We heard coming from off stage a clear, bright, distinctly American voice:

"*I hope you don't mind the awful Time I take!*"

I was thrilled to hear the words I had worked so diligently to re-produce, and here they were in that wonderfully musical voice of Gertrude Elliott herself. How glorious to hear my favourite character, the charming Mrs. Gracedew, speak the prose my Mr. James had written, to hear those words I had imagined so deeply come to life.

Even the white-haired Chivers was perfect in his answers to the voice of his mistress still off stage and wandering somewhere around the ground floor of the old house:

"*Oh, I quite* trust *you, mum!*"

And then the audience knew quite where we were, for we immediately trusted Chivers, and he trusted her, and so there we all were placed in Time.

I noticed how Nellie kept very quiet throughout the early scenes in which Mr. James had set up a dramatic confrontation between the grasping businessman, Mr. Prodmore, and his young and beautiful daughter over this lovely old house. Only the entrance of our hero—played by Sir Johnston Forbes Robertson—as the newly installed lord of the manor, gorgeous in riding boots and handsome old tweeds, was enough to make Nellie gasp and cause all the audience to break into applause at his first appearance. We saw right away how our young hero with his stoic, fine, and manly face was a good man fallen on hard times. Even his manner was charmingly respectful as he spoke of the ghosts of his ancestors. Of course, I knew what had caused this young lord's manner, but Nellie had to lean over to whisper loudly, "What's wrong with Sir Johnston Forbes Robertson? Why is he acting like that?"

"Like what?"

"Skulking around, hat in hand, kissing up to that horrid Prodmore."

"He's supposed to—"

Then Mr. Forbes Robertson began speaking again, and Nellie shushed me.

Of course the scenes between my heroine and Nellie's hero were wonderful, except the audience was still acting strangely, fidgeting at the actors' impassioned speeches discussing the wonders of the old house and the young man's financial predicament, as the two characters began to fall in love despite coming from such different places. I could even remember the stage directions and dialogue when the young lord revealed his willingness to sacrifice his home:

"*I see something else in the world than the beauty of old show-houses and the glory of old show-families. There are thousands of people in England who can show no houses at all, and (with the emphasis of sincerity. [sic]) I don't feel it utterly shameful to share their poor fate.*"

I was startled to find that the speech, which I knew was meant to show the young lord's disregard for the past and his willingness to give it all up, had made the audience burst into applause.

I was disappointed that Nellie was one of the loudest applauding the wrong speech; I worried that she would never understand Mr. James and his heroes and would probably miss the subtleties of the play's ending.

But by the last scene, I saw how the actors did indeed achieve everything Mr. James had wanted. They made the play come alive. How impassionedly Mr. James had spoken the stage directions! How much I had wanted to see the play performed! Our hero, Yule, was there in the centre of the huge stage, after the horrid Prodmore had scurried away, defeated. And now there they were, the two lovers, and we could see it all for ourselves, as Yule spoke:

"*With this heroic Proof of your Power, this Barren Beauty of your Sacrifice? You pour out Money, you move a Mountain, and to let you 'go,' to bow you stupidly <u>out</u> and close the Door <u>behind</u> you, is all my poor Wit can think of? You're the most Generous, you're the Noblest of women! The wonderful Chance that brought you here—!*"

And now, when my heroine and her hero embraced and went off to save their house, Nellie and the rest of the audience had forgotten their earlier burst of radical support and were happy that their hero was about to be made very happy.

Indeed, the enthusiastic applause at the curtain and the many, many curtain calls would have made my Mr. James happy, too. How I wished I could see Mr. James, but I did leave a note for him at the Reform Club to tell him the play had gone so well! Gertrude Elliott was a tremendous success, and the Cora actress, excellent.

Mr. James replied that very night, addressing me as he always did, with the formality we all used in those days:

Thursday midnight

Dear Miss Bosanquet

All thanks for your note, which adds to my regret that in the midst of the assault & complication of people that I had to deal with after the play this afternoon I couldn't get at you without the dangers of exposing myself to more people & more publicity. And then when I <u>could</u> sneak down I had ceased to expect you to be *there. I judge that the business did go off [inserted] very decently well this afternoon—if the testimony of a crowd of kindly friends & well-wishes signifies anything, & it is (the small comedy) very honourably acted, though Miss Gracedew will be very much more effective for she clearly had [sic] a great personal success)[sic] when she is [sic] less nervous. She was unendingly so today. But alli [sic "all is"] well that ends well, & I'm very glad you & Miss Bradley were in or [sic] it of it.*

I foresee that I shan't get home again till late next week. So I hope you will be able to stay on in town. I will give you due further news. I enclose a cheque for £1.15, & am yours very truly

Henry James

I wondered what Mr. James had meant. Had he intended for us to go back stage and bother the actors, rubbing shoulders with Miss Elliott and Sir Johnston Forbes Robertson? Is that what he meant with what I assume was meant to be written as *"in it & of it"*?

Over breakfast in our hotel the next morning, I enjoyed reading the reviews out loud to Nellie, as if we had been actors in the production. I clipped the reviews. As we checked out of the hotel, Nellie once again urged me to consider moving to London. She had an artist friend with a delightful little flat in Chelsea, which might soon be available. Might we stop by on the way to the station?

Of course, it was not on the way, as I well knew from my years at university. Nellie really had very little idea about London, its huge size and huge crowds, its traffic and noise, how hard travelling from one place to another was. But then I saw the tiny basement rooms on Lawrence Street, that charming street, which seemed so private and full of secrets waiting for me to discover. Chelsea was teeming with artistic energy. Every person we met seemed to be an artist or writer. The flat was too good a place to pass up; we vowed that we would find the money somehow, and I was sure my old friends who still lived in Bloomsbury would not mind if I came back to live nearby. They might like Chelsea, too!

It turned out that our decision to move was a fortunate one, for as soon as we settled back into the quiet routine of Rye, Mr. James fell ill. The doctors could not decide what it was, whether it was digestion, heart, or age. Something was making it impossible for the Master to continue working, even dictating. My heart went out to him; he seemed to feel so low, with the new volume of short stories complete and the prefaces finally through proofs. And now, after only a few matinée performances of "The High Bid," there would be no more possibility for his plays to be produced.

Still, I do remember one bright spot in those dark days, for there had been a day when Mr. James was able to dictate a remarkably long response to a letter.

I had come to Lamb House that cold blustery morning early in 1909 to check on Mr. James' welfare about a month before "The High Bid" was staged. When I rang the bell, Mrs. Paddington answered; Mr. James came down the stairs and welcomed me in. He was dressed in his usual neat fashion but with a warmer jacket than usual and an extra scarf about his neck. Even though he looked a little pale and tired, he bubbled over with enthusiasm and wanted me to come upstairs and see something.

As we went up to the Green Room, Mr. James told me that he had received a letter from Bernard Shaw.

A letter from George Bernard Shaw? From the theatre critic and newly successful playwright? I was thrilled! I hoped that Mr. James would write back to this famous man, since I had been told that Bernard Shaw was a source of the new energy that was changing London's theatre scene. His serious reviews had brought attention to startling, realistic playwrights, such as Ibsen and Chekhov.

Mr. James rummaged around on his desk.

"Here it is! A letter arguing several points with me about 'The Saloon.'"

I hoped the Master had not seen me shudder when he mentioned the "Owen Wingrave" ghost story he had turned into the play Mr. Forbes Robertson did not want to produce.

"I sent the script to the Incorporated Stage Society, which turned me down and asked Mr. Bernard Shaw to write the rejection letter." The Master waved the letter, and I thought: Oh dear! And then I thought: Oh my! Here is someone as prolific as my Mr. James!

Mr. James went on. "Wait until you hear this! He takes me to task, saying my play has been 'sticking in his gizzard.' He disagrees with me about my characters and what I make them do, how I make them more desperate and hopeless than they really are, says I don't know much about human nature, about men or women. Here's a really good bit."

Mr. James began to read aloud from Mr. Shaw's letter:

"'Why have you done this? If it were true to nature—if it were scientific—if it were common sense, I should say let us face it, let us say Amen. But it isn't. Every man who really wants his latchkey gets it. No man who doesn't believe in ghosts ever sees one.'"

I knew Mr. Bernard Shaw was more optimistic than my employer and that Mr. Shaw believed in the power of the common man, or, if the common man were not strong enough to save himself in these days of struggle, well, then his sister would be the one to do it. Mr. James especially wanted me to see how Mr. Shaw thought girls like Nellie and me were the heroes of the day. I found myself delighted to hear such appreciation of the small, daily revolutions happening because of the work of the New Woman.

Mr. James read another excerpt:

"'Families like these are smashed every day and their members delivered from bondage, not by heroic young men, but by one girl who goes out and earns her living or takes a degree somewhere. Why do you preach cowardice to an army which has victory always and easily within its reach?'"

"There," Mr. James said. "He stirs my thoughts so much, I want to write back as soon as I can. I've been thinking over what I want to say. Can you stay and help me write my reply?" He looked so eager and so forlorn at the same time that I agreed and sat down right then to the typewriting machine.

He moved to a nearby arm-chair and sat—not his usual habit for dictating—but apparently he was still too weak to write out for himself all that he wanted to say. Nevertheless, in a strong voice, he asked if I was ready and then began one of his most extraordinary dictations: a ten-page, densely packed letter.

I knew much of the origins of the play we were discussing; in fact, I had been involved in its creation, red ink bottle and pen and ruler in hand, marking Mr. James' stage directions, as I had done with "The High Bid." He had taken the ghost story, "Owen

Wingrave," and pasted its pages on large paper and dictated to me how to convert the short story into scenes and dialogue.

In his letter, Mr. James began modestly, politely, not self-consciously, but soon he was proclaiming that for him, the author's response—neither the audience's response nor the critics' but the creator's—was the only view that mattered. His argument went on to his own work, whether a play, novel, or short story, for he wanted to be persuasive. As I listened, I found myself becoming more and more involved. His words towering up and up became the kind of flight that made my heart beat faster, even as I typed steadily, wanting very much not to make any mistake or erasure on a letter to Mr. George Bernard Shaw himself.

Mr. James paused, then spoke. His words were even, careful:

"Capital B, Underline *But*, *if you press me, I quite allow that this all shifts my guilt only a little further back and that your question applies just as much, in the first place, to the short story perpetrated years ago, and in the re-perpetration more recently, in another specious form and in the greater* Open Parenthesis *(the very great alas* Close Parenthesis*)* Quotation *"maturity of my powers* Full Stop, End Quotation.*" And it doesn't really matter at all, since I am ready serenely to answer you* Full Stop."

The Master paused, for he was not as serene as he might have wished to be:

"*I do such things because I happen to be a man of imagination and taste, extremely interested in life, and because the imagination, thus, from the moment direction and motive play upon it from all sides, absolutely enjoys and insists on and incurably leads a life of its own* Comma, *for which just this vivacity itself is its warrant* Full Stop. *You surely haven't done all your own so interesting work without learning what it is for the imagination to* Underline *play with an idea* Dash—*an idea about life* Dash—*under a happy obsession* Comma, *for all it is worth* Full Stop."

He paused to rest, turning over Mr. Shaw's letter, while I rolled in a new sheet of paper. He spoke without disturbing the flow of his argument:

"*Half the beautiful things that the benefactors of the human species have produced would surely be wiped out if you don't allow this adventurous and speculative imagination its rights* Full Stop. *You simplify too much, by the same token, when you limit the field of interest to what you call the scientific* Dash—"

The Master paused in his argument with Mr. Shaw's use of science as opposed to the power of spirit and imagination. I wondered if Mr. James knew about the discussions of the scientific merits of ghosts and apparitions in the meetings of the psychical researchers as described in the journals his brother had given me.

His silence continued. Was that the ending of his letter? His appeal to the blessing of imagination? What kind of argument would that seem to Mr. Shaw, whose work was intended to do good right here, right now? Mr. James was very still, breathing quietly. I read the current page over for mistakes as I waited for the Master's closing ovation. His letter did not quite feel finished. This argument would not do. I looked up and saw that Mr. James was exhausted from this effort after days of silence. But I could also see that he had more to say. With a deep intake of breath, he began again:

"*And if you waylay me here, as I infer you would be disposed to, . . .*"

He paused. I wondered: Had I said anything aloud unconsciously? How had he guessed my thoughts?

"*. . . on the ground that we* Quotation *"don't want works of art* Comma, End Quotation," *ah then, my dear Bernard Shaw, I think I take such issue with you that* Dash—*if we didn't both* Underline *like to talk* Dash—*there would be scarce use in our talking at all* Full Stop."

I laughed out loud at this, and Mr. James and I exchanged glances.

"That ought to catch him, don't you think?!" Mr. James said, chuckling.

And so we finished up the letter and sent it out.

For me, that was one of the most thrilling of days with the Master. Never had he seemed so lucid, so direct in explaining the force behind his art, behind his works' most difficult complexities, his most discouraging plots, his unlikable, tragic, wrong-headed heroes, stubbornly un-triumphant. How I wished I could have made a copy of that letter before it was sent, but at the time, I was sure Mr. James' correspondence would be saved and eventually published.

I was wrong. Now, fifty years later, as I look back, the most curious thing is not that these two masters of literature corresponded,

but rather that Mr. James' letters to Bernard Shaw were not published in the first collection of the Master's letters or in his family's
subsequent collections, though I clearly remember I had selected
and prepared copies of Mr. Shaw's letters when I worked for the
family after Mr. James' funeral.

Now that I think about it, I suppose the omission was an early
sign that something was wrong with the James family's stewardship
of Mr. James' legacy. Was Mr. James' family still trying to erase any
possible smudges from the Master's record, as they had in ignoring
his friendships with divorced women writers, as they had in refusing
to taint his memory with examples of his affections for young men?
If that letter simply disappeared, then perhaps no one could find
a connexion between Henry James—the Master—and the threat-
ening, low-class radical, the socialist, the theorising, scandalous
George Bernard Shaw.

I am glad I remembered that particular dictation so well many
years later, when Mr. Leon Edel came to me as a young graduate
student writing about Henry James and the Master's dramatic years.
I liked young Edel, and I thought he might be the person to add
to the story. And so I hinted to Mr. Edel that there might have
been some sort of a correspondence between the two great men.
He jumped at this news: How? Where? I sent him to the Great
Man himself, to Bernard Shaw, who had kept copies of his own
correspondence, including his letter to Mr. James and the Master's
response.

Thus began Mr. Edel's amazing run of luck.

I am glad I took the step, but how strange to think my little
push rather launched a young man's career—and also that, if I had
so chosen, I could have supplied Mr. Edel with other missing pieces
as well.

15

"The Outcry"

1909

Form alone takes, and holds and preserves, substance—saves it from the welter of helpless verbiage. . . . There is nothing so deplorable as a work of art with a leak in its interest; and there is no such leak of interest as through commonness of form.

—Henry James
Letter dictated to Theodora Bosanquet
For Hugh Walpole

Mr. James did have a lighter side, and he could be brave. He had been so damaged by his first foray into the theatre many years before, however, that the few matinée-only performances of "The High Bid" in London did not assuage his disconsolateness, despite the times Nellie and I repeated our raves about the opening performance. Still, Mr. James could not resist the call of the theatre when the scandal broke about the decision by the Duke of Norfolk to sell Hans Holbein's painting "Christina of Denmark, Duchess of Milan." Allan Wade and others at Charles Frohman's Repertory Company wanted the Master to write a play about the infernal Yankees who were swooping in to cart off our sedate, private collections of British art.

Mr. James' secret love was the theatre, despite his lack of recognition there. He came alive with Allan Wade's persistent request. I was delighted to return to take dictation and then, under the Master's direction, to colour-code the stage directions even as I was also typing the constant stream of correspondence we sent from Rye to London about this new play, "The Outcry."

It was such a thrill to sit at the Remington when Mr. James dictated a play, not dictating, really, but more like performing the play, shifting from role to role, the timbre of his voice fluctuating from stalwart Lady Sandgate to conniving Lord John to the rich, manipulative American. I tapped away while also serving as his audience—his audience of one. I remember how he paused once in an unusual way that made me look up. Mr. James was smiling, a sly, impish smile, as if he were teasing me. He shifted from his neutral, script-direction voice but with more than his usual resonance:

"*GRACE,* Miss Bosanquet," he said, signaling the beginning of the character's speech.

I sat up. I knew Mr. James could already tell that Grace, Lord Theign's steadfast daughter, entranced me. The Master's body shifted, becoming more gently framed, his notes in his left hand, his right hand moving gracefully as if to duplicate the feminine determination he had created for Grace:

"*The Duchess will never convince me of anything but that she simply* Underline *wants* me Semicolon *; wants me for my Father's so particularly beautiful position, and my Mother's so supremely great people, and for everything we have been and have done, and* Underline *still are and* Underline *still have* Colon:"

I was smiling as I typed, my fingers moving gracefully with my own feminine determination, feeling Mr. James absorb my delight. We continued, and then his voice turned arrogant as Lord John negotiated with Lord Theign for Grace's hand, yet Mr. James was smiling again in that strange way:

"*LORD JOHN,* Miss Bosanquet.

"*Why* Comma, *tacked on to a value so great and so charming as Lady Grace herself* Comma, *I dare say such a sum as Nine or Ten Thousand would serve* Full Stop."

I had to stop. Had Mr. James somehow heard the conversations between Nora, Clara, Nellie, and me? Was he speaking about us? Was "The Outcry" only about the art heist the Repertory Company wanted to expose? Or was Mr. James also saying we women were the art that our families haggled over and sold?

Oh, I did love this play. I would almost jump up with delight when aging Mr. James turned himself before my eyes into the youthful, impudent Hugh Crimble, the art appraiser who eventually wins Grace's hand for love, not money. Mr. James spoke in Hugh Crimble's voice, denouncing the invading Yankee buyers of our patricians' art:

"... *if we don't* Underline *do something* Exclamation Point, Dash*!—of more and more* Capital B *Benders to come* Colon *: such a conquering horde as invaded the Old Civilisation* Dash*—only armed now with huge cheque-books instead of spears and battle-axes* Full Stop."

Oh, we had such a good time with that play! But Mr. James made me wonder, too, as I often did. After all, he was an American, a Yankee, a member of the *"conquering horde"* invading the *"Old Civilisation,"* albeit hardly with a cheque-book. Yet, sometimes Mr. James seemed so English. I often wondered if, perhaps, it could be that the Master was neither. It seemed as if he were always striving, as if he held within himself the deep pain that he could never feel truly whole in either place.

We finished "The Outcry" towards the end of 1909, and then the work dropped off again.

When I look back now and remember how my years with Mr. James came to that first long interruption, I can see how even then I was affected by working with him. The more I absorbed from Mr. James, the greater my desire to write, the greater my ambition. After I bought my own typewriting machine, I wrote more and more, trying many kinds of writing—poems, plays, essays, and book reviews. It was then I first became a published writer.

But even more important, once I had left my rooms in Rye and moved back to London, I could follow every sort of writer, even the most outrageous, whether it was my ignored and strident Suffragette friends writing and printing out lengthy outpourings to demand Rights for Women or whether it was George Bernard Shaw as he went from being a well-respected critic and playwright to becoming a socialist and, thus, less respectable. As George Bernard Shaw grew more and more outspoken, radical even, I still never lost my own admiration. I seem to remember that I was happy that my employer, too, was not put off by Bernard Shaw's socialist rantings.

My own drama became quite intense that winter when my old friend, Clara Smith, came down to Rye. Nellie became so jealous she could barely speak. Perhaps the very frank (and sherry-aided) talk that Nellie and Clara and I had late into the night was the source of the seediness with which I finally awoke the next morning. What a talk that had been! Clara's frankness was refreshing after Nellie's usual, delicate avoidance of real talk, but even I had been surprised.

Of course, we were not worried that being educated women meant that our internal organs would rot away, that we were sure to have sex problems, that we would never be able to feel what a real woman would feel. Though we had never wanted to marry and have children but preferred, instead, to spend our lives with each other and with meaningful work, we knew that we were still women, that we still had deep feelings, were still able to be soft and loving, were still able to love. It did not matter whether it was a man or a woman as long as we found the right person. Clara even outdid Nora with her talk of sex appeal and the latest psychological theories about inverted women. Clara was amazing. It made me want to leave backwards Rye even more, to see for myself what was happening in London, in the world, what was happening for women, for lovers.

As it happened, Nellie and I were to go up to London sooner than I had anticipated. As winter and then the late spring dragged on in cold, gloomy Rye, Mr. James had very little work for me. He seemed discouraged, tired of it all, and unable to write. Once again, I was not sure what to do. I needed to pay my rent.

I was lucky. Clara, who was always up on the latest things, told me about an opening with the new, much-talked-about Eleventh Edition of the "Encyclopædia Britannica." This new edition was to be a great master-stroke of salesmanship for its new publishers. Mr. Horace Everett Hooper, an audacious American businessman, had added an all-American advertising campaign, teaming up with Editor-in-Chief Mr. Hugh Chisholm, who embodied the respectability of the London "Times" and the "Britannica." The Eleventh Edition would still have all the very latest information set out in tidy, manageable paragraphs and with each entry written by the person in the world who knew the most about that subject. Here was a perfect arrangement for England and its manly scholars, who were broad, deep experts on singular subjects, but this would also be a grand achievement for the entire British Empire, which spanned the globe, reaching into every culture and civilization, ancient and modern.

And so, as the year moved on into the summer, I found myself back in London among Miss Mary Petherbridge's "girls," who by now were highly trained young women working at a frantic pace to keep up with all the changes, additions, and corrections coming in from across the English-speaking world for the "Britannica." Now, my indexing skills were finally put to use. My task was simply to note every name and nearly every noun, proper or otherwise, and then to find and reference every possible cross-connexion between each and every subject.

We young women were all at work on "the greatest intellectual project of the Age," as the advertising claims would have it. The Eleventh was to be produced, not slowly, taking years, volume by volume, with the index to follow like all the previous editions. Instead, the Eleventh would be published all at once—all twenty-eight volumes—with the index included at the moment of publication.

At first, things went swimmingly. Readers could buy the encyclopædia "on time" and have it delivered (by freight, postage paid) along with a handsome oak bookcase, which was a great selling point and had already been manufactured. But then it turned out that Mr. Chisholm had assigned too many entries and had allowed his specialists too much sea room for their subjects. The overages piled up. A great pall descended over the "Encyclopædia Britannica" offices as the intended twenty-eight volumes swelled to twenty-nine. The books would not all fit into the stylish oak bookcases already waiting in warehouses. Mr. Hooper, the American entrepreneur, showed his true worth with a brilliant solution: change the thickness of the paper! And so, the "Britannica" came to be printed on onion-skin, the thinnest of the thin.

All those alarms and panics were only hearsay to us mere indexers toiling away up on the upper floors of the "Britannica" offices. I was amused by the flutter I found in Miss Petherbridge's workrooms. What a different atmosphere American bustle and push had produced! I understood some of the discomfort my fellow indexers felt at the change of pace, for I'd had some experience with this through Mr. James and his fast-paced American friends. I tried to reassure the other women: If we did succeed in meeting the impossible deadline, then we would be paid handsomely. And pay was what I needed, for Mr. James, after so many months, still was not requesting my services.

But as much as I loved London, my heart remained with Mr. James in Rye. I was always ready to return. When Christmas came, Nellie and I rode down to Rye, our very first time to be invited there as a couple. We had no idea it was to be our last visit together to Lamb House.

The little train was quite stuffed with holiday revellers and smelled of cinnamon, pine boughs, and wet wool. I felt like the amused outsider looking in on something cosy and quaint, as if I were living in Mr. James' essay from "English Hours," where he described for American readers how much we English like to wallow in our Christmas:

"There was a kind of wonder indeed that England should be as English as, for my entertainment, she took the trouble to be."

Mr. James had been ill that fall. I had not seen him for several weeks and did not know what to expect, but when we arrived from the dark, damp streets, we could see that he had laid on the English Christmas cheer in every possible way: fires snapping in all the fireplaces, the greens winding up the bannister, making the entry hall smell wonderful, and the dining-room lit with many candles. The table was set with linen, and the old silver shone, and each place had beside it a Christmas cracker, one of the shiny red-and-green paper cylinders filled with small surprises that I remembered from my childhood.

All fall, Mr. James had stayed on alone in Rye, and now apparently needing my help with his new book of short stories, he had sent for me again. Of course it meant that I, too, would have to work in Rye over the holiday. Still, he wrote that he wanted to be sure that I would have a real Christmas, and so he invited Nellie and me for a feast.

The roast beef with Yorkshire pudding was most delicious, and we guests held aloft many toasts to friends far away, to the season, to the King, and even to the flaming Christmas pudding. He presented us with gifts, which we opened at the table. The packages were identical and a little disappointing when Nellie and I each found a satin-covered box for a lady's gloves, so impersonal, like a gift for the housekeeper. In fact, as it happened, it was the same gift he had presented to me the year before! Perhaps it was the Master's one idea of a gift for ladies.

But that did not matter. We laughed over our pudding, and when we pulled our crackers with a great pop and a puff of smoke and more laughter, each of us found a little paper mask inside. I made a great gruff show of my lion-tamer's face, pulling it on with the elastic behind my bun and feeling the top-hat part to be sure it was straight. Nellie's Egyptian slave girl was amusing, with long black hair and a veil that hung over the girl's sweet, laughing mouth.

Mr. James' was the best. He had us roaring. He faced away to pull on his mask, and when he turned back, he had become a white-haired, round-faced, pink-cheeked washerwoman. He even pulled the raffia corkscrew curls down on each side so that they boinged. We laughed so hard that Mrs. Paddington came in to see, and Mr. James insisted that we send Burgess upstairs to bring down the shaving mirror. When he saw himself, Mr. James roared with laughter and boinged his curls a few more times. "Why," he propounded, "don't we all wear masks and change them as we do our clothes?"

That Christmas in 1909 was the last time I saw Mr. James for more than a year, since soon after that, his brother became very much more ill and came over for the European treatments to slow his advancing heart disease. In the spring of 1910, the family arrived in Rye and took Mr. James away with them for many weeks to Switzerland and Germany, to Baden-Nauheim, to try every specialist, all to no avail. I agreed to tend to details in London for production of "The Outcry."

Then there came an interruption to everything.

I remember that day, May 6, 1910, very clearly, all these decades later. I think we all do. I was working late at the "Britannica" offices, finishing up indexing for some volume, and when I came out to the street, I heard a murmur, a sound of many people gathered not far away. I turned and walked in that direction and found a crowd at the Buckingham Palace gates. A posted notice said the King was ill. From the uneasy talk, it seemed he was not expected to recover this time. He died that night.

I wondered what difference the death of the King could make. The "Britannica" would go on, we were nearly finished with the texts, and royal mourning requirements would not affect publishing enterprises. Still, I was uneasy.

The next morning, I felt sympathy for the girl behind the counter in the tea shop where I was waiting for my order. She wailed and wrung her hands over her trays of rolls and scones: "Oh dear, oh dear! The King is dead. Whatever will become of us? Whatever shall I do?"

An impatient man behind me in the line growled, "Keep filling the orders, dearie. Keep pouring tea."

The mourning regulations disrupted Mr. James' plans to return and oversee production of "The Outcry," which he had finished in 1909 and which was to be presented at His Majesty's Theatre. Now, all theatres were closed and shuttered for the required months of mourning.

For months, I had no opportunity to be with Mr. James, who only sent messages to let me know he was not well himself, and then a final brief wire to say he was sorry not to see me in person to say good-bye, that he was sailing to America to be with his brother. The Master had been so ambitious for his great project, the revision and gathering of all his best writing into one handsome set, the New York Edition. I knew, however, that the sales for the first volumes had been disappointing. Perhaps that was a great part of the reason for his breakdown and the loss of will that had stopped his writing.

That hiatus in our work created the personal financial crisis that put me back in London in 1910.

At first, Nellie and I lived in two tiny rooms in a large, ugly building grandly named Kings Cross Mansions, but soon we happily moved ourselves to three rooms in a basement flat off Lawrence Street in Chelsea. Now on my own, I was slow to find work, since I was not sure when Mr. James would return and need my full commitment again. I felt at loose ends, unraveled, unable to start anything, unable to finish anything, but so relieved to still have the work indexing the "Britannica's" Eleventh Edition.

I was quite good at my job; the supervisory staff would use me to check on the others. One evening, when I stayed late at my work with the other indexers, Mr. Chisholm, the editor-in-chief, walked past my desk. Then he turned and came back.

"Miss Bosanquet, isn't it?"

I nodded. My usual restraint with older, formidable men once again became active. I said "Good evening" with another nod.

"Your work here is quite satisfactory. I've been wanting to speak to you."

I caught my breath, waiting for what might follow from this handsome and unpredictable man. Even my expectation of surprise was over-reached.

"We have a problem in the 'H-Hubris to J-Jerusalem' volume. Well, actually, several problems. That indexer doesn't quite have a grip on his tasks, and you are so quick at this. I'd like for you to take a look at his work, see what you can do. All very hush hush, of course. We can't let the indexer know that he's letting us down."

I imagined Mr. Chisholm's unsaid words: "And we can't entertain the thought that someone like you, a mere woman, could actually do this job better than a man."

Nevertheless, I took on the additional task, looked the other indexer's work over, and quietly corrected his mistakes, re-indexing articles where he had missed many minor cross-references and even a few major references.

Then I came to the long section covering three members of the James family in the United States. But now, I found myself not only struggling with the problematic work of the male indexer but also facing lapses and errors in the essays themselves. Whoever had written about Mr. James, Sr., and about the Professor had done a middling job. They had said enough, praised enough (for my taste anyway, though probably not enough for the family).

However, the entry for Mr. Henry James, Jr.—my Mr. James—was not acceptable. It was short and complained of the dense difficultness of his language, his too-many words. His plots were unbelievable and often repetitive, even his nationality was ambiguous. (What was he, anyway—neither American nor British? Some strange mixture?) Mr. James was neither popular nor famous in either country. The "Britannica's" author sounded peeved that he (the famous expert of something or other that the entry's author claimed to be) had had to waste his precious time writing about this nobody.

I wondered: Am I the first person to read this entry? If I have the courage to fix it, would anyone notice or complain? Should I gather my courage and give it a try?

I pushed aside the other pages of notes, found a clean sheet of paper, rolled it into my typewriting machine, and, before taking much more thought, began to type. I used the previous writer's paragraphs and stodgy tone about Mr. James and the Master's origins and early life, and I stayed with the expert's listing of the Master's early stories and novels. But when the entry came to Mr. James' later writings, I let myself go:

"As a novelist, Henry James is a modern of the moderns both in subject matter and in method. He is entirely loyal to contemporary life and reverentially exact in his transcription of the phase [sic]. His characters are for the most part people of the world who conceive of life as a fine art and have the leisure to carry out their theories. Rarely are they at close quarters with any ugly practical task. They are subtle and complex with the subtlety and complexity that come from conscious preoccupation with themselves. They are specialists in conduct and past masters in casuistry, and are full of variations and shadows of turning."

I especially liked that phrase, "shadows of turning." I liked how it called up "The Turn of the Screw," Mr. James' most talked-about work with its ghosts and shadows.

It was fun to add elements, to emphasise the parts of the Master's legacy that I valued, not what others thought he should be famous for. I spoke of his heart, his spirit, and how he wrote to enable us to become more conscious, to pay more attention, and how his reputed difficulty was because we had to learn to read him with that same attention that he put into his writing. I wrote of his methods as only I could, mentioning his idiosyncrasies, the little details only I knew.

I kept on through the evening, thinking this might be my only chance. When I had finished correcting the entry, I went ahead and indexed it with all the others, put it on the completed pile, and continued with other entries. No one ever mentioned the piece, and so I came to be the entry's anonymous author.

I was occasionally also openly working for Mr. James. His British agent, Mr. Pinker, at first was frantic when he did not receive word from his client about the proofs to the new book. He asked me to come to his office to help him, and I arranged to arrive late one afternoon after I was through at the "Britannica."

We had met, but Mr. Pinker (short, stout, perspiring behind piles of manuscripts) shook my hand and peered up at me as though he had never seen me before, as if I were some saviour angel summoned from the wilderness.

"What am I to do?" he asked plaintively as he handed me a letter from Macmillan listing several unanswered questions. They had tried writing to Mr. James; now, with no answer, they had to come to Mr. Pinker. There was no more time—the presses were being held until they could be sure about the order for the stories in this volume, about which story was to begin the collection, which one to end it.

As I looked up from the letter, prepared to answer, Mr. Pinker went on, "And the corrections to the text from the copy editor, so many. What do you think Mr. James would want us to do with those?"

"That's easier," I said. "I still have the originally dictated pages. I can look back and see if I might know what he meant."

"Would you? Could you? Oh! Wonderful! But Miss Bosanquet, what about the order of the stories? Can you tell us what to do with that?"

"I believe Mr. James meant the order of stories to be as he gave them to you." Knowing Mr. James as I did, I felt bold enough to go on. "As a writer myself, I'd say, 'Leave it as it is. It's a good arrangement.'"

Later, after we had solved the remaining questions, Mr. Pinker walked me down the marble stairs to the street entrance for his office. He thanked me and politely asked what I was working on (probably hoping to hear that there was more of Mr. James' work in progress, but of course there was not). I was thinking of how Mr. James would often counsel the young male writers who came to him, saying, "Don't be afraid to just begin."

For once, I overcame my reticence and spoke: "I'm working on a little book of my own: it's a story in letters, which I'm writing with a friend."

"Charming," Mr. Pinker said. He looked interested.

"Perhaps you've heard of my friend," I said. "Clara Smith? She works for Lord Milne, the Home Secretary. We've been writing to each other ever since we were up at Cheltenham. Now that I have more time to spend on my own writing, our idea of a novel in letters seems a good one."

For months, I'd had this idea, but when I first tried to enlist Clara's help, she thought I was daft: "What? A novel in letters? Dora, that's so quaint! Even eighteenth century! 'Samuel Richardson' and 'Clarissa'!!"

But since Mr. Pinker seemed interested, I sketched out our novel. He nodded, especially when I told him about basing the novel on our real experiences of working with our famous men, using the people we had observed as starting points for our narrators.

"Ah," he said. "You have such interesting people to use, don't you. I'd be willing to give it a look when you have a few chapters."

I was thrilled. Before we had even finished a first version, we had an agent interested! I could hardly wait to tell Clara.

But the novel was one more activity in a busy life. I was surprised to find how quickly my time became filled, what with working for the "Britannica" by day and devoting my free hours to the Cause. Clara had introduced me to the founder of the Women Writers Suffrage League (WWSL), a section of the WSPU, the Women's Social and Political Union. We were all proud to be known as "Suffragettes" as the papers were calling us. Now, we were immersed for the first time in the political world, which was nothing like living in Rye or recording Mr. James' memories of past writing adventures in his prefaces. Instead, London in 1910 was a world of women and politics and ambition, and my long-time friends were at its centre.

Besides her job with Lord Milne, Clara was writing for a women's newspaper. Early on, she recruited me to write articles on suffrage issues, in particular about Mrs. Pankhurst and her courageous efforts again and again to disrupt the Parliamentary hearings that were to deal with the Vote for women, protesting that they were unfair. She would insist: With no women present, how can the Parliamentarians hear anything?

But my most ambitious idea had been that novel in letters with Clara.

Clara, however, still needed some persuading.

"I'm happy to hear about Mr. Pinker," she said. "But Dora, this idea of writing it all in letters!—Why in letters?"

"You've often said how much you liked my letters when I first was living down in Rye. And I don't have the usual trouble with my writing when I'm writing to you. A letter seems to flow out of my pen, but a novel would be very different. At least, after listening to Mr. James and his theories, I'm sure we can't jot down whatever comes into our heads. We need to have an idea of what we are writing, a plot. Something has to happen."

"Well, not the usual silly romantical fluff! You know, boy meets girl and on. Right?"

I thought Clara had a good question. "No, we can't do that, but without the convention of letters, who are we? Maybe letters are only a place to start. I've always thought I'd like to imagine being a man—"

"Dora, not that again!" Clara liked to tease me whenever I would start in on how the world ought to be, if only the men would be different.

"Don't worry, I wouldn't be a very manly man. No cigars and no broken hearts. No, I'll write as if I were one of Mr. James' sensitive observers, a quiet man who listens, sees, and understands."

"So, a man who has all your good qualities."

"Well, if I'm to make someone up, he might as well be good, or at least someone I can imagine."

Clara lit another cigarette. "Then who am I?" She drew in the smoke, held the flavour, let it go. "I shall be a Bad Woman. No, I don't know how to do that. I don't want to be a melodramatic sort of girl. I'll have to write from what I know."

"We can write about us, the working girls doing the sorts of tasks we do. I've never seen a novel about a woman working in an office, a female assistant or a secretary. Your work with Lord Milne, arranging his meetings, watching after him. I think you could create a wonderful character. I know—" I realised I really did not want to deal with men and women in love affairs. "We could be brother and sister! That would remove any expectation of romance. You could 'know' something—"

"Maybe we could discover someone's secret, come across—"

"Yes, yes! You could describe who they are, what they're doing."

"And as the clever observer, you could figure it out, tell me something hidden that I can't see. But we need to have something happen that surprises our readers, some discovery that our words lead them to make, like in Mr. James' stories, where it dawns slowly on readers what is happening, and there's always a handsome young man who is quite benighted by his beautiful male-ness—"

"Oh, Dora, you know too much. But we can't write like Henry James, can we?"

Clara had never really liked to read the same books that I read. Besides, I had a different fear: Sometimes I felt as if I could only write like Mr. James. I had sat there for too many hours, days, years, taking it in, taking it down, that complex interweaving of thought and word, the Now interspersed with the Long Ago, very few signpost adverbs, too many repeated pronouns, too many repetitions. But I always knew who it was he meant his readers to care about, wherever we were. I suppose my mind had worked that way already before I came to the Master, but now I knew I was caught in his spell after all those hours, my fingers tapping, his feet pacing, his words coming fast, his words staggering.

Now, Clara had another idea. "We'll have them never meet. Brothers and sisters do that here in London, between all the goings-on, all the parties and invitations."

"So," I said, "they can have very different friends, live in different worlds. I'd like to imagine I'm part of the artistic world of writers and artists, Chelsea and the Embankment—"

"And my character will be in the social set, Belgravia. You know, I don't think I've ever read a book about a brother and sister. Do you think we can actually do it?"

"Yes!! I think we should do what Mr. James was always advising in those endless letters I used to type: 'Don't be afraid to just begin, not to wait for any ideal *readiness* to begin, but to let a beginning *make* that readiness.'"

16

"A Round of Visits"

1909

But one appearance more vividly even than the others
stared out at him. "I really think I must practically have
caused it."

—Henry James
"A Round of Visits"

Clara had introduced me to the Women Writers Suffrage League and their meetings to prepare for yet another big march. However, my first assignment for the WWSL was not writing. In those days, we spent most of our sessions making banners and signs. I'm not much for designing or sewing, but in the weeks before the march, we would all gather every night to help out, talk, and support each other.

I had never before heard such talk—never anything this open and clear and persuasive. It was as if I were being made anew. This was true for all of us led by the older, wiser women, by Mrs. Pankhurst and others. And so it was that I found myself inspired by all those women writing, editing, publishing, and being published as I was working on my own writing. Listening to them, I began to work harder on my stories and articles. I was ready to try anything: I even wrote poems or the beginnings of poems.

One day, I received a wire asking my help the next morning, down in Rye, if possible.

The trip down was dreary, and Rye seemed more isolated and provincial than ever in contrast to the busy streets, the liveliness of London. Now that Nellie had moved permanently to our flat in London, I had not been back to our little studio on Watchbell Street, not even to visit.

As I approached Lamb House, there was a smoky pall in the air: something of burning leaves but more of the burnt-cardboard and scrap-paper smell of the trash barrel, or even, as I felt with a pang of remembering, of the acrid smell the day after my own home had burned down, so long before.

How desolate that had been, with Father wringing his hands, saying over and over how sorry he was, how he knew he should not have given up the house, should not have let it out to those people, all the very points I had thought. Everything had been unchangeably lost, and everywhere, that smell of loss and destruction. Now, as I trudged up the steps of Lamb House and raised the familiar knocker, the smell was so strong that I almost expected to see something floating in the damp mist: a burnt scrap, a singed corner, or even a darkened page.

The housekeeper brought me in and took my things, then pointed to the parlour, where there was a low fire in the grate. I stood there, rubbing my hands before it.

Mr. James came slowly down the stairs. I could hear his progress, not a limp exactly, but heavy steps halting. When he came in, I was surprised by his appearance. He was not dressed for visitors but in a soft faded shirt, an old waistcoat, and a dressing gown—and his face—his face had undergone a huge change. It seemed swollen and blotchy. There were deep, etched lines, and under his eyes were heavy pouches, circles. He had been ill, unmistakably, but still he was the kind host. His fine fingers played and fidgeted during his offer of something to warm me, over the question of my wet things, my boots, which steamed when, with his encouragement, I rested them on the fender one after the other.

But before I could inquire after his health or even begin to ask after him, his gloom seemed to lift, and he began to ask more about me. Was I comfortable then in the crowded metropolis? Was I financially, monetarily, economically sound? Soon we were talking easily of my flat on Lawrence Street in Chelsea, of how much I enjoyed Chelsea and its almost village-like charms in the midst of London. Mr. James did not know much of the artists' enclave there, but he promised to come and have me show him around whenever his health and strength returned.

I asked then about what the doctors were saying about his illness, and he told me that they thought it was something to do with his heart, something he had expected at his age and with his family history.

"My brother's heart is also quite weak, you know. He's tried the various remedies here and in America, but with no success. But for me, those treatments, those consultations and appointments are so expensive. I can't afford any more expense right now."

He sat deeper in his old chair, speaking rather distractedly, almost to himself.

"It's the New York Edition, our great endeavour these last years. It turns out to have been a great financial disaster for me, nothing like the resource I had hoped. Instead, the royalties for the whole thing last year came to less than six hundred dollars. I've received the cheque from the publisher, and what with the payments for permissions and the delays, and whatever else they want to deduct, it's too little. I wouldn't be telling you, except that you have worked with me on so many phases of it—the prefaces, the corrections, the galleys—Really, would you have ever thought? The total payment is less than what I earn for a single story in a magazine here, when they take one. Oh, it's hardly bearable."

He sighed deeply and stared into the fire for a long moment of petulant silence.

I hardly knew what to say or do, but soon enough he gathered himself again and stood to walk back and forth. He began to explain why he had wired for my help; it was not that he had more work.

"No, no, work is at a standstill right now. I can't make myself do new work."

Instead, he needed help with a small matter, something for the editor of the soon-to-be-published volume of new stories, "The Finer Grain," they were calling it. Did I remember?

Of course I remembered the stories written in-between the bursts of play revision and script preparation the year before. The stories— "The Velvet Glove" and "Mora Montravers"—had been so exciting.

"Now, I need your help, because I've made a terrible mistake. Two days ago, I had a sudden desire to clear this place." He gestured around the slightly stuffy, cluttered room.

"And as George was conveniently burning a quantity of old brush and dead leaves back in the alley, I carried all my old rubbish out and threw it on the bonfire. Really, it was most amazing, and it was somehow right—all those years and years of letters, papers, old scraps of stories and notes, everything that I'd finished with."

I imagined the scene—the cold grey day, the smouldering ugly fire, the darker pungent smoke fitfully blowing back and forth as some papers caught quickly, and others smudged and smoked and partially burned. Did Old George have to keep turning the bonfire as Mr. James sent more and more piles of papers to be burned? Or did Mr. James come out himself to put the papers on the flames, to make sure that every word was consumed?

Mr. James went on. "For, you see, in the flurry and enthusiasm— over-enthusiasm—to clear out all, all those years of words and words, to make sure that no prying eyes would ever see them, in the general tumult, I seem to have burnt up the carbon copy to 'A Round of Visits.' The very next day, the editor wrote to request another copy. Can you imagine? He needs it, and so in short, I need to make a copy. Would you be so kind?"

He went to the desk and brought out the story, then hurried about to find me a bite of lunch and get me settled, even though clearly he was too tired and too weak to be doing much of anything.

Before many more minutes had passed, I was once again there alone in the Green Room, our old comfortable place of work. Now, it was dusty, cold, unused. Nothing seemed to have been moved from the last time we had worked there. I sat before the typewriting machine and began making a fresh copy of the story, thinking how sad it all felt and how the story matched my feelings.

Mark, the narrator, is called to visit an old friend, who has been seriously ill. The story grows dark, when Mark's financial reversals force him to flee back to America after he has spent his life in England. I wondered: Would Mr. James also have to go back? Were things that desperate for him? As I typed the sentence when Mark first sees his friend after his friend's illness, the day outside the Lamb House window seemed suddenly to grow darker:

> *"You must have been ill indeed."*
> *"Pretty bad. But I'm better. And you do me good"*— *with which the light of convalescence came back.*
> *"I don't awfully bore you?"*
> *Winch shook his head. "You keep me up—and you see how no one else comes near me."*
> *Mark's eyes made out that he* <u>was</u> *better—though it wasn't yet that nothing was the matter with him. If there was ever a man with whom there was still something the matter—! Yet one couldn't insist on that, and meanwhile he clearly did want company. "Then there we are. I myself had no one to go to."*
> *"You save my life," Newton renewedly grinned.*

And so I typed on into the afternoon, through Mark's discovery of the revolver under the sofa, through the crashing entrance of the police and the authorities, the shock of the single shot. Really, it was a most disturbing story.

When I stopped to shake out my cramping hands, to take a stretch and move around the room, I noticed the unnatural silence of Lamb House. There were no sounds of Mr. James' usual, busy life—the visitors, the chaos of his ongoing work.

Without his work, what would happen to him? Had I abandoned him? Should I have waited longer before I left for the pleasures of London?

But after all, I had left with his encouragement. He had even offered to write a letter of recommendation. I believed him when he said there was no more work, and of course, again, as always, I did need the money. Perhaps if I could have stayed in Rye, I wondered, if I could have waited for him to resume his work, then he might have found a new project to sustain him, and he would not have been left at the mercy of his illness.

As I typed the final scene, the sound of the typewriting machine was abrasive in the quiet house:

> *The emissaries of the law, looking down at him, exhaled simultaneously a gruff imprecation, and then while the worthy in the high hat bent over the subject of their visit the one in the helmet raised a severe pair of eyes to Mark. "Don't you think, sir, you might have prevented it?"*
>
> *Mark took a hundred things in, it seemed to him— things of the scene, of the moment, and of all the strange moments before; but one appearance more vividly even than the others stared out at him. "I really think I must practically have caused it."*

And so, in much the same way, I had been wondering about my own role in the year of silence between Mr. James and myself and whether I held some responsibility for his decline. Of course, at that time, I was careful not to fill up all my time, for I kept expecting Mr. James to return from America. It was strange, but even though he was far away, I had such a strong feeling, a psychical sense that he was troubled. I tried to express my concern for him to my friends. One evening I said to Clara, "It must be painful for Mr. James to be watching his brother's long, inevitable dying, but I keep having this feeling that our Mr. James is the one who is really suffering."

Clara frowned. "Do you believe he's ill again? Remember last year when he had that long bout with a deep chest cold, and then that long time of collapse, when he never left the house?"

"But this time I don't feel that it's a physical pain. When I don't hear any response from him, not even to his agent's questions about the changes that I know he cares a great deal about, well, I wish I could send him some reassurance and hope. It's something Nellie and I have been trying a little, to send healing even from a distance."

Clara laughed, as she always did when I slipped and told her anything of my life with Nellie.

However, this time it was Nellie who found a way to answer my concerns. One evening when I returned to our flat from a meeting of the Society for Psychical Research, I found Nellie waiting up for me. I told her what I had learnt about current experiments to send psychical messages long distances, all very scientifically recorded and tested, so unlike our own little experiments at sending to each other. We used to try to wake at the same time. We would take the small, blank white card that we had left ready beside the bed the night before and, before even sitting up, would stare at the blank paper and then write down whatever we saw or imagined there—a shape, a letter, an image. I was not very good at this. All I could imagine was tea and toast. But Nellie with her painter's eye always got something: a pattern, a shape, or even a familiar object. The idea was to send something and to receive something. Sometimes I did receive what she had sent, for she was more psychical.

That particular night, we talked about whether or even how far we could send messages. I wondered if I might be able to receive something from far-away America, from Mr. James or his family (I knew the Professor and his wife had both been keen on distant communications), and I wondered if maybe I was in touch psychically after all, for I was feeling keenly that Mr. James must be suffering very much over there with his brother so very ill. But without any word, how could I know? I wondered if Professor James had already passed; I wondered if his psychical research friends were there with Mrs. James, trying the ultimate psychical experiments—the final test of all his books and theories. What messages might there be flying through all the ether around us?

Nellie thought she would like to try to connect with my Mr. James. Nellie believed she was a healer; she wanted to try healing Mr. James with her powers, but she needed me to help direct the sending. I in my practical way wondered if my role were not rather like finding the correct address. Very early the next morning (night there in America for Mr. James), Nellie and I sat in the dark with a candle and Mr. James' last letter to me spread on the little table between us. We held hands for a minute, then closed our eyes. Nellie began to speak in a low voice, at first of the dark and then of a journey over the ocean, that deep, slowly shifting world between

Nellie and me and my old employer. She spoke of clouds and colours. I could picture what she described about wafting and floating. I don't know how long we stayed like that, but I soon became stiff and uncomfortable. As I tried to stretch a little, my rickety chair gave a great creak, and I laughed.

That was it. I broke the spell. Nellie was insulted and hurt that I could not take her seriously. She would not let me explain.

We never knew if our sending did the Master any good. Days passed, weeks passed, and we still did not hear from Mr. James. I came to think he must have trusted me immensely to leave me with all the things I had to finish up and decide for him during all those months.

Yet there was one strange morning in late August 1910, when I awoke earlier than usual. As I lay in the dark, I thought I heard a voice, very quiet, a woman's voice I could almost recognise. I tried to make out the words, for there were only a few. I felt icy cold. But then the cat came in and broke the spell. I told Nellie I was sure then that Mr. James was in trouble, for the few words were only, "Now he's gone."

Nellie asked if I thought Mr. James had passed on, but I knew somehow that it was not our Mr. James. I guessed that it was his brother who had gone. The heavy sense of sadness lasted with me for a long time. Only work could lighten it. I continued with tasks for the Master's work, sending him the corrected pages, sending him notes and reassurances: I sometimes wonder if perhaps my letters back to him about the work I was doing were not a frail connexion that helped him during that painful time of his brother's passing.

17

"English Hours"

1910–1912

Doubtless, there is a certain initiation necessary for the enjoyment of Mr [sic] James. He presupposes a cosmopolitan outlook, a certain interest in art and in social artifice, and no little abstract curiosity about the workings of the human mechanism. But for speculative readers, for readers who care for art in life as well as for life in art, and for readers above all who want to encounter and comprehend a great variety of very modern and finely modulated characters, Mr James holds a place of his own, unrivalled as an interpreter of the world of to-day.

—Anonymous entry on Henry James "Encyclopædia Britannica," Eleventh Edition

C lara and I started in writing our fictional letters back and forth. I used what I saw around me to imagine myself as a man. I watched the men at my job, those I saw walking through London, or the ones I had seen at the "Britannica" who had come to talk with Mr. Chisholm about their essays. I noticed what they wore, how they talked and walked; I tried to imagine what it was that a man does all day. I wanted my character to be younger than my Mr. James by quite a bit, so I could not use too much of him or what I had observed from being with him for such a long time. No, it was the younger men I watched and listened in on—actually spied on. And as I wrote in character, I began to feel like a man.

Of course I could not wear trousers, but I did wear tailored suits with vests, and I liked to wear heavy shoes that tied. The winter was bitter cold, and so I was dressed in woollens and tweeds, dark skirts and jackets, and blended right in. I felt more comfortable among all those men when I was wearing a business-like suit.

These days it is not unusual to see working girls walking to their jobs, but in 1910 the streets were crowded with men. Men, men everywhere you looked, all alike in their dark suits and hats, hard hollow hats called bowlers. I did not wear a man's hat, but I did wear a mannish one of dark wool felt, fitted close to my head. It made me feel invisible and safe. When my friends and I look back at that time, it seems we were always doing things to feel safe, to become invisible. Were they so terrible to us, all those men? Would they have attacked us right there in the streets? Or was it public opinion we feared, afraid that we would be perceived as immodest, fallen women if we did not appear meek and reluctant to draw any attention to ourselves?

I felt so tall and strong. I did not think I had anything to fear, for my friends all valued my difference. They were different too, most of them living away from home, working in offices, being secretaries or aides. They were brave, yet we were all subservient, helping men in charge. At that time, only a few women were independent and confident enough to try life on their own, writing, editing, and publishing. I admired them, and I envied them, too.

I suppose, though, in that winter of the suffrage marches, we thought we could bring about change for us all with the cry everywhere of "Votes for women!" When the Women Writers Suffrage League and the rest of us gathered after work every night to plan and prepare for marches and demonstrations to give women the Vote, I am not sure we even thought about how that one change might in due course change other factors, other relationships, other arrangements. Of course, I still thought that even if we were successful, even if we got the Vote, whenever Mr. James came back from America, I would surely go back to working for him, as I always had, quietly taking dictation, helping him produce his books. Still, something was changing in me, now that I had time and space and was working on my own book. Yet, given so much unsettled with Mr. James, how could I think of starting anything new of my own?

Clara and I were always talking about writing and about the upcoming march, which sounded so splendid, with not only all the famous women who had made the books that changed my life but also younger women like Clara, who were writing but were still unrecognised. Clara was very persuasive, and so there we were, on a cold morning in February 1910, after weeks of preparation, gathering our hand-made banners and hurrying to the staging site on the Chelsea Embankment, only a few minutes' walk from our rooms.

After so many rehearsals, we gathered in good order even though it was still dark. This was the second women's suffrage march; the first, several months earlier, had turned out smaller than the planners hoped, with much opposition from the police and from politicians in both parties. I had heard the weather was terrible—cold, endless, pouring rain. We were not sure how many would turn out this time with the morning still dark.

But when we reached our appointed place, our white dresses moving, luminous in the dark, we were thousands, faintly glowing in lines, swirls, eddies, moving, stopping. It was all so quiet, only a constant murmuring.

Clara and I found our place and waited, silent.

The pre-dawn quiet held energy and strength, a thousand held breaths, ten thousand, as we waited for the signal to begin.

Policemen were everywhere, not against us but to protect us, I felt. They did serve to keep back the men who were watching, crowding the sidewalks and curbs, almost as many as we were, restless men, shoving, staring, calling out rude remarks.

Then the signal came from somewhere far up the line. We let out our breath and slowly, slowly began to move. Bands played somewhere, drums beat, and songs were tossed back and forth, some melodies starting up ahead, some beginning from behind. On we marched, not in step or anything of a military way, only our quiet walking, the pad of our feet and the rustling of our skirts.

Proudly I held up our banner proclaiming women writers, women who had worked unseen for years, for centuries. Only a few were famous, known by sight. The names of the rest of us were the names that had never appeared on our few published pieces or, in order to appear in print, had appeared only as initials or as men's names to hide our fatal female-ness.

I looked around and wondered: How many of us were those whose work was truly invisible, for we were editors, researchers, amanuenses, and literary secretaries—the "typewriters" for the many famous, erudite, creative men.

That bloody machine—that typewriting machine—how did that machine make it acceptable for us to hire ourselves out to offices and private homes, to become secretaries? In my father's day, the word "secretary" always meant a man, exactly as "writer," "poet," and "novelist" always signified a man. Yet here was a battalion of writers of every possible description, and all of us were women! How many of us were serving some other Mr. James?

I wondered, too: How many of these interesting-looking women were like me, on their own as their own financial support? How many of us were successful and able to support ourselves without a husband, father, or brother to help?

I looked along my row of younger marchers, neither famous nor distinguished, yet we were independent, self-supporting, and supporting each other. I found myself smiling, for I felt as if Mr. James, when imagining "The Outcry," had created Grace to be a woman who, that day, would have stepped out of her rehearsals to join us. I looked over at Clara and Naomi Royde-Smith, our friend who worked for the "Westminster Gazette." Clara smiled her tender smile as we marched on, the sound of our feet echoing between the office buildings.

That evening, we collected the newspapers and looked for articles about the day. Of course, the papers presented our march in the worst possible light, focusing on the skirmishes and arrests. Some papers even refused to cover it. This was discouraging, but our leaders simply began to plan another march. We continued on, in our small groups and large ones. However, King Edward's death in May 1910 did make a difference in our plans for marches. Some leaders, wanting to maintain respectability, cancelled all demonstrations until the end of mourning.

Then, at last, at last, Mr. James and I were back in contact. He began writing letters of instruction, sending wires about this project and that one. Reading them, I could feel that his energy was returning, that his own time of initial mourning was coming naturally to a close. I sent him the news about the cancellation and postponement of all dramatic productions, but he surprised me. Instead of dismay, he wrote of his excitement about a new project, a book to honour the memory of his brother and their father, a book of letters and memories.

I suppose he could have worked on this project and remained there in his brother's house, surrounded by the grieving family. At first, he did seem to be trying to work in America, leaving me with no hopes for my own employment. But soon enough I received a letter, in which he complained of how difficult it was to write, how he needed to return to his own world to do real work, and, as I added to myself with a little thrill, how he needed to get back to our old arrangements.

However, I knew that if Mr. James returned, the damp, cold winter in isolated, provincial Rye would no longer work for him. Surely he would fall ill again. It also would not work for me. Clara and I were deep in our novel, and I valued my connexions with other writers, with publishing friends like Naomi Royde-Smith. I had hopes for my own writing.

All of that would not be possible if I were back living in Rye.

I wrote to Mr. James and made my proposal, quite brilliantly, I might say. I would find us rooms or even a suitable flat in Chelsea, where we could keep the typewriting machine, while he could live in his old rooms at his club, with everything as he needed it. He would still have Lamb House and Rye, but his work would be in London, close to the editors and publishers, close to his writing friends, close to me. Before I wrote Mr. James about my plan, I looked around at available rooms he might like. Then I wrote, including the prices, which he found not to be an obstacle.

It is strange to think now what argument it was that worked to persuade Mr. James to this arrangement, which was so convenient for me. It was not my convenience that appealed to him; rather, it was that he could continue his connexion with his club, the Reform, where he had been a member during all his years living in England. He had kept a room there and had often written in the club library or some other quiet space. Whenever he was in London, he took his meals there with the other members and lived a quiet bachelor's life.

The Reform had been a good choice during the first years of the new century, when his method of dictating to the typewriter became essential to his creative process, because he had hired only men to be his secretaries. As men, those secretaries were permitted to enter the Reform Club's sacred male portals. Rye and Lamb House had provided the perfect balance to the arrangement he'd had with Miss Weld and me. But now that I was Mr. James' amanuensis based in London, something else had to be arranged. I saw the irony. After my months of organising to obtain rights for women, I had to search for suitable rooms so my employer and I could work because I was not to be allowed into the Reform Club, even to take dictation.

Clara and I had a good laugh over that.

Clara heard two rooms were available at the back of the building where Nellie and I lived, off Lawrence Street, near the Chelsea Embankment. When Mr. James arrived in London, I arranged for him to see the space. Though the rooms were small and dark, apparently he became quite charmed by the idea of them and by the idea of coming every day to work with me in Chelsea. Soon after that, we were able to find a larger flat around the corner in Carlyle Mansions, a handsomely reconstructed block of apartments that might do very well even as a place for him to live. I was curious how he would take to Carlyle Mansions, for the apartment was quite luxurious compared to our rooms in Lawrence Street.

That was the beauty of Chelsea—the wonderful mixture of old and new, with quiet side streets yet all the hubbub of London at your door, and the river with its bustle. You saw everyone there on the streets, a mixture of old and new, rich and not so rich, some living in the fancy houses, some in only two rooms and the bath down the hall. We all strolled about: the well-to-do, the toffs in their fancy clothes, the struggling artists, ink-stained writers, the working girls. I had hoped Mr. James would see the fun in it, and he did.

The leasing agent for the large and elegant flats told us about its name as he showed Mr. James and me around.

"Carlyle Mansions is named for the famous writer Thomas Carlyle. This site is where he once lived. Have you heard of him?"

I mumbled something, but Mr. James seemed to be more interested in the large, modern appliances in the kitchen and pantry. The agent continued as though we had answered no. "Thomas Carlyle wrote numerous books, I'm told, and though he was from the North, from Scotland, I believe, he was quite famous here. It was not a mansion, but nearly so. His writing made him piles of money."

The apartment agent went on, opening closets and doors, pointing out the large windows overlooking the river, the consistently warm steam radiators, the electric fixtures, the many modern conveniences that might appeal to an elderly man looking for comfort.

"They say Mr. Carlyle was a little man," the agent said, "I think, no more than five feet tall."

I quickly looked aside at Mr. James, who was not much taller, but the Master was not responding to the agent's silly talk. Instead, he seemed to be lost in thought. He looked especially at the room where we would be spending our time, commenting on the window and where we would place the desk, the typewriting machine, my chair ("your throne," he called it). He suggested that for his own comfort, we might add a wickerish sort of arm-chair, the sort he had seen in the shops in Sloane Square in Chelsea. I could tell that he was pleased with what I had found for him. He went on to make all the arrangements.

As we were leaving Carlyle Mansions, Mr. James talked about how when he was very much younger, he had met Mrs. Carlyle—Jane, he called her—and what an amazing woman she had been, much smarter than her husband and much the better writer.

That afternoon, I asked my women friends to tell me what they knew about Jane Carlyle, since I had never heard much about her.

"She's another invisible one," Naomi decreed in her loudest voice. "I wonder if she didn't write his stuff for him, the good stuff, anyway. What a mind! I bet they talked about everything, and her suggestions improved his work. I'm sure that at the least she edited him, edited every essay before it went out. She was a force."

I thought of my work with Mr. James, now that he was about to write his memories of his brother and his father. Would my responses be as helpful to him as my thoughts had been when we were working on the great projects, his revisions and the prefaces? I knew how much he liked the act of thinking out loud, especially with an audience. I used to think I was helping him, drawing him out, editing his flow as it came, my smooth typewriting responding to each shaped sentence, to every paragraph. Maybe he was about to lift the curtain on a whole new dramatic work.

18

"A Small Boy and Others"

January 1911–July 1913

. . . held it there, at every point, as a vast bright gage,
. . . in those beginnings I felt myself most happily cross
that bridge over to Style . . .

—Henry James, commenting on the
Louvre's ornate Galerie d'Apollon
"A Small Boy and Others"

And so, we were to begin our work again after more than a
year's hiatus. I felt quite comfortable, despite all I had done
in-between. I knew I would enjoy hearing Mr. James' reminiscences,
and apparently he came to this writing with new-found energy and enthusiasm. We usually worked every day for several hours, but that still
would leave me time for my friends and even time to develop my other
interests. Listening to his memories of the life and death of his brother
gave me more ideas, more evidence with which to investigate the spirit
world. Nearly every week I went to one lecture or another at the Society
for Psychical Research, or the SPR, as we called it.

I learnt that while Mr. James was staying on in America, he
tried to reach his brother from beyond the grave through séances

and other experiments his sister-in-law had set up. However, in his conversations with me, little of these experiences came out, at least not at first. No, as we took up working again, my two worlds were separate, and our two worlds were separate.

Some of the first lectures I had attended at the Society for Psychical Research had been about automatic handwriting. I had to try this out! I followed all the speaker's instructions and sat very still, trying to empty my mind. Nothing. I tried lighting a candle and staring into the flame. Nothing. I tried to imagine some sort of connexion with the spirit world, someone who had passed on. My mother? Nothing.

I dropped my head onto the paper and wept. Then something came—not my mother, not even a person, but I began to write as I had been instructed, as fast as I could, not thinking as the words or whatever it was came to me, but as if I were taking dictation, as I had so often, yet this seemed like a foreign language. I made squiggles and lines, dots and slants and circles, small ones floating above letters, I wrote all these strange letters and mysterious words as if my hand belonged to someone else, someone who spoke another language. I wrote these hieroglyphics fast yet evenly. I filled—that is, she filled, whoever she was—a whole page, and then she stopped. My hand stopped, and I took a breath. It felt as though I had not been breathing for the entire five minutes or however long I had been writing.

But what writing! The black ink on the stark page, the strange shapes. I had never seen anything like it. I certainly did not know what it said, what I had been writing. Was it mine? What was it? Whose writing was it? Whose voice? I kept staring blankly at the pages, and then I put the papers away. I wanted to throw them all out, but I did not dare do so. Perhaps the pages contained an important message for someone. For Mr. James? For me?

The next night, I tried again, and the next, but nothing came. Then, on the third night, it—they—she appeared again. I wrote as fast as I could, and the black ink spread on the white page like horrible insects, disturbed, maddened, crawling everywhere. I could recognise no word, no letter, even, it came so fast. Then it stopped and I sat up, drained. What did this say? What did it mean? I knew several languages, but what was this? Another alphabet? But how could this series of puzzling shapes and marks be a language or an alphabet? Perhaps it was a cipher, a code, and I was merely a conduit for a message. But what part of me knew this language?

I put the paper aside, knowing I would come back again to puzzle it out, and left for my other job, still with the "Encyclopædia Britannica."

That night, Clara stopped by to go to a lecture. "It's what you need, Dora. It will take your mind off your distractions."

The presentation was one of a series of lectures on Romance languages. I thought it would be on the poets of the Langue d'Oc, inventors of love poetry, but no, the professor began with a statement that the language he was going to discuss was curiously without artifice or any love poetry. Instead, Romany was a language for direction, for action, for mysticism. Saying this, he turned and began scratching on the blackboard. As he wrote and as I watched, I felt a shock, for he was writing the same shapes and marks I had produced in my experiment with automatic handwriting.

The professor explained that this language was more ancient than any of the known Indo-European group. Not even Basque or Occitan (Langue d'Oc) had such a long history. Scholars had traced Romany to fragments found in caves and burial sites, but it was not generally known as a written language. Its speakers were a nomadic collection of tribes, which stretched from the Ganges to Russia to the wilds of ancient Gaul. "We call them Gypsies," he said. "That's our word—not one of theirs."

Of course, as I listened, I was wondering how I had come to write this language. Where did it come from? And how was I to know what I had written? As the professor spoke, I took notes, scribbling frantically, writing down where the language was studied, where I could learn more. As it turned out, the experts were right in London, at the Society for Psychical Research. I wondered if I had unconsciously picked up some of the language while attending meetings or looking over articles, storing up the words in some hidden part of my brain. But that is not how we had been taught to think about our automatic handwritings. We were told that in the trance we were connected to the World Mind, the Collective Unconscious, tapping into some larger Shared Wisdom.

After the lecture, I went back and tried to read the gibberish I had written. In the SPR library, I found a Gypsy grammar and dictionary. I wondered how I ever came to know any of their language. I thought it was possible, this collective knowing business, but I had been trained as a scientist (well, actually, as a geologist) and needed evidence, proof, and a reasonable train of connexions. I thought about where I might have heard or seen Romany. I looked through experts' essays about the Gypsies in England, how they wandered, but not randomly, and I noted that one of their annual migration circles included Lyme Regis and the Devon coast. On the experts' maps I recognised the church and the old road through Uplyme, the one that passed our house.

My father, as the rector, would have given the Gypsies food and old clothing as part of his duty. An old memory floated up. I could catch the edge of it: darkness, that eerie clear dark of a late afternoon in summer, the tall trees, taller to me than they have ever been since, tall like dark spires against the light sky holding the last of the sunset. I remember thinking how strange it looked, the wrong way round. It seemed magical and a little frightening. Indeed, I should have felt frightened, since I was very young, and I was alone where I should not have been, for I had run away.

Now, looking back, I wondered how far away I had run.

I think this memory is from very long ago, from the time when my father first had his own church, before my mother was ill, before poor little Louis was born. And yet I was running away from something. Maybe they were trying to make me take a bath or comb my hair, maybe Nurse accused me of being as wild as a Gypsy. I would not listen or let her near, and so she had tried to lock me in my room, but I climbed out the window and ran away into the woods. When the house was out of sight, I stopped and sat down, trembling under a bush.

What to do then? I was free, but to do what? I began to make up a story about myself as a wild little Gypsy girl, who never had to take a bath or brush her hair. Soon, I was not afraid any more. I broke sticks for a pretend fire in my pretend camp and, wandering there and about, soon, I really was lost and wild. Our house was out of sight, and I had forgotten all about my unfair life.

Suddenly a girl appeared out of the shadows. She was about my size, with long black hair neatly braided. She wore a brightly coloured skirt and jacket and had a wonderfully dirty face. I remember her face. Her name was Dina, and as we played all that day, we spoke very little. Was I remembering a dream? Or did I make her up, her bright coloured clothes, her long dark hair, her face? Or did a book I had read turn into a memory from my childhood? I only know that when Dina led me back home (for of course she knew the way) and back to the certain punishment I faced, I had a wonderful feeling of not being alone any more. It was joy. I was happy. Nothing could take that joy away, not even Father's anger.

Nurse, who had caused me to run away, carried me back to the kitchen to be scrubbed. She was more angry at how dirty I was than at the fact that I had been missing all day. And when she heard my story of playing with a Gypsy child, she scrubbed even harder and rubbed me raw with the towel. I had gotten sticks and leaves caught in my long hair, and I screamed loudly when she tried to pull them out. Finally, in frustration, Nurse cut all my hair off very short. I remember that. Pictures of me from that time show a little girl with bangs and bobbed hair, when bobbed hair was not at all the fashion.

Was this a real memory? Did I really make friends with a little Gypsy girl? Why did they cut my hair so short, if not to rid me of the tangles, thorns, germs, and lice I might have picked up from such an unsuitable playmate?

Or maybe I'd had the scarlet fever and only imagined running away, but in that case, then, how did I learn those strange words that appeared in my trance writing so many years later? And besides, how could I possibly have learnt a language in only one day?

Clara was amazed when I showed her my trance writings. We took them to the next meeting of the Society for Psychical Research, where one of the experts told us that there are those who will believe anything and those who will believe nothing, but the SPR had to collect and study and prove scientifically, and so he took away my pages. That is how my small instance of trance writing became a part of the SPR Archive, which includes so many famous men and even a few women.

When the numbers of dead from the Great War were horrendous, the SPR added many other psychical experiences and puzzles to its records, as we searched for our lost loved ones, hoping for a few last moments of connexion. The lesson for me, though, from that trance handwriting was much simpler: Pay attention. We don't even know all that we know. And we don't know when we will learn something deeply disturbing.

Yet how curious it is that I was experimenting with my own psychical abilities when I was once again working with Mr. James after his experiences with his dying brother and, after that, with his brother's widow, seeking to contact the deceased.

Mr. James never spoke with me directly about his months there in America, but I could see from his behaviour when he returned that he was shaken. Something had affected him deeply. His dictations were different, more disconnected, more free-flowing, more personal. It was as if he were transported back across time and space to his childhood, and as I listened and typed away there in our rooms in Chelsea, I, too, felt as if I were there in the past with him.

He began with memories of his brother when they were very young boys, first in Albany, New York, and then in France. He explained his father's strange educational theories, which excluded schools. Instead, Henry, Sr. took Willie and Harry over to Europe to be taught French almost from their first words. The whole family with Mr. James' three brothers and his sister and their flurry of trunks and boxes and bags would board a steamer to be away for the summer or an even longer stay.

I should confess that, as entranced as I was with Mr. James' dictation, I sometimes found myself bristling at this history of the budding James intellectuals. Where were the younger brothers, Wilkinson and Robertson, who grew into the idealistic young abolitionists who volunteered (or were pressured by their father) to serve alongside Negroes during the Americans' Civil War in regiments composed largely of former slaves? And what about Alice, the youngest and a girl with nary a chance?

Mr. James dictated about that early household in such particular detail, remembering his soft-hearted tutor and how, when the tutor could no longer cram one more *mot* into Mr. James' young brain, the tutor would take young Willie and Harry out to walk on the esplanade and watch the handsome soldiers in their stunning uniforms, brilliant blues and golds. The Emperor was still revered in the France of the seventies, when Mr. James was a boy. Napoléon was still a hero, a figure to be admired. There were statues, paintings, and plaques to honour him everywhere. Whenever Mr. James watched the French boys playing, it was always the great Napoléon they discussed, arguing over whom they would cast as the Emperor.

After a morning of dictation, Mr. James would continue talking: "Later, when we moved to England—my father hoped it might be cheaper to raise our family here—I didn't like the English boys as well, maybe because my sympathies were still with my former French playmates. Whenever we played at war with pretend swords and valiant steeds, those English playmates regarded Napoléon as the great enemy and called the French 'Frogs.'"

Mr. James laughed at how puzzled he and his brave big brother had been. How could there be such a difference in the way the French and English boys treated them, when the two brothers were the same two boys? Yet I heard in his voice how he had felt the English boys' distance when he was young. Perhaps it was that he and the Professor were American boys not in regular schools that made them unpopular. Yet surely having Napoléon as your hero was not the way to win an English boy's heart.

Soon enough, his family moved again, this time back to America, to New York, then to Boston, and finally to Cambridge, where Henry, Sr. could write and discuss his ideas with the local Transcendentalists and host the visiting European worthies who might at last appreciate his strange, philosophical books.

One morning, the Master was dictating about how, as a very young boy, he first met among his father's visitors the famous greybeards, Mr. Emerson, Mr. Alcott, and Mr. Longfellow. Once, even the very aged Poet Laureate Alfred, Lord Tennyson came to visit. Mr. James was lost in his memories, describing his wonder and hero worship. His face took on an impish twinkle, as he abandoned his dictation, musing:

"When we were boys, we would recite the 'Idylls of the King' as a bedtime story, and here before us was the creator of that imagined kingdom. I had been scrubbed and brushed and dressed in my very best. I remember the jacket was a new one Papa had bought just for me on our way through New York City. My mother didn't approve, but I loved it—it was the brightest blue superfine cloth with the largest, shiniest brass buttons a young boy could desire.

"I could barely breathe that day when they brought us into the room where the famous author was sitting with my father. There was Lord Tennyson himself. He looked exactly like his pictures, with that long white beard and huge forehead. His eyes frightened me a little, deep-set under shaggy white brows. They bored right into me, it seemed. I wondered if Lord Tennyson could speak like other men, or if he would only speak in verse. I wanted to remember every word.

"I bravely spoke my memorised greeting with a stiff bow, and we all waited to hear what the Great Man might say. Lord Tennyson stared at me, then turned to speak to my father. The writer's deep voice sounded to me like what I imagined to be the voice of God."

There was a long silence, as I sat by the typewriting machine, listening. Then Mr. James lowered the pitch of his voice, as if he were Lord Tennyson: "'This boy—This boy is wearing the most amazing coat I have ever seen. Those buttons—they are majestic!'"

Mr. James was laughing as he told that story, and I laughed, too. Then the Master turned impish, saying, "And now I have a surprise for you, Miss Bosanquet." With that, he left the room.

A moment later, he was back, carrying a box, beaming at me. "Here! I knew I still had them." He opened the box and lifted out a framed photograph, which he proudly handed over to me.

"What do you think? Was I not the most handsome little boy ever, there in my new coat?"

In the photograph was a young boy proudly peeping out at me with his very handsome and well-buttoned jacket clearly visible. And there were the shiny brass buttons, gleaming out from the shadows of the old print, but as clear as the young boy's shy, sweet face.

"That's not all," Mr. James said, his words muffled as he leaned over, turning back to the box. He carefully lifted out a package in tissue paper, which he unwrapped. He opened out a small jacket and shook it.

"And lo!" he exclaimed. "Here is the very jacket! Here are the very buttons!"

Suddenly, all the years fell away. Before me was that smiling boy proudly showing off his buttons, wanting approval, waiting to be admired. It had made no difference—the passing years, the long-dead, disapproving mother, the strange, distant Papa with more ideas than heart. I could almost see for myself that small boy still trying to bring them all together, still hoping to be seen.

19

"The Ivory Tower"

April 1913 to 1914

Horton Crimper, among his friends Haughty Crimper, seems to me right and best, on the whole, for my second young man. I don't want for him a surname intrinsically pleasing; and this seems to me of about the good nuance. My Third Man hereby becomes, I seem to see, Davey Bradham; on which, I think, for the purpose and association, I can't improve.

—Henry James
Working notes for "The Ivory Tower"

There is something about birthday years with zeros in them that affect us all, even Mr. James. I noticed a change in his energy and focus as April 1913 drew closer and he would turn seventy. He had already surpassed his brother's age and was close to the age his father had reached. As Mr. James received more requests than usual for interviews and essays, I noticed he began to falter in the dictation of his memoir. He was more interested in the requests for new writing, new challenges. Plus, as I knew from typing the Master's correspondence with his agent, he once again worried about money. I had seen the signs before, when my employer stopped our work on one project only to delay picking up the next. For me, that faltering meant diminished income and my own fruitless search for other work.

One afternoon, Mr. James announced, after a dictation that was more halting than usual, "I'm going to take tomorrow morning for myself, Miss Bosanquet, and I have a new project for you. Actually, I believe it is Mrs. Wharton who has the project for you. She has requested your services for a few mornings, and you will begin tomorrow."

Part of me suspected a plan. Why was he trying to fob me off? Why would Mrs. Wharton need me? I'd never had any sense that Mrs. Wharton ever noticed me in all her chasing after Mr. James. I knew I was good at transcribing and taking dictation, but why did she ask for me when she had perfectly good servants and secretaries waiting for her at her huge house in Paris or accompanying her whenever she perched in the most elegant of London's hotels?

As I thought about the two of them, I began to feel a slow, deep anger. Why should I work for anyone but Mr. James? I was not a machine to be passed on, slightly used, when Mr. James no longer had need of me. I had already proved my competence at seeking other work when he had left me without making any arrangements for my well-being. But then, perhaps he never had wondered about me. Perhaps I was a part of the arrangements necessary for his working room, simply there, like the desk and the typewriting machine.

Nevertheless, the next morning I dressed with great care, choosing my newest white blouse and my cleanest blue skirt. I did my hair very carefully, using the new silver combs Clara had given me for my birthday. Yet I felt a murmur of resentment: Why should I care about what Mrs. Wharton thought about me or my looks? Still, I gave my boots another stiff brushing, picked up my notebook, and set off for Brown's Hotel.

Of course Mrs. Wharton was at Brown's, the most expensive, biggest, busiest of London's hotels, and of course Mrs. Wharton had the largest suite. Her maid answered the door, saying Madame was expecting me and led the way.

Apparently Mrs. Wharton was a late riser. She was waiting for me, still dressed in a grey lace-and-silk morning gown with silver ribbons and long, trailing sleeves. She was not as attractive as I remembered her from my few chanced glimpses. She looked older, and her skin was darker and more lined—she was no longer the radiant, vibrant woman I had seen at the train station with Mr. James and Mr. Morton Fullerton.

Now, she came to greet me with a handshake in that American way she had and gestured to a small table with even smaller chairs. "Come, sit here, Miss Bosanquet. I hope you'll join me in a *petit déjeuner*." She seemed to lean closer towards me to speak in her low voice, making me curious what work she needed my help with, but all this preliminary activity seemed to imply there was something else. I wondered if she and Mr. James were still close friends, if this had to do with Mr. Fullerton, whom I had seen leaving with her on the train two years before. She seemed almost conspiratorial.

As we sat down, her maid brought in a tray with a silver coffee-pot, a sugar bowl, rolls, three kinds of jam, and sweet butter, everything very Parisian.

"If you'd prefer tea," Mrs. Wharton said, "we have that for you as well."

Then Mrs. Wharton continued while I wondered how to go about eating and talking and listening at the same time, with such a small table between us.

"This is my usual time for breakfast, after my writing *au lit*." She nodded towards an open doorway, through which I could see a large bed, which looked strangely disheveled. Then I realised it was not that the bed had not been made up. No, the bed was covered with pieces of blue paper strewn randomly over its surface and even over the surrounding floor.

I was startled into asking, "Is that your writing?"

She nodded yes.

I leaned unconsciously towards the chaos, feeling, as anyone might, that I must help her right those surely mixed-up papers.

With a gesture, she stopped me.

"My secretary will be in soon. She'll collect and organise all this and type it up. You see, Miss Bosanquet, I also make use of the typewriting machine to speed my work. But now you must be wondering why I've asked Mr. James for your services this morning." She stirred her coffee and looked down, almost as if we were about to discuss something disreputable or shameful, a secret. Her voice became quieter. I had to lean nearer to catch her words.

"I'm sure you can be most discreet with what we are about to speak of here," and she looked up. When I nodded, she went on, "In your years with the Master, I'm sure you have seen enough to understand his hopes and disappointments."

I was ready to hear anything now. Was she to tell me of his personal affairs, of their unusual relationship? But no, it was the Master's writing that concerned her.

"He has revised and polished and then sent his great novels and stories again into the world, but they have not brought him the response he'd hoped for. I suppose you know about his old hopes for writing plays, for entering the dramatic world, how he'd hoped to make a success not only with the public but especially with his bank account?"

I nodded, for I remembered when I first came to work for Mr. James that his desperation to write for the stage was not only for the pleasure of the theatre but also because he worried about money.

Mrs. Wharton continued. "I believe, and this may surprise you, that he has worried about his finances for a long time. Even that last immense project, to collect all his work into one edition, even that was an attempt to improve his income. I think he is still worried."

I nodded, hoping to present myself as knowing but not too knowing.

"Miss Bosanquet, I'd like your help to change this situation for Mr. James. I have the good fortune to have sold a great many books and to have a most supportive publisher in Scribner's, who happens also, now, to be Mr. James' publisher. Together, our shared publisher and I have found a way to help our friend. We have arranged for the royalty payments from my most recent book to be offered to Mr. James as an advance payment of eight thousand dollars for his next project. I believe that he is finishing his memoir. Does he have another project in mind, an American novel? Am I correct? Would you reveal to me what he's working on? And do you think that this idea of mine might work for our dear, proud friend?"

"I don't believe—" I was struggling to find the words to make my response sound less incredulous. I could not believe anyone could or would offer such a large amount. Her largesse, her generosity, her nerve to imagine such a scheme, her having enough audacity to have already spoken with the publisher! I took a sip of coffee, drawing on the sweetness of cream and sugar. She needed me to answer. How could I pull all these alarms and doubts into some semblance of a reasonable response?

"Mrs. Wharton," I said finally, "this suggestion is so very kind, but to be honest, I can't imagine that Mr. James' new work would ever earn enough to pay back such a generous advance. I'm not sure that Mr. James would accept such an arrangement."

I stopped, unable to find more words without revealing Mr. James' great need for privacy, his deep sense of pride in spite of years of worries over money, his capacity for taking insult where none was meant, his great vulnerability at this moment of nearly completing his memoir. Oh, I was sure he would refuse this offer from another writer who was even more famous, from a younger writer, from a woman! Of course he would reject her.

Mrs. Wharton came back with an even more surprising suggestion: "We won't tell him."

I burst out laughing, but she went on.

"I know, though he's never said so, that you arrange all his business, attend to his correspondence, and so, you and I could do this and not let him know. You could let me know whenever he's sending finished work to his agent."

"But how do you know about my role? Have you talked with Mr. Pinker?"

"Of course! And Mr. James told me all about those months when you were the only contact with the publisher while the Professor was ill and after the Professor died, after Mr. James stayed on in America and never made contact. The publisher values your intelligence and your discretion at the highest, Miss Bosanquet. It was the publisher's idea that I should speak with you."

I felt wonderment at this whole scene. I was being asked to serve as the go-between for an arrangement to help Mr. James. I was being asked to serve as the one to make it possible for the

Master to finish the projects he had, maybe even a new novel. I have to be honest and say that I felt a surge of pride. Of course, Mrs. Wharton noticed my shift from scepticism to interest to agreement. She went on, making plans, arranging it all so thoughtfully that it seemed to me she had already settled everything before I agreed.

We finished laying out our plans. We shook hands on the results, and I took my leave, filled with wonder.

The walk back to Chelsea gave me time to grow more comfortable with the idea. I did think this might work, as long as Mr. James never got a hint. But to keep a secret from my long-time employer, one who saw everything, every impression, on whom nothing was lost, on whom nothing would be lost if the Master was truly, as I believed to be the case, as sensitive as his heroes. To do this, I would have to become more secretive and more subtle, even perhaps more like one of Mrs. Wharton's heroines.

The next morning, as I sat down with Mr. James, I was still wondering if I could keep all this hidden. He shuffled through his notes. He cleared his throat, as if to begin a long stretch of dictation.

"Miss Bosanquet," he said, setting his papers aside, "I wonder what project it is that my friend needs your help with, if you don't mind revealing your secrets to me?"

I almost gasped. How could he know what I had been thinking? Surely, he could not know.

"Was it something to do with her early-morning writings, those wondrous pages floating out from deep within her *boudoir?*" he asked, with a quick glance at my reddening face. "What project is it that she needs your help—our help—with, I wonder?"

I could not speak, I was that disturbed, unable to think of any sensible response.

"Oh, I know, I know. She wants you to keep it quiet. We writers don't like to reveal our ramblings when we're getting started. We are the most superstitious tribe." He looked at me again, as I continued to be unable to answer. His eyes twinkled. "Her methods are surprising, are they not?"

I suppose Mr. James must have thought I had reverted to our earliest days together, when I was so nervous with him that I could not say two whole sentences. Or did he think I was shocked that

Mrs. Wharton wrote in bed? Or perhaps shocked to learn that he knew she wrote in bed? To answer his question, I tried to think of something to say about her work. Did I even know anything about what she was working on? They were such good friends! He probably knew all the details, more than I did. I mumbled and hoped he would fill in my pauses.

"Yes, of course," he said. "It's something she doesn't want me to know about. Ah, you women and your secrets!"

I must have turned pale, for Mr. James chuckled.

"No, no, Miss Bosanquet, don't worry. I'll stop pestering you. You and I can go back to work," but then with a sigh he added, "though I am wondering what's the use of even trying again. They tell me no one wants to read long stories in serials running for more than two issues. Everyone's in such a hurry these days. Yet I have so many ideas for this one. It will be even longer! I wonder if I should approach Mr. Pinker to try our publisher again, for an advance and straight publication, straight to the book. This new tale might work that way, straight out as a novel, don't you think?"

I nodded in encouragement. He began pacing with his old enthusiasm. I took a breath and hurried to prepare the paper and carbon for Mr. James' dictation of his first ideas.

This was always an exciting moment for me, starting a new work. The room seemed filled with electricity, as if a storm were gathering. I bent to the machine, waiting. I realised I was holding my breath.

The Master began with a name. He often used the name of a character to begin his dictation of notes—but not the main character's name, no, he saved that for a few paragraphs into the piece. It was the process he had used with me many times before, from the first stories and novellas he mapped out for me whenever we needed a rest from working on his revisions and the New York Edition. This process had worked for him in years past. I was excited to find us here again at this same beginning point, and this time—at last— he was beginning a new novel.

Each time Mr. James had begun a new project, I had hoped it would be a novel, only to have my hopes dashed. I had felt despair when he returned from America the year before and was working on his brother's letters and the memoir, for I had wanted so much to be his audience, his assistant on another novel. I was afraid I had come to him too late. Many times while supposedly working up a short story with a restricted number of words, he would lament over his failure to keep within the limits prescribed, only to keep on going, making his tale as intricate and as long as he wanted, with no fear of his editors refusing him. I knew from the correspondence I had typed that the editors complained mightily as the number of pages grew astronomically. Yet every time the work remained a tale and not a novel.

I could feel his excitement for this new project. Mr. James had approached his publisher about an advance, and it worked! Eight thousand dollars! Mrs. Wharton was a genius to have thought of this support. Her arrangements made the spring and early summer of 1913 a period of good work for Mr. James and for us. She had made it possible for the Master to relax into his writing and forget financial difficulties.

He began calling this novel "The Ivory Tower," a phrase which in those days had not yet come to have quite the sense of precious isolation that it has since taken on. No, to him "The Ivory Tower" would have his meaning, something to do with the sanctity of the artist and his desirable retirement from the hurly-burly of commerce. As with his other titles, Mr. James had chosen this one less for its meaning out in the world than for the inner meaning contained within his tale, for its physical embodiment as a real, gleaming object of importance in the story and a symbolic object, but not to be obvious, not showy and barking its importance. Rather, the title hid the secret that underlay the story's plot complications and hid the letter revealing the origins of the enormous American grubby, ill-gotten, new wealth that would be the spring behind the plot.

But how ironic that his rich American friend's scheme had made this very novel possible. Could it be that the Master really did know?

And so in that spring of his seventieth birthday, Henry James was happily at work on a new novel, and I was happy to be there with him.

Mrs. Wharton tried other ploys to honour her friend on his seventieth birthday. She had been unable to obtain for him the Nobel Prize in Literature with its generous prize money, but her next idea was to write to his many friends and set up a fund in his honour. She actually began such a project, but before she succeeded, Mr. James got wind of it from his nephew in New York and frantically stopped it.

However, before he quite succeeded, his friends had collected quite a sum, enough for his old friend and the most expensive of portraitists, John Singer Sargent, to paint his portrait. Mr. Sargent refused to take his fee; the funds were used to present the Master with a "golden bowl," a teasing reference to his novel, but in fact this gift was a very handsome, silver-gilt reproduction of a Charles II cup on a salver. Mr. James graciously accepted the bowl and the offer of the painting. Indeed, he enjoyed many, many hours with his old friend, posing for that portrait. For me, however, those hours given over to the portrait were unpaid hours. Once again, I needed to find other work. I was glad he was dictating notes for "The Ivory Tower" not down in Rye but in our working room in Chelsea. In my off hours, I was able to keep up with my friends, serve as executive secretary of the Society for Psychical Research, and even have time for suffrage meetings.

Indeed, we Suffragettes had come back strong after that strange period of mourning and the "Suffragette Truce" following King Edward's death. The Women Writers Suffrage League's fierce desire to be recognised and heard in that most male domain inspired me. It seemed strange to be making plans for the marches and painting banners in the evening but to be back sitting at the typewriting machine and listening to the Master dictating the next morning—and stranger still when I had to soothe Mr. James after a Suffragette wielding a butcher's cleaver horribly slashed Mr. Sargent's painting of the Master at the National Portrait Gallery.

I found time to write my own short articles and book reviews, which my friends published. Sometimes there would be a longer break in Mr. James' work, when he was off to visit his young friends. Now back in London, he was swept up in the city's social life, especially with all the young men writers coming to him for recognition and praise. They wrote and called, they interrupted our dictation, they spirited him off for afternoons or whole weekends to visit with all those hungry, handsome young men in the countryside at Queen's Acre—Howard Sturgis's house on a single acre, which bordered Windsor Castle, hence the name, or "Qu'Acre," as they called it.

I suppose I was glad of the time for myself. I even attempted something longer of my own, a suffrage work I called "Lesbia." Though the prospect of so many pages to fill out and so many characters to create excited me, I felt daunted as well. What was this? A novel? A play? I wondered if I ought not to decide before I began. But then I felt urged on to write as I wanted by Mr. James' voice echoing in my ears from those mornings as he went on, sketching out his notes for "The Ivory Tower," celebrating his muse and his freedom now to write without restrictions. Was it his genius? Voices? Something he heard? Saw? Felt? His angel? His muse? Could I have it, or her, too? Was I a part of his muse? Or, for him, did speaking aloud release him, make it possible to write, to create?

Thinking my own thoughts, I typed steadily ahead while he struggled with beginning a new novel after so many years. He was newly inspired, newly energised. The dictations went slowly but steadily. It was as though he'd had the story deep within himself, waiting to be pulled out, and all he needed was to work out the details. I had never before worked with him on anything like this or a process like this, for these were notes, really notes. It seemed in the dictation as if he were trying a little of this, a little of that, a name, a place, seeking what followed what.

I liked how he set out each scene, for it was like a play, the way he structured his preliminary notes, how he sketched the scenes with the main characters in mind and then added other characters to build his story.

As he went on, I began to see what this project was going to be about, this new novel. But I worried that he was building the same old story of the sensitive young man lost among the predatory others, the story he had told in so many ways so many times. Here were good and evil again, America and Europe again, yet I could see superficial differences in these new characters. As the Master began to work his old magic, I could see how he changed his themes. This time, he turned the tale around and reversed his basic premise.

This time, it was the young American who had lived his whole life away in Europe, who was the pure, uncorrupted character, the heir, the artist-hero, while the enemy was the character who had stayed on in America to become very rich and corrupted not by Europe but, rather, by America's sudden wealth, its changing morality, the ease in grasping huge fortunes, money at the expense of others, using others for no other reason than to obtain great wealth. Ah! "The Ivory Tower" was going to be a different story. I grew very interested as the searching process of the notes unfolded. I felt proud and moved that I was to be a part of the process.

We worked hard at "The Ivory Tower" day by day in our rooms perched over our little, lively Chelsea streets. Mr. James worked steadily, dictating the whole outline and then settling into Book One. I felt his sense of urgency, which seeped into my own work during the book's early months in 1914. I began to write other pieces, all the while trying to finish "Lesbia," which had become a play. What I remember now is the sense of time rushing past, of wanting to send my own experiences out into the world, trying to express what we women, and especially we women writers, were feeling during those struggling days. There were afternoons when I left Mr. James and his dictation so that I could meet and work with the Suffragettes, my friends. The unfairness of our differences felt like a blow. We women wanted so little, yet the reactions against us were so massive, even brutal. Our efforts met with beatings, unjust arrests, even physical brutality as the gaolers shoved feeding tubes down the throats of the brave heroines who went on hunger strikes, when hunger and self-starvation remained their only resistance tool.

We in the Women Writers Suffrage League were working with women's organisations from every part of Britain. We would march and gather for speeches. But I think it was our writing that made the most difference. We wrote all the time, read each other's writing, commented, agreed, disagreed, and when we were able to, we published each other. There were not many women in positions where they could publish other women, for publishing was a man's world. Women graduates were still denied the degrees, labels, and connexions that Oxford and Cambridge provided male graduates. We women writers had few places to secure a toehold for even the smallest step up. We had to do whatever we could for each other.

I entered several pieces in a contest Naomi Royde-Smith and "Westminster Review" were sponsoring. There was to be a prize, ten pounds to the winner, quite an inducement in those days. The challenge was to write in the style of a famous author on subjects of the day. I wrote two different pieces and carefully hid my identity from my friend by using two made-up names. I even borrowed two different typewriters to mask my identities, and I posted my submissions from two different pillar boxes. My first attempt went well. Imitating Thomas Hardy was easy. I chose bleak subject matter and set the story in Wessex with bleak characters whose names were equally bleak. I sent my story in and began on my next entry. I wanted to try Mr. James' style, but how would I choose a suitable yet current topic?

At that time, the horrors of the Great War and the next war were yet to come. To us now, it might seem strange that I chose as my subject the failing diplomatic drama unfolding around us in the summer of 1914. But at that time the puzzling headlines seemed only to be incomprehensibly intricate maneuverings between civilised people, all of whom had known each other since childhood and had even played together as children. I knew from reading the society pages that these players had loved and envied and hated each other, had visited each other's country estates, perhaps even married and made secret diplomatic arrangements. The news and society pages did not point to a moral centre, a hero, or a heroine in those early days of broken promises, renewed alliances, and accusations. "Sabre rattling" still meant soldiers of friends and foes practicing on parade. Indeed, at that time before the horror, the socially connected intrigue among the highest class, which was so interconnected by personal and national history, could seem like an appropriate subject for a novel or late short story by Henry James.

I remember how excited I was, waiting to see the results of my two entries in Naomi's contest. I was disappointed the morning of the results. My parody of Mr. Hardy ran on the page for the runners up. That meant my Jamesian story had not made it, even though I had felt it was a much better entry. But wait! There was a notice printed near the first-prize winner's piece: "We're happy to announce a further prize, a grand prize-winner, and for reasons of space, will be printing this remarkable, quite good piece in tomorrow's paper—look for it!"

The next morning, I was the first to open the paper. There it was: "The Four Faces" in all its glory, and a fine paragraph from Naomi praising it.

I crowed over this with Clara and then folded the paper so that only its title showed. I tucked the newspaper under my arm and walked around the corner with my usual promptness. I thought I might somehow cleverly set the newspaper down in some conspicuous place so that my employer, whom I had so cleverly imitated, might happen upon it.

But this was not to be. The Master was already deep at it, pacing back and forth. I had to sit down immediately to my machine. I thought I would never have a chance to see his reaction to my cleverness.

That morning went at a furious pace. At our usual halfway break for tea, Mr. James came over to me with an amused expression and said we would be working on a little something new when we began again. After I had put fresh paper into the machine, I was startled to find myself listening to the remarkable sound of Mr. James dictating to me the first lines of my "The Four Faces."

We went on for a paragraph. Then he stopped, saying, "This one's very good as an imitation, don't you think, Miss Bosanquet?" I knew then that he suspected something, for he was laughing and shaking his head. I still could not tell whether the Master knew "The Four Faces" was my work. He went on to point out the various cleverness that he saw in the parody—the changing identities, the repetitions, the alliterations, all the usual things his friends and enemies parodied about his work.

"But this story is different," he said. "This writer has chosen a subject I have never dared to approach—the imperial line of succession and the intricate moralities of international diplomacy. She has taken it to a higher level, into realms I've never dared, higher even than Lord Milne and the House of Lords. It's the diplomacies

of imperial ambitions from the four allied countries. I wonder—"
He turned to face me. I held my breath. "I wonder if you know the
authoress. Tell me, Miss Bosanquet, is the author your charming
friend, Miss Clara Smith, the one who works for Lord Milne? She
would certainly have the right perspective for such a piece, and she
did replace you for a short time, I remember."

Clara! He thought the author was Clara. I was safe!

He went on. "I wonder if she'd like to know that I know and
admire her work—"

As I nodded yes, he began to dictate a letter to Clara.

Mr. James went on at such length praising Clara that I wondered if, after all, the Master had not lovingly ensnared me in one
of his intricacies. Perhaps he knew I did not want him to know that
I had written the piece, but he had wanted me to realise he had seen
it, admired it, and respected what I had accomplished. He would
have wanted me to know he had appreciated my having hidden my
identity so well, for, of course, if my name were known, "The Four
Faces" would become a subject for hilarity over the notion that Mr.
Henry James' amanuensis had won the grand prize by writing a
parody of her boss.

20

"The Sense of the Past"

Summer 1914–Autumn 1915

He disappears into the Past, and what he has wanted is that his companion shall know he is there ; shall be able to give that account of him if he is missed or wanted ; shall also perhaps be able to take in all, whatever it is to be, that may yet happen, and believe in his experience if he ever rises to the surface again with it.

—Henry James
Working notes for "The Sense of the Past"

We tried to keep on with life as normal when war was declared in August 1914. We all felt such a sense of unreality: This could not be a real war. This war would be over quickly, and then we would all go back to being England, France, Germany, Belgium, all of us return to being the mixture of friends, old schoolmates, ancient allies, and, for the Royals, even relatives. My friends in Germany wrote to say how distressed they were. They could not believe it, either. Each morning, the newspapers bore more evil news, while day after day the weather was ironically beautiful, each day more perfect than the one before.

The Americans kept out of the war, proclaiming peaceful-sounding rhetoric, baffled by our swift divisions into friends and enemies, all along the old lines. Only Americans were neutral. They were to be watched.

As an American, Mr. James became an alien noncombatant. He was required to report regularly and to register whatever whenever wherever he was going any time an official asked. Worst of all, Lamb House was no longer a sanctuary. Mr. James had to reduce his trips to Rye and could travel there only at restricted, prescribed times. Rye had become militarily important since the coast across the Channel nearly opposite Rye was the scene of some of the fiercest fighting. The little town of Rye filled with soldiers and military vehicles; the harbour was restricted, with the beaches swathed in barbed wire. Barriers and militia hampered any travel by road. It could take hours to pass all the check points and reach the town.

At first, Mr. James was angry, but as he began to follow the course of the battles, he grew interested in what was happening and was eager to observe. He wanted one last trip to Rye, and so we went, taking our bicycles for our favourite ride slowly down through the steep Rye streets, through the old Land Gate, and out towards Hastings. The golf course was deserted and showed signs of neglect. Some of the fairways had been turned back into pasture, with new fencing, wallow troughs, and manure piles.

We rode slowly. Though Mr. James was feeling better now that he could use nitroglycerine whenever he needed it for his heart, he had never recovered his old strength. We stopped to rest on the last sandy buttress raised to hold back the highest tides and propped the bicycles against a lone tree hanging precariously on the steep-sided levee.

"Can you see anything over there?" he asked as we scanned the Channel's hazy brightness of sea and sky, and, beyond the Channel, the War.

As our breathing stilled, I heard it, the low, dim booming, a constant visceral growl that could only be the guns. Even if we could not see, we could hear, and we could feel the horror. Mr. James was quiet. I waited for his words.

"I've only known wartime once in my life," he said quietly, haltingly. "It was when I was a young man, before I knew I was a writer. I did not go to war. Neither my older brother nor I went. But our younger brothers did. Oh, Wilkinson and Robertson were so excited and sure and manly and beautiful and strong. So young. It was our mother and father who urged them to go, my father and his theories, my father, who believed war would help his sons become strong. How terrible it must have been for my brothers, so young, to be sent off with hopes of becoming heroes and saving the Union. It was a terrible war, and they were hurt, wounded, frightened, starved, so far from home, so far from the safety we knew. Terrible."

He was quiet a moment, and I heard again the sound of the guns.

"And now it's come again," he said, "even here to Rye, even to us. Sitting here, I feel the War so keenly." He stopped talking and began again, more softly, more haltingly, reluctantly. To my surprise, he began talking about me.

"You know, Miss Bosanquet, I'm concerned for you. I want you to think about finding other work. I'm afraid I can't go on with 'The Ivory Tower.' It's not working. It's not right—my characters, my story. Not now. The War is here, our War, England's War. Readers over there in Boston and New York will not understand. I don't have the heart to go on with a story about America and its wealth. My heart is here. My country is here, my country is England. I'm even thinking of taking a step they will not understand back in America."

I sensed how desolate he felt and, if he were giving up his work, how desperate. He could not do that, he should not. No matter how terrible the War was, his work was important. I would have to find some way to help him shift away from "The Ivory Tower" and its now-awkward premise of a poor young man repulsed by America and its obscene greed. Mr. James' hopes for that novel would never work for him now, not with these feelings.

"Mr. James," I said, "my place is with you. With whatever work you are doing."

"But I know you need paying work. You need steady, paying work, especially now. I would like to keep on, but I can't be sure I have the heart for it, the push I would need to start anything else."

"Maybe," I said, stalling for time. "What if—Maybe if you went back to something not tied to the present time, maybe if you return to the novel about time travel. 'The Sense of the Past' is not about the present."

He looked away towards the sea, shaking his head, no, no.

"All these years," he said, "you've been working with me. You're still young, you have your own life to live. I would think you'd want to settle down somewhere, pursue something of your own."

"But," I protested, "this is my work! This is our work! I want to work on whatever you are writing, even if the work is not steady. For now, my work is with you, wherever you work, whatever it is that happens. We are fortunate: we work well together!"

There was a long silence. I ran my hand back and forth across the sand where we were sitting, smoothing it, smoothing it. The sound of the waves—that uneven, rhythmic hushing—seemed louder than the muffled explosions from across the water.

He took the silence as our final agreement. With a sigh, he said, "Well, then, I suppose it's settled. You are right. We're fortunate, I'm fortunate. I'm glad. But now, we'd better go back. I'm afraid I'm rather tired."

"I know an easier way." We mounted the bicycles, and I led the way round on the flat to the Land Gate. Soon, we were home again.

On the train up to London, as Mr. James slept in his corner, I thought over our conversation. I wondered how I had been strong enough to step out of my usual role. What had I done? "Our work," I had said! But it was true: The Master needed me. He had needed me from our first days, but now, he needed me even more.

On the spur of the moment, I had come up with an idea, another way back to the writing he had begun that could avoid the present chaos and confusion. Instead, we could work on "The Sense of the Past," set long ago in that *"palpable imaginable visitable past"* he had enjoyed creating in many of his stories. That novel's imagined premise of time travel would take us even further and further from the day-to-day struggles of the unreal autumn of 1914.

Yet when we returned to London, the manuscript for "The Sense of the Past" was nowhere to be found. Mr. James had apparently left it at Lamb House in Rye. I went back to the grim, closed-up house and began my search, even including the Garden Room, but with no luck. Then I remembered one last place—the tall, wooden cabinet behind his writing desk. But it was locked, and the key was not hanging with the others. I did not have much time before my train would depart to figure out where he might have left the key. I wished for Nellie and our combined psychical powers to see where the key might be. I stood quietly there in the dark and then sat in his chair and stared at his desk. It came to me. I opened the small drawer on the right. Yes, the key was there. I opened the cabinet and found the manuscript with all the pages he had dictated. They were stacked and tied up, exactly as I had left them.

Now, we had another novel with a manuscript to work on. We spent the mornings in his sunny rooms in Chelsea, and then in the afternoons, while I typed the new pages and his increasing correspondence, Mr. James found other work to do in wartime London. The city was crowded with the War's first casualties and refugees from Belgium. Mr. James would return from his afternoon walk filled with stories of conversations with refugees and wounded young soldiers. He was very concerned for the children and the women who had lost everything. He began to write essays again, this time an article about the Belgians in our midst, which was well received.

As the War went on and on, Mr. James began to visit the soldiers' hospital nearby to talk with the wounded young men. He took small presents, sweets, and comfort. He wrote their letters for them. A young journalist heard of Mr. James' work on behalf of the refugees and the wounded. He asked for an interview with the famous, elderly novelist, who was not even English, who was doing his part. Mr. James was charmed by the young man and apparently charmed him in turn, for the reporter returned several times to add to his story. One day, Mr. James handed me several of the young man's pages and asked me to take dictation: he had a few words to add to the journalist's article. After nearly an hour, the article had grown from a few to many, many pages, but Mr. James was pleased.

"There!" he said. "Now, our journalist friend has the story exactly as it happened, as I described it to him."

I could only smile, wondering how the young journalist would explain his strangely enlarged assignment to his boss. Nevertheless, the article with Mr. James' amendments was printed, and it brought Mr. James even more letters.

The War was not over by Christmas, as we had hoped, not at all; instead of letting up, the battles seemed to be growing more deadly. There was talk of how America would have to enter the War soon. England sent her most capable and wealthiest politician, Lord Rhondda, to meet with the Americans, but the Yankees held back. They even held back after the Germans torpedoed the *Lusitania,* the neutral passenger ship carrying Lord Rhondda and his daughter back home. The *Lusitania* sank off the Irish coast, within sight of the fishermen and rescuers who rushed through heavy, cold seas to save as many passengers as possible.

Mr. James pointed to the newspaper story with its photograph of the young woman wrapped in blankets, reunited with Lord Rhondda after a long night. He wondered if I had ever met the wealthy diplomat's daughter, Margaret, who was a leader of Suffragettes in Wales. I looked at her brave face in the photograph and said I wished that I had met her! He smiled.

"Someday," he said, "you'll come to know her. I'm quite sure."

As the winter went on, more and more young men were called up or volunteered. It was strange for us women. We had worked so long and hard to obtain the Vote, to retain our own property, to earn academic degrees like the men, and then to be paid a proper wage. All our efforts were thrown aside; everything was about the War. In a burst of patriotism, we women cancelled our suffrage marches; even our regular assemblies and meetings ceased.

Women everywhere turned away from each other and returned home, turning towards our brothers and cousins and lovers as they were leaving for War. I went to my aunt's house to be there with my cousin, Victor, on his last home leave before he was sent over. Victor was my favourite boy cousin. Like his sisters, I was in tears. By then, we knew the War was not going well. More and more often, we saw shades drawn over windows; more and more often, we saw families dressed in black. Like so many other families, our family bravely sent our Victor off. That night, I returned to the flat, feeling especially low.

As the weeks passed, I watched Mr. James also lose his enthusiasm for the War. Nevertheless, with much heartiness, he helped his young manservant, Burgess, prepare to go by paying for his kit and shaking Burgess' hand most manfully on that last morning. Still, I could tell Mr. James felt uneasy on little Burgess' behalf.

My psychical abilities haunted me. Everywhere around me, there were losses and sorrow and ghosts. Not that I was actually seeing ghosts, but I often had that edgy feeling. One night a few weeks after Cousin Victor had left, I awoke in the dark, sure that I had heard something, felt something. A few days later, the word came that Victor had been killed. Then Mr. James' Burgess returned from battle, wounded, peppered with shrapnel, and deaf. The Master visited him in Leicester when he could, taking Burgess every little comfort: special soaps, soft clean pajamas, his favourite candies—bulls' eyes peppermints, bags and bags of them. Mr. James would say again and again, "It feels as though I can't do enough for him, poor little fellow. I should have kept Burgess back. He is so young, so small."

"But you couldn't have," I would say. "They all have to go."

"I know. Burgess is so proud to have served!"

"What's to become of him?" I asked, measuring my words.

"I'll have Burgess back here! That is, if he wants it!"

Several months later, Burgess returned to us, his deafness abating.

I believe it was Burgess who led Mr. James to envision his own sacrifice, to feel that he, too, had to do something.

One morning, I arrived at work to find Mr. James dressed very formally, ready for some important occasion. He showed me the text he had prepared for me to type while he would be out for a few hours, but he gave no more explanation of what was taking him away from our routine. I did the few tasks, a little retyping of his arrangements with his agent for his new book. I was finishing that work when the Master returned, all bustle and pomp.

"Well, I've done it!" he announced. "I'm an alien no more! Miss Bosanquet, I'm proud to announce that I've been made a citizen of your country!!"

He and I brought in Burgess and Kidd, the cook he had in London. We, his long-time English help, proposed a toast with our tea. The Master told us about the ceremony, a private one arranged for him by his friends, Prime Minister Herbert Asquith and the minister's wife, Countess Margot Asquith, right there in the prime minister's office. Mr. James explained that his new citizenship would not change much, and it should not be such a surprise. Ever since the Great War started, he had been feeling more and more like he was part of our poor, beleaguered country. America's cold, slow response to our plight had only made it clearer to him that his heart was with us in England.

We were all surprised that his naturalisation created such a press clamour. Yet Mr. James remained steady through it all, including the recriminations from American papers. I noticed that his letters from Cambridge, Massachusetts, and New York City were fat and numerous. I could imagine what his family was saying.

We kept to our old rhythm of working in the mornings, even though his health was precarious as the autumn of 1915 shifted into winter. He suffered three bouts of pleurisy and a painful recurrence of the shingles. Yet he kept on with his work and with his visits to the men in hospital. Nothing was changing in the trenches, except that there were more and more young men to visit in hospital, more drawn shades, and more and more families dressed in black. It was a dark time. Only Mr. James' writing seemed to brighten his mood.

Part of my own urgency during those last weeks of his life and of our work came from the outcry that overwhelmed him, overwhelmed us, overwhelmed his work and our work, as his family and friends from across the ocean turned on him viciously, their horrible tirades rejecting him as the treasonous turncoat who had spurned their American purity and holiness. We Europeans, we English had corrupted him. Yet though the Americans rejected Mr. James as evil, he received accolades from English newspapers.

He never spoke directly to me about what his former countrymen were writing. Still, I could not help but see that he was faltering in his work.

One morning, I came in early and found a copy of the "New York Sun," which I read while I waited. Then I understood. Of course, Mr. James would not be able to write after the terrible things they accused him of, even saying his writings—all his writings—all his great work was nothing but the silly scribbling of an effeminate expatriate. He did not matter. He was not even an American. He had probably never, ever been an American.

Several of his English young-men friends were very sweet. They knew how he had suffered from being so unlike the ideal American man. They supported him in his loyalty to his adopted country.

I am sure it was part of Mr. James' reticent nature not to display his passions, not to be seen going around with anyone or to have some handsome young man come to Lamb House or come to Carlyle Mansions. From my time with the Master, I knew of only one or two possible special friendships. Of course, I knew about Morton Fullerton, but I had wrongly appraised that relationship. The Master's secrets were safe, even from me. Yet I do believe Mr. James knew about me and even encouraged my love affair with my beautiful painter, Nellie. Perhaps my risking social censure with Nellie explained my years of work with Mr. James, for no other woman spent as much time with the Master.

Mr. James' other friends also rallied to support his naturalisation. Mrs. Wharton once again came to his rescue, as she had many times before, when he had been struck down by illness, by a lack of understanding, by rejection, even by depression. As the storm over his defection and his apparently abandoning his country rose around us, Mrs. Wharton's intervention once again buoyed Mr. James. The threats from German torpedoes and the stalemated War in France made it impossible for Mrs. Wharton to come over from Paris, but what a wave of letters and wires she sent. One morning I was startled to find Mr. James holding a letter out to me.

"From Mrs. Wharton?" I said.

"Yes," he said. "This one's for you. She enclosed it in one for me."

Later, when I was by myself, I opened the letter. I found that Mrs. Wharton had addressed me as the most intimate of conspirators. She had bounced back from the disappointment of Mr. James' aborted birthday fund-raising surprise and wanted me to correspond with her directly, to report to her on Mr. James' health and spirits. And, she said, she had enclosed something for me. Out of her feminine envelope fell a money order, more than I had seen in a long time, enough to pay for all the wires I would ever need.

I tucked the money order away. Later that day, I replied to Mrs. Wharton that I would try, that Mr. James did seem even more alone than ever, that he did need us, and I would be her agent with him, to find for him whatever he needed, watch over him and his household, his health, and report back every few days or weekly.

I did feel a bit disloyal to Mr. James. Oh dear, what if he knew! But I thought Mrs. Wharton was right. There was no one else in England to keep watch over and help the Master now that the War was stretching on and on and now that contact with his family back in America was uncertain.

"I'm puzzled about this story," he said several days later. "Am I wandering more? It seems harder to bring my characters to make their point. Each scene seems to spread and spread, more and more with every minute."

I started to speak, but he lifted his hand as if to stop me.

"Miss Bosanquet, you're a writer. After all these years, I realise how I've made use of you unconsciously." With a pleading look, he asked, "Is it true that this novel is going nowhere? Am I going around in circles, wasting my time, wasting your time? Shouldn't I give it up during this War of Horrors? Who wants to read a story about long ago, a ghost story that's meaningless to anyone but myself?"

"Oh, no!" I protested. "What you're writing is very important because, these days, everything else is so unreal. The real has become the horror. You know this from your long conversations with the wounded. Don't you see? Your writing takes us to another place, another time, where today's horrors don't exist. 'The Sense of the Past' reminds us that we don't have to be trapped by today's world of circumstance and guilt. Each of us can be like your hero, can step back and see more, see another possibility, see other possibilities."

That was as long a speech as I had ever made to my employer. He looked away, gently shaking his head, no, no.

I tried another tack. I picked up the stack of typed pages and slowly fanned them, fanned them again until I saw the page I wanted. "Here, let me read you a passage from your notes about your hero's hopes for a relationship with Nan. This writing is so far from the War, so close to our daily lives. This might show you what I mean." I found the section where Mr. James was contemplating what his hero must do:

I want to make it that this "nothing" is but the fact of his seeming to feel more confidence, as it were, the harder and the harder, that is the more wonderingly and conceivingly, so to speak, he looks at her. I don't want to drag out such indications more than they will bear, this being already at the longest stretch; but can't I put in still, for firmness of ground promptly provided, that the <u>search</u> of her, even though still mute, though I abuse of what mutely takes xxxxx [sic] place, puts, or glimmers its promise of putting, the <u>relation</u> with her on a different sort of basis, and so, and so, begins to give me the key, the pitch, begins to slide them into what is to come.

How strange, I thought, for me to be telling Mr. James what to do by reading to him what he himself had written!

But this effort also made no difference. The Master bent forward, as if exhausted, still shaking his head, no, no.

I felt haunted. Days passed. I could feel the change: As the Great War wore on, the Master was abandoning his own inner war.

He set aside the novel and spent his days writing to his remaining friends in America, urging them to support America's entry into the War. He wrote articles for the papers, he wrote letters-to-the-editor, but to him, all this felt useless. Often, when I would arrive at the flat to work, I would find that the Master had already given up for that day. He would ask, instead, if I would walk with him, for he needed more and more exercise to keep up his heart.

Our walks were slow and strangely without direction.

21

"The Altar of the Dead"

December 1915

"Why, they 're Dead, sir—dead these many years."
"Indeed they are, sir, alas," I could but reply with spirit ;
"and it 's precisely why I like so to speak of them!"

—Henry James
Preface to "The Altar of the Dead"
The New York Edition, volume 17

Mr. James' spirits in those December days were low, and he suffered a return of his old illnesses, particularly his stomach. With each new death, each funeral, he would stop eating, stop writing, stop walking. I remember how sad and discouraged Mr. James was when he came back from the beautiful funeral in Westminster Abbey for the recently killed young poet, Wilfred Owen. Once again, the writing helped. This time, the request was for an essay—a serious, extended essay on Wilfred Owen. Mr. James set everything else aside and began immediately.

The Master had had a difficult time that autumn. His visits to the wounded in hospital had tired him, and his worries over becoming a British citizen added more stress, paper-work, and intense discussions with his friends. Finally, all that was behind him. Then, one morning, Mr. James was floundering in his dictation, his words somewhat slurred. He paused, then stopped. By this point in our work, he was no longer pacing. He usually sat as he dictated. That morning, he let his notes settle onto his lap. I waited, attentive, but the words would not come.

Then, on December 2, when he was in a more cheerful frame of mind, he was felled by a stroke, with some temporary paralysis. He had awakened to a strange feeling and fell when he tried to stand. He called for help. Between them, Burgess and Kidd lifted Mr. James back to bed and made him comfortable. They called his doctor and sent for me in my Lawrence Street rooms nearby. I hurried over. It was shocking to see the Master there in his brown woollen robe, slightly rumpled hair, with such an expression of dismay.

I cabled right away to his family, so far from London and from our struggles with the War. Mrs. James wired back immediately that she was determined to risk all perils to come over. She had promised Professor James that she would look after his brother. She would be on the next ship sailing, war or no war. We could expect her the following week.

That stroke passed rather quickly. By that afternoon, Mr. James was able to talk with us quite lucidly, and we even did a bit of work on his essay about Mr. Owen. But the next day was worse. A second stroke made it difficult for Mr. James to move, yet he retained his speech.

Then, one morning, I awoke to yet another dark, windy dawn. The winter storms were still arriving one after another, and the wet, cold streets seemed empty as I walked the few blocks to Carlyle Mansions to be with Mr. James. Burgess let me in. I knew immediately from Burgess' grim silence that it had been a bad night, for Burgess had none of his usual smile and shared jokes. The doctor was leaving.

"It's bad, Miss Bosanquet," the doctor said. "Perhaps another stroke. I hope his family will arrive soon. I don't think he's going to pull out of this one."

"What should we do?" I tried to cover the anxiety in my voice.

"Whatever he wants or needs to make him comfortable. Let him tell you if he can."

That week, we tried our best to keep Mr. James' household working in a normal fashion, but it was difficult. Everything was upset, confused, and there was no money, for Mr. James could not write clearly, not even to sign a cheque. Yet we established a daily rhythm. In the morning, Burgess took care of the bathing and dressing, and Kidd fed Mr. James. In the afternoon, the Master and I went on with his work. At any point in the day, Burgess and I would bring out the typewriting machine, and I would take his dictation to calm him whenever he felt agitated or lost. His great mind was wandering, as Mrs. Wharton and I had most dreaded.

And sending Mrs. Wharton the news—How I dreaded that.

Dictation seemed to work. He would become lucid and reconnect to the work he had been doing at the time of the stroke. He did not want to add corrections to the Owen essay, but rather, he wanted to return to "The Sense of the Past," the time-travel novel he had set aside. I brought out the notes, but he dictated without looking at them. The scenes he spoke are muddled. The dialogue between the hero and the woman he loves is problematic. He left some sentences incomplete. Readers will surely misunderstand some sentences. He left some deep feelings hidden. He discarded phrases. The text is misty and disconnected.

I kept trying to bring him back to some real, physical aspects of what he was writing, but he would brush away my words and questions. He knew what he wanted to write. He did finish the Owen essay, a beautiful memorial. With that essay, Mr. James became an English voice for great loss. We English welcomed the Master's words, which comforted, healed, and inspired us.

As the days passed, the damage of the strokes became more apparent. He lost his way more often, and his speech grew less clear. Sometimes he would be gruff and not want to work; sometimes he would be most insistent that we record it all. We in the house followed the Master's lead as best we could understand him. With Burgess and Kidd and the nurses helping, we lifted him and carried him wherever he wanted to go. He liked best to be out of his bedroom, sitting up on a day-bed in the dining-room with its windows looking out over the river and the trees along the Embankment.

As we in the household waited for his sister-in-law and niece to arrive, the Master's thoughts sometimes made a kind of sense yet were confused. He wondered about Mrs. James' travel across the sea. Would she arrive soon? Was all in readiness for her? He confused places—London, Boston, Paris—and mixed up times. He had forgotten that a war, the Great War, prevented quick jaunts across the Channel or back and forth to America.

At last, on December 11, we received a telegram announcing his sister-in-law's expected arrival two days hence. The flat was immediately in a bustle, everyone polishing, dusting, hurrying to be ready.

Mr. James and I were sitting quietly in the midst of this commotion when, from the other room, we heard a great crash of something heavy—china or glass—that had fallen and broken.

"Oh, no!" Mr. James called out. "What is it?"

I hurried to check and found the maid with the pieces of a large broken platter in her hands. "It is only one of the plates," I said to reassure Mr. James. "No one's hurt."

"Please tell me it's not one of the Paris plates!" he moaned. In fact, it was one from a set he'd had since he was a boy. I thought I might distract Mr. James by showing him his sister-in-law's telegram. "Mr. James," I said, "I'm not sure you had a chance to see this. Do you see that her ship arrives tomorrow?" I read the telegram to him. He was silent. He sat leaning against the pillows, propped up. He still seemed agitated, staring out the window at the ships moving up and down while icy rain rattled against the blurred glass.

Burgess and I thought we might try the typewriting machine again, this time with a letter. Its familiar *tap-tap* had seemed to help Mr. James feel more at ease during those weeks of struggle after his first strokes. I sat at the typewriting machine and rolled in two sheets of fresh paper. I spoke quietly, hoping to soothe him:

"Shall we begin again where we left off the last time? What would you like?"

A ravaged face turned to me, his beautiful eyes now haunted, red-rimmed, crusted.

"Can we—Do you know where we stopped? No, I want to—"
He paused, frustrated. His brow furrowed in concentration. His
right hand, partly paralysed, was jerking up and down, almost as if
he were leading a phalanx of soldiers marching in time. He seemed
to be drifting back to childhood years, when he and William and
the French boys they lived among had played at being Napoléon.
He began to speak, to dictate:

> *They pluck in their terror handfuls of plumes from the
> imperial eagle, and with no greater credit in consequence
> than that they face, keeping their equipoise, the awful
> bloody beak that he turns round upon them. We see the
> beak sufficiently directed in that vindictive xxxxxxxxx
> [sic]intention, during these days of cold grey Switzerland
> weather, on the huddled and hustled after campaigns of the
> first omens of defeat. Everyone looks haggard and our only
> xxxxxxxx [sic] wonder is that they still succeed in "looking"
> at all. It renews for us the assurance (divinity) that doth
> hedge a king. . . .*

He lay back against the pillows and coughed a dry, harsh cough.
Then he turned towards me, chuckling, lifting his hand but not
like a man directing a march. For a few moments, he spoke with
surprising lucidity:
"Miss Bosanquet, did you ever think I would write such an introduction!? My sister-in-law would lock me up if she saw this one!"
I smiled at his staid yet whimsical comment in what was to be
our last shared joke of friendship. I read Mr. James' words back to
him. He was still the Master, the child/man in the captured memory with his own acute observation and clarity, as if he were sitting
once again, dictating from his wicker chair.
Mr. James smiled. "I wonder what made me think of that
scene from so long ago, from when we were playing at Kings and
Queens—" He was as alert as ever, each word clear, nary a muddle.
"We must have read every book ever written about the Emperor.
How fascinated I was with Napoléon when I was a boy, when all of
Paris was formed by his influence. The Emperor's motto, his golden

insignia emblazoned on every royal entry, on every black iron gate or doorway." He paused, breathed deeply, his voice still clear and strong, determined, even commanding. "I remember so well how we children fought over who was to be the Emperor, over who would write out the imperial decrees and copy Napoléon's signature. Well, that introduction is a good start—"

Mr. James closed his eyes, seemingly exhausted by his effort.

I wondered where this strange communication had come from. In the meetings of the Society for Psychical Research, I had heard reports of the white light, that last image seen as we die. I had also heard stories of people in their last moments, who saw their long-deceased loved ones waiting for them and calling out their names. Was this a response to such a calling out?

I usually made a carbon copy of everything Mr. James dictated, and that morning was no exception. As I rolled out the two sheets of white paper and removed the carbon, I wondered if Mr. James would ever look at this piece of his writing. Would he ever revise it for me to type again? I looked over to the day-bed, where Mr. James was lying sideways, his eyes closed, his mouth slack, a little twisted still with the partial paralysis from the stroke. Was this paper the record of his last words, his last thoughts? If this dictation were going to be his last, even as strange as it was, would those words someday come to mean something more?

I took the pages to our working room. I felt an inconsolable sadness when I looked around at the air of disuse, an unkempt feeling I knew so well. The room was not dusty or disordered, but it felt as though life had left it empty and echoing, as if everything of his life had already moved out. It is probably silly to think of a room as alive, but looking around at his wicker chair with its usual cushion, the battered black and vermeil inkwell on the dark wood table, I felt a shiver. I knew he would never come back. He would never again sit at that table, writing.

I set the original of that dictation on top of the few recently dictated pages and the waiting revisions and corrections. I placed the carbon copy between two pages of my note-book to carry safely home. I had the strong feeling that even I would not see that room again for a long time.

As I waited out that quiet afternoon two days before Mrs. James was to arrive, I wondered: Did the Master believe in the Afterlife? In the haze and weakness left from his stroke, was he lost between This World and the Next? As the daughter of a minister, I had taken down other deathbed messages and knew that last words are often recorded without the listener realising her role. Yet as I tucked away that carbon copy, I had every hope of helping Mr. James return and continue dictating.

That step was furtive and not what I had been trained to do, but some deep urge drove me: I cannot really say that I wanted it for my research on behalf of the SPR, for at that time I was doing very little research. No, the tug came from a far deeper empathy between speaker and listener, between the speaker and his addressed audience of beloved siblings at a dark distance, and between the speaker and the listener sitting attentively nearby.

22

"The Death of the Lion"

February 1915

*How can one consent to make a picture of the preponderant
futilities and vulgarities and miseries of life without the
impulse to exhibit as well from time to time, in its place,
some fine example of the reaction, the opposition or the
escape?*

—Henry James
Preface to "The Death of the Lion"
The New York Edition, volume 15

The confusions, misunderstandings, and bitterness started
the afternoon of the arrival of Mrs. William James, tired,
chilled, and bearing a most critical attitude. I was there at the flat
with Mr. James' staff to meet her. We began all wrong, all three of
us trying to talk at once. Then in her most chilling with-servants-
I-know-best tone, Mrs. William James ordered us all about, Kidd
back down to the kitchen, Burgess out to search for the rest of their
boxes and trunks, and for me: "Miss Bosanquet, you are dismissed
for today. You may return tomorrow at eleven, when I will instruct
you on your further duties."

With that, after years of cordiality, including when I had helped
Mr. James host Peggy, her daughter, Mrs. William James turned
away from me, as if I had become a speck of dust to be brushed
aside and forgotten.

From that point on, for days and weeks, I knew little of Mr. James from my own impressions. Instead, I often learnt what was happening from his friends, as they contacted me, wanting to talk, hoping that I might know more. From them, I learnt that the family's first actions were to remove the Master from the front rooms of his flat, where he had so enjoyed the light and had been comforted to have his staff and his visitors around him. Mrs. William James hired more nurses—strangers—to watch after him night and day. She could pay for such services by signing his cheques.

All I could do was wait and think and remember. I was glad I had been there to take down his last dictations and, the day before Mrs. James' arrival, take down the Master's strange two letters to his deceased older brother and his sister. I was glad I could be there for him in those few final days of lucidity, yet I was left to puzzle out the meaning of those letters: Did they pull together threads of his life in a way we, each of his friends, had missed, having seen only one thread at a time? Were the two letters that followed his description of *"plumes from the imperial eagle"* any less or more meaningful than other deathbed moments, with their solemn reaching for those who have gone before?

I still felt how much I wanted to protect him: I knew Henry James in a way no one else could, not his friends, not even Mrs. Wharton, and especially not his family. But I was helpless, powerless. As an outsider watching the comings and goings, I perceived that his family was embarrassed by Mr. James, alarmed by his friends, and even distrusted the poor, wounded soldiers Mr. James had visited in hospital during those last months. I heard about the many people who came to his door to ask after him, many of whom were turned away without thanks or even a kind word. Some turned to me after there had been a notice of his illness in the paper, but I had to tell them I knew nothing more. I, too, it seemed, was locked out.

Looking at the carbon copies of the final dictation and the two letters that I had kept from those two days brought back the pain not only of losing him, dear friend to me that he had become. No, the pain was more about the pushing away, his family's rejection of me and of all I stood for and the loss of all Mr. James had tried so hard to create, encourage, display. Openness to all experience, to all consciousness—that was his religion, his passion. Mrs. James' small minded-ness was a sharp reminder of how the world was, how his memory, his passions, his work would be mauled and torn by those who thought there was something wrong with a writer who did not want to be popular, did not want to write like everybody else, did not care to be easy to read.

Poor Mr. James, isolated in his confusion, his way lost, was wholly dependent on his sister-in-law, who refused to acknowledge Mrs. Wharton because she was a Fallen Woman, the subject of gossip but not because Mrs. Wharton's husband had taken an expensive house in Boston for his mistress. No, the reason was Mrs. Wharton's independence, her insistence on living apart, outside her own country and in, of all places, Paris. And Mrs. Wharton wrote books. And such books! No, Mr. James' friends were not fit people for his sister-in-law. And so, the Master spent his last days without visitors, without news reaching his friends, without their gentle words reaching him.

Mrs. Wharton continued to write to me for word of him, but now her letters came to Lawrence Street. I had to answer that I, too, was being kept away, that my news came only from neighbours. Mrs. William James did call to ask for my help several times during that long month of Mr. James' passing but never for me to come and see him. No, it was as though they were ashamed of his state, of his weakness. They had no idea about how many of us loved him.

I was surprised when Mr. James' niece, Peggy, arrived in London. She came over to my room to ask for help with Mr. Gosse, who had insisted that they needed to answer what Peggy called "some official sort of rubbish, a summons or something." She brought me to the flat and the empty dining-room, the table piled high with unopened mail. They handed me a huge envelope with the Royal crest embossed in scarlet and gold.

"You must know how to answer this sort of thing," Mrs. William James said. "Tell us how to put these people off. I can't be bothered with such foolishness." Then she mumbled something about "never having had any such attention for dear Professor James" and left me in wonder to break open the Royal seal.

Inside, sent directly from the prime minister's office along with Prime Minister Asquith's personal note was a most amazing summons for Mr. Henry James, Gentleman, to appear at Buckingham Palace to receive the highest award possible for a literary man, the Order of the British Empire! Our Mr. James was to be knighted by the country he had recently joined as a citizen. How proud Mr. James would be. Then, with horror, I noticed the envelope's date: it had been sent two weeks before! The family had held this noble proclamation from the King for more than a week! I was furious that they could be so rude, so insulting to our country, so insulting to Mr. James and to his great work. I was further furious that I could not even begin to express or explain the *faux pas* to two silly Americans, who knew nothing, NOTHING of England, of our traditions, of our long history of honouring our writers. We wanted to honour Mr. James, but his silly, jealous sister-in-law was trying to prevent us, because Professor James had never been so honoured.

I realised I had to calm down, or I would be of no help to Mr. James and would also harm myself.

I went to find Mrs. William James and Peggy, who were seated in his dressing-room, sorting through the Master's clothes as he lay in the next room. I gave myself a shake and asked meekly, "Might I speak to you a moment about this 'summons'?"

They nodded yes.

I began with how important a figure Mr. James had become in his adopted country, how much we respected and honoured him. The envelope, I said, was an official document. I explained knighthood.

They spluttered, went off on some foolishness of "above himself" and not the "American" way and how the Professor never wanted any of that rigmarole.

I merely stood and nodded. My approach, the only way I could see to persuade them, was to insist that the polite and proper thing to do, even for an American, was to respond to the letter and to accept the invitation. Even the least of invitations deserves a response, I said, and since Mr. James was the person to whom the invitation had been addressed, we should make every effort to ask him what he wanted.

That worked. I marched past the two women, bearing the formal envelope and letter with all its golden imprints and seals and presented it to Mr. James, who was sitting up with his covers tucked around him.

The Master welcomed me and took the envelope. With glee, he read the good news from his old friend, Mr. Asquith. He agreed to accept and asked me to see to it. Imagine! I could tend to the details to arrange for the Master, for Mr. Henry James, to accept his position as a Knight of His Most Royal Majesty in the Order of the British Empire, to join the ranks of our other famous writers.

Yet I was also frustrated, since I had waited for weeks to be asked, knowing how many projects the Master and I had left incomplete. Probably much of that pile of unopened correspondence was from his agent, Mr. Pinker, or perhaps even from publishers and editors. I knew Mr. Pinker wanted to bring out a volume of Henry James' letters right away. He had told me before how many of Henry James' friends he had heard from. They all seemed to have been saving their letters for such a book.

Then there were the several volumes in progress. I was able to complete Mr. James' introductory essay for the Rupert Brooke poems, since I had taken that project back to my flat before I was kept away. I was well-meaning, but the day I arrived to ask for a sheet of Mr. James' letterhead to send the essay off, Peggy let me know that I gave her the impression of being above myself.

That was bad enough, but then came the day the first copies of a reprint of one of his earlier American novels, "Roderick Hudson," were delivered to me at Carlyle Mansions. Mrs. William James wanted to order many more copies to distribute. I intervened. The book was hideous, a cheap edition full of errors, and Mr. James would have hated it. I was sharply reprimanded by Peggy, who seemed to feel again that my efforts were a presumption on the part of a lowly secretary.

Of course, it took some time to arrange the ceremony for the Order of the British Empire. By the time the appropriate English officials could present the Order to Mr. James, he was spending more and more time in bed. There were still moments when Burgess and Kidd saw a spark of his old brightness, such as when the dining-room door was stuck and the Master stammered, "The door will be all right, as long as Kidd and Burgess, who are invaluable, are on the same side as myself."

Yet, as I made the arrangements for the official presentation at Mr. James' flat, I had no way of knowing how he would be. I had set the time for the morning, when he would be awake. The presentation was to be very brief. I had insisted to the family that there be some sort of formality. It would not do to have the Order of the British Empire presented to Mr. Henry James by way of the mail. I imagined that the James ladies might not even open the box but instead might fling it onto the pile of unanswered mail, as they had done with the official letter.

When the time came, I made sure I was there, and I invited in Burgess and Kidd. The nurses who were attending the Master stood about, and Mrs. William James and Peggy interrupted their business of packing up his things for a few minutes to stand at the doorway. In the midst of the War, the presenter was not the prime minister or even his assistant but, instead, two very handsome, young *aides-de-camp* in full-dress uniform, all very proper.

Mr. James was sitting up, and he had insisted on being washed and shaved for his presentation. When the beautiful young men came in, he looked at them, his face glowing. One of the young men read the proclamation, while the other stood at attention, giving us the feeling of what a more public proclamation might be like. When the reader finished, we all applauded, even Mr. James' sister-in-law and niece. Afterwards, Mr. James asked to see the official proclamation, and the young man came to his side and leaned over him. As Mr. James reached for the paper, his hand trembled. The young man leaned down to him and held the proclamation steady for Mr. James to see. The Master stared at the scrolled design, then turned towards us and made us all smile, asking us to spare him his blushes. We who knew the Master knew what this last gesture of recognition and fame meant to him.

But before long, Mr. James appeared to doze off, and we staff filed out in the absence of any graciousness offered from the family. They had gone back to their packing. Mr. James' moment of glory was over.

After that day, I expected, wished, hoped to be called over to help, but there was no word. I was left to imagine the worst.

Mrs. William James had the Master put into bed and left there alone. When Mr. James seemed to forget where he was and tried to get out of bed, Mrs. William James had him tied in, in restraints. I heard this from Mr. Henry James' friend and neighbour, Miss Sargent, who lived in his building and had gone to see how he was. Mrs. William James told her everything and even showed her the pitiful spectacle.

Yet I had become *persona non grata* because I had been trying to see to his needs and to what he might have wanted. I never saw the Master alive again.

From Miss Sargent, I heard of the Master's last days, of his struggle for breath, his apparent loss of consciousness, then his efforts to be back among the living. How hard it was for me to hear of those terrible, final struggles.

At last it was over. He died at five o'clock on February 28, 1916.

It took more than a day for Mrs. William James to let me know that my employer was gone, and in the strangest way imaginable: she sent personally to invite me to view the body. Of course, I wanted to go to pay my last respects. She was animated when she met me, even giddy. I wondered if she had been drinking or had come unhinged. Her warmth was strange after her coldness at the presentation of the Order of the British Empire. She led me to where Mr. James lay in state with a dark cloth over him. I was not sure I wanted to have this image of him replace my memory of the Master alive.

"Beautiful, is he not?" Mrs. William James said quietly as she lifted the cloth from his face. "At peace, like some marble statue. We made a death mask so everyone will remember his beauty and striking elegance like some ancient emperor, Caesar or Napoléon."

I thought how strange he looked—not like a statue but something waxen, made, made up. They had put some sort of cream on his face, which was bland, blank, shiny. Perhaps it was an overlooked leftover from the masking so that the plaster would not stick. I felt growing horror as I looked at the doll figure lying before me. They had dressed him into some image they had of who he was—the sweet, weak, younger brother, powerless, unable to make it in America, where a successful life was difficult. A man had to act like a real man in America. The little brother was too weak to survive. He went to Europe, where he became softened, weakened, even corrupted. Now they could tidy him up in death, arrange him into the figure they wanted him to be.

Where was my Mr. James? Where was my strong muse, my powerful, intellectual friend, confidant to authors, politicians, rulers? Where was the writer who best portrayed the changing world we now lived in, with all its complexities, its beauties, its cruelties? Where was the man who never looked away no matter what horror, what weakness, what moral illness his words revealed? Where was the soul who looked so deeply into the human heart and came back with such true mirrors for us to contemplate?

I looked away from that strange face and left the room. As I departed, Mrs. William James asked me to come back later that day for a "little work" to sort a few of his papers. I was struck by the inadequacy of her request. I knew as his aide and confidant that he had left an enormous number of projects unfinished. "Little"!! How that word, "little," horrified me! But I quietly, even meekly, agreed to return whenever they would allow me.

I spent the rest of that week in Mr. James' flat, sorting his correspondence, writing letters, finishing legal arrangements with his editors while, around me, I heard the banal sounds of the two American women packing, sorting, tossing away Mr. James' favourite possessions. I found myself growing more and more angry at them, at his loss, at our loss, at their ignorance of what was important to him and of what mattered. They hardly spoke to me, they were so caught up in their own busyness. I made many decisions on my own, using as reference all the discussions Mr. James and I had had.

Each morning, if the first mail arrived at the same time I came in, without thinking, I would go through it, as I had when Mr. James was alive and away from Lamb House. I had been expecting an answer to a question I had sent to one of his publishers. I was in the foyer searching through the mail when Peggy snatched the letters from my hands. Fury filled her eyes.

"What do you think you're doing?" Her voice rose. Burgess and Kidd could surely hear her, wherever they were. "You leave at once! You are no longer needed here, Miss Bosanquet. You are not wanted, you and your pushy, bossy, interfering way, acting so proper, when you are really interfering, intruding, taking over everything. What right do you have to touch anything here? It's ours, not yours. These letters belong to our family." Letters in hand, she spread both her arms. "This is our furniture, our art, our books, our papers, all ours. Nothing is yours. You'll know soon enough, you interfering schemer!"

With that, Peggy stalked out. I slunk away, feeling ashamed at her accusation that I was the most presumptuous and interfering of lowly secretaries. My cheeks burned, as if I had been slapped. I could tell my face was scarlet.

Soon enough I learnt what she was referring to, when I heard from Kidd how generous Mr. James had been to all his staff, this trinket to Kidd, that legacy to his dear Burgess Noakes, even something fine for Old George Gammon, the gardener. How nice that he remembered all these friends in his will. Yet for me, not a word.

I tried to imagine reasons. I had to remember that I had been with the Master for only nine years. I was not a servant to be provided for after he was gone. Instead, I was skilled and trained, his trusted amanuensis. Leaving something to me could have been seen as an insult and also, since I was a single woman, as deeply inappropriate. Or perhaps Mr. James had meant to do something very personal and sweet but then the stroke interfered. Whatever the reason, I felt desolate, abandoned, bereft.

The morning of the funeral, March 3, was dark and wet. The rain came down heavily, making it darker. With such weather, I wondered if anyone would attend. We did not need to worry about filling a large space, since Mrs. William James had decided that having his service and burial in Westminster Abbey was out of the question. It would have been too expensive. Besides, her husband's younger brother belonged at home in America, in the little Cambridge graveyard, there with his family.

They chose to hold his funeral at the rather small parish church nearby, St. Michael's, with the simple Anglican service read by its minister, no pall bearers, only family and friends, and nothing extra— no wreath, no flowers, and no eulogy because that might cost extra. Mrs. William James expected that no one would come. From her point of view, the pouring rain was perfect: it would keep away anyone who had heard of the service or had planned to come. Yet when I reached the low, stone church porch and shook out my umbrella, there was hardly room for me in the steady, silent line of mourners in dark, wet raincoats and hats. We were all there. I was glad Mrs. William James had indicated a place for me in the second pew behind the family and alongside Burgess and other familiar faces.

Hardly an empty seat remained by the time Burgess and I had found our places. Many mourners, the older men especially, held their hats and bowed their silver heads as they stood along the sides and back of the little church. Squeezed into the second pew, I knelt and said my usual hypocritical minister's daughter's prayer: "If You are there, please forgive me and keep me safe." I crossed myself in the shabby Anglican way I had learnt.

As I settled back and looked around at the smoky candles, at the heaps of unsolicited flowers on the Master's casket and felt the murmuring stir of too many people crowded, steaming, I wanted to cry out. We all did. The family finally filed in, and there was a stirring and a whispering and that long pause as we all tried to bring ourselves back from our own private wars and losses, back to this moment, this black box placed before us in the stuffy silence, for there was even to be no music, only that silence, until at last the familiar, somber words began.

After the benediction, as we were filing out and sharing greetings in low voices, Mr. James' friends took me by the hand, first this person, then that one, asking if I was to be the one to arrange for publication of the Master's letters. Each of these friends seemed to assume the family might ask me. Mr. James' friends—many of whom were "different," who had chosen their lovers as they did, as they must—had long treasured this letter or that one, in spite of Mr. James' often expressed wish, "This is to be destroyed as soon as read."

The Master never wanted a commemorative volume about his life or a collection of his correspondence. Yet surely there would at least be a book of letters. Did I dare hope the family might ever consider me to arrange a compilation? I wondered, hoping that I might once again assist Mr. James in choosing what he might want to share. I knew there remained some copies of the letters Mr. James had written, and I knew the Master had not destroyed every letter sent to him, for letters are memories, comforts we keep from the difficult times to buttress us when other difficult seasons appear.

23

"Henry James at Work"

1916-1924

At the beginning he had no questions of compression to attend to, and he "broke ground", as he said, by talking to himself day by day about the characters and construction until the persons and their actions were vividly present to his inward eye. This soliloquy was of course recorded on the typewriter.

—Theodora Bosanquet
"Henry James at Work"
The Hogarth Press

When, shortly after the Master's death, I was instructed to return to Carlyle Mansions to "help with the letters," I thought I might be finishing details of Mr. James' correspondence, not that the family would embark on publication of his collected letters so soon after the Master's death. I arrived to find piles of Mr. James' letters waiting on every surface. Mr. Percy Lubbock was waiting, too, with his own stack, a not very high stack. The family had chosen him as editor. Mr. Lubbock explained my job. Simply put, I was the copyist. With a surge of shame, I remembered how I had fantasised about being an editor.

Mr. Lubbock was clearly embarrassed to have to explain my tasks: I was to retype the letters he had chosen and sometimes only parts of letters. He explained that he was not actually doing the choosing; the family had selected the names he was to include. He had given them suggestions, but the final choice was theirs. He shook his handsome young head as if sad that it had come to this. I think we both understood why Mr. James had insisted on keeping his letters private and, in turn, had insisted on destroying his friends' letters.

However, I knew that in spite of Mr. James' instructions, no one would destroy a letter from the Master. Mr. Lubbock made two piles—include and exclude. With choking apprehension, I saw that we were exacerbating the terrible loss begun on that dark November day back in 1909, when Professor William James was so terribly ill and the Master in his deep depression had gone out to the burn barrel and flung, dumped, thrown, piled up, and burned it all, burning so many letters—piles and piles of them, so many piles that he could not ignite the heavy stacks of paper. And then came the re-enactment burning in 1915, during his last visit to Rye. As Mr. Lubbock and I sorted letters to retype for publication or to return uncopied, I watched the rejections pile up in a terrible literary shunning, as every mail brought more and more letters for us to shun.

A copyist has no say. Yet who knew the Master's correspondence better than I? Especially in Mr. James' last years, when he had taken to using dictation as his chosen way of writing more letters to more of his friends because he had that old trouble with his hand cramping up whenever he wrote too much. I think, too, that he had grown accustomed to the ease of dictating and was no longer so wary about using my services when writing to his friends, though this was seldom the case with his family. From the piles of typewritten pages, I could tell that many of the letters had come from my typing on the Remington.

I brought in my Oliver typing machine and set it up in the library on a folding table, while Mr. Lubbock sorted and decided. As I began retyping texts, I could not help but notice which recipients the family had chosen and who was missing. Typing on, I wondered: How did they make their choices? It seemed clear they had chosen those with famous names, with a few glaring omissions, for only the most respectable of men were to be included as correspondents with Mr. Henry James.

The "included" pile contained only a few women who were not the Master's relatives. A bachelor, no matter how old, sending or—worse!—receiving letters from a woman would be shamefully improper, though the second volume did include quite a few letters to Mrs. Wharton and a few to Mrs. Dew Smith (whom Percy listed as Mrs. Dew-Smith), but there were few to the Master's other dear women friends. Very few letters had been chosen from an addressee not living in England or America. The letters were about insipid subjects and flattering to the recipient or written in the most general way. No letters were personal, but then, perhaps that would have been Mr. James' choice. No, these were letters other people had saved. But where were the funny, quirky letters that I remembered, when I had typed responses to his friends or to other writers or to critics? Where was that long rant about the future of the theatre he had sent to George Bernard Shaw?

Surely it was not Mr. Lubbock who was choosing, it was Mrs. William James. Even the letters to famous people were only to the people well-known in America. Few letters had been chosen for intrinsic interest, with few of them describing how Mr. James thought, how he solved a difficulty in his writing. No, mostly these were insipid letters of puffery, which gave more credit to the people addressed than they had deserved.

I protested to Mr. Lubbock that what we were doing was a travesty, but he answered very practically that it was not our money Mrs. James was spending. With that I had to be content.

It did not take long, this retyping. I went into our working room for one last time and saw that our typewriting machine—my link with Mr. James—had been removed. The room felt strangely barren. Soon enough, I reached my last day working at 21 Carlyle Mansions. Each day there, I felt more and more angry as I passed the half-filled boxes, rubbish, and packing excelsior. Mrs. James and Peggy were tearing through Mr. James' things, as if little mattered to them.

Mrs. James was there and sorting among the piles of books and papers. "Miss Bosanquet," she said, "I believe this will be our last request of you. I want you to pack up these few random things, now that we're done with the letters." She put her hand on a pile of note-books stacked beside Mr. James' travelling trunk. How many times I had seen Burgess bring out that trunk, had even helped pack it with whatever Mr. James would need for his time away from Lamb House, his dip-pens and inkwell, that special, heavy paper he had liked so well, books, letters to be answered, more books, and the note-books. The note-books always went into the trunk.

I had often seen the Master bent over his note-books, searching for some long-ago memory, an idea, a funny story, finding where a thought had begun, remembering who had given him the first germ, that prick of inspiration. He would select one of the note-books, leaf through a few pages, and find whatever he wanted. He could remember almost to the day. These were treasures. I felt honoured to be the one to preserve them so others in the future could see and understand Mr. James' initial creative process.

"You can bundle them into that old trunk. I still don't know what we're going to do with everything. It's too much."

Mrs. James left me surrounded by piles and went out to other, more important packing.

I touched the old trunk, rubbing my hand along its scarred top, the battered old leather and wood. Like a captain's sea chest, it had seen a lot, had been carried through many adventures. But those were all adventures of the heart, requiring the courage of his spirit to see and believe and express things as no one else could. I could save it all for posterity, pack the trunk full of Mr. James' most personal words: the note-books, the early versions, the tries of unfinished work, even those last novels, "The Ivory Tower" and "The Sense of the Past." Here was the right place for all that to rest.

I found the originals of the last typewritten dictations in a pile Mrs. William James may have intended to bury in the trunk. I looked through the pages, somewhat comforted that I had selfishly saved the carbons. Had Mrs. James thought the Master was losing his mind at the end? Did she want to keep the weakness caused by his stroke hidden from the world? Were his very last dictations—those last two letters after his description of *"plumes from the imperial eagle"*—strange ramblings? Or was he in touch with those who had passed on? I could feel the Master's spirit around me as I packed. It was as if he were standing by his desk, one hand on books and papers, pensive, pausing between thought and speech.

During those days, as I re-typed the Master's letters and thought over his life, I realised there were images and voices I wanted to see examined, unfolded, shared. I began to want to tell my own story about the Mr. James whom I had known. Little by little, I began to put together my thoughts and memories. I let this slip out one day to Mr. Lubbock, and he asked most respectfully if he might see the work when I was done. I had not even started, but I did keep patching pieces together, looking back through my diaries from those first days, remembering all the little moments that had come to be so dear. I started working it up into an essay, "Henry James at Work," which I took to Mr. Lubbock, who wanted to send it off to editors he knew back in America. They in turn wanted to publish it in a small magazine, "The Yale Review," at one of the American colleges. I did not think very many people would see the essay, but I was wrong. Some friends from America brought it over to London, so there you are.

Before long, "Spectators"—our novel in letters, Clara Smith's and mine—came out in its own blue cover that spring of 1916. It was not much of a splash, for during the War was the wrong time to publish such a silly little book. The reviewers made a quick morsel of it and passed on. But one reviewer perceptively wrote that the second name on the title page—not the famous Clara Smith, who was known to be the assistant to Lord Milne, but T. Bosanquet— was "quite quaintly a woman." Apparently this T. Bosanquet had written the letters supposedly penned by a man-about-town, who followed the latest poets and novelists.

Bereft and out of work, I was glad once more to find steady employment through Miss Petherbridge in a Red Cross project, for which I was indexing refugees and their needs. Then, in 1924, I received a note from a young friend of Mr. James', the daughter of Sir Leslie Stephen, to whom Mr. James had introduced me many years before in Rye. Sir Leslie Stephen's daughter had written several books, novels of her own, and was about to embark on an adventure. She wanted my help. I made my way to Bloomsbury to meet the famous daughter, Virginia Woolf.

I arrived for our appointment early. I felt sweaty and unattractive as I walked up Paradise Road along the edge of Mecklenburgh Square in the early afternoon heat. I climbed the steps, rang the bell, and waited. A very young, harried maid opened the door. When I stated my business, the young woman said Mrs. Woolf was too busy to see anybody.

"But she sent for me," I explained. "She expects me."

The young woman took me through the central hall to the stairs that led down to the ground-floor basement. We passed through several rooms cluttered with papers, past a young man taking a greasy, black rag to a large press with rollers and wheels and shiny metal. He answered the maid's question with a nod.

"Mrs. Woolf, she's back in the last store-room," he said, "but she won't want to see you. She's writing."

I thought, How could anyone be writing in this confusing place? We found Mrs. Woolf sitting in an old arm-chair, papers in her lap, papers on the floor. She looked up, her eyes wide, like a hunted animal.

"Mrs. Woolf," the maid said, with a tone of voice I had never heard from a servant. "I've had to look everywhere to find you. This visitor says she has an appointment, and you were nowhere to be found. Why must you hide down here? Not writing, I hope! You know Mr. Woolf is very strict about how much time you spend writing."

Mrs. Woolf, apparently startled, hid what she was working on (clearly it was a piece of writing) under a cushion. She stood up to greet me. She was very tall, but not as tall as I am, and was a bit gawky, stooping under the low ceiling of the basement room, but her handshake was warm and welcoming. As she led me back upstairs, she explained their publishing project. We passed several small rooms, each with boxes, paper, and books.

Mrs. Wolfe pointed proudly to a press with shiny black paint and bright metal. "Later today I'll finish composing a long essay we're publishing. Here, these are the type trays. We were lucky the man who sold us the press had good taste in fonts. We have several that will work for the new booklet format we have in mind."

After climbing the two sets of stairs to the living quarters on the second floor, we settled into a bright room at the back of the house. She explained what she wanted from me: something like the essay I had published over in America, the one about my Mr. James.

She could not take in the fact that I was not American. "I assumed you were American, since Mr. James—He is or he was American. Many of us love his work and want to know more. That's why I wrote to you. And here you are, having had a tour of Hogarth Press for yourself, Miss Bosanquet." (We remained at the level of "Miss" and "Mrs.") "You can see that I'm ready for your work."

I wondered, What could she—this well-off, well-connected woman—want of me? She seemed much younger than I, though I later learnt she was a few years older. But I had been on my own much longer. I wondered what her life was, married, there in a large flat in Bloomsbury. Why did she need to be so taken care of, protected, coddled? Was it illness or perhaps something else? She was very quick and very scattered in our first conversation. I was fascinated.

She explained why she and her husband had returned to London, why they had bought a printing press. Indeed, it was a question of her health. Her husband felt it would be good for her to have something to do, something active, something physical. The doctors thought writing made her nervous and upset. At last, she said, they had found a different doctor, one who understood. This doctor allowed her a certain amount of writing each day if she would also make sure she took daily exercise outside. They had tried living away from London. She was glad to run the press and to be back in town, where she felt easier and not exiled as she had been in Hampstead. With the press, she would be physically active, setting type and moving heavy trays. She would not always be up there in her mind.

I am sure she did not tell me all this that first morning, but I remember that I felt a strength in her. Later, she certainly had strong ideas about my essay and the small book it became.

"I've read what you've written about Mr. James," she said. "But there's more to say, isn't there?" Hers was such a charming way of talking to a writer.

"We can't make your book too long. I have this idea, to do a series of three or four booklets to come out at the same time, or nearly so. I want to publish my ideas about the novel, about how it has changed, moving away from Mr. Thackeray and Arnold Bennett, as it must. I thought I saw in your short piece that you could tell us what Mr. James thought."

She looked up at me, pausing for breath, and went on.

"I do think Mr. James saw something new coming. He was already creating a new form for us. Is that not right? Do you think you could expand your 'Yale Review' essay? We would need it to be at least three times as long. Would that give you enough space to tell us more about Mr. James' process, about what was behind his most unusual style, and even why he used dictation?"

Mrs. Woolf was interesting me more and more. At first, I had been thinking that I had said all I wanted, all I knew, all I thought. But as we continued talking, I found myself growing excited about what I could write, how I could extend my little essay to describe Mr. James as a writer and not simply provide more details of our daily life, as the editor at "The Yale Review" had wanted.

Mrs. Woolf was apologetic when she explained how short a time I would have, but I thought the deadline would not be a problem. We shook hands over our agreement. I was thrilled. I would have a book published by this new publishing house, The Hogarth Press, and would be edited by this brilliant writer. Like my article, the book would also be called "Henry James at Work."

Oh, but it turned out to be so hard to write more and to write quickly! I found myself procrastinating. Self-doubt descended. Had I already said everything I knew? Could I go deeply into new ideas about Mr. James that I had not really thought about? Where was the line between scholarship and prying? Mr. James was very private, and so was I.

I met several times with Mrs. Woolf to discuss my first efforts. She seemed to like what I did write, but she always seemed to be wanting a deeper analysis of the work Mr. James and I had done. At one point, I threw the pages with her suggestions down on her desk, put the cap back on my pen and sat back, angry, defiant, and discouraged. I could not do it, whatever it was Mrs. Woolf wanted from me. I did not know enough. Mr. James had been too secretive about his process, and I had come to him too late, after he had written his masterpieces.

"Too late." What a terrible phrase.

Yet I had made an agreement with Mrs. Woolf that I would write about Mr. James and how he worked to reveal an understanding that would be important or meaningful. I was afraid, no matter how hard I tried, no matter how many pages I wrote, that I would never be able to reveal anything. He had not revealed anything to me, had he? All those years, through the illnesses, the mourning, the discouraged times, his deepening sense of failure—I had known and understood all those times, but that was not what Virginia Woolf wanted. Perhaps, though, if this new printing project was Mrs. Woolf's attempt to overcome those dark places that consume writers, it might help her to know how Mr. James alternated his long, intense periods on stories or a novel with working up something do-able, an essay or some other short non-fiction piece. I wondered if knowing more about Mr. James might help this astute but troubled writer.

"Tell me," she would say, "tell me how he did it. What was his process? What made him write those great, intricate, opera-like novels, with all those voices simultaneously singing amazing sextets and octets like Mozart, individual voices, individual stories, destinies, ambitions, desires, each with its own line, distinct, and yet all braiding, weaving together? How did he do it?"

It was possible, I thought, that I had learnt something while Mr. James and I worked on the New York Edition. As Mr. James wrote the prefaces, he was talking to me, with me, about his process, about what he had been doing, what he had been striving for. I had noticed the changes in his *oeuvre*, beginning from the earlier years, when he had started out with smaller pieces, to the big canvases of his novels dealing with types of people, hordes of people, and bigger ideas—politics, art, and drama. I had begun working as his amanuensis when he was writing the preface to "The Tragic Muse," one of those "loose baggy monsters." (Was that Mrs. Woolf's term?) He wrote that he had consciously shifted towards smaller pictures, impressions, the novellas, and the short stories in the nineties. For me, his prefaces for the smaller works had felt like hymns or prayers. He seemed to know this when he returned after years to the stories he liked best, the ones about young children or men and women in distress. There, in those prefaces, he seemed to feel his work was good.

How could I write about such a huge topic? It was not the change in subject matter. Mr. James had dictated to me how he had tried a different process, a way to remove the author's voice. How could I capture the revolutionary vision of what he called in his preface to "Maisie" his *scenic system*?

I went back and re-read that preface, which I had typed: "*Going over the pages here placed together has been for me, at all events, quite to watch the scenic system at play. The treatment by 'scene,' regularly, quite rhythmically recurs ; the intervals between, the massing of the elements to a different effect and by a quite other law, remain, in this fashion, all preparative. . . .*"

I looked again through the volumes of the New York Edition, twenty-four volumes, all those words from Mr. James. At the time of publication, I did not have the funds to buy a set, but with the payment from my last work for Mrs. William James I purchased my own dense volumes of the New York Edition, the masterpiece Mr. James and I had wrestled with, our big effort editing all the works he cared about the most from his *oeuvre*. That was his legacy, how he wanted to be remembered. Those books in their handsome bindings had also become my legacy, the only physical legacy aside from his letters to me and a few typescripts that I had from my time with Mr. James.

I wondered: Which is the more immoral literary act—illuminating a puzzling piece of writing from Mr. James' *oeuvre* or revealing secrets he perhaps wanted to keep private? We readers love to have personal secrets revealed; we love to find that an author's feet are made of clay. But most important of all, what would Mr. James think? I wondered what Mrs. Woolf would say; I sent a note to her, asking to meet again.

This time when I rang the front door-bell, Mrs. Woolf answered. She was wearing a coat and scarf. Pulling on a velvet hat of warm brown, she came hurriedly out and began walking down the sidewalk. I caught up with her.

"Now I can get away!" she said. "If I'm walking, they can't be expecting me to report in. It's making me crazy—'Don't do this!' 'Don't do that!' 'Drink this!' 'Eat more!' 'Drink milk!!'—I can't stand it. Whenever I've had one or two bad spells, it's always because I'm writing too much." Her hands were churning the air. "What does that mean, writing too much? How can I live any other way?"

She left no time for answers.

"When you're writing, Miss Bosanquet, do you have this sort of trouble with your people, trouble ducking away from them to secure time to think?" She paused, looked at me, hard, but left no time for breath. "No, I don't suppose you do, but then I don't know anything about you. How do you live? Are you alone?"

She waited; she apparently really did want an answer. I struggled against my own wish to remain private, to keep my own secrets.

"No," I began. "I live with another woman."

"Servants? I don't suppose you need anyone to take care of you?"

I laughed at the strangeness of this thought. "No, I've been on my own, had my own place ever since university."

"How did that happen?"

I answered before I could think. "It was Mr. James who made it possible. I was alone for the first time when I came to Rye. I lived in a boarding house and worked every day as his amanuensis. It was Mr. James who supported my special friendship with his friends' daughter. You would think both our families might have prevented us. My family had always intervened before, but by that time my father had given up on keeping me apart from my lovers."

"Lovers!? Really?"

"Some were pashes, schoolgirl crushes; some were my dearest friends. But if I would feel too much for another woman, my father or, more often, her father would make us separate."

"When was this? It sounds so Victorian—"

"I came to Mr. James in 1907. My mother had died years before, and I kept the house for my father until I escaped to university. By then, my aunts had tried and failed to find me a husband. When I went to Rye, I was on my own. Mr. James made my life possible. He was the famous, slightly eccentric bachelor in little Rye and could do things others could not. Nellie—"

Mrs. Woolf and I were standing at the edge of Mecklenburgh Square. A black cab, still relatively new to London, lumbered by. I could feel my voice about to tremble, for I still felt bereft even though my Nellie had decided to leave for her own life quite a while before. "Nellie—Nellie was an artist. Mr. James supported us in finding a small studio for her painting. I could arrange to spend more and more time there, and finally I was living there, and she with me—"

Mrs. Woolf was not interested in Nellie and me, in the difficult details of making our life together in provincial Rye in 1908. She circled back to Mr. James.

"Why, Mr. James knew your friend, Nellie, was that it? What did he think of you two together? Come to think of it, why did Mr. James, with his reputation—How could he have a woman for his personal secretary?"

The answers were intertwined: my romantic life, his friendships. During Mr. James' lifetime, love between men was considered shameful and punishable by imprisonment. But there was no law against women loving women. It was Mr. James who had freed me to live, to love Nellie, my special "chum," as he used to call her. I had often wondered about Mr. James' story describing a woman artist's studio. Had he been affirming the intimate situation between Nellie and me so he could observe us? Was he always an experimenter with people's feelings? Was Mr. James like the conniving villains in his own novels? Were Nellie and I in some way one of Mr. James' research projects?

But I never breathed a murmur of those thoughts to Mrs. Woolf.

Instead, I said, "I think he was comfortable with me. I was his amanuensis the longest. Perhaps it was because I was 'different,' or perhaps because women typists were so much less expensive than men when Mr. James faced a very extensive, expensive project, the revision of all his greatest books."

I did not reveal how glad Mr. James was when Nellie and I set up housekeeping, how he helped ease our way with Nellie's father. I hid Nellie's and my passions from Mrs. Woolf, this most curious woman, who, as a writer of novels like Mr. James, would want more. That day, as Mrs. Woolf and I walked back, she went on about troubles keeping good help, while I was wondering: Would she and I ever return to Mr. James and his work? And my essay?

I wanted to describe for Mrs. Woolf the new method Mr. James had developed, how he would push himself deep into his "*scenic system*," when he dictated by acting out for me the various parts. But then, when I was sure Mrs. Woolf had forgotten about my book, she stopped.

"Whatever am I going on and on about? We need to go back, we need to see about your book. Have you brought pages for me? What do you have for me today?"

We turned around and walked back. Her questions turned sharp and straight to the point. She listened to my concerns. She helped me find what was needed.

I had been stuck on how to move from the excited discoveries during my first days with my famous employer, while he was laying out the way his writing had changed as he moved from the shorter pieces to his experiments with the dramatic method—the blessed "*scenic system*" that had pleased him so—and then moved on to dictating while acting out the parts as he created new scenic works. I had been stuck on how to narrate the weeks and months of daily minutia, the repetitive tasks that were endlessly the same, those months that were crucially important to the work but which had become a blur. And how should I deal with the months when the Master was away travelling? Or when he was discouraged and not working at all? Those times were part of Henry James at work but not part of my project with Mrs. Woolf.

She was quite clear: "Nobody wants to read about minutia. We only have so many pages, so many minutes of the reader's attention. Keep your story focused on what is important, what mattered to Mr. James, what matters to you. You're a writer, too—I've seen your novel in letters. Very clever, really. Too bad it got lost in the clamour of the War." She paused. "Miss Bosanquet, I know you know things."

As we walked back to Mecklenburg Square and Hogarth Press, she began to talk of her own work. "I have my own points to make. These booklets seem the right way to do it; no big blasts of brass announcing my own ideas. We have heard enough of that from everyone else. No, this is right, and you'll be early in our new series of booklets, with Henry James, who was able to look at his own writing and try something new. I like how you've taken a tone that is sitting right there beside the reader, not donnish at all."

We both laughed. I did not need to tell Mrs. Woolf that I had never even been allowed to sit in a seminar with a don. My university education was all laboratories, field work, and huge lecture halls. I imagined Mrs. Woolf's experiences were similar.

She answered my thought. "Not that I would know about 'donnish'! I spent those years with my family. Everything I know I had to learn from my brother and his friends. No, your tone is right. Continue. Continue on to the end. People always want to know about the end, about last words."

I returned to my flat to work again on my book, once again to face Mr. James' last days. What should I say? Until Mrs. William James arrived and kept me away, Burgess and I had protected the Master at the end of his life by keeping away the vultures and journalists who wanted to see the Great Man in all his dying. I returned to those days, to the copies of the deathbed dictations I had kept as an expression of a great soul still speaking, still creating even out of the confusions of illness and weakness, but *not* as evidence of some huge delusion. Mr. James did not lapse into a belief that he was Napoléon or that his family was somehow related to the Emperor. Only persons who did not really know the Master could believe such a thing, but I did not want to take a chance on any misunderstanding.

It still rankled that the James family did not respect Henry James and his work. How delighted I was to find this strange, brilliant woman, who wanted to understand Mr. James. Her position as daughter of the greatly respected Sir Leslie Stephen would make any book from her press respectable and worthy of notice. That Mrs. Woolf wanted to know more about how Mr. James wrote, about how he thought—That was the most exciting part.

I had been amazed during my first visit to find Mrs. Woolf ensconced in a store-room in order to create a writing space of her own. But I doubted that life had ever required Mrs. Woolf to work for hire. She probably would not know that we typist secretaries studying the Curtis Method had been trained as copyists. Our eyes were always to be on the words—our male bosses' words—to the left of our left elbows. We watched neither our fingers nor the emerging typescript. Our eyes never searched for where to reset the fingers of our left hand after we had thrown the typewriting machine's carriage when the bell signalled the end of a line. Oh, no, we copyists never looked at the keyboard. We worked by the sound of the carriage bell and the blind feel of the nib on the home key for the left index finger so that all the other fingers of our left hand would hover correctly over their own keys.

But my work with Henry James was different.

I was a copyist only in the afternoons, when I retyped Mr. James' revisions, my eyes following his handwritten changes as my fingers found the keys. But in the mornings, I was no longer a reader of handwritten words. True, I was typing. But I was also a constant listener, with my eyes free to watch the Master. Ours was a subtle dance. I was the observing audience, interested, attentive, present but not too obvious. As the days and weeks passed, Mr. James became more and more the performer, with our working room turning into his stage. Increasingly, he acted out his scenes, absorbed in each character he played, changing between them, his voice shifting from male to female, the tone shifting from rage to petulance to gentleness. He became his characters, concentrating on each one yet simultaneously subconsciously attentive, as every professional actor is, to how his scene played with his audience.

I wondered if Mrs. Woolf could understand what Mr. James had meant when he said "*scenic system.*" She seemed so utterly intellectual, of only the mind and not the body. I was not sure she could imagine the theatre I had attended every morning, watching and listening to the Master perform.

But I kept on writing my essay, as Mrs. Woolf had instructed. Soon, I found my voice, writing first about coming to work for Mr. James and then describing his many friendships and how important they were to him. My essay became more and more an overall look at all Mr. James' writings and especially his letters. I worked diligently, trying to find the right balance. Mrs. Woolf encouraged me. This was what she wanted, more about his writing process, how he would work things out in his notes. And so, I avoided his last illness and his death but retained the section about the Master's posthumously published novel fragments. She liked that.

"It's about as long as we can handle," she said. "Remember, it's a booklet. But why not have a few more paragraphs about his being an American? What did he think of the English? Why are so many of his heroes misplaced Americans?"

"They're not, really—"

"Well, then, there's your ending. Tell us what we have all been wondering about your Mr. James. How did he feel about adopting our country? Think of the uproar Mr. Pound made, saying that his naturalization was 'America's intellectual death warrant.' Think of Miss Rebecca West's little book. Tell us: Was Henry James American, or was he English? Why do we English think he writes mostly about Americans? Who was he really writing about?"

Her casual, thrown-out questions gave me the idea for ending "Henry James at Work" and allowed me to avoid any decision about revealing the Master's last two intriguing letters. I could speak more generally but deeply to his core character:

"His Utopia was an anarchy where nobody would be responsible for any other human being but only for his own civilized [sic] character. His circle of friends will easily recall how finely Henry James had fitted himself to be a citizen of this commonwealth."

24

"The Wings of the Dove"

1927–1933

> *It [*the initial idea*] stood there with secrets and compartments,*
> *with possible treacheries and traps ; it might have a great deal*
> *to give, but would probably ask for equal services in return,*
> *and would collect this debt to the last shilling.*

> —Henry James
> Preface to "The Wings of the Dove"
> The New York Edition, volume 19

I t was not until I began to work with Leon Edel, a young
scholar, in 1929 that I came to see the obvious: In time,
Henry James, the Master, the *Cher Maître,* would receive affirma-
tion of his rightful place as a progenitor of the modern novel. Yet at
the time leading up to Mr. James' death, his fame was evaporating,
his books were not selling, and his friends editing magazines could
not promise him that they would publish his new work. Henry
James was a failure to his family, a rapidly fading falling star, and a
figure of fun for younger novelists and reviewers.

When Mr. Lubbock and I were editing the Master's letters
shortly after Mr. James' passing, I realised, and I think Mr. Lubbock

also realised, that we were beginning a new vision, which—albeit flawed—we hoped would continue to build. Mr. James' friends and I wanted to be sure the Master's work would not be demeaned any further. At the time, I knew the public mostly misunderstood Mr. James, but I felt that if I could keep his family from destroying everything, then in the future there might emerge a younger scholar—someone brave—who would be able to use everything we had saved. That is why I carefully packed that sea trunk as the family was leaving. And that is why, at the first chance I had, I knew I would test out any young believer in Mr. James. If ever I found someone worthy, I would make sure that scholar learnt about the last dictations by Henry James.

Thus, my question when I met Mr. Edel was this: Should I trust him?

Mr. Edel came to me in Paris in 1929. He was quite young—only twenty-one. I was delighted to find a young person reading Mr. James. Mr. Edel, a brilliant young Jewish boy, was working on an advanced degree at the Sorbonne. He had discovered Mr. James' writings on his own and found a puzzle to be solved. Why, he wanted to know, had the novelist written so much about the theatre, especially the French theatre? Mr. Edel knew of rumours that Mr. James had written plays. Whenever Mr. Edel interviewed Mr. James' old friends, they would suggest he find Miss Bosanquet. And so, he did.

I was not hidden. I was writing my own essays about Mr. James, all of us were, trying to keep his memory alive. I did not want to add to all those dreadful anecdotal memoirs that were written at the time. Instead, I wanted to keep Mr. James' *oeuvre* alive.

Young Leon Edel wrote to me very politely, and we arranged to meet. He was surprised to find that I was living in Paris. But he should not have been. Everybody lived in Paris in those days, *toujours gay* after the Great War. Paris was cheap. We were all saving money by living where we could enjoy the chance to be light-hearted and, for me, writing, writing. I was trying everything then, poetry and another novel. I do not remember much about that novel, only that I gave the best scenes to tall, dark-haired, smart characters, while the blonde fluff-heads caused trouble and were unfaithful. I was still bitter, apparently, over Nellie's departure from my life during those still-dark days of the War after Mr. James had passed away.

Reviews, too. I was writing for a new weekly, "Time and Tide," edited by our friends from the Six Point Group, especially Margaret, Lady Rhondda, whom Mr. James had "introduced" to me when he showed me her photograph after her rescue from the torpedoed *Lusitania*. While I was in Paris and writing for "Time and Tide," Lady Rhondda's father had passed away, leaving her with an enormous fortune. I wrote for the magazine, covering women, such as Harriet Martineau, and I wrote the first review for Mrs. Woolf's "A Room of One's Own." I even reviewed books on Henry James and sent everything off to Winifred Holtby and Margaret, Lady Rhondda, who were having a large effect from their "Time and Tide" offices on Bloomsbury Street.

I led two lives in Paris—a daytime work life in Reid Hall, arranging conferences and support for university women as part of the International Federation of University Women, a job that had grown out of our work as suffrage pioneers in Britain. The movement had spread with the Americans' help all across Europe. I was good at writing essays and speeches for our leaders, though of course I never gave any speeches, for I was still shy among strangers, but I was good at organising our office. My work with Miss Petherbridge, where I had learnt to index and manage an office, was paying off as our women's organising picked up after the Great War.

We fought to make fairness to women a part of the post-war treaties and agreements. How heartbreaking it was when we travelled to see the losses in Eastern Europe—in Germany, Hungary, and Poland, all so demoralised, so ravaged. Yet a new hope for women's recognition emerged in desolate country after desolate country.

That was my day work. The nights—Oh, Paris nights! Now that I was alone, I could stay out all night, I could do anything. I laugh in making that comment, for I was and still am also the constant observer, still the shy, self-conscious spectator. Maybe it was my height or my Britishness, but there in Paris, I was even more self-conscious. I would go to the American Café with its English-speaking events and listen to others reading their bad poems but completely lose the courage to read my own work. Yet still, I would go; still, I wrote.

As I sat waiting for Mr. Leon Edel, I wondered which version of me he expected to meet. I remember he was surprised that I had arranged for him to come to Reid Hall, the handsome, comfortable complex that a group of very rich American women had bought so that young American women could come to Paris to study and have a safe and comfortable place to stay. It was a lovely building, old stone and rose brick, a low two-storey structure built around a flagstone courtyard open to the sky, with tables set out under the trees and flowers in large pots.

If I surprised Mr. Edel, he also surprised me. His letter had been very competent and sounded as if it had been written by a man much older and much taller. He was slender and dark, intense, with a slight build, and in his student jacket and scarf, he seemed to me very dapper and handsome, shining and clean-shaven with lovely brown hair, lots of it. We shook hands, and as we sat at a small table, I had one of the girls bring us tea in a flowery pot and two of their tiny, perfectly round French tea-cups.

"Tea!?" he exclaimed, surprised. "Of course, now that I've met you, I can tell that you're British, but I'm still adjusting to the idea that you're not an American."

But why had he assumed (as Mrs. Woolf had, too) that I was not English? He went on in a voluble flow of words. "I don't know why I thought you were American, assumed you were, but when Mr. Percy Lubbock first suggested I ask for your assistance, he never said—And I suppose I thought you English girls would not have taken such a job. But forgive me, I'm being terribly rude. I'm afraid it comes from my work in journalism. I'm always asking questions!"

After the first awkwardness, it became a bit easier. My restraint began to thaw as we talked. I nodded and encouraged him to tell me more about himself. Why had he come? I knew only that he had arrived at the Sorbonne after his years at McGill University. I learnt that he was a younger brother. In fact, he thought that he had first become interested in Mr. James as also being a less famous, less successful younger brother.

"My brother and I both went to university after the War," he said. "There was not much money, not enough for both of us. I've paid my own way by writing for the newspapers whenever I could find assignments. I guess that's how I've trained myself to be curious, from having worked as a journalist through my years at university."

He looked around at the comfortable AAU accommodations for American women studying in Paris. "My younger brother had an easier time—he's at Oxford now. I've come to the Sorbonne as a less expensive alternative. My French is very good if you discount my Canadian accent from having grown up in Montreal."

I wondered if there were other reasons his brother was the only one to be at Oxford. There were still quotas, I had heard, maybe even at Oxford. How many young Jewish boys were allowed to go to our universities? But I kept my questions to myself. I knew from my own work with universities everywhere how many obstacles there could be—and not only for Jews. It was even harder for young, brilliant women.

Listening to his story, I asked, "How did you decide to write about Mr. James? As a topic, Henry James seems pretty far afield for a young man from so far away."

He explained how he had come across Henry James during his years at McGill. He had needed a subject for a thesis; his professor had sent him off to find information on the French theatre and its influence on modern drama. Some articles mentioned that, as a very young man, Mr. James had sent notices back to the papers in America, full of enthusiasm for the Paris theatre. This had caught young Edel's interest, and, after he had read several of Mr. James' novels, he felt he had found his subject.

His voice became more energetic: "But I never knew much about when Henry James began writing his own plays, until I began to look a little deeper."

Mr. Leon Edel seemed to expect not to be believed when he mentioned the literary historical figures he was describing. It was as if his were a theory from some place far away and long ago, as if he were holding the facts of Mr. James' life at a distance, studying them. I wondered: Would he take hold of this dream of mine, to keep Mr. James alive? Could he be the one? Did this young man have it in him?

It was hard for me to let go of all that I knew. I had been quite disappointed in what others had written about Mr. James and his work, the whole magnificent range of it. Most writers in the fifteen years since Mr. James' death wanted to speak only on one or another aspect of the Master's *oeuvre*. Perhaps this young man was different. I was excited, too, because here was someone who liked and respected Mr. James and who came from the world of professors and writers and critics.

Yet when we were meeting face to face, it seemed he, too, was thinking only of what had already been done. I felt that what I had in mind seemed impossible: How could I persuade him to step up? How could I help him see what an opportunity awaited him? Could I lead this young journalist along? Might I feed him interesting tidbits? I was quite sure he would love a mystery to be solved. He could act as the reporter, be the one to spy things out.

The second time I saw Mr. Edel, I was back in England. We met at Crosby Hall, on Cheyne Walk, near 21 Carlyle Mansions, where Mr. James and I had worked as long as we could—But perhaps Mr. Edel did not know that. The young man and I sat by the fire in the Great Hall. It was a bitter day along the Embankment. He seemed very un-British in his heavy woollen, Nanook-of-the-North great-coat.

I was a little more forthcoming with what I wanted. Soon, he asked a question that gave me the chance to lead him along. He was speaking of George Bernard Shaw, saying how he had been surprised after reading Shaw's reviews that there were no letters between the two men. He was direct: "Didn't they know each other? Didn't they meet?" His voice was a touch exasperated. "I wish I could find out if they met!"

I laughed. "Many times, I am sure."

He startled. "But if that's so, why has Mr. James' correspondence and his friendship with George Bernard Shaw never been mentioned?" Mr. Edel sounded very excited.

"You've studied the letters, but only the published letters." Perhaps my voice carried a tone of bitterness. "Surely you know that published books don't always tell all the truth. When Mr. Percy Lubbock and I suggested to Mrs. William James that we ask Mr.

Shaw for letters, she objected. She was vociferous! 'No theatre people!' she said. 'I will not have it. They have no role! They would be of no interest!'"

"What?" Mr. Edel's voice was almost a yelp. "Of no interest? How could she believe that?"

"The family was very careful about which letters they would print. They wouldn't allow the least breath of scandal or gossip. No letters could contain hints of what a wonderful friend Mr. James had been to the theatre and to many of its most colourful participants. The family wanted the letters to paint the portrait of a very serious, important man and only that. For them, 'serious' and 'theatre' were opposite words."

"I've never seen anyone write about this or even mention it. I wonder—Oh, Miss Bosanquet, this—this could make my study of Mr. Henry James' play-writing years famous!"

I nodded encouragingly as Mr. Edel jumped up. He paced about, excited with the thoughts of what he had discovered, what it might mean, must mean for his career.

"But where to find those letters!?" he exclaimed. It was almost as though he needed to leave right away to go in search of them.

"I'm sure Mr. Shaw still has them," I offered. "Why don't you ask him?"

Leon Edel stopped in mid-pace and came closer. "George Bernard Shaw!? I don't know—He's so very famous."

"If you don't ask, how will you know?"

"Do you really believe Mr. Shaw would see me, talk with me? Could I, could you—Could I use you as an introduction? This would be the making of my thesis, my book, the making of my career. Miss Bosanquet, I can't tell you how important this is! Thank you, thank you, my dear Miss Bosanquet!"

As a budding scholar, Leon Edel came to use his journalistic self to serve his art. George Bernard Shaw was delighted to have this eager young man interviewing him about his early days in the theatre. In 1895, George Shaw had been one of the theatre critics at the raucous opening night of Mr. James' first play and had seen for himself the disastrous response from the rowdier part of the audience. Now up in years, he was full of memories. He talked, oh, he talked, as Leon Edel was later to tell me, talked and talked, with many useful details Mr. Edel could use to imagine that pivotal event. And more importantly, as Mr. Edel later told me, "Mr. Shaw even remembered the letter—the exchange of letters I had mentioned—but he couldn't put his hand on Mr. James' special letter among the piles of his papers."

George Bernard Shaw did find Mr. James' letter to him, the one I had typed back in Rye many years before. He sent it along to the young scholar, as Leon Edel later wrote to me, crowing of his triumph. He had wanted to wait to publish this rare piece of theatre history, knowing that Mr. James had burned all his correspondence including the original letter from Mr. Shaw. Leon Edel had quite a scoop in his hands. The way he handled it would foreshadow how he used the other discoveries he made, the other secrets that I helped him find, the parts of dear Mr. James that the Master wanted the world to know.

At first, Leon Edel did not publish anything about that correspondence but instead used it to strengthen his thesis for academia. Later, he published his research in a more accessible form for a general audience and, thereby, led the rest of the world to see Henry James in a most interesting role of an elder literary advisor, who presented his thoughts on French and English theatre to young George Bernard Shaw.

I was surprised to have to wait as Mr. Edel built his reputation carefully, but Leon Edel did eventually do the right thing. Before long, we all began to read his constant stream of articles on Henry James and the Master's influence on British theatre.

Leon Edel came to see me again in 1931, when I was in Paris, working for the International Federation of University Women. I had recently returned from travelling in America, giving my little talks on Mr. Henry James at Wellesley College and at a meeting in Providence, Rhode Island. I had kept in touch with Mr. Edel, sending him my published essays on Proust and Beckett. I knew he would be interested. I had even sent him my review in "Time and Tide" about Andre Maurois' new theory of literary biography, "Aspects of Biography," asking Mr. Edel if he had ever thought of writing such a biography, hoping, hoping I had found the scholar who would keep Henry James as he truly was and perhaps even bring my Mr. James alive.

When Mr. Edel came to me again on a clear, crisp November day in 1931, he had his many questions about Mr. James and the Master's play-writing, but of course I knew only about Mr. James' last years, his second season of writing plays. Mr. Edel and I met at Café Deux Magots not far from Reid Hall. He seemed most attentive, asking for more and more stories of my time with the Master. I still did not completely trust Mr. Edel; he was so young, and what could he know of the difficulties Mr. James had faced?

But Mr. Edel was persistent: "Why did Mr. Henry James stay away from America all those years?" and "Do you think I can do more with this? I want to do the plays, be the man who knows."

He seemed more interested than before in telling me what he was thinking, what he was about to do. He was young and not under suspicion from his family and friends, as Mr. James had always been, not accused of being different, of being corrupted by Europe and by the sort of men to be found in England and on the Continent. Leon Edel knew nothing of that fear. His fear was that there would be no jobs for him, now that he had found his subject; he worried that no university would be willing to take a chance on him.

"Miss Bosanquet," he said, "I'm running short of time and must return to Canada to find paying work. I've been turned down again for any sort of fellowship, but you could help me. You must have some sort of record of those years, some notes you've kept. I've read your booklet, and I'm sure that there is more—I mean, you must have more to say. Do you think there might be something for me, for my project?"

I still was not sure of him, or of myself. Did I want to give it all away? Maybe I wanted to write a bigger book myself, more about Mr. James' way of writing, what it was he was doing—not only those lessons I had learnt from the words he dictated for the prefaces but also what I had learnt when he would take the first notes for a new story and then expand and expand.

Did I trust Leon Edel not to take it all for himself?

"I'm sure," I said to the young scholar, "that my notes are mostly not of much use to you and your thesis about Mr. James' years of writing for the theatre. After all, I was not there for the majority of his plays."

"I'm sure your more recent experiences would be most useful."

"Perhaps I could copy out the relevant passages for you. I'll be returning to London soon, after this round of meetings and the big conference in Geneva is over."

He was ebullient. "That would be most kind of you. And if I may ask, urge you, please to include every scrap of a note or a mention of anything. You may not realise—I mean, something that might not seem of importance to you, well, it might be the detail that would reveal all."

I thought: Reveal all? What was it he might be looking for? I felt myself bristling: Mr. James was right to burn all those personal notes and letters before the scholars and biographers got hold of them.

And so, I was careful as I typed out passages from my journals and diaries and sent them to the young scholar. I took great care to include every bit of the theatrical detail. He was most appreciative. I must admit that Mr. Edel was—and is—very good at ferreting out original material. He kept coming back and back. I suppose I was his first source, and may even have been the best source (because my material was both new and direct from Mr. James) for his career as the premier Henry James scholar.

After Mr. Edel finished his thesis on the dramatic years, I suggested he publish it along with an edition of those plays. "Mrs. William James has passed on," I said. "For permissions, you'll need to contact the Master's nephew, Henry James."

Mr. Edel looked surprised.

"Yes. Named for his uncle and grandfather, but they call him Harry."

"Would you, could you—"

"Of course I can give you his address. I wrote to him when his mother died. He has some sort of well-connected job in New York. They were all so proud of him."

Leon Edel came back to thank me before I left Paris. We walked from Reid Hall to our favourite café. In the evening light, Paris looked more beautiful than ever. I suppose I had let down my guard in the glow of our farewells, or maybe it was the wine, for I found myself speaking without too much thought:

"I love to imagine Mr. James walking here, as a young man— He must have been very beautiful."

"Beautiful? Was he? I've never seen photographs of him when he was younger. I wonder if there are any."

"Oh, yes. Once, he showed me a photograph taken when he was a young boy, and I saw lots of old photographs when I was packing his papers and the note-books into his old trunk."

"A trunk, filled with—?" Leon Edel leaned forward in his excitement, interrupting me.

"Well, the trunk was not that large, actually more like a sea chest with travel labels pasted all over it. He used it on every trip in those years. I always packed all the note-books for him, in case—"

"Note-books!? He kept note-books? You put note-books in a trunk? What was in them? Were they diaries?"

"No. Mr. James destroyed nearly all his really personal things, and I'm pretty sure he never kept a diary or a journal. No, these were working note-books, like composition books, where he would jot down his ideas. It was a long-time habit. I saw them many times—volumes and volumes. When we were working on the prefaces, our first work together, he set the note-books in stacks around his writing desk. Sometimes, he would pause, go over, and check in a note-book for a detail."

"Did you ever see inside one of them?"

"No. No, he was very private. He would prepare his notes for our work before I came in. I never had the opportunity. At the end, we were in such a hurry, packing everything away."

"Do you happen to know if he kept note-books while working on the plays, back long before you came, back in the nineties? I would be so thrilled if you can remember that detail."

"I don't know. When he was working on the prefaces, his order was mostly chronological. I came to him when he was dictating his preface for 'The Tragic Muse.' Do you know that work?"

"Of course! His love affair with the French theatre! But a little heavy-handed, I thought."

"Have you read the prefaces?"

"No, I read all the James novels in the McGill Library, but they didn't acquire the New York Edition."

"If you have a chance, you should study that preface. It has much to say about Mr. James and his theories about the theatre. He had already given it quite a lot of thought, before he wrote that novel, long before he wrote the plays. Perhaps you have not seen his prefaces about the shorter works he wrote after his plays, after his first dramatic years?"

"I've been looking only at the plays, at his strange and, to me, sudden attempts to write dramas. My questions are all focused on the time before and during."

"Have you wondered why he stopped?"

"Of course—that disastrous first night! That was certainly enough for anyone. He'd struggled all along with the form and the British theatre conditions, the audiences and their suburban train schedules, but that night must have destroyed him. Psychologically, it must have been a death."

"I have a feeling," I said, "that it was not only that night which turned him back to his other writing. You see, it might be that he actually continued with his dramatic experiment by transferring all that he'd learnt into the writing of his shorter novels. Mr. Edel, look to his prefaces."

Leon Edel was gathering his papers and putting on his coat in too much of a hurry to listen to my theories. Perhaps a beginning researcher has to focus on his own theories and not let his own ideas be tainted with anyone else's.

"Miss Bosanquet, I must leave you now. I hope I can see you again. You've been enormously helpful. I must go back soon to America. I want to see about that sea chest of yours. I wonder how I might see it." He was talking to himself. It seemed almost as if I no longer existed. His focus had completely changed. "I wonder where it could be." He looked at me in horror. "You don't think they might have destroyed it?"

"I'm sure they've forgotten all about that sea chest. It's probably in some basement or attic. If you like, I'll write to Harry James about you and your project with the plays, but it will be up to you to ask about the sea chest. You may use my name. He'll remember."

Before long, with Mr. James' nephew at his side, Mr. Edel went down into the store-rooms at Harvard University to search for the sea chest. He wrote me that he had found the note-books, as I had said, and went on about how young Harry James was very impressed with his scholarly work on the plays. The two arranged to publish the plays, and Harry James offered future help after Mr. Edel returned to Montreal.

Mr. Edel also wrote that he was excited about the possibilities of editing and publishing the note-books, but this was not to be, at least not immediately. Those were dark days for Mr. Edel, since he was still looking for paying work. His Sorbonne degree did not lead to professorial posts in Canada. In fact, he sounded rather desperate. This was after the Crash, 1932. Everyone was looking for work. He was lucky he could make his living as a journalist. I watched for his by-lines. Then came years of silence, for we in England were in the midst of our own dark days.

25

"The Aspern Papers"

1946-1956

*There are parts of one's past, evidently, that bask consentingly
and serenely enough in the light of other days—which is but
the intensity of thought ; and there are other parts that take
it as with agitation and pain, a troubled consciousness that
heaves as with the disorder of drinking it deeply in.*

—Henry James
Preface to "The Aspern Papers"
The New York Edition, volume 12

Life intervened. The sea chest remained in a storage
room at Harvard, for Mr. Edel had his study on Mr.
James and the dramatic years to finish and then the even more
daunting task of finding and editing all the plays. He kept in touch
as each change in his fortunes came about—first the publishing of
his thesis and then, after my connecting him with the James family,
his pursuit of the other facets of Mr. James' life that interested him.

After he published the complete edition of all Mr. James' plays
with the publisher I had introduced him to and after he had moved
to New York, with permission from the James family, he began the

biographical articles and essays that made his career as the Henry James Professor at New York University. He married a doctor, also very smart, a psychiatrist trained in Freud's theories, as many in that field were in those days. I followed her career as well.

Mr. Edel wrote that we had apparently both done well, for each of us had found a new life. I had sent him a letter from a cruise ship in the Mediterranean, my first cruise with Margaret, Lady Rhondda. With his quickness, Mr. Edel saw right away what that postmark meant and what my letter about my new arrangement said. For me, life had taken an amazing shift, as I found myself with one of the wealthiest women in Britain—in the world, even—travelling on our own without any struggle of pretending.

I had become the companion and dearest friend of my Margaret, Lady Rhondda, with all that this involved—great travel, great conversations, and shared work on her magazine, "Time and Tide." This meant lots of typing and editing, as well as my own responsibilities as head of the "Time and Tide" Book Department, where I decided which books to review and recruited the best reviewers. Margaret had started the weekly as an alternative newspaper when we women finally obtained the Vote, since the main-line papers were abuzz with how women needed to be told what to think and *how* to vote. Surely we women could not think on our own. By the mid-1930s, "Time and Tide" had become a well-respected weekly. I was busy and happy.

In May 1937, Mr. Edel was in London on a Guggenheim Fellowship. I was again able to help him with copies of my letters and more diary passages, which seemed pertinent.

When I invited him to a big party at "Time and Tide," he asked if he might bring his wife. I was delighted. That evening, I was watching for them to arrive. I wanted to be sure he felt welcomed, and I was curious to meet his wife. We had reorganised the editing floor of "Time and Tide" for the party so that guests entered the festivities as soon as they came through the doors. It was a loud and smoky affair, catered, with plenty to eat and drink. Mr. Edel paused on the threshold, surprised, I suppose, for I had not made it clear that "Time and Tide" was mostly women, who were well-known, even famous, and good, loud talkers.

So there was my Mr. Edel, and beside him was the most gorgeous creature I could imagine, tall and stately with dark dark hair, not bobbed as so many of us had taken to. No, she had wound her hair up into a crown of braids that made her even taller. She was dressed very studiously. She looked European, even distinguished, and her face was luminous, with eyes that could watch and look and see into you. I shook his hand, and he introduced her as the doctor that she was, and she shook my hand. I brought them over to find glasses of wine—or was it to be something stronger? And then we talked there, in some hidden corner of the offices, out of the chaos. His glorious wife looked around and listened while Mr. Edel and I caught up.

"Miss Bosanquet," he said. "I've wanted to ask you—" He looked over to his wife, who was watching the room, but she turned to us. "We were curious about something that Mr. Harry James and I found when we opened the sea chest. I did not really have a chance to look at it, only a glance, but it seemed to be pages from your typewriter, something Mr. James had dictated at his deathbed. Do you—Well, of course, you remember."

He took in more of his drink and went on. "It seemed something of a Napoléonic fragment that I saw, and clearly you had typed one signature as Napoléon. Can you shine any light on that strange matter?"

His wife nodded and leaned forward, expecting me to tell all, I suppose.

Instead I had a question of my own. "Did Mr. Harry James see it, too?"

"Oh, not at first, but I was exclaiming so. He came to see what it was. He snatched the papers from me, and that was the end of our work. Without so much as a comment, he gathered up everything we'd taken out and packed it back into the chest. Yes, he did see the pages."

By then, his wife was listening. I sought an elusive escape. "There at the end, things were very confusing. Burgess and I were trying everything we could do to try to help Mr. James. We used the sound of the typewriter to calm him down if he got to feeling agitated. Perhaps you know how it can be—" I looked to his wife as if for confirmation from a medical personage. "Sometimes, there at the end, things seemed all a muddle. We would do anything we could to make the Master comfortable."

She nodded, and we went on to other bedside, last-words stories. Soon, I was able to usher them over to meet Margaret, who wanted to introduce Mr. Tom Eliot, who did not like parties, and his friend Mary (who did), and to Mr. Ezra Pound, who did not like Margaret, but our food was good (for we had a good supply of everyone's favourite liquour), and there was Miss Veronica Wedgwood, so elegant and brilliant, and then some of our oldest friends, such as Mrs. Rebecca West, and even the publisher Mr. Rupert Hart Davis. Really, it was a great success, and I believe the Edels were very pleased.

In late 1939, when the War came, Mr. Edel was sent on assignment to Paris. I lost contact with him when Paris fell. With his dangerous, perhaps even secret, work, he stopped writing his charming letters to me.

We in London celebrated Mr. James' Centennial Birthday, even though it had to be in a small way because we were in the midst of the Second Great War. On April 13, 1943, about fifteen of us gathered for dinner. We spoke with such pathos and feeling for the Master and raised many toasts to his work, his life, and his sweet soul. As the party was winding down, there came to be talk of what we would do about Mr. James' *oeuvre* and reputation after the War.

One suggestion came from someone with the BBC, who thought that I, with my low-pitched voice, should read Henry James on the radio. That would be a sign that civilisation had at last returned! I laughed, but, no, they all loved the idea. The man from BBC said he would be in touch. Rupert Hart Davis said, "But how about that book of yours, the one you did for the Woolf woman. Maybe you could read some of 'Henry James at Work.'" They all thought this would make a terrific BBC programme, and they said Mr. Davis should publish more of my reminiscences about Henry James, more of what I had to say. It all ended with more toasts and more silliness.

Eventually the BBC did get back to me.

But before that, when at last I was able to contact Mr. Edel once again after the War, we arranged to meet. It was 1949. Leon Edel had just published "The Complete Plays of Henry James" and came to sign a copy for me. We were savouring before-dinner drinks at the Ivy, one of our favourite restaurants, Margaret's and mine, cosy and elegant. Strange to say, five years after the War, it still seemed incredible to me to have good Scotch for the asking. I began by telling him all about the Centennial Dinner and how we had missed him and had sent a few toasts his way.

"Was the War really so bad here, Miss Bosanquet? How close was it to you?"

"Our flat in Maida Vale was partially destroyed, bombed during the Blitz. We moved everything twice."

Mr. Edel looked frightened. "Everything? Your notes and diaries, they survived, I hope."

I thought it strange he did not ask about where we were in the house when the bombs fell and if we had been hurt.

"A few of my diaries were destroyed."

He looked even more concerned at my answer.

"But luckily, not the ones you want. A friend had borrowed some of my diaries. Those were safe."

He looked relieved, then a little ashamed, "And you and Lady Rhondda, were you both all right?"

"We were away from home, thankfully. But what about you, Mr. Edel, how did you survive? I lost track of you once you went to Europe. I tried to send you letters, but they came back."

He looked away, then back. "I was luckier than most. They took me into a journalists' unit. I was trained, then sent off, you know, here and there—"

From his practised way of evading a question, I wondered if, with his very good French, he had been recruited into the intelligence services, something secret; but of course he would never tell.

He went on, "When I was demobilised and sent back to New York, I found another surprise waiting for me. I'd wanted to keep on with my work on Mr. James, only I'm stymied, Miss Bosanquet." Mr. Edel was charming, leaning a little towards me, his quick dark eyes so expressive of intelligence, and his manner of we-two-know-about-this confiding only in me. "I returned to Harvard to examine the sea chest, expecting to use Mr. James' note-books, the ones you'd put me onto. But they were unavailable. Unavailable!" He looked in my eyes, searching for what? For recognition of his disappointment? Of his expectation of failure?

"What does that mean?" I asked. "'Unavailable'?"

"It means others had them, were using them, and had them set aside for their personal project—those Harvard professors who never gave me anything, who ignored my articles, who never knew what treasures Harvard kept in that store-room until I took Harry James down to find that chest. *They* had that treasure trove in hand, and woe unto any non-Harvard imposters and interlopers."

"I'm so sorry." I tried to imagine his disappointment. But there was more:

"I was furious, those fellows who were sitting safe and sound with some sort of medical deferment, pawing through that chest for all those years while I was stuck in the War, and now they have published an edition of the note-books. That was two years ago! But those are *my* note-books, *our* note-books, Miss Bosanquet, the ones you first told me of. Those two would never have paid a bit of attention before my first visit. Now, everything is lost."

"Not really lost, is it?" I said. "Now, everyone can see them."

"Oh, no. Those two have their own organisation of the note-books, their own notes and ways of using the note-books."

I was surprised. "Why? What were you planning to do with them?"

"Well, first, use them to throw more light on his plays, my specialty. And then I'd like to build on my research, all the people I've talked with, the correspondence I've copied, and then write a comprehensive study, a full biography. Not an edited collection like this—" He tapped the dust jacket of the volume he had signed for me. "I want to do a full biography, a study in five volumes!"

"Of Mr. James? But the Master never wanted anyone—"

"I'm sure, if I could have talked with Mr. James, I could have changed his mind."

I thought to myself: Yes, Mr. Edel, you probably would have changed the Master's mind.

I found myself offering solace, offering help. "But you can write a comprehensive biography. I'm sure you can. You can build on all the work you've done and go back to the family, enlist their assistance."

"There's an idea. You're right. If I can persuade the family to place a restriction on using the materials, then they will all be mine again—except for those note-books, but never mind them."

I agreed to give Mr. Edel copies of some of my notes. I was sure that he was once again on his way. Soon enough, I heard from him. He had secured the family's permission not only to publish editions of the Master's letters and his short stories, but also, as he was so proud to let me know, to be the official biographer of Henry James. Ah, he was charming, that young rascal, and very ambitious.

I watched his career rise, though with not so many letters written to the Master's aging amanuensis, who had helped him early on. But Mr. Edel would still send along his questions: Who was Mrs. So-and-So? Did I ever notice Mr. James wearing a certain tie pin, perhaps made from a Roman coin? Did I remember it?

I followed Mr. Edel's articles in those days after the War, but here in London, life was still very difficult; sometimes, even correspondence seemed impossible. Whenever I found the articles he told me about, it seemed that Mr. Edel's research was a little like his work as a journalist, with each new piece presented as part of a puzzle devised by Leon Edel, the sleuth searching for clues to Mr. James' hidden life.

In time, I noticed a shift in his work. Back at Lawrence Street so many years before, I had spent many hours listening to lectures at the Society for Psychical Research in the early days of Dr. Sigmund Freud's conquest of the psychological world. I thought I recognised the Freudian basis in Professor Edel's choices of explanations for the James family. I wondered: Was this the influence of his Freudian-trained wife? Mr. Edel seemed to be adding theories and explanations to his previous straightforward fact-finding searches, almost to be looking for evidence to support psychological theories about the young boy, the powerful mother, the distant father. In 1955, he even published "The Psychological Novel: 1900–1950," which indicated where he was probably headed.

I did not like it. Of course, I still thought I knew more than Leon Edel. I still had hopes of what I could do myself with what I knew. However, it was too late, for as I grew less trusting of

Mr. Edel, it seemed that I was less and less able to do what I had dreamed of: to write my own book with our secrets.

Mr. James and I had kept our deepest passions secret. As I have said, in England, before and even after the Second Great War, it was a crime for a man to love another man, though it was not legally dangerous for a woman to love another woman. As soon as Freudian psychology took over, our passions became a sickness. Many people held that such love was against Nature and against God. We were back to "inversion" and other derogatory terms from the turn of the century. Many of us—Lady Rhondda, my lover, our friends—were once again afraid, as had been true at the time of Henry James and his friends.

Now, Mr. Edel was bringing his wife's psychological stance to researching the biography. What would he be saying? Oh, not about the mother, the father, but about the deepest springs of the Master's creative art? In the early and mid-1950s, artists were also suspect, their lives, their work revealing evidence of sickness clearly to those who knew how to read it. And so, as Mr. Edel more persistently sought to have all my diaries from those years with Mr. James, I grew more persistently reluctant to share them.

In 1956, the BBC invited me for a third time to talk about the Master. It had been almost fifty years since I first started to work for Henry James. I found myself thinking once again about the sea chest and the Master's last dictations with his last two unusual letters. There we were, Leon Edel and I, each with our knowledge of Mr. James' secrets, illicit passions, all that his letters and note-books might reveal, in spite of the Master's direct orders to burn everything.

And here I was again, sitting with those dictations among his last writings. I would have to decide: Was this evidence of madness, of a sick mind? Did it expose egomania? Was it evidence connected to that self, to those selves he had kept hidden? Did it reveal a monster? Or was this merely a mind ravaged, a mind where linkages no longer flowed as they had before. Was the writing in those last dictations like all those strange novels with their strange images, almost as if the writer had been possessed? Or, did the last dictations reveal something else, evidence of the world after death that Professor William James had postulated?

After the Great War and then this Second Great War, we knew more about the season of dying. I had seen so much of it. Part of me had gone on keeping the carbon copy of those last typed pages, still hoping to keep faith with that Other World.

But maybe those last dictated words were the Master's summary image of himself and his works as part of a grand enterprise, a campaign, a series of battles, all planned out and prepared for, fought valiantly against every kind of weakness and trouble, all to achieve the grand structures that were his books, his creative life, which was his life.

I was thinking about this once again in 1955, as I prepared for my presentation on the BBC. I had read for the BBC before, and we had done one taped, two-hour interview some months before at my flat, but this time, in rehearsal, I seemed to fail at everything I wanted to say. Michael Swan told me that I read too fast, as everyone does in rehearsal. He was the narrator and the author of one of the newest books on Henry James. I was extremely nervous. Everything was new to me—the tiny room where I was to sit, the half-finished look of the walls, no paint, white dotted tiles everywhere, an old beat-up wooden chair, a small table, the huge microphone towering over everything, and that closed-in feeling after they shut the door. They gave me earphones, put them on me, so they could talk to me from the control room. I was uncomfortable, could not breathe, and did not know how to talk to the engineer, for my little box had no windows. The air felt old, used, dusty, unnatural, used up.

The voice through the earphones was kind but hurried.

"Lean into the microphone, Mrs., uh, Miss Bosanquet, and read your piece."

I cleared my throat.

The voice shouted, "No, no! Never do that. You have to do all that before we record!"

I smoothed out the papers I had been clutching.

The voice came again. "What's that noise? You must hold still. This microphone is the newest, the best, the most sensitive. It will pick up the smallest sounds."

I held absolutely still and stiff and began to read the words before me, the ones I had written. I felt like wood, like stone, trapped, enclosed, and waiting for that voice to crash into my ears. But I made it through to the end. I was safe.

Or so I thought.

This time, the voice through the earphones was quieter, but the tone was one of reprimand. "That will do, Miss Bosanquet." I could hear the rustling of papers. "Please look over the notes I've made so you can be better prepared tomorrow."

Defeated, I went home to revise.

26

"The Beast in the Jungle"

June 1956

*You will be feeling a great void now; but you will
have happy & dear memories of the long years of your
collaboration with one of the wisest & noblest men that ever
lived. We who knew him well know how great he would
have been if he had never written a line.*

—Edith Wharton
Letter to Theodora Bosanquet

I walked slowly back home to Arlington House, carrying the script I had written, knowing I would have to decide what more I wanted to say. But how could I decide?

I let myself into the apartment, which felt dark and empty. I remembered that Margaret was staying late at "Time and Tide," probably meeting some of our authors for drinks, even for dinner at the Ivy. The quiet stretched out before me as I went to the back of the flat and to my own room, to my own night's work. I had decided I would look back over the letters I had from Mr. James and the carbons I had secretly kept. Maybe seeing the Master's work afresh, reading his words anew and weighing them would help.

What was it I wanted this broadcast to do? What was I trying to accomplish years after the Master's death? What had I always been trying to do? Help him? Protect him? Save him? Even when I began our work together, I knew Mr. James needed my help. I felt his gladness that I was there. I understood him, I think, in some way not deeper than his friends but more than they, for I knew him in all his moods and strengths and illnesses and disillusionments, his triumphs, his joys.

I had continued protecting him, first by saving the living, complex, contradictory parts of him from his family's small-minded vision of who he was, saving the larger Henry James, who was so much more than the ex-American who had turned his back on his own people. He was a writer for the world, a writer who had begun the modern novel, who had brought a new largeness to the form. I was also still protecting the deeply passionate man.

I thought about the exclusionary guidelines Percy Lubbock had been forced to follow in choosing the Master's letters and then how each new scholar and critic had come to me, asking but not saying his real questions: Did Henry James ever love anyone? Was all his life only about the work? Even today, England and the world still punish men like Henry James, with his deep passions. Those scholars never saw me; their use for me was only to frame their own versions of Henry James. I brushed aside their prurient speculations, the ugliness, for the world cannot yet see the full complexities of a man, such as Henry James, with all his strengths and triumphs. Instead, the world is led to see sickness and shame.

I took down my James boxes and set them on the bed. The first box held some queries from Leon Edel—Professor Edel, as he now was. I could smile at his title but not at Mr. Edel's reluctance to speak of Mr. James' passion, the Master's great heart. Instead of portraying a feeling, caring man, Professor Edel seemed to be depicting Mr. James as cold and analytical. Perhaps Leon Edel had lost some of his own heart during the War, or perhaps he had suffered too many life disappointments, which had forced him to become hardened, to insist on being the only one to use the Henry James papers so that he could become an esteemed professor.

Then I came across a copy of a letter from Mr. Pinker, Mr. James' agent, who had heard somewhere that there was another unfinished manuscript. Mr. Harry James, the nephew, wanted to know if there were anything to this rumour. I remember thinking with some cynicism: Mr. Harry James thinks there's more money to be made. My reply had been short.

Harry James' letter back to Mr. Pinker was a bit dissembling. Mr. Edel told me about this exchange when he was working on the biography and had access to the James family's letters to Mr. Pinker as well as, finally, all the papers at Harvard. The letter bore the coldness of the family's shame at the Master's strange deathbed words, which Harry James insisted must be kept secret:

Mr. Harry James wrote to Mr. Pinker after learning from Mr. Edel about the Master's last letters, saying this was "so slight an indication of whatever may have been my Uncle's intention, that I fully agree with what I infer were my Mother's and Mr. Lubbock's opinions. . . ."

I thought again about Mr. James' intention. Those last dictated words would have meant something different to the Professor and Henry James' sister, Alice James, compared with Mrs. William James and Harry James. The remaining James family did not even begin to understand the Master's importance and stature until long after his death, and even then, they remained ashamed of him, of his choices. They were ready to hide away his life, his true passions—Ah, not the young beautiful men Mr. James so admired, though the family was ashamed of them as well. Rather, it was the Master's choice to stay in England, to write novels, to write shockingly good, strange, not-for-the-young-girl novels. The family's embarrassment over the Master continued with wanting to control his unpublished works and particularly the previously ignored materials I had packed up with such care—the letters, note-books, and fragments. Of course, it was their legal right to decide who would see what, who could use those largely unread words. Now, that material was in the control of Professor Edel, the official biographer, who would willingly follow the family's posture of secrecy to shield shame. Yet those last writings were Mr. James' legacy as much as his unfinished novels. Mr. Edel had written to me about those "Napoleonic fragments," as he called them, which he had seen at Harvard and which he promised to use "with discretion."

There was nothing to be done.

Only, there might be.

Perhaps I could do something in my reading for the BBC and open up a new vision of Henry James to BBC listeners around the world.

What if I were to read from the Master's deathbed dictations?

I found the typed carbons.

Staring once again at his typed words, I realised that they harboured the way for me to have my say in how we remember Henry James. I would read his last professional, dictated words and, thereby, make Mr. James' last written piece part of the public record. The family, Professor Edel, and all the other biographers would have to take Henry James' last pieces of writing-as-dictation with his professional amanuensis into account. I would introduce the reading in such a way as to emphasise my interpretation countering the family's shameful view and the Freudian interpretation from Professor Edel, with his eagerness to make a name for himself.

I would make sure Mr. James was perceived as I wanted and that his words were understood. I would take my part of the Henry James story back for myself.

But if I chose to read those unpublished dictations on the air, then wouldn't I be the one not respecting the Master's desire for privacy?

Yet those last writings were Mr. James' legacy as much as his unfinished novels.

Sorting once again through my own papers as I ruminated about the BBC programme, I thought back to that trip the Master and I had taken in returning to Rye—our bicycle ride to the Channel, our conversation by the sea. We could hear the sound of guns thudding, low and rhythmic, more of a physical pressure than a real sound, an ominous far-off presence. We had been working on "The Ivory Tower" about the American obsession with business and success, but Mr. James could not go on. That novel no longer fit him. America was no longer important to him; his country of birth had lost its moral direction.

He spoke about how he and his brothers used to play at war when they lived in France, how the French boys knew all about war, having grown up with families torn apart by the movements of armies, how the James brothers loved to watch the French boys play with tin soldiers, setting them up in ranks, knocking them down. The French boys always talked of Napoléon, not as the emperor but as the general. Younger than the others, Henry James vowed to learn all he could about the French boys' mysterious hero.

That day by the sea, the Master wondered how he could keep on with our work, all those words, when there was such horror over there across the Channel, a horror made by men. What could he write that would matter? I had never heard him speak like that in so low a voice, so discouraged, so tired. In the past, when he had stopped writing, he never mentioned his desolation but would only tell me not to come in for a day or two. But this was different. What had he been hearing? Was it our guns? Was it the enemy's? Whose friend was down in the mud, struggling to breathe, his blood around him, the earth taking him back?

Remembering that day years later, I felt sure Mr. James could sense his own death looming. I have always felt gratified to have had those moments when he expressed his trust in me, when he entrusted me with his work, when he let me pick up what he offered and carry it forward for him. I realised that I had kept the carbon copies of those last writings with implicit agreement from Henry James, when his body was deserting him, leaving his mindful soul exposed.

The BBC reading would allow me to continue our agreement. I saw what I was to do. I would be keeping my word by making sure the Master's very last formally dictated writing was understood as it was dictated from the complex world of his soulful imagination. I was a good editor. I could adjust the script I had written for the BBC to accommodate new material from the Master. I could include his deathbed dictations.

I would begin with an excerpt from the first dictation, which was rather long. I wanted it as a message for the James family, Mr. Edel, and other James biographers and scholars. These were his words, the Master's strangely moving power, yes, but not ravings.

No, these were striking, forceful images, the sort he always used. I remember thinking as I chose that first passage: I want that "*bloody beak*" of the "*imperial eagle.*" I want the terror, the plucking!

I found myself thinking of Mr. Edel and his energetic, almost frenzied snatching at facts. I wanted Mr. Edel and his colleagues to know that as Henry James was dying and as the family was gathering, perhaps the Master did feel the first omens of defeat and of death, but he was warning his family of his intentions, even then. He was playing his part with assurance. The family needed to face him, still in all his powers.

The next day, my final BBC taping, I felt strangely calm as I sat in front of the microphone. The narrator, Michael Swan, read the words I had written for his part, the introduction to Mr. James' last days:

> Miss Bosanquet said that even when he was confined to his bed during his last illness the impulse to write remained and he would dictate to her.

Sitting in the silent cubicle, I began reading my own narrative:

> But on the evening of December 11th, he appeared to wish to dictate. He was very ill, the stroke which had partly paralysed him had been followed by embolic pneumonia. And on that day he'd been wandering in delirium, quite unconscious of his actual surroundings or the persons he had in, and the typewriter was taken into his room and he dictated.

Michael Swann picked up his narration:

> It is not possible to give the whole of this strangely moving and absolutely characteristic final dictation of the Master. One may call it a vision—a vision in which he sees his own utterly dedicated life as in some way paralleled by the career of Napoleon. Here is a short passage from the dictation.

I took a deep breath and read from Mr. James' text:

> *They pluck in their terror handfuls of plumes from the Imperial Eagle, and with no greater credit in consequence than that they face, keeping their equipoise, the awful bloody beak that he turns round on them. We see the beak sufficiently directed in that/vindictive [sic] intention during those days of cold, grey Switzerland weather, on the huddled and hustled after-campaigns, the first omens of defeat. Everyone looks haggard, and our only wonder is that they still succeed in looking at all. It renews for us the assurance that the part played by that element in the famous assurance [sic], divinity that doth hedge a king.*

I stopped as planned, and Michael Swan came in:

> The next morning Henry James again wished to dictate, and again he spoke as if motivated by some deeply rooted empathy to enter the mind of Napoleon. He dictated two letters, the first concerned with the decoration of the royal palaces in Paris.

Sitting there in front of that dreaded microphone, I thought how Mr. James would have loved to hear these words read over the radio, these playful and charming words creating roles, once again giving parts to his brother and sister, William and Alice. I began again to read the Master's words:

> *Dear and most esteemed brother and sister. I call your attention to the precious enclosed transcripts of plans and designs for the decoration of certain apartments of the palaces here, the Louvre and the Tuileries, and I beg you to let us know from stage to stage how the scheme promises, and what results it may be held to inspire. It is, you will see, of great scope, a majesty unsurpassed by any work of the kind yet undertaken in France. Please understand I regard these plans as fully developed, and as having had my*

last consideration and look forward to no patchings, nor perversions, and with no question of modifications, either economic or aesthetic. This will be the case with all further projects of your affectionate Napoleon.

I smiled as I read, thinking how even here Mr. James was scoring his points over Balzac with Mr. James' own great scope and his own collected works. He was scoring over his family and even over the Jamesian scholars. He had been clear: "*No patchings, nor perversions.*" And at the end, even saying, "*This will be the case with all further projects.*"

As Michael Swan's voice came in, I thought about how the next letter was not as metaphorical, except for the conceit of writing to deceased people and Henry James' treating the legacy of his writing life as if it were his Empire to be doled out to descendants. I wondered if his sister-in-law had ever read the Master's letters written many years before in fun to his brother and his nephew.

Michael Swann was finishing his section of my script:

The second letter was written as from Napoleon to his brother Joseph and his wife, persuading Joseph to accept the throne of Spain.

Then I read more of the Master's text:

My dear brother and sister. I offer you great opportunities in exchange for the exercise of great zeal. Your position as residents of your young but so highly considered Republic at one of the most interesting minor capitals, is a piece of luck which may be turned to account in the measure of your acuteness and your experience. A brilliant fortune may come to crown it, and your personal merit will not diminish that harmony, but you must rise to each occasion. The one I now offer you is of no common cast, and please remember that any failure to push your advantage to the utmost will be severely judged. I have displayed you as persons of great taste and judgment [sic]. Don't leave me a sorry figure in consequence, but present me rather as your fond but not infatuated relation, able and ready to back you up, your faithful brother and brother in law, Henry James.

I caught my breath. I could feel tears gathering.

My voice had become husky, but I had kept on, determined to reach the end. I had practiced that strange, playful recapitulation of the childhood theatrics of Emperor Napoléon, his brother (Joseph-Napoléon Bonaparte), and King Joseph's wife (Julie Clary) played by William, Henry, and Alice James. I had dared to speak out in public in the voice of Henry James, the devoted middle sibling in that three-some.

I breathed in deeply the quiet of that checkered room with its softened echoes.

Afterword

An Amanuensis for an
Amanuensis for an Amanuensis

The Story behind This Book

Author Susan Herron Sibbet (1942–2013) described *The Constant Listener* as "an imagined memoir." She based her novel, which is written in the voice of amanuensis Theodora Bosanquet (1880–1961), on extensive research in the Bosanquet and James Collections at Harvard University's Houghton Library, as well as on other sources. Bosanquet kept a page-a-day diary during her years working for Henry James (1843–1916), and she carried on a prolific correspondence with her women friends in London about her work with James in Rye.

In many ways, *The Constant Listener* is the PhD thesis Sibbet never completed. She graduated from public high school in segregated Alexandria, Virginia, in 1960 and attended first Brown University and then the University of Virginia, when UVA insisted that its women students could major only in nursing or education. When Sibbet applied for graduate school in English literature, no English-literature professor at the University of Virginia would write her a reference letter, because she was a woman. Nevertheless, Sibbet went on to become the second woman to receive a Woodrow Wilson Fellowship; she completed some of the writing on her thesis about Henry James. A poet, Sibbet earned an MA in English literature and an MA with a concentration in creative writing before San Francisco State University established its MFA in Creative Writing.

Susan Sibbet died from cancer in August 2013. We had been best friends since first grade. For decades, I had encouraged her with this book, suggesting (along with others) that she apply for a prestigious Bunting Fellowship (now, regretfully, discontinued) at Radcliffe, where she could research the James and Bosanquet papers. While at the Bunting Institute in 1992, Susan composed some of the first writings that, much transformed, appear in this book. She received other fellowships to work on this project, including at the Headlands Center for the Arts in San Francisco and at Stanford University.

But life intervened, as it does, with busy children, grandchildren, her husband's work, her poetry and poets' group, and her own work as long-time mentor for and teacher in California Poets in the Schools, as well as cofounder and copublisher of Sixteen Rivers Press.

As I look back over our sixty-plus years of friendship, I can see now that in Susie's efforts to complete *The Constant Listener,* her greatest strength—her endless extrovert energy—also became her greatest obstacle. The Bunting Fellowship required that she rein in her sociability, seat-belt herself to a chair, research the James and Bosanquet papers, and begin to produce a manuscript. The other fellowships had similar expectations.

In the mid-1990s, Susie stayed with me for several weeks at my small farm in Appalachian Ohio. I would not engage with her during the day. She wrote by hand on my front porch and had only monosyllabic cows for a daytime audience. She worked on *Theo,* as we who knew and loved Susan all called this project. In the evenings, she and I had an ongoing discussion: What would have been the effect on James if his amanuensis were not merely a typist—a blank wall—but, instead, an intrigued listener? Wouldn't that have affected James's dictation and, therefore, his writing?

In the summer of 2011, for several weeks, Susan and I shared Heinrich Böll's Cottage on Achill Island, Ireland, where Susan worked at the Nobel Prize–winning author's desk overlooking the Atlantic. By then, Susan had fully recuperated (or so we thought) from stage 1 cancer. As during the extended visit at my farm in Ohio, I was an enforcer. Once again, I refused to emerge from my room until 6 p.m. This time, Susan had only monosyllabic sheep for distraction. She wrote.

In early 2013, the cancer reappeared, this time in Susan's lungs, this time as stage 4. I was living in Ha Noi, Viet Nam but with more scheduling freedom than Susan's husband, David, and their grown children. I went to San Francisco in January 2013 for an extended stay with Susan during chemotherapy so that David could travel for his work. Susan and I had not spent so much time talking since eighth grade. We were both aware that stage 4 cancer brings apprehension and a keen consciousness of time.

One day, I asked whether I might look at whatever Susan had written for *Theo*. I had read pieces of the manuscript but had never seen it as a whole. She went to her study and returned with two black, snap-bound PhD binders. While she napped, I sailed through the first binder, delighted by the voice and the unfolding story. I penciled in a few small suggestions. Then I opened the second binder: There had been too many of those life interruptions. The text was chaos, utter chaos, but redeemable chaos. That evening, I asked Susan whether she would like me to work on the manuscript together with her by e-mail.

From January to May, I immersed myself in James's and Bosanquet's texts on the Web and in Susan's narrative. As the weeks progressed, so did Susan's cancer. News came from David that cancer had appeared in her brain. I became brazen in rewriting, editing, researching, changing, correcting. Yet with all the shifting of chapters and paragraphs to fit what I call "psychological logic," with all my cutting of repetitions, combining repetitive sections and sentences, and rewriting sentences, in truth, I wrote only a half page of new text.

In May 2013, I returned to San Francisco, a USB in hand. By then, Susan had had brain radiation and was entering hospice care, but as far as I could tell, the cancer had not affected her mind. She and I printed out the full manuscript so that she could hold *Theo* in her hands. My additional half page was printed in yellow. Aside from some of the epigraphs, that half page was the only section for which I felt I needed Susan's permission. She made her way through the typescript, adding comments and changes on sticky notes. She, David, and I defined David's role as literary executor and my continuing role as editor. We three had long discussions about publishing *Theo* and about *Theo*'s formal identity as *The Constant Listener*.

Since Susie's death, I have checked and fine-tuned the manuscript, aligning it with James's and Bosanquet's diaries and writings at Harvard's Houghton and Widener Libraries. During that visit four years ago, in May 2013, when Susan held a complete draft of her manuscript in hand, we chuckled at the irony that she had finally become the successful amanuensis for Theodora Bosanquet and that I, in turn, had become Susan's amanuensis.

Lady Borton
Summer 2017

Acknowledgments

Author Susan Herron Sibbet held a fellowship in 1992 at the Mary Ingraham Bunting Institute, now the Radcliffe Institute, to research in the Theodora Bosanquet Papers and the Henry James Papers at Harvard's Houghton Library. The fellowship provided sufficient travel funds to research in libraries in England and to interview James's biographer, Leon Edel, in Hawaii. Sibbet was always clear that the Bunting Fellowship was the impetus for *The Constant Listener.*

Artist-in-residence awards at the Headlands Center for the Arts in San Francisco and a stay at the Heinrich Böll Cottage on Achill Island, Ireland, enabled Sibbet to work on the manuscript, while her time at Stanford University provided a community of writers. Sibbet was also appreciative of these opportunities and grateful for assistance from staff and colleagues.

Susan Sibbet was particularly grateful for the consistent support from her husband, David Sibbet, and from her writers' group in San Francisco.

Archivists at Harvard's Houghton Library and Dartmouth's Rauner Special Collections Library were helpful with checking details in the manuscript and compiling the notes.

Special thanks are also due to Gillian Berchowitz, director; Ricky Huard, acquisitions editor; Nancy Basmajian, managing editor; Sally Bennett Boyington, copyeditor; Beth Pratt, production manager; and their colleagues at Ohio University Press for turning Sibbet's manuscript into this handsome edition of *The Constant Listener.*

Notes

Susan Herron Sibbet did extensive research for *The Constant Listener* in the Theodora Bosanquet and Henry James Collections at the Houghton Library of Harvard University while on a Radcliffe Bunting Fellowship in the early 1990s. She also spent extensive time researching in many libraries in England, where she visited sites (particularly in Rye and London) described in this imagined memoir. In addition, she traveled to Hawaii to interview the famous James biographer, Leon Edel, who appears as a character in the narrative.

For consistency in quotations, we have used Henry James's style in *The Novels and Tales of Henry James* (New York: Charles Scribner's Sons, 1907–9), the twenty-four-volume New York Edition (hereafter abbreviated as NYE), because Theodora Bosanquet worked on those texts. The NYE includes James's prefaces but not all his novels and tales. British style choices of that time differ from current American scholarly style in several details, including spelling, contractions (such as "should n't"), hyphenation of compounds (such as "note-book"), capitalization, and the use of quotation marks for titles. Quotations from James's other published work follow the publishers' styles. Published James quotations are in italics. Fictional dialogue by James is based on archival research; those quotations appear in roman type, with annotations (see below) for quotations by James taken directly from Theodora Bosanquet's diaries. Henry James's published work is in the public domain; readers can download the Master's works from the Web.

Theodora Bosanquet's papers are in Harvard's Houghton Library (hereafter abbreviated as HOU, with a finding aid at http://oasis.lib.harvard.edu/oasis/deliver/~hou00370). The collection includes many handwritten diaries, though some diaries were destroyed during the Nazi bombing of Britain. Most entries are only a half-page or a page long and not descriptive, although the far fewer typed entries from 1912 through 1914 are more expansive. Some of Sibbet's *The Constant Listener* is based on Theodora Bosanquet's *Henry James at Work* (Hogarth Press, 1924, published by Leonard and Virginia Woolf), a small book on which Bosanquet based other published writings and her BBC interviews about James.

✳

Page vii: Epigraph, "We who knew him well," James HOU b MS Eng 1213.3/276.

✳

Chapter 1: "The Tragic Muse"

This chapter builds on *Henry James at Work* and particularly on diary entries for October 10–12, 1907, which describe Bosanquet's arrival in Rye, her first acquaintance with the Green Room and Mr. James's Remington, and her first dictations. Subsequent diaries indicate that Bosanquet constantly borrowed books from James and that he was personally acquainted with many of the writers mentioned, being particularly close to Edith Wharton. Sibbet simplifies James's dictation style for easier reading. In the entry for October 11, 1907, Bosanquet noted, "He dictates considerately, slowly & very clearly, giving all the punctuation & often the spelling."

Page 1: Epigraph, James, preface to *The Tragic Muse,* NYE, 1908, vol. 7, v.

Page 4: "I rejoice to hear," James, HOU b MS Eng 1213/4.

Page 7: "PREFACE / I profess a certain vagueness," James, preface, *Muse,* v.

Page 8: "And I remember well the particular chill," James, preface, *Muse,* vi.

Page 9: "It seemed clear that I needed big cases—," James, preface, *Muse,* viii.

Page 10: "Maimed or slighted," James, preface, *Muse,* vi.

Page 10: "Preserved *tone*," James, preface, *Muse,* vii.

Page 11: "There need never," James, preface, *Muse,* viii.

Page 11: "Nothing can well figure as less 'big,'" James, preface, *Muse,* viii.

Pages 12–13: "And we look in vain for the artist," James, preface, *Muse,* x.

Page 13: "I fairly cherish the record," James, preface, *Muse,* xi.

Page 13: "She is in the uplifted state," James, preface, *Muse,* xviii.

Page 14: "Her measure," James, preface, *Muse,* xviii.

*

Chapter 2: "In the Cage"

The diary entry for August 22, 1907, contains the job interview with Henry James. Other scenes are imagined. Nora first appears in the diary on October 10, 1902, where she is described as looking "awfully clever," while Clara Smith appears on October 14, 1902, but without any description. Ethel Allen, Bosanquet's first love, appears in the diary first on December 28, 1898, with jealousy surrounding Ethel soon a persistent diary theme, as in, for example, this entry from December 10, 1900: "I managed to tell her [Ethel] what I wrote last night—ie [*sic*] that I'd better keep out of the way & that I knew the reason I'd behaved so badly was jealousy of Jessie."

On January 5, 1903, Bosanquet's stepmother, Annie Bullen Bosanquet, asked whether Ethel was Bosanquet's "greatest friend." Bosanquet replied in her diary, "I should say she [Ethel] is most decidedly [my greatest friend]. Nora & I are too much in love with each other to be friends—yet." Ethel Allen and Bosanquet remained friends after Bosanquet moved to Rye and London. Allen died suddenly on July 25, 1913, while still in her midtwenties, after surgery.

On October 25, 1949, when Bosanquet was almost seventy, she wrote in her diary: ". . . we sorted masses of letters from Ethel Allen into dated piles. What a frustrated creature she was, & how sad many of her letters are. I looked at some of my own to her, how egotistical and raw."

Page 15: Epigraph, James, preface to *In the Cage,* NYE, 1908, vol. 11, xxi.

*

Chapter 3: "What Maisie Knew"

According to Bosanquet's diary, James began dictating the preface for *Maisie* on January 2, 1908; Henry James remarked on January 8 that this preface was "giving him more trouble than all the others." He finished it on January 18. The adventure with Max is not mentioned in the diary but may have been described in a letter to Ethel, Nora, or Clara. James sometimes mentioned Max in his letters. In Bosanquet's entry for November 7, 1907, James commented that he did "better with dictation than when he wrote by hand: 'It [the writing] seems to be pulled out of me.'"

James wrote a letter by hand to William James on October 17 and 18, 1907, a week after Bosanquet's arrival in Rye: "I am having a good deal of decent quiet & independence, without invasions from London & a new excellent amanuensis from thence, a young, boyish Miss Bosanquet, who is worth all the other (females) that I have had put together, & who confirms me in the perception, afresh—after eight months without such an agent—that for certain, for most, kinds of diligence & production, the intervention of the agent is, to my perverse constitution, an intense aid & a true economy. There is no comparison!" (Henry James, letter to William James, October 17–18, 1907, in *The Correspondence of William James,* ed. Ignas K. Skrupskelis and Elizabeth M. Berkeley, vol. 3, *William and Henry, 1897–1910* (Charlottesville: University Press of Virginia, 1994), 490–91.

When preparing a new novel, James dictated comprehensive notes (not to be confused with his notebooks or with a draft), while he explored the novel's themes, characters, and situations. In her 1946 BBC broadcast, "Henry James at Work" (HOU b MS Eng 1213.4/9), Bosanquet added that James burned his notes as soon as he finished dictating a novel. Thus, James's only extant preparatory notes accompany his two unfinished novels, published posthumously: *The Ivory Tower* (New York: W. Collins Sons, 1917) and *The Sense of the Past* (London: W. Collins Sons, 1917).

Bosanquet's diary entry for October 12, 1907, says, "[James] remarked that his former amanuenses had never at all fathomed what he wrote & made many 'exceedingly fantastic mistakes.'" On October 14, Bosanquet added, "[Mrs. Bradley] told me that Mr. James had dismissed one or two amanuenses because they dared to suggest things! He says he likes a 'girl without a mind.' Fancy any one though having the cheek to suggest a word to Henry James— that master of words. He goes in more than I had noticed for alliteration & I didn't quite like 'a fine purple peach' which occurred this morning. Peaches have too mellow a colour to be called purple."

Page 29: Epigraph, James, preface to *What Maisie Knew*, NYE, 1908, vol. 11, viii.

Page 33: "That is we feel it when," James, preface, *Maisie*, xxii.

Page 34: "I have already elsewhere noted," James, preface, *Maisie*, ix.

Page 34: "Once 'out,' like a house-dog," James, preface, *Maisie*, ix.

Page 35: "The seed sprouted," James, preface to *The Awkward Age*, NYE, 1908, vol. 9, vi.

Page 36: "It fell even into the order," James, preface, *Age*, vi.

Page 36: "It was not, no doubt, a fine purple peach," James, preface, *Age*, vi.

*

Chapter 4: "The Awkward Age"

The Bosanquet Papers contain two boxes with photographs of relatives and local scenery from her childhood; young Theodora appears with a schoolboy haircut from about age four to ten. A photo album contains the exquisite, handmade "The Three Bears" (1886) in pen and ink and another exquisite, handmade pen-and-ink and watercolor picture book, "The stories of Naughty Jim and Cruel Edward (undated)," both by Bosanquet's parents, F. C. T. [Frederick Charles Tindal] Bosanquet (1847–1928) and G. M. [Gertrude Mary] Bosanquet (1854–1900). Queenie first appears in a diary entry on January 1, 1901, again on May 11, 1901, and elsewhere in the diaries. The scenes with Aunt Emily and Queenie are imagined. The diaries show that Bosanquet often borrowed a new book each time she went to Lamb House, including books James introduced. He would suggest she read one of his previously published works that he was about to adapt to another genre. Bosanquet's diary entry for December 14, 1907, notes that James had always "held aloof" from fountain pens because they would not "work properly." She applied "gentle persuasion." On December 17, she noted, "Mr. James gave me a 2nd fountain pen to use gentle persuasion with. I tried the (apparently novel) experiment of putting some ink in it, after which it worked admirably!"

Page 37: Epigraph, James, preface to *The Awkward Age,* NYE, 1908, vol. 9, v.

Page 47: "One could count them on one's fingers," James, preface, *Age,* ix.

Page 47: "Inevitable irruption of the ingenuous mind," James, preface, *Age,* ix.

Page 47: "The ingenuous mind might," James, preface, *Age,* ix.

Page 47: "That is it would be, by this scheme," James, preface, *Age,* x.

*

Chapter 5: "The Spoils of Poynton"

Bosanquet noted on October 20, 1907, that she had had "supper with the Bradleys, very nice, the daughter [Ellen Bradley, "Nellie," whom Bosanquet occasionally referred to in her diaries as "Nelly"] was there, quite pleasant, much older than I'd expected." On December 30, 1907, Bosanquet attended a dance and was entranced as she watched Nellie dance and flirt: "It made me devoutly thankful that I hadn't met her [Nellie] there for the first time, for I shouldn't have dreamed there could be the slightest common meeting ground for us if I should also have been in abject terror of her." That same evening, Bosanquet first met Mrs. Dew Smith, whose tea party as Sibbet imagines it incorporates details from many such Rye tea parties. Percy Lubbock, editor of the first edition of Henry James's letters, wrote Mrs. Dew-Smith's name with a hyphen. Mr. Bradley should not be confused with the Shakespearean scholar, A. C. [Andrew Cecil] Bradley (1851–1935), whom Henry James knew and who was occasionally a walking companion for James in Rye. A. C. Bradley never married and lived in London.

Page 50: Epigraph, James, preface to *The Spoils of Poynton,* NYE, 1908, vol. 10, xi.

Page 51: "The air as of a mere disjoined," James, preface, *Spoils,* v.

*

Chapter 6: "The Story in It"

Bosanquet's first extant diary begins in June 1898. The second diary begins on March 12, 1900, with her mother's death from complications due to influenza. Entries on October 23 and 25 and November 2, 1907, describe the conversion of "Covering End" to *The High Bid* and marking the play's stage directions with red ink. The entry on December 16, 1907, mentions revisions and another letter to Mr. Forbes-Robertson, whose name Bosanquet wrote without the hyphen. For Ethel Allen, see the explanatory note to chapter 2.

Page 60: Epigraph, James, preface to "The Story in It," NYE, 1909, vol. 18, xxiii.

Page 60: "Everything counts," James, preface to *Roderick Hudson,* NYE, 1907, vol. 1, v.

Page 61: "Art of representation," James, preface, *Roderick Hudson,* v.

Page 61: "Causes the practice of it," James, preface, *Roderick Hudson,* v.

Page 61: "A wondrous adventure," James, preface, *Roderick Hudson,* vi.

Page 61: "That veiled face of his Muse," James, preface, *Roderick Hudson,* v.

*

Chapter 7: "The Real Thing"

On November 26, 1908, Bosanquet noted that she had read *The Real Thing* to the Bradleys. She recorded her trip to the Blomfields' house on January 5, 1908, including James's surprise visit: "In the afternoon, I went to call, at tea-time, on Mrs. Blomfield. They live when here in a house right on the edge of Point Hill, with a ripping view. Mr. James took the house once for a summer & describes it in his preface to *The Spoils of Poynton*."

Page 67: Epigraph, James, preface to *The Real Thing*, NYE, 1909, vol. 18, xxi.

Page 68: "The prick of inoculation," James, preface to *The Spoils of Poynton*, NYE, vol. 10, vii.

Page 69: "Life being all inclusion and confusion," James, preface, *Spoils*, v–vi.

Page 69: "life has no direct sense," preface, *Spoils*, vi.

Page 70: "I saw clumsy Life again at her stupid work," James, preface, *Spoils*, vii.

Page 70: "But ten words," James, preface, *Spoils*, vii.

Page 70: "One had been so perfectly qualified," James, preface, *Spoils*, vii.

Page 70: "Fatal futility of Fact," James, preface, *Spoils*, vii.

Page 71: "Renews in the modern alchemist," James, preface, *Spoils*, ix.

Page 72: "Scenic system," James, preface, *Maisie*, xxii.

Page 73: "Secret of life," James, preface, *Spoils*, ix.

*

Chapter 8: "The Ambassadors"

The diary entry for January 27, 1908, notes that Bosanquet had begun taking dictation for the preface to *The Ambassadors*; on January 29, she commented that James had said there were "too many things to say about 'The Ambassadors'" and that "they get 'congested.'" She reported looking with Mrs. Bradley on December 12, 1908, for a possible studio for Nellie and recorded beginning tenancy on January 11, 1909. The entry on August 7, 1908, describes washing up in James's bedroom after typewriter repair. A chocolate treat appeared on October 26, 1907. On January 3, 1909, Bosanquet wrote, referring to an unnamed story: "Mr. James had done a lot of his story last night & we raced along. He says he wants to do three or four, & finds his only plan is to write them himself—it keeps him more within bounds—and then dictate them. Hope he'll remember to pay me for copying them! He forgot the last. He is so kind in providing chocolat for me."

Henry James's gift of roses along with a follow-up check-in accompanied by his niece, Peggy James, appears in the entry for July 30, 1908. Bosanquet mentioned Peggy James often in connection with walks and lunches during April in her five-line calendar-diary entries for 1913.

Page 74: Epigraph, James, preface to *The Ambassadors,* NYE, 1909, vol. 21, v.

Page 78: "There were some things," James, *Ambassadors,* 217.

Page 79: "Live, all you can," James, *Ambassadors,* 217.

Pages 80–81: "Drama of discrimination," James, preface, *Ambassadors,* xiii.

Page 81: "As always—since the charm never fails," James, preface, *Ambassadors,* xvi.

Page 81: "The reader's friend," James, preface, *Ambassadors,* xix.

Page 81: "Something of the dignity of a prime idea," James, preface, *Ambassadors,* xxi.

Page 82: "I shall have to tick-out," James, letter dictated to Bosanquet for William James, November 13, 1907, Skrupskelis and Berkeley, eds., *Correspondence of William James,* 3:351.

*

Chapter 9: "The Saloon"

According to Bosanquet's diary, on December 1, 1907, James began sketching *The Saloon* from "Owen Wingrave"; he worked on "patching" the play on December 28 and was "almost finished" with it on December 31. On February 20, 1908, James worked on revisions and said *The Saloon* was "eagerly accepted" by the chairman of the Stage Society, but Henry James had withdrawn the play, "not thinking the conditions favourable—acting wasn't good enough." Bosanquet's diary says that James began "amplifying" *The Saloon* on April 16, 1908, and notes on April 17 (Good Friday, which James referred to as a "double distilled Sunday") that the play was "much improved," that "Owen's <u>death</u> is made much more comprehensible." Bosanquet underlined the stage directions on Easter, April 19, and typed copies of the script on April 20, 21, and 22, 1908. The diaries record many visits with Nellie to mediums, palmists, and séances.

Page 84: Epigraph, James, preface to "The Author of Beltraffio," NYE, 1909, vol. 16, viii-ix.

Page 86: "A plain but ample country-house," James, stage description, The Saloon, in Leon Edel, ed., The Complete Plays of Henry James (Philadelphia: J. B. Lippincott, 1949), 651.

Page 86: "What is important being," James, stage description, Saloon, 651.

Page 87: "The whole place betrays a little," James, stage description, Saloon, 651.

Page 89: "So bare an account," James, preface, "Beltraffio," viii.

Page 89: "Dramatise it, dramatise it!" James, preface, "Beltraffio," viii-ix.

Page 90: "He turns to the portraits," James, stage direction, Saloon, 674.

Page 90: "Which embraces thus," James, stage direction, Saloon, 673.

Page 91: "What do I care for what you 'see,'" James, speech by Owen, Saloon, 673.

Page 91: "What do I care for the Demon," James, speech by Owen, *Saloon,* 673.

Page 91: "Caught up and extinguished," James, stage description, *Saloon,* 673–74.

*

Chapter 10: "The Lesson of the Master"

A gap follows Bosanquet's diary entry for April 26, 1908. Bosanquet's long entry for July 10, 1908, describes a visit on June 6 to Uplyme and one of her few extant references to her brother, Louis, who would have been thirteen years old: ". . . found pour little Louis there & a nurse, he seems very quiet & obedient, & the fact that he can come in to meals & behave shows some measure of intelligence." Louis Reginald Bosanquet died in 1917 and was buried alongside his mother in Uplyme. Theodora Bosanquet's diary for 1917, a tiny two-by-three-inch calendar, has few entries and does not mention her brother. A longer diary may have been among the volumes destroyed during the Nazi bombing of London.

On July 16, 1908, Bosanquet committed to buying the Oliver with regular payments. Her entries record incipient women's suffrage activities in Rye as well as the invitation to join a newly formed local society and serve as its secretary. On November 14, 1908, she noted that Mrs. Wharton was staying with Mr. James, but Bosanquet did not see her and only heard "the snorting of her motor car."

The entry on November 21, 1908, records other interrupting visitors: "Mr. James tiptoed to the window & looked out cautiously. 'Motor people,' he remarked, 'two of them, done up in goggles etc.'" James had forgotten he'd invited them to lunch. He complained that the automobile made Rye too accessible to Londoners and violated the town's isolating protection that he so valued. The imagined electrification scene reflects Sibbet's research at Lamb House in Rye.

Page 92: Epigraph, James, *The Lesson of the Master,* NYE, 1909, vol. 15, 76.

*

Chapter 11: "The Bostonians"

James's publisher excluded *The Bostonians,* Henry James's novel about the feminist movement, from the New York Edition for financial reasons, much to Henry James's disappointment. Thus, unfortunately, there is no preface for *The Bostonians.* On August 14, 1908, Henry James began his preface for *Daisy Miller.* Peggy James arrived on July 11, 1908, with plans on July 12 to attend the "'suffrage' meeting" at Mrs. Dew Smith's on July 13. That entry includes a description of the meeting on the "Salts" and a note that Bosanquet walked back to town with the speaker, while the entry on July 14 refers to her article "A Suffragette."

Bosanquet first mentioned William James on December 23, 1902, four and a half years before she met author Henry James, noting that she was "much interested in [William] James's 'Psychology,'" which had been published in 1890, with a shorter version brought out in 1892. On January 1, 1908, Henry James wrote to his brother about William James's pending visit to England. Bosanquet first met William James on July 18, 1908. She described her interest in his work in psychology in a diary entry on July 27 and had conversations with Professor James about spiritualism on August 1 and 9, 1908. On August 5, Bosanquet turned down work with Professor Bradley because, she wrote, "there's too much of it."

Page 100: Epigraph, "She [actress Elizabeth Robins] has lately hurled herself," letter from Henry James, dictated to Bosanquet for William James, November 13, 1907, in Skrupskelis and Berkeley, eds., *Correspondence of William James,* 3:352.

*

Chapter 12: "The Reverberator"

Bosanquet's diary entries fret about finances and the gaps in work caused by James's depression and travels with Mrs. Wharton. On November 16, 1908, Bosanquet described meeting Mrs. Wharton: "Introduced to Mrs. Wharton, fairish, bright hazel eyes, much more wrinkled skin, looks tired, quite pleasant. I was an awkward fool as usual." Mrs. Wharton's biographers and Mrs. Wharton's writings and letters describe her frenzy in 1908 in response to the dual worry of her husband's increasing bipolar, manic-depressive illness and her own flaming, secret affair with William Morton Fullerton. Bosanquet would not have known about these aspects of Mrs. Wharton's life. The Bosanquet diaries contain no mention of the imagined hat scene, although Bosanquet may have described this caper in letters. Bosanquet noted that on March 5, 1908, James began dictating the preface for *The Reverberator,* and he continued with that dictation on March 9.

Page 112: Epigraph, James, preface to *The Reverberator,* NYE, 1908, vol. 13, v.

Page 113: "Reader's friend," James, preface to *The Ambassadors,* NYE, 1909, vol. 21, xix.

Page 113: "Or that no less a pounce," James, preface, *Ambassadors,* xix.

Page 115: "In consequence of dispositions," James, preface, *Ambassadors,* xix.

*

Chapter 13: "The Private Life"

James began dictating the preface for "The Private Life" on July 29, 1908. For some time, Edith Wharton did not share with James news that her marriage was disintegrating and, simultaneously, that she was consumed by a passionate affair with William Morton Fullerton, an American expatriate who had had multiple secret affairs involving both women and men and with whom James had conducted an intimate correspondence some years before. In late 1908, one of Fullerton's disaffected mistresses (thought by some scholars to be Henrietta Mirecourt) stole Fullerton's correspondence and threatened blackmail, using Wharton's passionate letters.

Faced with exposure of an affair she had tried to keep secret from staff, servants, and close friends (including James), Wharton arranged Fullerton's payment of the bribe with assistance from James, who facilitated a publishing advance to Fullerton for a book about Paris, with Wharton putting up the funds for the advance. Fullerton paid the bribe of £1,000, for which he secured the incriminating letters. He refused to return Wharton's letters to her and never wrote the book. In 1980, three hundred of Wharton's letters to Fullerton were discovered. Many date from 1908 to 1912, the period of their extended relationship.

On June 1, 1909, Wharton seems to have ended the sexual relationship, as recorded in her famous poem, "Terminus," about a last, wild night of lovemaking with Fullerton in a seedy railway hotel at Charing Cross. A letter handwritten by James to Wharton on July 26, 1909, mentions Fullerton's acceptance of the Wharton-James rescue plan: "I could really cry with joy for it!—for what your note received this noon tells me: so affectionate an interest I take in that gentleman. How admirable a counsellor you have been, & what a détente, what a blest & beneficent one, poor tortured & tattered WMF [William Morton Fullerton] must feel! It makes me, I think, as happy as it does you." See Lyall H. Powers, ed., *Henry James and Edith Wharton, Letters: 1900–1915* (New York: Charles Scribner's Sons, 1990), 114–15.

Page 121: Epigraph, James, "The Private Life," NYE, 1909, vol. 17, 246.

✻

Chapter 14: "The High Bid"

On October 23, 1907, less than two weeks after arriving in Rye, Bosanquet began taking dictation for conversion of James's tale, "Covering End" (which had formerly been a one-act play, *Summersoft*, written for Ellen Terry but never produced), into a three-act play, which became *The High Bid*. Her diary entry on November 8, 1907, provides background about James's work on *The High Bid* for producer-actor Johnston Forbes-Robertson and notes, "Play finished!" on November 12. On February 20, 1908, the diary quotes James regarding possible production of the play in London: "'I shan't be there, to kowtow or anything. I shall make arrangements for you to rise and kowtow as a collaborator!!'"

On September 12, 1908, James heard that *The High Bid* would run for only six matinee performances (in actuality, only five) because of the ongoing sold-out show, *The Passing of the Third Floor Back*, for which Forbes-Robertson was both the producer and the lead actor playing the role of Jesus. On August 22, Bosanquet had quoted James's comment about Forbes-Robertson's role: "Jesus Christ is the main character & of course one has to realize that He's a 'formidable competitor'!!"

According to Bosanquet's diary, on September 14, 1908, Forbes-Robertson postponed *The High Bid* matinées because they might "injure the run" of *Passing*. Nevertheless, James made changes to act 1, while on September 15, James said, "I don't want to have any further communication with Forbes Robertson. I shan't answer his letter of yesterday."

Bosanquet's diaries show an early interest in George Bernard Shaw. The Shaw-James exchanges occurred between January 17 and 22, 1909. On January 22, 1909, James received news that the first of the proposed six matinées for *The High Bid* would be on February 18, 1909. The imagined scene between Bosanquet and Forbes-Robertson is based on reviews of James's early efforts as a playwright.

Page 132: Epigraph, letter from Henry James to G. Bernard Shaw, January 20, 1909, in Edel, *Complete Plays*, 645.

Page 138: "I hope you don't mind the awful Time I take!" James, speech by The Voice, *The High Bid*, in Edel, *Complete Plays*, 555.

Page 138: "Oh, I quite *trust* you, mum!" James, speech by Chivers, *High Bid*, 555.

Page 139: "I see something else in the world," James, speech by Yule, *High Bid*, 581.

Page 140: "With this heroic Proof," James, speech by Yule, *High Bid*, 600.

Pages 140–41: "Thursday midnight," James, letter to Bosanquet, February 18, 1909, HOU b MS Eng 1213/16.

Page 143: Letter from G. Bernard Shaw to Henry James, January 17, 1909, in Edel, *Complete Plays*, 643.

Pages 144–45: Letter from Henry James to G. Bernard Shaw, January 20, 1909, in Edel, *Complete Plays,* 645.

✷

Chapter 15: "The Outcry"

Bosanquet alluded to a conversation with Clara and Nellie about "sex problems" in her entry on January 24, 1909. On December 24, 1908, she mentioned Henry James's Christmas gift of a "glove box" as "just the sort of thing one would give an illiterate house- keeper." A year later, on December 25, 1909, she mentioned a second "glove box" and described a Yuletide dinner, including Mr. James's washer-woman mask. James's letter to Edith Wharton on December 13, 1909, mentions "Yule-tide observances" with Bosanquet and a "pal & second-self of hers (a lady-pal)." See Powers, *Henry James and Edith Wharton,* 130. Bosanquet's diary entry for May 7, 1910, mentions the "Black-bordered 'Times' announcing the king's death" and the chatter at tea stalls. Several of Bosanquet's diaries were lost during the Nazi bombing. Nevertheless, on October 24, 1913, she mentioned a conversation with Mr. Pinker, "pledging myself not to traffic in any way but through him in stories or articles."

Page 147: Epigraph, James, letter to Hugh Walpole, May 19, 1912, in *Henry James: Selected Letters,* ed. Leon Edel (Cambridge, MA: Harvard University Press, 1987), 400.

Page 148: "The Duchess will never convince me," James, speech by Grace, *The Outcry,* in Edel, *Complete Plays,* 770.

Page 148: "Why, tacked on to a value," James, speech by Lord John, *Outcry,* 775.

Page 149: "If we don't *do* something," James, speech by Hugh, *Outcry,* 785.

Page 152: "There was a kind of wonder," James, "London," *English Hours* (London: William Heinemann, 1905), 2.

Page 153: "Why," he propounded, "don't we all wear masks," James quotation, Bosanquet Diary, December 25, 1909.

Page 156: "As a novelist," Anonymous, "Henry James," *Encyclopædia Britannica,* 11th ed., vol. 15, "Jacobites" to "Japan," Project Gutenberg, http://onlinebooks.library.upenn.edu/webbin /gutbook/lookup?num=41264.

Page 161: "Don't be afraid"—A variation of this quotation appears in a letter from Henry James to Edith Wharton on October 29, 1909, regarding the Paris book Morton Fullerton was to write to pay off his "pacte with his fiend [*sic*]": "I would urge him not to wait for any ideal readiness to begin it, but to let a beginning make that readiness, which I shall defy him then to distinguish from the ideal." See Powers, *Henry James and Edith Wharton,* 125–26.

✳

Chapter 16: "A Round of Visits"

On April 29, 1902, Bosanquet recorded "House on Fire—cannot save it." Her diaries are missing, beginning in early May 1909 until the typed entries start on April 11, 1912. The diaries that do exist record that Henry James was often ill, suffering from head colds, shingles, digestive disturbances, and possible heart problems. They also record the interest she and Nellie shared in possible psychical communication.

In November 1909, suffering from depression—perhaps due to poor sales of early volumes in the New York Edition—James burned his papers, particularly his correspondence, including letters from Edith Wharton and from other close friends. However, Wharton did save James's letters, although she may have destroyed some of the correspondence that she considered too sensitive.

Page 162: Epigraph, James, "A Round of Visits," *The Finer Grain* (New York: Charles Scribner's Sons, 1910), 185.

Page 166: "You must have been ill indeed," James, "Visits," 175–76.

Page 167: "The emissaries of the law," James, "Visits," 184–85.

✳

Chapter 17: "English Hours"

Bosanquet's typed diary pages record James's visit on April 11, 1912, to a possible flat above the one rented by Bosanquet and Nellie. Later entries refer to James using two empty rooms on their floor; on January 13, 1913, Bosanquet mentioned the visit to Carlyle Mansions, where James lived until his death. Naomi Royde-Smith appears in the entries quite often, with gatherings hosted on October 23 and 24, 1913. The women's suffrage movement was active in Great Britain and the United States until the beginning of World War I; movement activities resumed after the war.

Page 170: Epigraph, Anonymous, "Henry James," *Encyclopædia Britannica*.

*

Chapter 18: "A Small Boy and Others"

Bosanquet's typed entry on January 13, 1913, indicates that *A Small Boy and Others* was all but finished and Henry James was working on proofs of earlier sections; another typed entry on April 3, 1913, announces that the book was out. Diary entries for September 9 and 10, 1908, recount that Professor William James had sent Bosanquet a report by Mrs. Holland on automatic writing, which Bosanquet and Nellie tried. Professor William James had introduced Bosanquet to the Society for Psychical Research. In a letter to Bosanquet dated October 27, 1911 (HOU b MS Eng 1213/39), Henry James refers to Bosanquet as the "Remington priestess."

Page 178: Epigraph, James, *A Small Boy and Others* (New York: Charles Scribner's Sons, 1914), 346.

*

Chapter 19: "The Ivory Tower"

Edith Wharton arranged the advance of $8,000 ($4,000 upon signing and $4,000 upon completion of the manuscript) for Henry James in a letter on April 29, 1913, to Charles Scribner, who was dubious about Wharton's secret scheme. Scribner's publishing contract with James was for *The Ivory Tower*, which James abandoned as inappropriate during World War I. He died during the war. During James's decline, Wharton made arrangements through Bosanquet secretly to assist James's housekeeper, Kidd, financially with care for Kidd's mother. The extant letters do not mention the publisher's advance.

As noted above (see chapter 3 descriptive note), at his death, James left two unfinished novels—*The Ivory Tower* and *The Sense of the Past*. James usually destroyed his notes (not to be confused with his notebooks) once he had completed a manuscript. However, James's extensive notes for each of these novels' themes, characters, plots, and subplots still exist. For Bosanquet's papers regarding *The Ivory Tower,* see HOU b MS Eng 1213.4/1; for *The Sense of the Past,* see HOU b MS Eng 1213/73. See also Bosanquet's 1946 BBC presentation "Henry James at Work" (HOU b MS Eng 1213.4/9). The Bosanquet diary for 1914 is a tiny calendar book with five lines a day. The entry on July 19, 1914, runs into the five lines for "Memo": "Mr. James is going to take at least a day for meditation on the form of 'The Ivory Tower' which is baffling him—the relation between 'dialogue' & the analysis of states of mind: 'I so hate crude elementary narrative.'"

Bosanquet's typed entry on April 3, 1913, reflects James's distress at turning seventy and the misinterpretation of his refusal to have contributions raised by Edith Wharton put toward commissioning a portrait by his friend, John Singer Sargent. Sargent waived his fee, and the flurry subsided; subsequent diary entries record that James enjoyed sitting for the portrait. On May 4, 1914, Mary Wood (a.k.a. Mary Aldham) slashed the painting with a butcher's cleaver in one of several suffragist actions at museums in London. Bosanquet's handwritten entry on May 4, in her five-line calendar-diary notes, "Mr. James' portrait slashed at Academy by unknown female. Horrible." The next day, she added, "H.J. took 'outrage' very calmly."

For his birthday, James's friends gave him a reproduction of a Charles II bowl. On April 20, 1913, Bosanquet noted in a typed entry, "[James] was pleased, too, by the actual list of names, representing as it did practically all the literary and artistic 'celebrities' of the day as well as many personal friends. But there has been a good deal of heart-burning among some of his friends over the omission of their names. . . . The really sad part about it allis [sic, "all is"] that Mrs Wharton, wishing to associate herself with the American offering, didn't join in the English one, and now that the American one has been crushed (by his nephews) her name doesn't appear at all, though she is his best friend really. He is very sorry about it and all the more so as he has had a very much hurt and resentful letter from her." (Powers's *Henry James and Edith Wharton* does not contain this letter.)

A few lines in Bosanquet's calendar-annotation diary for June 12, 1915, note, "H.J. expresses approval of Prize Essay—says it is good." Sibbet has imagined the scene with Bosanquet's entry in the competition.

Page 187: Epigraph, James, *The Ivory Tower,* including the notes (New York: Charles Scribner's Sons, 1917), 271.

*

Chapter 20: "The Sense of the Past"

Many of Bosanquet's diary entries refer to James's health, stating that he was in bed or "feeling 'seedy'" (with "seedy" being a word Bosanquet often used for herself and her close friends). She referred to James's attacks of shingles on October 20 and November 13, 1912. For the Bosanquet-Wharton correspondence (including Bosanquet's letters) regarding James's health, see Powers, *Henry James and Edith Wharton,* Appendix B, 361–92. For Wharton's original letters to Bosanquet, see HOU b MS Eng 1213.3/255–83.

Victor appears often in the diaries from 1908 and 1909. He reappears in diary entries for April 24 and 25, 1914. He signed up for the Irish Guards on October 4 and received his commission on October 18. The entry in the five-line calendar diary for May 22, 1915, records news that Victor had been killed.

On July 28, 1915, Bosanquet noted, "HJ much in request for interviews on account of his naturalization. Quite ebullient." The letters from Edith Wharton to Bosanquet testify to the constant, mutual attention with which the two women tended to Henry

James; they provide the basis for Sibbet's imagined scenes. James burned much of his correspondence in November 1909, including his letters from Edith Wharton. He burned subsequent correspondence in October 1915, during his last visit to Rye.

Page 201: Epigraph, James, *The Sense of the Past,* including the notes (London: W. Collins Sons, 1917), 286.

Page 204: "Palpable imaginable visitable past," James, preface to *The Aspern Papers,* NYE, 1908, vol. 12, x.

Page 211: "I want to make it," James, unpublished, draft notes for *The Sense of the Past,* HOU b MS Eng 1213/73.

*

Chapter 21: "The Altar of the Dead"

Bosanquet read from Henry James's final dictations during a special BBC broadcast, *Recollections of Henry James in His Later Years,* which was hosted by Michael Swan on June 16, 1956 (transcript at HOU b MS Eng 1213.4/20). Bosanquet's thirteen lengthy letters to Edith Wharton, which were written between November 4 and December 28, 1915, detail Henry James's failing health and Mrs. William James's exclusion of both Bosanquet and Wharton from news about the Master. See Powers, *Henry James and Edith Wharton,* 367–89.

Page 212: Epigraph, James, preface to "The Altar of the Dead," NYE, 1909, vol. 17, vii.

Page 216: "They pluck in their terror," James, dictation ("Deathbed Dictations"), December 11, 1915, HOU b MS Eng 1213/75.

*

Chapter 22: "The Death of the Lion"

The Nazi bombing of Britain destroyed Bosanquet's diary for 1915, the last full year of James's life. Edith Wharton's letters to Bosanquet

(HOU b MS Eng 1213.3/255–83) testify to the efforts of both women and James's household staff to support the Master during his final illnesses. They also reveal that Wharton offered financial support so that Kidd (James's cook/housekeeper in London) could retain hired help to assist her in tending to her ill mother and, thus, free her to be available also to care for Mr. James. The best description of James's last days and Bosanquet's and Wharton's exclusion is in Bosanquet's thirteen lengthy letters to Wharton from November 14 to December 28, 1915 (in Powers, *Henry James and Edith Wharton*, 367–89). Wharton's response to Bosanquet on March 1, 1916, immediately after hearing news from Bosanquet of James's death, is telling: "We who knew him well know how great he would have been if he had never written a line."

Page 219: Epigraph, James, preface to "The Death of the Lion," NYE, 1909, vol. 15, x.

*

Chapter 23: "Henry James at Work"

Several of Bosanquet's diaries were destroyed during the Nazi bombing of Britain, including the volumes from the beginning of 1918 until November 1920; 1923; and from early in 1924 until July 29, 1924. Sibbet based her imagined scenes with Virginia Woolf on research into the early days of Hogarth Press. Percy Lubbock's two-volume collection is titled *The Letters of Henry James* (New York: Charles Scribner's Sons, 1920); for Virginia Woolf's letters to Bosanquet, see HOU b MS Eng 1213.3/284–90.

Page 230: Epigraph, Theodora Bosanquet, *Henry James at Work* (London: Hogarth Press, 1924), 9.

Pages 233–34: "Plumes from the imperial eagle," James dictation, December 11, 1915, HOU b Ms Eng 1213/75.

Page 239: "'Scenic system,'" James, preface, *Maisie,* xxii.

Page 245: "His Utopia," Bosanquet, *Henry James at Work,* 33.

*

Chapter 24: "The Wings of the Dove"

Bosanquet's diary notes that James began his preface to *The Wings of the Dove* on January 19, 1908, and finished it on January 26. Her diaries for the period covered in this chapter were destroyed during Nazi bombing. Edel's earliest extant letter to Bosanquet is dated January 21, 1952 (HOU b MS Eng 1213.3/72), long after Edel had published substantial work on James but before publication of the first volume of his five-volume biography of James. Sibbet's imagined scenes for this chapter are based on research in the *Time and Tide* archives and on interviews with Leon Edel in Hawaii in 1992.

The Bosanquet diary for 1915 contains an obituary clipping from the *Daily Mail* for Henry James, III (Harry), with a handwritten date, December 15, 1947. Harry James had received a Pulitzer Prize in 1931 for his biography, *Charles W. Eliot, President of Harvard University.*

Nellie Bradley does not appear in the later, extant Bosanquet diaries until June 13, 1949, when Bosanquet heard that Nellie was in a nursing home—"quite bedridden" in Rye; Bosanquet commented that she was not sure Nellie would want to see her.

Page 246: Epigraph, James, preface to *The Wings of the Dove,* NYE, 1909, vol. 19, v.

*

Chapter 25: "The Aspern Papers"

Bosanquet's diary says James began the preface for *The Aspern Papers* on January 15, 1908, but then contracted influenza and was unable to resume work until January 19. He soon stopped but then picked up work on the preface again on February 22. On April 13, 1943, Bosanquet described the centennial dinner, while later entries mention subsequent gatherings.

As a follow-up to the centennial dinner, Bosanquet presented "Henry James at Work" on the BBC as a live broadcast on October 20, 1946 (HOU b MS Eng 1213.4/9), with the text printed in *The Listener* on October 31; she read "Studies in English Letters" for the BBC on January 21, 1947 (HOU b MS Eng 1213.4/10), and presented "It's Good English" on the BBC on April 27, 1948 (HOU b MS Eng 1213.4/14). Leon Edel edited *The Complete Plays of Henry James* (Philadelphia: J. B. Lippincott Company, 1949).

Page 259: Epigraph, James, preface to *The Aspern Papers,* NYE, 1908, vol. 12, vi.

*

Chapter 26: "The Beast in the Jungle"

Bosanquet's diary entry for August 19, 1954, notes that Michael Swan (author of *Henry James* [1952]), Geoffrey Taylor, and a sound engineer visited Bosanquet's flat for two hours to record tape for an upcoming BBC broadcast. She wrote, "I practically read the St. Anne's talk & added a few more bits." For the St. Anne's talk, "Henry James," see HOU b MS Eng 1213.4/15. Indeed, most of the transcript for the 1956 BBC broadcast came directly from the St. Anne's talk, which itself was based on *Henry James at Work* (Hogarth Press, 1924).

It is clear that the two Bosanquet typescripts in the "Deathbed Dictations" are not and could not be the actual dictations (or copies) from December 11–12 because both documents have within them lines of narrative clearly written by Theodora Bosanquet in past tense (after the fact) to describe those two days. Bosanquet may have used James's process of destroying original notes once a final text had been prepared. When the impossibility of the typescripts being original copies of dictations was pointed out to the Houghton staff, one archivist responded, "Ah, Henry James remains mysterious, and Theodora Bosanquet also remains mysterious!"

Page 269: Epigraph, letter from Edith Wharton to Theodora Bosanquet, March 1, 1916, in Powers, *Henry James and Edith Wharton,* 391. For the original Wharton letter, see HOU B MS Eng 1213.3/276.

Page 271: "So slight an indication," Michael Anesko, *Monopolizing the Master: Henry James and the Politics of Modern Literary Scholarship* (Redwood City, CA: Stanford University Press, 2012), 69.

Pages 271–72: "Napoleonic fragments," Leon Edel letter to Theodora Bosanquet, September 29, 1952, HOU b MS Eng 1213.3/75.

Pages 274–77: "Deathbed Dictations," James with Bosanquet's narrative, "Dictations," December 11–12, 1915, HOU b MS Eng 1213.4/75.See also *Recollections of Henry James in His Later Years*, compiled and introduced by Michael Swan, produced by Douglas Cleverdon, BBC, June 14, 1956, transcript, HOU b MS Eng 1213.4/20. Theodora Bosanquet's typescript for the BBC broadcast in 1956 differs from the BBC's transcript for the entire broadcast. The text in this chapter of *The Constant Listener* is taken from the complete BBC transcript.